SECRETS

OF THE

CRONAL

THE SWORD OF DRAGONS

BOOK 3

Jon Wasik

For my Starshine

My Muse, my inspiration, my one and only ever after

I couldn't do this without you!

Also by Jon Wasik

The Sword of Dragons *(Reading Order)*
Rise of the Forgotten – The Sword of Dragons Book 1
The Orc War Campaigns – A Sword of Dragons Story
Burning Skies – The Sword of Dragons Book 2
Secrets of the Cronal – The Sword of Dragons Book 3
Advent Darkness – The Sword of Dragons Book 4

Project Sirius
The Awakening

Chronicles of the Sentinels Trilogy
Legacy
Retribution
Champions

CONTENTS

ACKNOWLEDGMENTS

Thank you to my parents for their undying support and encouragement. To my sister Tanya and her family, for always encouraging me. To my wonderful Starshine, Beck Wasik, for believing in me every step of the way, and helping me through revision after revision, cover designs, layouts, and everything in between!

Thank you Wayne Adams and Danielle Lirette for toughing it through the first round of beta reading. Thank you to Chloe for making such incredible maps!

Thank you to all of my blog and Facebook followers, you all rock!

And as always, thank you to the Welts family, especially Nick and Natalie for listening to all my ideas, for beta reading, and for cheering me on!

SWORD OF DRAGONS CHARACTER REFRESHER

Cardin Kataar – Trusted as the Keeper of the Sword, Cardin has had the Sword of Dragons for nearly a year, and has gained considerable power. At the end of the Battle for Maradin, Cardin discovered that he has the ability to use both star magic and dark magic. Not officially a member of the Warriors, he acts under the direction of the Allied Council.

Kailar Adanna – Kailar's ability to use magic was thought to have been taken by the Star Dragons at the end of the Battle for Archanon, but upon seeing Nuuldan during the Burning Skies, she discovered that she can use dark magic. Currently a probationary member of the Devor Warriors' Guild in order to prove herself.

Letan Velethar – A Lieutenant in the Devor Warriors. With the destruction of his hometown Corlas, he was transferred to the Tieran Port Guild, and is directly responsible for Kailar.

Sira Reinar – A skilled and cunning Warrior, Sira's leadership abilities have taken her far within the Guild. She has commanded the group attached to Cardin Kataar since the beginning of the Orc War Campaigns.

Reis Kalind – A non-magical Warrior, Reis has struggled to prove himself against Mages all of his life. Currently at odds with Cardin after having discovered Cardin kept a vital secret from him during their voyage across the sea.

Anila Kovin – One of the Covenant's most trusted guardians, Anila served as guard over the imprisoned elf Baenil for nearly a decade. She is considered a half-breed, half-Mage and half-Wizard, and hides this from everyone for fear of being ostracized by society at large.

Dalin – While originally assigned by the Wizards' Guild to train and watch after Cardin, he now feels replaced by Endri, a Star Dragon sent to help Cardin come to terms with his new dual powers. Since Endri's arrival, he has spent most of his time with the Wizards.

Elaria – A gifted explorer, Elaria is a Dareann Elf who keeps finding herself drawn into the struggles of Halarite. First she was manipulated into helping Kailar attempt to kill Cardin, and then she returned to Halarite to find and rescue Baenil.

Baenil – A member of the Dareann College of Serelik, Baenil is an archeologist who was caught exploring the catacombs beneath Archanon and was forced by the Covenant to help them uncover ancient secrets. He was rescued by Cardin on Trinil, and has since returned to the College. After a decade of imprisonment, torture, and forced labor, he struggles to regain his full sanity.

King Eirdin Beredis – The most beloved ruler of Tal in centuries, King Beredis has recently found himself under severe criticism following the multiple wars and cataclysms that have befallen Tal and the Allies.

Prince Idrill Beredis – A young, power-hungry man, Prince Beredis continues to earn the ire of his father, who continually tries to educate him to become a better ruler. The Prince seeks any opportunity to claim the throne as quickly as possible.

Wizard King Sal'fe – Ruler of Falind, Sal'fe has used the Staff of Aliz to continually heal or even resurrect fallen soldiers and Warriors in battle from all of the kingdoms, often charging considerable sums of money to the other three kingdoms. He has since used Falind's burgeoning wealth to vastly improve the quality of life for his people, among other, less overt pursuits.

Queen Sechel Leian – Ruler of the eastern kingdom of Erien, Queen Leian now rules from the northern city of Lassil, after her capitol of Maradin was flooded by a tsunami, and then further devastated in the fight against the undead.

Grand Master Wizard Valkere – The oldest living Wizard, Master Valkere is wise but cautious in dealings with humans. He was present 3,000 years ago when the Sword of Dragons was hidden on Halarite. He is a proponent of the return of the Wizards to Halarite, and is spearheading the effort to rebuild the ancient Grand Wizard Hall in the north of Tal.

Master Wizard Syrn – One of the eldest Wizards, Syrn helped contact the Star Dragons during the initial Sword of Dragon crisis. Since then she has served the Grand Master, despite opposing his policies of returning the Wizards to the fold on Halarite.

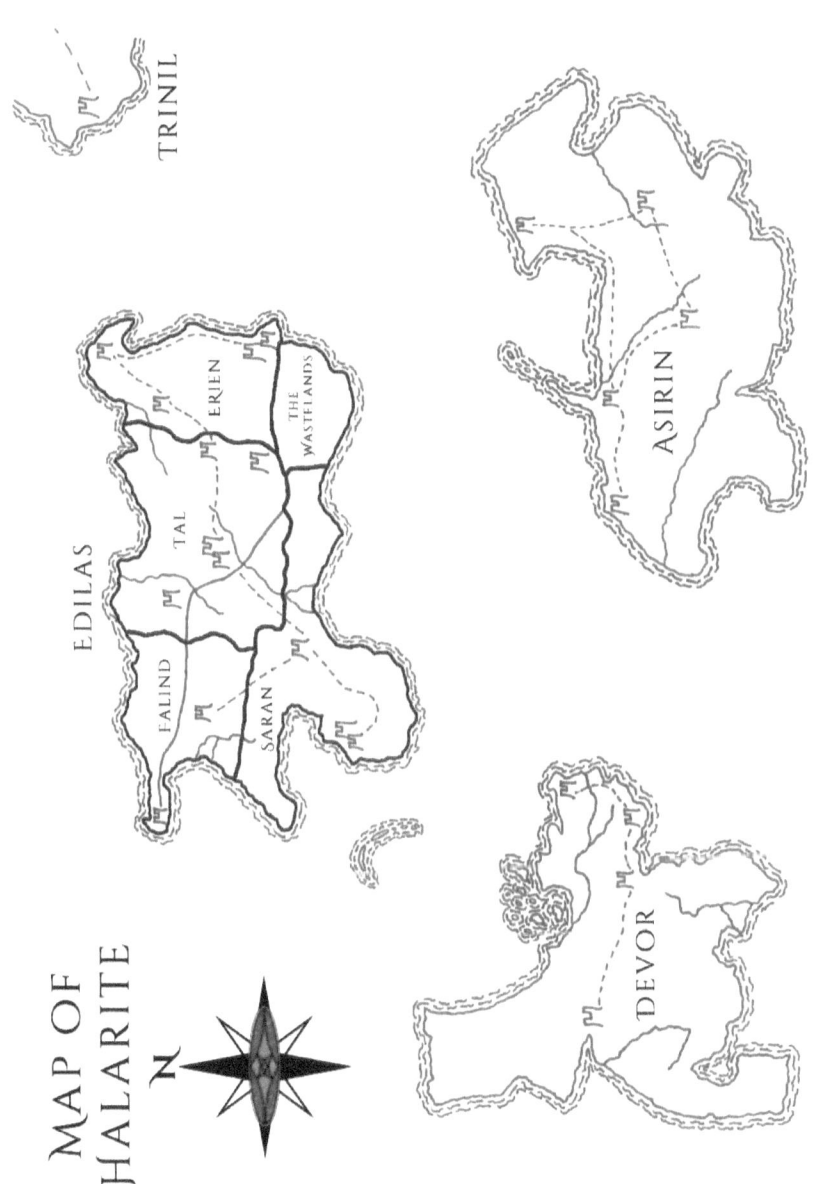

MAP OF
HALARITE

N

TRINIL

EDILAS

FALIND

TAL

ERIEN

SARAN

THE
WASTELANDS

ASIRIN

DEVOR

EDILAS

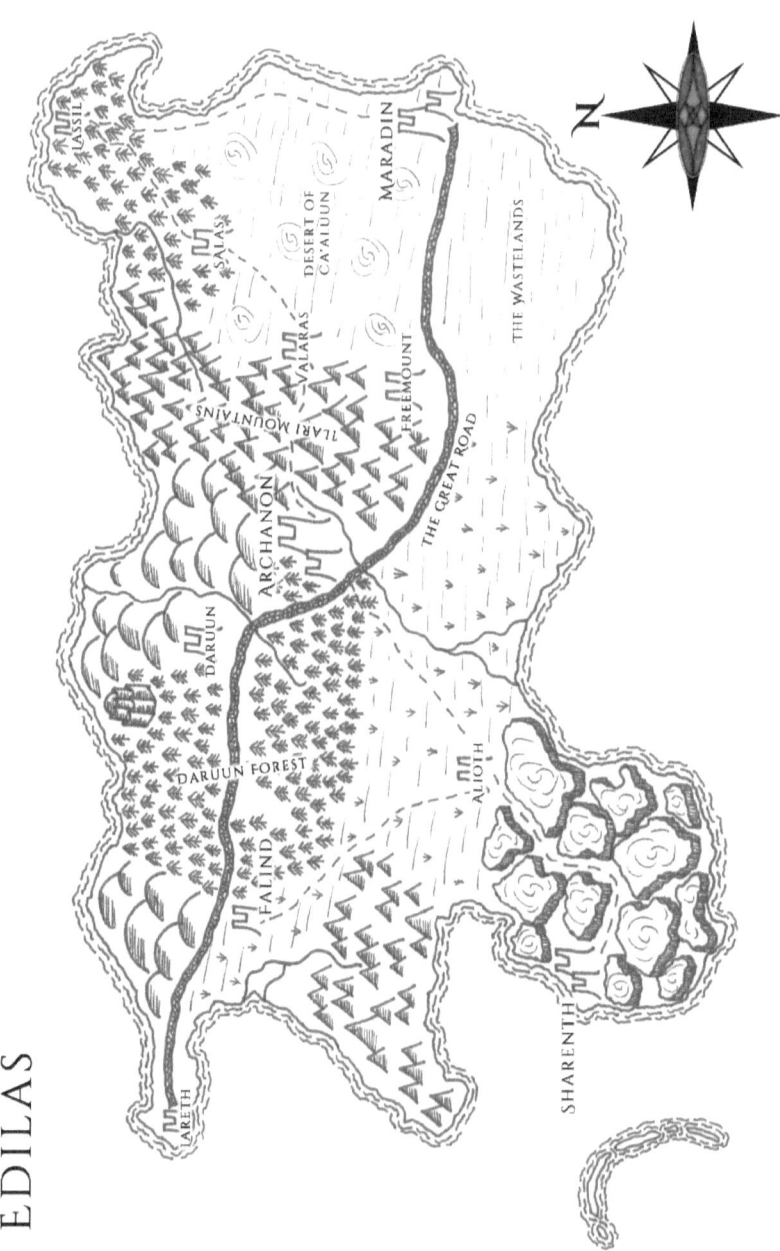

DEVOR

CYRSTAL BAY

CRYSTALLINE PEAKS

CRYSTALLINE FOREST

AGRIAT ISLANDS

BARRIER MOUNTAINS

TIERAN PORT

CORLAS

NEOLAS

EDINGARD

CENTRAL PLAINS

FROZEN PEAKS

PLAINS OF GLASS

N

SECRETS OF THE CRONAL

In the darkest shadows, a spark of light is blinding;
Within the brightest light, darkness prowls.

It began in the shadows of history. In the earliest days of Halarite, when the world was steeped in superstition and fear, one man dared to step outside of his station and learn everything he could about the universe.

Zairel had an infallible memory, and sought out every legend, story, and bit of history that he could find, and recorded them all in great volumes of books, the first ever historical recordings. He spoke to countless sages, the eldest of elders, and numerous scholars, until there were no more stories to find. In time, all came to revere his knowledge of history, and he became the most sought-after teacher on Halarite.

But he was not satisfied. Zairel recognized that there was more to the world than superstitious stories. He sought greater knowledge, until he and his most trusted friend, Degrin, made an incredible discovery – the Cronal. Said to be written in the language of the gods, Zairel and Degrin deciphered the Cronal, and learned the truth about ascension.

Zairel and Degrin established the Order of the Ages, with knowledge as its founding pillars, and ascension the goal of all who followed them. They believed that the greatest figures from history had already ascended to become gods, and were worthy of worship. Preaching that society should follow the example of the gods, Zairel decided to spread knowledge to every corner of the land.

This led Degrin and Zairel across the great Desert of Ca'aluun, to the hidden kingdom of Erien. It was there that Degrin, whom many believed had always been a demon disguised as a man, turned on the people of Erien and threatened war.

Zairel, desperate to keep the peace, sacrificed himself to destroy Degrin, and in doing so, secured his position as the sixth god of the Order of the Ages.

But with Zairel's death came a warning – darkness could never truly be destroyed. If the people of Halarite strayed from the light, Degrin would return, and the kingdoms would be cast into shadow.

While some believed that the Six would step in to stop Degrin, the Covenant feared that humanity would be on its own, and the world would fall mercy to the whims of the first and darkest demon.

Chapter 1

THE SEAL OF THE COVENANT

In an insignificant corner of Tal Kingdom, on a cold, cloudy spring morning, Prince Idrill Beredis folded his arms around himself and cursed his fortunes, or lack thereof.

He was in the tiny little village of Eskra, far to the southwest of the great First City of Archanon, on the very edge of his kingdom. No, not *his* kingdom. Not yet, anyway. It was still his father's, despite his best efforts.

Now, at his father's command, he toured the kingdom, surveying the damage caused by the meteorite storm three months ago and reassuring the peasants that the throne would still take care of them.

Running his fingers through his shoulder-length hair, the Prince grumbled under his breath and wiped his face. This was the job of a subordinate. Governor Maral, perhaps, or even one of the kingdom's Warrior Commanders. He should be at home, resting his feet near a fire, feasting on fresh game or other, more enjoyable meals.

The village was small, consisting of single-story buildings constructed around a basic dirt-road infrastructure. It had no more than a hundred people living in it, and that number was much lower than it was the previous spring. Winters usually resulted in a few deaths every year, but after the cataclysmic meteor storm, after so many had perished in the fires and explosions of the falling rocks, more fell to starvation and exposure.

The death toll was staggering.

One such meteorite had struck not far from where the Prince now stood in the village square. In fact, from the small wooden pedestal that he stood upon, he could see the charred remains of the house where the meteorite had hit. He shuddered at the memory of the first streak of fire that arched across the sky above Archanon.

Looking down at the gathered villagers, he pushed the memory to a dark corner of his mind and began his prepared speech.

"People of Eskra," his tenor voice called out. "I know how much the world has changed. I know how frightened you all must feel. This past year has brought several disasters upon our people, and many have turned to violence to express their fears."

He paused to look into the eyes of his subjects, but saw that they were not comforted by his words. They were angry, and terrified, and as they shifted uncomfortably, he had the distinct impression that they wanted to throw him off of the pedestal.

Gulping, he looked above them to avoid their stares completely, and continued on, "Let me assure you, the throne of Tal will protect you."

"Like you protected my father," a young man bellowed from the crowd.

One of the Prince's guards stepped forward to try to stifle further outburst, but then a woman cried out, "Or my daughter?"

"Be silent!" his guard demanded. Two more guards stepped forward, resting their hands on the hilts of their swords. They all wore the splendid, ceremonial steel plate and mail armor and a black and silver tabard bearing a mountain crossed by a pair of swords.

The guards normally instilled respect and reverence from the rabble, but today, their commands were ineffective.

"We're starving," another peasant whined from somewhere.

"Where's the food we were promised?"

"We were guaranteed tools to plant new seed last month, where are they?"

"You can't protect us, no one can."

The voices continued, on and on, asking where their promised provisions were, or why the throne had not paid the Falind's Wizard King Sal'fe to use the Staff of Aliz to resurrect their fallen, or when they would get any of the help that they, and every other village, claimed to need.

While the voices grew louder and bolder, the crowd surged in around him, closer and closer, until the rest of his guards surrounded his pedestal and pushed back against the mob. "Get back," the Captain demanded. "You shall not approach the Prince!"

Anger boiled, and Idrill felt a fire light within. Before the crowd could surge forward again, he snarled, "That is enough!" When no one listened, he looked down at the Captain, one of the only Mages in his guard, and stated, "Captain, draw your sword!"

Enough people heard his command, and suddenly all protest ceased. The Captain gaped back at him. "My Lord?"

"You heard me." He planted his fists on his hips. Prince Beredis wore one of his finest forest-green tunics and leather trousers, and his boots, though muddied, still looked finer than anything the rabble wore. He had to remind them that he was their Prince, and they would suffer for their disrespect.

In an obvious flourish and with deliberate delay, the Captain drew his longsword and held it in both hands. He glanced furtively at Idrill, who glared warningly at the Captain, before he channeled magic into the blade, setting it humming audibly.

Looking out to the crowd, though still avoiding their eyes, the Prince held his chin high. "The next person that speaks without my consent shall be arrested. After that, any who attempts to approach me will receive a far worse punishment. Is that clear?"

There was a low grumble of discontent amongst the crowd, but none actually spoke out against him. He waited, almost wishing someone would say something, but no one did.

Feeling flustered, he forgot his prepared speech, even though he had already delivered it to over a dozen villages and towns. There was a time when he would have punished anyone who spoke out against him, but he grudgingly admitted to himself that in this case, he couldn't very well punish an entire village, not when he only had a dozen guards to protect him.

Worse still, Idrill's father had threatened to announce succession to someone outside of the family if the Prince didn't 'learn his lesson.' His visits to the outlying villages was meant to be an example in humility for him, but all it did was further fuel his hatred for the King and his weak ways.

If only his father hadn't survived the poison. Idrill would be King now, and none of the disasters that befell them would have happened. *Damn those Wizards,* he growled inwardly.

When no more protests arose, he nodded. "You have forgotten your place in this world. Disaster is no excuse for such conduct." He almost took pieces of his speech and told the crowd that the throne would take care of them, but he knew that the kingdom was spread thin on resources, and the coffers were empty. Only force could keep the populations in line, force that his father was unwilling to use.

The people would suffer, and there wasn't anything anyone could do about it.

So instead, he said, "Violence and protest will only make your lives harder. So do your jobs. Plant your crops. Tend to your livestock. Make new tools. You will survive this, and the throne will protect you."

He could see the dissatisfaction in everyone's faces, and many looked ready to protest, but the Captain brandished his sword. On the outskirts of the gathering, he could see several Warriors also patrolling, and he knew that they would obey his orders. The villages were simple farmers and craftsmen, and he realized that they wouldn't stand a chance against the well-armed and well-trained Warriors, even in so small numbers.

If only he could take the throne. He could wipe Eskra off the map and warn all other villages of the price of defiance.

Without another word, not caring that his speech was incomplete, the Prince stepped down from his pedestal and moved towards the Captain. He stopped and waited impatiently. The Captain, realizing what Idrill wanted, shouted into the crowd, "Make way!"

As the villagers reluctantly parted, the guards surrounded the prince, and they pushed their way through the narrow corridor. The Prince avoided everyone's glares, knowing full well that if he met their eyes, violence would ensue, and he would have to explain it to his father.

When they finally made it past the villagers and out of the square, he hurriedly led his entourage towards the carriage. He needed to leave the village quickly, he needed to escape an otherwise dark fate.

When they reached the caravan, they were surprised to find a single young boy waiting for them. He wore a black tunic with red trim and similar trousers, and his boots were muddied from running errands. Even before the Prince could see the logo embroidered into his right breast, he knew that the boy was a squire from the local Sanctuary of the Order of the Ages.

The Captain brought the procession to a stop, and then stepped forward to meet the boy, his sword still drawn. Could the young squire be a threat to Idrill?

"What is your business with us, young man?" the Captain demanded. The Prince scoffed, thinking, *he's not a man, not by a long shot.*

The boy presented a sealed letter in his left hand. "I have an important message for the Prince, milord. From the Sanctuary."

The Captain regarded the letter for a moment before he sheathed his sword and took the offering. After examining it for a moment, the Captain nodded and said, "You may go."

Without another word, the boy nodded and ran towards the Sanctuary east of the convoy.

Returning to the procession, the Captain presented the letter to the Prince. "My Lord," he nodded at the seal.

Idrill regarded the seal with unexaggerated surprise - it belonged to the Covenant, the leaders of the Order of the Ages. How could the boy have been given such a letter? Members of the Covenant rarely visited the smaller villages, and he knew that all three of them were currently in Archanon meeting with the Allied Council.

Hesitantly, the Prince took the letter from the Captain. He pulled out a small dagger and used it to break the seal, and then unfolded the parchment.

Its contents were simple, 'Come to the Sanctuary at once. Enter alone.'

The Prince frowned, and then showed it to the Captain, who read the letter and likewise furrowed his brow. "My Lord, with respect," the Captain hesitated. "This seems a little suspicious."

"Indeed," the Prince nodded. "However, it does bear the Seal of the Covenant. Their signet rings are closely guarded."

The Captain nodded, and then awaited Idrill's orders. The Prince considered his options, recalling that his favor with the Covenant had suffered last year when he had declared the elf, Elaria, to not be a demon. However, in light of events that followed after that, with the discovery that the Covenant already knew about elves, Idrill began to care less about his popularity with the religious leadership.

With that in mind, he was tempted to disobey the summons, but his curiosity was too great. The Covenant was reaching out to him, and did so in a tiny village rather than in Archanon. Was it urgent? Or did they wish to speak to him far from his father's ears?

Nodding, the Prince ordered, "Take me to the Sanctuary."

The building wasn't far from their caravan, but he had given it little notice before. Accustomed to the Grand Sanctuary in Archanon, this one seemed underwhelming at best. It was a small, cylindrical building, built from wood imported from the forest to the north, and painted a light, almost-white color. The conical rooftop had a steep pitch, which was said to help ascending souls focus into the ascension crystals at the top of every ceiling of every Sanctuary in the world.

The Sanctuary in Archanon had multiple windows, both on the walls and in the domed ceiling, but this one had no visible windows. It seemed depressing in comparison, and he felt dirty even thinking about going inside.

They came to the only visible entrance, and he realized that once inside, he could walk from one end to the other in only a few dozen steps. Why would a Covenant member be waiting inside this decrepit, diminutive place?

The Captain stood next to the Prince, his sword hand resting on the hilt of his weapon. "Are you sure you wish to go in alone, Sire?"

The Prince looked at him and raised his eyebrows. "This is a place of knowledge and worship, Captain. If anyone dares attack me from within, they will deserve the wrath that the gods shall bring upon them."

They were hollow words, and it was likely that the Captain knew that. Never-the-less, Idrill did his best to keep up the appearance of a pious monarch.

Drawing in a deep breath, and resting his hand on the small dagger on his belt, the Prince stepped up to the heavy wooden doors and pushed them open.

The sight within was as underwhelming as outside. Every Sanctuary was a safe haven for knowledge, for books, and this Sanctuary was no different. Without any windows, the only sources of light were multiple torches and candles spread throughout, giving a very low ambient light.

Like spokes on a wheel, bookshelves starting at the outer walls ran inward, but the Sanctuary was so small that the shelves ran only five feet, and were likewise five feet tall. In the center of the Sanctuary was a wide pedestal with a wooden stand in the center. This was where the village cleric would read to the masses and interpret the books for them.

The Prince respected any cleric that could successfully teach the peasantry. After all, how could you make complex ideas understandable to such simple people?

He looked around, expecting to find at least the village cleric, but no one was inside. In fact, he realized he had not seen the cleric at the town square, either. That was more than a little unusual.

Idrill gripped his dagger tighter, his eyes darting about the room. Was this an assassination attempt? He turned to look at the Captain, but at that very moment, the double doors slammed shut, and the lock latched.

He felt his chest tighten, and he fumbled while drawing his weapon. Without windows, there was no way a wind could have blown the doors closed from within. He stumbled towards the doors, but before he could reach them, an inhuman voice shouted, "Stop!"

The Prince instantly obeyed the order, but then frowned. Only one voice had ever been able to make him obey without question like that, and that was his father's. But this voice was chillingly different.

Idrill turned towards the altar to find a tall, intimidating figure glowering at him.

The owner of the voice hid his face beneath the hood of a black robe with dark-red trim, and the Prince relaxed when he saw the Order's logo, six red lines expanding out from a central point, on the right breast of the person's tunic. It was a member of the Covenant after all.

The silence grew like a void between them, and the Prince wondered who should speak first. He was aware of the dagger in his hand, so he lowered it and relaxed his stance. "I apologize," he bowed slightly. "I did not realize it was you." He wished the person would pull their hood back to reveal their identity. There were still only three members of the Covenant, but the lack of light helped conceal their body form.

"I would not expect you to recognize me," the voice spoke again. It was distinctly male, but it was not one of the voices the Prince expected. The inhuman quality he swore he had heard before was gone, and now it sounded familiar. "You, like the rest of humanity, have strayed."

The Prince tilted his head to one side. "Strayed? Strayed from what?" Quickly growing annoyed, he stepped forward threateningly. "Why have you summoned me here?"

The figure stepped around the altar and raised his hands to draw his hood back. When the face was visible, the Prince drew in a sharp breath. "You…"

It was Pevrin! The same Covenant member that had convinced the Prince and several others to capture Elaria just before the Battle for Archanon.

"You recognize me after all, child?"

The Prince started at being called 'child.' "Of course I do," he fumbled over his words. "You were banished from the Covenant. How do you still possess one of their seals? How did you come by those robes?" He grew angry when he realized the gravity of Pevrin's actions. "How dare you summon me under false pretense! How dare you show your face in this place of sanctuary. How dare-"

"Be silent!" Pevrin roared, the inhuman quality returning. The seemingly ordinary man's eyes suddenly glared with a bright-orange glow, startling Idrill.

Snapping his jaw shut, the Prince gawked and his stomach twisted. Never before had he seen someone's eyes glow, and Pevrin's glow did not fade. In fact, the brightness grew so intense that Idrill had to shield his eyes.

"I warned everyone," Pevrin shook his head, his voice returning to normal. "I warned that if you strayed from the teachings of the Order, darkness would return." He folded his arms and glared down at the Prince, the glow fading just enough that Idrill no longer had to protect his vision. "Halarite stands upon a threshold from which there shall be no return."

Frowning, the Prince shook his head. "If you are referring to Elaria and the elves, you are alone in your assessment that they are demons."

Pevrin's eyes flashed again. "That is merely *one* of your

transgressions, boy." Who the hell was he to call him 'boy?' "One of many committed by all but the most devoted followers. If the people do not return to the teachings of the Order, the demon will return. You know of whom I speak."

When Pevrin's words registered, a cold, dark pit formed in his chest. He lowered his arms and looked down, shock taking hold.

"Degrin…" He shivered when he spoke the name, remembering all of the horrible tales the clerics had told him when he was a child. Of the destruction it was said would be wrought by the first evil one, if he should return to Halarite.

That was why so many people were turning back to the Order fervently, and protesting violently against anything that went against their teachings, including the Allied Council's cooperation with the elves. They believed that the meteorite storms and the appearance of the Dark Dragon, Nuuldan, was the beginning of the dark times foretold by the Cronal and the Covenant.

But then, another thought occurred to the Prince. The glowing eyes, the apparent power beyond his normal measure, and the fear his presence instilled. Something had changed drastically within Pevrin.

If it even is still Pevrin, he realized with a start. Stepping forward, he dared to look into the glowing eyes. "Who are you?"

A gust of wind swirled throughout the Sanctuary, extinguishing most of the candles and some of the torches. But the light inside grew brighter. Not from Pevrin's eyes, but from his entire body, which was alight with the same intense orange glow. He raised his arms up, and as he did so, his body lifted off of the ground, rising closer to the ascension crystal in the ceiling.

In complete awe, the Prince stared helplessly, fearful of what might come next.

The inhuman quality of Pevrin's voice returned when he spoke. "I am Zairel."

Idrill stared dumbly. It took several moments for the words to register, but they couldn't be true. The Prince had, after all, begun to doubt the existence of the gods. Yet there was no denying the powers displayed by Pevrin, far beyond even that of a Wizard's.

Cracks appeared at the edges of Pevrin's eyes, as if the power within was too much for his body to contain. As if the power could explode out at any moment.

With no powers of his own, the Prince could only imagine what the display of magic felt like. All of the hairs on his arms and neck stood up on end.

This was power. *Real* power.

This was a god.

Dropping the forgotten dagger, the Prince fell to one knee and bowed his head. "My deepest apologies, my lord. I did not recognize you in the body of Pevrin."

The god did not speak at first, and Idrill prepared to be struck down for his insubordination and doubts.

When Zairel spoke, his voice returned to Pevrin's normal tone. "This one sacrificed his soul and body so that I might return. I am humanity's last hope, and I have chosen you to help me bring humanity back to the light."

Feeling his heart stir, the Prince smiled and dared to look up at the god. "Me, my lord?"

A crooked smile crossed Zairel's face. "You once served the gods loyally. I will give you a second chance, just as I am giving humanity a second chance. Do you accept this responsibility, boy?"

Cringing inwardly at being called a boy again, the Prince nodded. "I do, my lord. I do whole-heartedly."

The cracks reappeared around Zairel's eyes, and his crooked smile grew further. "Good. You failed with poison last year." The Prince's head snapped up in shock, but then he realized that of course a god would know. What surprised him further was when Zairel continued, "Your father has been one of the greatest sources of heresy and must be eliminated, so that you may take your place upon the throne and return Tal to its pious roots."

Though still shocked, the Prince couldn't help but smile. With a god on his side, he would finally take his place upon the throne. He could rule the land with the iron grip that it needed.

This time, no one could stop him.

Chapter 2

BROKEN WINGS

The wind howled and whipped past Cardin Kataar's ears, a wide, child-like smile plastered upon his face. The renewed spring grass beneath his feet was a blur as he ran faster than he had ever run in his life, faster than even a horse! His almost-black hair had grown out a little, and at these speeds, he could feel the wind tugging on it, just as it tugged on his blue tunic and brown trousers.

South of his hometown of Daruun in the wide open grassy plains, Cardin let magic flow freely into him from the Universe. Just like he'd done in the Wastelands at the end of the Orc War, he used that power to give strength to his muscles, allowing him to run faster than any human was meant to.

While he channeled ever more power into his legs, a voice spoke from everywhere and nowhere at once, a voice that spoke within his mind. *"Your strength does not just lie within your muscles,"* the voice spoke, somehow taking on the tone of a strong, confident, and wise man. *"There is greater power in the Universe than you know. Greater power within you."*

Gritting his teeth, Cardin thought to himself, *"How the hell am I supposed to know what that power is if you don't tell me?"*

Of course, the being that spoke to him couldn't hear his thoughts.

Cardin hadn't yet learned how to project his thoughts to others. Never-the-less, as he tried to run faster, the being replied as if he had heard Cardin's thoughts, *"Trust in the Sword of Dragons. Trust that when you are ready, when you open yourself up to new possibilities, the Sword will give you the knowledge you seek."*

Not much good that would do. The Sword of Dragons, a claymore-sized weapon strapped to his back in an enchanted scabbard, seemed to have a mind of its own when it came to giving him new powers.

No, he thought to himself. *I need to stop thinking that way. It doesn't give power, it teaches.*

That was the first lesson that was pounded into his head by his newest trainer, often anytime Cardin failed. Knowledge truly was power, and the energy needed to use that power was always available. He just had to learn how to open himself up to it.

A great shadow passed over Cardin, blocking out the noon sun for a moment. Without breaking stride, he looked up to witness a majestic sight. With verdant scales gleaming in the daylight, the Star Dragon Endri soared overhead, his leathery wings outstretched to catch the wind.

The giant, wondrous creature looked down at him, and even though hundreds of feet separated them, Cardin lost himself in the dragon's eyes. Pin-pricks of ardent green light in deep, endless black, as bright as the strongest stars in the night sky.

Then the dragon's eyes darted ahead of Cardin. *"Pay attention!"*

When Cardin looked down, he had only a moment to react to a boulder in his path. On instinct, he surged energy into his legs and leapt as high as he could.

The ground sank below him at a dizzying pace, as did his stomach. He could have easily flown with the birds!

Except that he wasn't actually flying, and his rise from the surface slowed, and then stopped. His momentum was not lost, and the ground still rushed by beneath his feet, just as it rushed up at him.

Panicking, he wondered how he could land without breaking a leg. He looked up at Endri, hoping the dragon would swoop down to save him, but the dragon merely soared on.

"Believe in yourself," he heard Endri's voice, the wind whistling in Cardin's ears now suddenly lost as the moment drew to a crawl. The dragon's wings fluttered lazily on a breeze as his starry eyes bore into

Cardin's soul. *"Trust in the Sword. Trust in your powers. Trust in the stars."*

Cardin looked down at the approaching ground, a patch of dandelions giving his landing target a sharp yellow hue. He closed his eyes and drew his consciousness into himself, just as his Wizard friend Dalin had taught him at the beginning of the Orc War.

Beyond his eyelids, he could see the ebb and flow of magic around him, and he could feel the energy pulsing through the world, like a living being with a heartbeat.

Power. Energy. It wasn't just people that were made of magic, it was everything. From the tallest dandelion to the smallest pebble, magic was everywhere.

With moments to spare, he called to that power, from further away than he had ever done before, and willed it to create a cushion for him.

It worked! He landed hard, jarring himself and almost buckling his knees, but he kept running, his momentum carrying him past the dandelions at blazing speeds.

"Yes!" Endri called down in excitement, letting out a teeth-chattering roar that set Cardin's ears ringing. *"You have done it!"*

Echoing the dragon's roar, Cardin gave out a loud whoop, pumping his fist into the air. "Yeah!"

Having flown much further ahead, Endri banked sharply, until he shot behind Cardin at extraordinary speed. Keeping his senses extended beyond himself, Cardin felt the sharp, focused power of the dragon as it turned into another, lazier bank to come up behind Cardin.

"Now try it again," Endri called down to him. *"Jump, but this time, use your magic to propel you higher, not your muscles!"*

A wide grin spread across Cardin's face. He was climbing a gentle hill, the crest coming up fast, so he drew magic in at a rate that would peak at the top of the hill. The yellow dandelions had given way to older ones, their white seedpods exploding into the air as he raced past.

If he jumped from the top of the hill, he knew he could get even higher. Maybe even as high as Endri flew. He coaxed the magic at the top of the hill to build up, like a snake coiling up before striking.

When the moment came, even he wasn't prepared for the results. He leapt forward, planted both feet firmly in the ground, and then while he pushed with his magic-enhanced legs, he released the gathered power at the top of the hill and let it spring him up. The effect was incredible, his stomach dropped, and the ground fell away as fast as a loosed arrow.

His jump took him at least twice as high as the last one, and as he reached the peak of his arch and started to fall down again, a pang in his stomach reminded him that he didn't have wings. But fear quickly turned into determination. Cardin knew what to do, and this time, he would do it gracefully.

Using the magic in the world around him, he angled his descent, increasing his forward momentum while slowing his downward momentum. When he touched down, it was a gentle but fast landing. His legs almost couldn't keep up, even magically enhanced, and he felt himself slow down.

The shadow overtook him again, the great dragon flying overhead. *"Wonderful, human!"*

I can go higher, Cardin thought to himself. He knew he could. The Sword had been given its powers by dragons, so maybe, just maybe, he could fly too!

He remembered the dragon avatar he had summoned at the Battle for Maradin, remembered what it felt like to have wings, to soar through the air with the ground an afterthought beneath him. He wanted to feel that again. He *had* to feel it again!

Cardin prepared another coil of magic ahead. He had run in a long, slow curve, and was now racing back towards Daruun. Maybe he could even jump so high that he could land in town.

When the moment came, he leapt with all of his strength, willing the magic to push him further and further. His stomach felt as if it dropped away as quickly as the ground, but it wasn't enough. He knew his arch would carry him higher than the last jump, but he wanted to go higher. He wanted to touch the clouds!

So he willed more power around him to push his body up. He could feel that power, not so much pushing at his feet as it was catching his soul and carrying him upwards like a powerful wind.

More, he thought hungrily. *I can do this!* Endri was just ahead of him, his head craned beneath him to watch Cardin come closer and closer to his flight level.

Cardin tried to draw more power to him, but where could he get it from? There was nothing up here, high in the sky, other than himself and Endri. He tried to draw more power from the Universe, but he didn't know how. He was so close, he couldn't stop now!

Until he felt the sudden clasp of cold and emptiness, gripping his heart and his stomach. The complete reversal of everything he had known all of his life.

The absence of energy, and the sudden strength it gave him.

Dark magic.

No!

His powers faltered, the push against his soul stopped, and his arch ended. That's when he looked back down, just as he began to fall. Endri roared in surprise, and Cardin let out his own alarmed cry. He'd lost his connection to magic!

"No!" he shouted. "No, no, no, I can't stop!"

He doubted that Endri could hear his cries, but he didn't know what else to do, he was useless without power. The ground raced up at him, and unlike before, time wasn't slowing down. He was dead...

Until the magic sparked within him again. His connection to the Universe suddenly returned like a splash of water in his face.

In a panic, Cardin forgot to use the magic on the ground to cushion him, he just pumped as much strenth into his legs as he could, and braced himself.

When he hit, he immediately felt and heard the sickening crack of one of his legs breaking, sharp pain shooting through his entire being. He tried to tuck and roll, hoping his forward momentum would diminish the damage, but after only a moment of intense pain, he gave up trying to hold his legs in, and his body flailed about. He bounced again, and again, his hands and arms and head and legs, even the broken one, slapped the ground.

Something else broke, but by then, agony washed away all other sense, and all he knew was that he hurt everywhere.

Cardin must have blacked out before he skidded to a stop. All he felt was that cold inside of him, slowly fading into the background, like a dull ache in his soul.

When he awoke, it was to the sense of warmth coursing throughout his body. He became aware of the pain again just as it left his limbs. He opened his eyes to find Endri towering over him, his eyes fixed on Cardin.

When he looked down, Cardin could see a green glow encapsulating his body. The same green glow he'd seen when he healed the burned girl during the meteorite storm. Once again, Endri healed his wounds.

"I should make you do this," Endri spoke to him through his mind. Dragons never spoke aloud, Cardin had found out. They only ever used mind communication, while their mouths were used for eating, drinking, and occasionally roaring, a throwback to their primal days.

Thankfully, they could hear just fine. "Kinda hard to do when I'm unconscious."

Endri shook his head. Whatever focus he needed to heal Cardin, it seemed to barely distract the dragon. *"You should never have fainted."*

"Hey," Cardin glared up. "I didn't faint. You try staying conscious when you break every bone in your body."

He didn't know how it was possible, but Endri rolled his star-eyes. *"Do not be so dramatic, human. You only broke fourteen bones."*

"Oh, only," Cardin rolled his eyes right back at the scaly beast. "Have you ever broken a bone?"

"More often than you care to know," Endri shook his head, before he looked towards the city. *"And yes, it hurts."*

Suddenly another thought occurred to Cardin, and a concerned frown crossed his face. "Wait, how do you know how many bones I broke?"

The dragon looked down at him, and then slowly sat back on his haunches. *"I can see through anything."* The dragon's eyes darted downward and then back up at Cardin.

Feeling his face turn bright red, Cardin stammered, "Uh, anything?"

If dragons could grin, Endri certainly did. In Cardin's head, he heard a great bellow of laughter, while Endri echoed that laughter verbally in an awkward, deep-throated chuckle. *"No, not really. You humans are surprisingly gullible."*

Cardin's face grew warmer, and he shook his head. "I swear, I'm never going to get used to you having a sense of humor."

The green glow subsided, and the last ache faded. Cardin rolled over and pushed himself up. Nothing hurt, nothing was sore. Endri had done an amazing job healing him.

Craning his neck up, Cardin said, "Thank you."

Endri tilted his head to one side, and then nodded in a human-like gesture. Cardin had grown accustomed to the dragon's attempts at human gestures over the past three months.

Three months since the skies burned, since Maradin, and since Nuuldan.

It felt like a lifetime ago.

Looking back up at the Star Dragon, Cardin regarded Endri, and wondered if, after such a relatively short time, he could consider Endri a friend. Could a human be friends with a dragon?

Shaking his head, he started to turn away, but then noticed something on Endri's chest, just beneath his right wing joint. The scales were lighter on his underside, but looked harder, like a kind of armor that nothing could penetrate. Yet, something apparently had.

Pointing to the damage, Cardin asked, "What happened there? And how did I never notice it before?"

Endri tried to look down at his chest, raising his wing up enough to touch the spot with his right front claw. The dragon shook its head and looked down at Cardin. *"That was a result of Klaralin's final attack."*

Cardin remembered that night, when Klaralin was defeated and the Battle for Archanon was won. Moments before Sal'fe had used the Staff of Aliz to finally end Klaralin, the ancient enemy had sent a blast of black and purple energy at the jade dragon, and managed to actually wound him.

"The wound hasn't healed yet?" Cardin wanted to reach out and touch it, despite it being too high for him.

Endri recoiled and covered the wound. *"No. The magic Klaralin used against me was far more powerful than anything we have seen from a human. This wound cannot be healed through magic, and may never properly heal."*

Cardin felt in awe, but he also felt very frightened. It was a reminder that he still had barely scratched the surface of the magic he would someday be capable of.

Shaking his head, Endri asked, *"What happened to you back there? You were doing so well, and then it felt as if you had disappeared from the Universe. I felt a cold absence in your place."*

His spirits darkening further, Cardin looked away. The moment flashed through his memory, and he felt the darkness threaten to take over again. "It…"

He couldn't finish, but Endri did for him. *"It was dark magic."*

That much would have been obvious to the dragon. This wasn't the first time the darkness had asserted itself at a key moment of training. Every time it did, Cardin's connection to regular magic was severed.

"It was like the other times, but worse," he admitted, staring at a blade of grass. "I couldn't feel anything. Except for the emptiness."

After a moment of silence, Endri said, *"We have already established that dark magic and star magic coexist within you."*

Shaking his head, Cardin replied, "No, they don't. Not anymore, if they ever really did." He flailed his arms about and asked, "Why does it keep happening when I need my powers the most? It's like the stronger I become, the stronger the darkness becomes. What if it happens in battle? How do I stop it from happening?"

Endri's tail twitched. He knew what the dragon's answer was.

"I do not know," he admitted. *"You are unique, Cardin Kataar. I wish I had the answers for you, I really do."*

Cardin looked down again, tears threatening to come forth from the pressure building up inside. Things were getting worse, not better. And he saw no end in sight.

He was losing his powers as fast as he was gaining them.

Suddenly he was aware that Endri's presence felt closer, and he looked up to find the dragon's head level with him so that he could look one starry eye into Cardin's. *"We will figure it out,"* he said softly. *"I promise you, I will not stop until we solve this riddle."*

Warmth coursed back into Cardin's soul. He felt a smile creep across his face and into his heart, and he reached a hand out to pat Endri's muzzle, but then stopped suddenly. Blushing, he looked sheepishly into the dragon's eye. "Sorry…"

The dragon's mouth stretched into an approximation of a smile. However, before he could say whether he was okay with the intended action, they felt a sudden burst of magic.

Cardin and Endri looked east at a large wall of light that had appeared a few hundred feet away. He tensed for a moment, recognizing the feeling and the sight of a portal stirring up magic all around them. He reached for the Sword, ready to defend against anything that came through. Endri likewise stood to face whatever came through.

Much to his relief, it was another Star Dragon that emerged. With scales as blue as the deep sea, and eyes to match, the newcomer was about half the size as Endri, and had fewer spines around his body. Did that mean it was younger than Endri?

The blue dragon stopped the moment it cleared the portal, which closed instantly behind it, and stared at Endri. All Endri did was stare back, but after several moments of silence, Cardin realized that they conversed privately.

Feeling excluded, Cardin barely resisted the urge to demand that they include him. Why had the dragon arrived, and why didn't it move or do anything else? Did he not care that Cardin was there? Did he not care about the Sword? Was he there to report a sighting of Nuuldan?

Then, with a quizzical look, he wondered if the dragon was even a he.

After several more moments of embarrassed silence, the blue dragon finally broke eye contact, and looked directly at Cardin. Through his blue, star-like eyes, Cardin felt the power of the Universe pulsating, just as he always did with Endri.

Nodding, the dragon spoke to him through his mind, the sound of a female's soft, though younger voice echoing in his head. *"It is an honor to be in your presence, Keeper of the Sword. I apologize if I was rude, but I have little time. Please, excuse me."*

Without another word, the blue dragon turned on the spot and summoned another portal, stepping through immediately. Just as suddenly as she had appeared, she disappeared, leaving no trace behind.

Cardin looked up at Endri with a frown, and saw that the dragon stared after the blue one silently. He hadn't been around dragons long enough to be able to read their facial and body expressions well, but he had the sense that Endri was disturbed by whatever the visitor had told him.

So Cardin cleared his throat. "What was that all about?"

Endri shook his head and sighed deeply, an interesting sound to hear in one's mind. *"She informed me that our efforts to locate other Star Dragons in the Universe have faltered."* Endri looked back up to where the giant portal was moments ago. *"Alone, we are vulnerable to Nuuldan. He is too powerful for any one of us, and many of us remember just how influential he could be."*

When Endri didn't continue, Cardin prompted, "What do you mean, influential?"

Shaking his head, Endri stood up and sauntered towards Daruun. When Cardin realized where the dragon was headed, he had to jog to catch up. *"Any dragon can become Dark, like Nuuldan. If singled out and alone, a dragon can be influenced or coerced into tapping into dark magic."*

Feeling himself tense, Cardin thought back to his last magic-fueled jump. When he'd felt the cold, empty pull of dark magic. "I could see why that's frightening."

For a moment, they walked in silence towards town, Cardin's thoughts wandering back to three months ago. To when he had first discovered that he had the same kind of power as Nuuldan. To Endri's arrival, and learning what having dark magic really meant.

He didn't know that Star Dragons could turn dark. Then again, he didn't know much about the history of the dragons. Every time he asked Endri, the dragon gave him bits and pieces, but never about the Civil War or the forging of the Sword of Dragons. Never anything about Nuuldan or the Dark Dragons.

All he told Cardin was that dark magic was supposed to be the opposite of star magic, both terms he had only learned in the past few months. They weren't supposed to be able to be used by the same individual, they were supposed to annihilate each other.

That was why he feared it more than ever. If Cardin let dark magic into his soul, what would it do to him? What happened when two kinds of magic destroyed one another? What did it do to one's mind?

Could he become insane? Or evil?

Absently he reached back and touched the handle of the Sword, wishing he had never allowed Dalin to convince him to pick it up. Suddenly, he didn't want to have anything to do with it.

Now, more than ever, he wanted to find Sira. He wanted to hold her in his arms, and just forget about the Sword and Endri and Nuuldan. He needed peace, if only for a moment.

Chapter 3

SHADOW'S DAGGER

Kailar Adanna shifted anxiously, her legs growing uncomfortable from crouching for over an hour. She grumbled inwardly and shifted her posture as much as she could, but she had to remain hidden.

She, along with Letan Velethar, crouched behind a crate next to one of several businesses in the port city of Tieran. While her dark hair and clothes helped conceal her, it was almost for naught against Letan's bright red hair and beard.

The two of them stared over the crate at a warehouse across the main avenue of Tieran, lit up only by torches. She glanced eastwards, but the predawn glow had not yet arrived.

They were running out of time. Absently she gripped the edge of the crate, the wood feeling smooth and slippery from condensation. If their source was correct, one of the most wanted men on Devor was in that warehouse, and she meant to put an end to their pursuit tonight.

They were accompanied by an entire Warrior unit, under Letan's command of course, and their troupe had surrounded the warehouse in secret during the night. Their source, a criminal they had arrested and convinced to spill his guts about his cohorts, was inside meeting with their quarry. He was supposed to have gone in to confirm that their target was indeed hiding in there, and then come out to give them the news.

That had been over an hour ago, and Kailar wondered if their source had betrayed them. She wouldn't be surprised if he had, but that just meant they were going to have to do things the hard way.

Shifting anxiously again, she let out an audible sigh.

"Would you relax," Letan commanded with a whisper, never taking his eyes off of the warehouse.

Kailar pushed her hair behind her ear and shook her head. "No, I won't."

Finally breaking eye contact, Letan frowned at her. "Even when we first met, you were never this anxious."

That was saying something, considering she was a wanted criminal herself back then. Technically, she still was, as far as Falind Kingdom was concerned.

Kailar searched for Letan's eyes in the low light, the closest lantern several feet away. Those eyes usually helped soothe her nerves in tense situations.

But nothing could make her relax tonight. To say that their target was one of the most wanted on Devor was a bit of an overstatement. Egil was only one of hundreds of leaders amongst the criminal underground. But Kailar had wanted to hunt him down ever since their first encounter on the plains west of the Barrier Mountains.

"I won't let him get away," she growled.

"I know you won't," Letan set his hand on her shoulder and squeezed. "But don't forget your promise."

Rolling her eyes, she nodded and whispered, "I know, I know. We want him in a dungeon, not a grave."

Their eyes fell again upon the warehouse. It was a two story building just off of the docks in Tieran, and it reeked of fish. She still found the smell to be wretched, and whatever appetite she had once had for fish died on her voyage aboard a ship from Edilas to Devor.

Unfortunately, fish was the primary source of food in Tieran Port. Since the Warriors of Devor often met there, thanks to her ability to create portals, it meant that if she wasn't out hunting the criminal underground, she was in the port, swimming in that stench.

She had quickly gained favor with Commander Kent Qerlin when she told him the extent of her powers. In fact, over time, she had discovered that she retained many of her former powers granted by the Sword of Dragons. The only difference was that, thanks to the Star Dragons a year ago, she no longer used normal magic. Instead, she drew her power from another source altogether.

Darkness.

Dark magic was something she had only heard of when she learned about the Sword of Dragons. Klaralin, under the guise of a creepy old mentor, had told her how the Star Dragons feared dark magic, and that they had once warred with Dark Dragons over control of the Universe. Dark magic, he had explained, corrupted Star Dragons, distorted their minds and destroyed their identities.

But for her, it was a second chance. One that she didn't intend to waste.

Knowing Letan would object, she didn't bother to tell him her plan. She simply stood up and walked towards the warehouse's front entrance.

"Kailar!" Letan hissed.

She glanced over her shoulder and called back, "Make sure no one escapes."

Whatever objections he had were lost as she confidently strode forward. She gripped the hilt of her Guild-issued longsword and drew it, preemptively channeling dark magic into the blade. The steel hummed quietly, excited by the built-up magic.

Maybe she should have come up with a plan. But their quarry knew who she was, probably every criminal knew her by now, and she would use that to her advantage.

Opting for a dramatic entrance, she lifted her left hand up and used her new powers to blast open the double doors, sending splinters of wood spraying inside.

The warehouse was poorly lit within. It was one of several along the shoreline of the port, but this one was easily the largest. There were crates and barrels scattered everywhere, and there would have been lots of places to hide, except that her method of entering was unexpected and didn't give the occupants time.

It didn't help that the dozen men and women inside held the only lanterns in the entire warehouse, offering an easy target to hone in on to her right. She immediately saw their informant, a stout man already cowering away from the others. And in the center of those others was *her* target.

Egil.

Drawing their weapons, the criminals scattered, but she didn't care about the rest. Egil stared at her wide-eyed, and he mouthed the word 'you' with terrifying, quivering lips. She grinned at his disheveled appearance, his tattered untucked tunic and mud-soiled trousers, remembering from their first encounter how much he cared about his image. Now he looked like he lived on the ragged edge, as well he should have. Ever since Kailar had regained her powers, she had helped organize the disparate Warriors of Devor and led them on an encompassing campaign to finally end the chokehold organized crime had on Devor.

The days of open crime were gone. Their time living in comfort was over.

Then Egil looked over at her informant and scowled. "You idiot," Egil shouted.

Two of the others stayed near Egil, their loyalty outweighing their fear of Kailar, and they placed themselves between her and her target.

Kailar stalked towards them, her rage and anticipation giving her senses an edge. Egil started to back up, and then he turned and ran.

Her built-up fury unleashed, and she barreled forward. "Get back here!"

Though she could not sense their presence through dark magic, the two defenders were both Mages, and they released arcane attacks upon her. She thrust her hand out and cast a shield, easily absorbing their weak attacks. Then she swung her sword and released a destructive wave of energy that sent the two sprawling and destroyed several crates, sending their goods, mostly salted meats, flying.

Egil was already at one of the back entrances, opened earlier by the fleeing criminals. He stopped short when he looked outside, and Kailar heard shouts from the other Warriors as they rounded up Egil's cohorts. Her target must have realized that there was no escape.

That didn't stop him from trying. He glanced at her as she rushed towards him, and then he ducked outside into the dark of night. Incensed by the thought of his escape, she channeled as much power into her legs as she could and ran faster. She was outside in a heartbeat and caught a glimpse of Egil darting down a narrow street into town. The Warriors were too busy with the other criminals to have noticed.

"I said get back here!" she barked and took off after him. He wouldn't escape!

Thanks to her unnatural speed, she caught up fast. She could have tackled him, but she wanted to humiliate him more.

Coming to a sudden stop, she jabbed her sword at his feet and released a weak blast of magic. The ground exploded beneath him and sent him stumbling down onto his face. He was stunned for a moment, but he recovered and scrambled to his feet, glancing at her in terror.

Kailar released another blast, this time just ahead of him. The bright flash and echoing boom stunned him, allowing her to catch up in just a few strides. She placed her sword over his left shoulder, the edge of her blade pressed against his neck. His rapid breathing froze.

"It's over," she growled.

He tried to turn his head back to look at her, but feared for his neck and couldn't. So she carefully maneuvered around to face him, the tip of her sword now pushed against his chest. His focus was on her sword, but when he looked at her, she grinned.

"Did you really think you'd get away with threatening me," she asked, pushing her sword point into his chest. She must have broken skin, because he cried out in pain and a bit of red soaked into his dirty white shirt.

She savored the moment, soaking in the fear on his face, the color of his blood. She wanted to end his life, and all it would take was a little bit of extra pressure, or perhaps a quick discharge of magic...

And then the man whose life she had taken in a nameless easement in Edingard flashed through her memory. Her grip on her sword softened, and she pulled it away. Staring down the length of it, she saw the cowering look on his face and realized that she had taken it too far.

Maybe he deserved it. Maybe she should have just killed him. Or taken an arm off, or better yet a leg. He couldn't run if he didn't have both legs.

But she'd promised Letan. More than that, she'd promised herself to try to be better. She had a purpose again, a reason to move forward, to keep going and try to do what was right. She had power again, and she was in a position to make a difference. Where she had failed in the four kingdoms, she had the chance to succeed on Devor.

And it started with arresting Egil.

Drawing her sword up beside her, she sighed. Then she looked around and realized there were no other Warriors nearby. Egil had somehow made it past her companions, and she had blindly pursued him further than she realized. Kailar would have to handle Egil herself.

"Turn around," she commanded.

Egil was panting heavily. He winced and clenched at his chest. "You're not gonna kill me?"

"Not this time. You're going to spend the rest of your life in the dungeon." She smiled. "Or worse."

He glowered at her. "You think you've won?" His commoner accent was stronger than she remembered. "You've declared war, you kn-..."

Kailar felt a sudden sense of danger, and a flash of movement in the light of the everlasting torches caught their attention. On instinct alone, Kailar raised a dark shield around her, barely in time to stop a pair of daggers from stabbing into her. In fact, their tips penetrated her shield!

Feeling suddenly fatigued from the power of the assault, Kailar leapt away while swinging her sword at the wielder of the daggers, a tall, slender figure clad in all black. Her shield had barely stopped the assailant, but they hadn't lost their grip on their daggers, and were ready to attack again in a heartbeat.

She couldn't tell if the assailant's clothes were cloth or leather, but their head was wrapped in black as well, leaving only a slit for their eyes to peak through.

Kailar tried to ask who they were, but then heard a shuffle behind her. She ducked and spun around, swinging her sword just as another assassin tried to impale her from behind. Her swing caught the assailant in the shins, and with a magically-enhanced sharpness, her sword cut right through the attacker's legs.

Kailar raised another shield just as a bolt of lightning lanced out at her from the shadows of an easement across the street. She turned towards that assailant, only to mentally stop.

"Lightning?" she wondered out loud. Only Wizards could use elemental magic!

Only it wasn't a Wizard that stepped out of the shadows, it was another darkly-clad assassin. That assassin likewise wielded two daggers, but that was the first time that Kailar noticed a fiery-orange gem embedded in the hilt of each dagger, and that the daggers' blades were a dark color, much darker than normal steel. She glanced at the first assailant just as he leapt at her, and noticed the same gems in their weapons.

Already growing tired of the exchange, Kailar released a wave of purple-black magic from her sword, catching the first assassin off guard and flinging him down the roadway away from her.

Which left one. Or so she thought. From the shadows of other alleys and easements, and from the rooftops, several more assassins appeared, surrounding her. A curse escaped her lips, and then she noticed that Egil was gone. Were they working for the little rat?

The assassins all wore the same clothes, and while not all of them sported daggers, every weapon she saw was made of darkened steel and had a gem embedded in them.

But they did not attack at first. One of them walked over to the man she had just sent flying and leaned down to check if his chest rose or not. When it did not, the other assassin stood back up and glowered at her.

Though she could only see their eyes, she recognized what was in them, beyond the anger.

Fear.

Whomever they were, they didn't expect her to have the kinds of powers that she had. This pause in combat allowed her to get her bearings, and she was able to count seven total assassins still alive or still a danger to her.

This wasn't going to be easy, especially if they had elemental powers on their side. She decided her only chance was to unleash the full extent of her powers. Coaxing dark power into her sword, feeling the emptiness within her growing, she prepared to strike.

But the lightning attack had attracted further attention. The sounds of rushing footsteps caught everyone's attention as several Warriors, led by Letan, came running from the warehouse.

Realizing they were outnumbered and outmatched, the assassins all relaxed out of their combat stances and looked at each other. It was then that she felt a stirring, though with her new powers, all she could feel was the pressure of energy against her absence.

One by one, they each turned on the spot, and disappeared into quickly-summoned shafts of light. The last one bent down to collect the one she had killed, and then they, too disappeared into shafts of light. Moments later, all traces of them were gone, except for the legless assassin a few feet away from her.

It was only then that Kailar noticed the predawn glow growing. Letan came to a stop and looked at her in breathless shock.

"What in the Six was that all about," he breathed.

"Were those Wizards," another Warrior asked.

She shook her head, and looked back at the legless assailant, their daggers out of their reach. "No," she said. "I wouldn't be standing here if that many Wizards had attacked."

With determination, she walked over to the legless assassin and pushed the tip of her sword against their throat. The assassin was surprisingly calm, and didn't make sound, despite their grave wounds. They were highly disciplined, and well trained.

With rage seething inside, Kailar said through gritted teeth, "You have no idea how long I've wanted to find that man, and now you let him escape. You had better tell me who you are, or you'll get to feel every bit of pain I ever wanted to inflict on him."

The assassin remained stoic as the Warriors encircled them. The commotion had apparently attracted the attention of several residents as well, no doubt startled from sleep by the sounds of combat, as front doors opened and curious onlookers gawked out.

The assassin's eyes furtively looked around, their stoicism suddenly replaced by terror. Realizing the assassin would say nothing, Kailar pointed her sword aside and reached down to unmask them.

Before she could even touch the assassin, Letan yanked her back and shouted, "Look out!"

There was a flash of heat, and bright blue flames suddenly engulfed the assassin. This time she actually screamed in agony, and everyone backed away from the surprising intensity of the fire. But the scream was short lived, and within moments there was nothing left but a pile of ashes.

Everyone stared in stunned silence, and Kailar and Letan exchanged horrified glances. "Did...did that really just happen," he asked.

On any other day, she would have had a sarcastic response. Not this time.

With the assault over, Kailar stared at her sword for a moment, and noticed there was still some blood on it from when she had taken the assassin's legs out. Absently she pulled a cloth out of her pouch and wiped the blood off.

"Who were they," Letan asked her. "Why did they attack you?"

Kailar looked at him evenly and replied, "I don't know." Sheathing her sword, she looked at the daggers left behind and frowned. They looked like they were made of the same metal as that which Klaralin's orcs had wielded, but she didn't remember the orcs ever using daggers. "But I'm going to find out."

Chapter 4

UNREST

The short walk to Daruun was enough for Cardin to mentally recover from his shattered bones. Spring was in full swing, but it was an unusually cold spring this year. He tried to sniffle away allergies, and thought to himself, *if not for the reprieve from winter's cold, I'd hate spring.*

Archanon, nestled in the foothills of the Ilari Mountains, still had snowfall on the cold days, but thankfully Daruun wasn't likely to get anymore snow.

Endri strode behind him, his steps light for a creature of his size, but he still shook the ground. When they reached the edge of town, they looked to one another.

"I promise you, the other Star Dragons are searching for answers," the emerald dragon spoke, his star-eyes piercing into Cardin's. *"We will not abandon you or give up on you."*

Cardin smiled, feeling the darkness in his heart lift just a little. There was always a feeling of elation and warmth in a Star Dragon's eyes, and sometimes Cardin thought it was the only thing keeping him sane. He walked over to Endri's right front paw and rested his hand on the dragon's lower leg.

"You've no idea how grateful I am that you are here," he craned his neck up to look at his newest friend. His voice shook a little as he spoke. "I don't know…I'm not sure what to do. How to get through all of this."

Endri crouched down low, so that Cardin didn't have to strain his neck. When the dragon's snout came close enough for Cardin to touch, he wanted to reach out and scratch the side of the dragon's cheek, like he would a dog.

"I do not know what your future holds, Cardin," Endri's mental voice was soothing and encouraging. *"However, I promise you I will stay with you until we find out."*

Suddenly the dragon's stomach audibly grumbled. Cardin grinned and looked back into Endri's eyes. "Well, maybe not *always* with me. Sounds like you need to hunt."

Endri's scaly lips curled back into a smile. *"Indeed,"* he replied, and then stood back up to his full height. He looked into town, and motioned his head. *"Besides, I think you two might need some time alone."*

Cardin followed the dragon's gaze to find that a crowd had gathered to stare at Endri. Even after several months of training Cardin, people were drawn to the Star Dragon in wonder. Cardin searched the faces, hoping he knew exactly of whom Endri spoke, and felt a broad smile cross his face when she pushed through the mass of people and walked towards Cardin with purpose.

With shoulder length platinum blonde hair and striking blue eyes, Sira Reinar always took Cardin's breath away. He wanted nothing more than to hold her in his arms. No, not hold her, be *held* by her, now more than ever. He looked up at Endri and smiled. "See you later tonight?"

"Of course," Endri replied, turning around carefully so as not to hit Cardin. Once he faced away from Daruun, Endri sprang into a full run, and moments later he spread his wings and leapt into the air. Cardin watched the dragon grow smaller and smaller as he picked up speed and altitude.

Then he felt the familiar, fierce presence of his love, and he turned to Sira as she came up beside him.

Without a word, he wrapped his arms around her, not caring how awkward it felt in her duty armor. He squeezed as hard as he could, and though she was surprised at first, she returned the embrace.

Cardin closed his eyes and didn't let go, he didn't want to let go. He wished he could just stay in her arms forever, forget the world around him, forget the war that raged in his soul.

But he knew the warmth couldn't last forever. She loosened her grip on him and whispered, "What's wrong?"

Cardin released his grip on her and pulled back just enough so that he could stare into her eyes. As much as he wanted to tell her what he felt, what had happened during training, how the dark magic had asserted itself again, he couldn't find the words, and just stood with his mouth hanging open.

That's when he noticed that the crowd was still gathered, but now stared at them instead of the dragon. Feeling his face grow warm, Cardin smiled sheepishly and shook his head. "It's…a conversation for later. Are you still on duty?" He looked down at her armor, but then felt his heart skip a beat.

Pulling further away, he looked closely at the brooch that held a white cape in place around her shoulders. The brooch was that of two bronze swords crossed in front of a shield, and though he had never actually joined the Warriors' Guild, he knew exactly what that meant.

"Lieutenant?"

A broad smile lit up her face, and she nodded rapidly. "Yeah, I just got the promotion and was coming to tell you!"

"Congratulations!" He surged forward to embrace her in a much more energetic hug. He felt her bounce up and down a little beneath his embrace, her exhilaration resonating through magic. If he hadn't been so preoccupied with his own issues, he might have felt that energy earlier.

When he pulled away again, the smile on her face faltered a little, and she lowered her head. "Yeah, well, it was almost a promotion of necessity."

A dark frown overtook his face, and his stomach sank when he realized what she meant. "Oh no, don't tell me…"

She nodded and looked at him with worried eyes. "The Tal Commanders have elected our very own *beloved* Commander Kale to assume the rank of General." The sarcasm in her voice when she said 'beloved' echoed his thoughts. It was a worst case scenario.

The search for the missing General Artula was ongoing, but no one had seen him since the meteor storm. Before the skies burned, most of the Allied troops had still been camped in the Wastelands, having just defeated the orcs, and several meteors had struck near the camps. Many feared that General Artula was killed by one of those meteorites.

Now there was little hope of finding him. With no successor appointed ahead of time and the next highest rank being that of Commander, the Guild fell back on the old tradition of Commanders electing one another.

A block of ice formed in the pit of Cardin's stomach and a sour taste reached his mouth. "Of all the Commanders in Tal, why did it have to be him?"

Sira took Cardin's hand and tugged him in towards the city. "Outside of Daruun, he puts on a totally different face," she explained, steering them around the crowd and towards home. "He's become quite the politician."

Cardin squeezed Sira's hand in an attempt to be reassuring, but he really just wanted her to reassure him. "That's the last thing we need."

She nodded. "I know. And naturally, he selected his favorite Lieutenant for promotion to Commander."

Another scowl crossed Cardin's face. "Really?! It should have been Kellis. He has seniority *and* he's the best we have."

They walked along in silence after that, not letting go of one another's hands. He couldn't feel her skin through her gloves, but it still felt nice. To finally be able to express his feelings for her again, in the open and unabashed, was a great relief for him, especially now. Especially given everything they faced.

He should have never walked away eleven years ago.

When they were halfway home, Sira suddenly said, "I envy you." She paused when he looked at her in shock, and amended, "Sort of."

Laughing a little, he asked, "How so?"

When she looked into his eyes, he saw genuine terror in them. "You don't have to answer to him. You don't have to take orders from him. Well, not exactly, anyway."

With a playful smirk, he replied, "I thought I only took orders from you."

With a shrug, she nodded, "So long as he doesn't reassign me, yes."

Squeezing her hand again, he shook his head. "Surely the King won't let that happen. He knows that we make a great team." Staring ahead, Cardin tried to push down the anxiety swelling up within. "I need you, Sira. Now more than I ever have."

The moment he said that, she stopped and tugged at his arm to bring him around to face her. "Okay, I can't just let that go. What's going on?"

Feeling his cheeks burn red, he looked down at their hands and reached out with his other one to take her free hand. "It's nothing new," he said, working up the courage to look into her eyes again. "More nightmares. More fear. More darkness." He still couldn't look into her eyes, worried that somehow the darkness within him could spill out into her soul.

Sira let go of his hand to lightly touch his chin, gently coaxing him to look at her. "Hey," she whispered, "I know you're afraid. I know this is all too much for one person to handle. But you're not alone, remember?"

He smiled and tried to look down again, but she wouldn't let him. "Say it," she insisted.

After a moment of allowing himself to be lost in her blazing blue eyes, he nodded. "I know. I'm not alone."

Leaning in, she closed her eyes and gently kissed him. Only for a moment, but that moment was all he needed to dispel the darkness.

The moment was shattered by distant shouts and the sound of boots running past them. A dozen on-duty Warriors ran through the intersection they were closest to, heading from the Guild fortress towards the center of town. More shouts could be heard from that direction, panicked and angry.

Sira groaned. "Now what?"

Together, they broke into a run, Cardin resisting the urge to use magic to get to the disturbance faster.

Towards the town square, and near the only surviving bridge crossing the river after the meteor storm, they saw that a crowd had gathered, much larger than the crowd that had gawked at Endri. They surrounded someone or something, but he couldn't see over their heads. The only thing he knew for sure was that their shouts were angry.

Panic and fear had grown strong in the general population, and already the Warriors and local soldiers of every major city in the four kingdoms had been forced to dispel riots. Religious extremists rallied people towards hatred and mistrust, and Cardin wondered if this was just another religious riot.

As soon as the Warriors ahead of them reached the crowd, they pushed their way through, yelling, "Make way!" above the discontented throng.

The Warriors were angry, too. Not only could Cardin hear it in their voices, but he felt it in their magic and saw it in their light. This was not a normal riot.

He stopped, allowing Sira to pass him, and closed his eyes. Reaching out with his soul, he searched for the epicenter of activity to try to figure out what was going on.

Finally, he felt two familiar points of energy at the center of the crowd.

Elves.

There was a third presence with them, but it was unlike anything he had felt before, like a void, present and absent all at once. He wanted to explore that new sensation, but he didn't have time. He had a terrible feeling he knew who the elves were, and they were in danger.

Without another thought, Cardin opened his eyes and leapt high into the air, using his powers to boost over the crowd. The first thing he saw in the center was Elaria's bright-orange hair and her scale armor, its color matching the greens of the grass fields surrounding Daruun. The other elf he had felt was Baenil, the elf that had been held captive by the Covenant for almost ten years. The third person with the elves was decidedly *not* an elf, as he was considerably shorter and much hairier.

Slowing his descent with magic, Cardin felt shocked by what else he saw in the shrinking circle enclosing the arrivals. Reis, sword drawn, was hunched over a wounded man, who was writhing in pain on the ground in a growing pool of blood.

When Cardin landed, the crowd immediately grew quieter and stopped pushing inward. The elves and their companion were surprised by his landing, but Elaria quickly smiled and breathed, "Cardin!"

He noticed that she had drawn her two long, curved daggers, but they were not bloodied. The short, hairy person, however, did have blood on his short sword. Cardin glanced at Reis and the wounded man, and noticed a dagger next to the man.

He looked again to the new short man, and took a moment to take in exactly what he was. If Cardin had to guess, the man was just under five feet tall, and was very well dressed in clothing that bore earthy dark blues, greens and browns. His hair and beard were a neatly-trimmed dark red, and the whites of his eyes surrounded pitch-black irises.

The newcomer appeared to be very fit, and looked like he knew how to handle the fine-steel short sword clutched in his right hand.

The crowd grew noisy again, so Cardin turned away from the newcomer and shouted, "That's enough! What's going on here?"

The din ceased again, if only because of his growing reputation and his powers. Then again, if they were angry about the presence of elves, these same people were likely not happy with his presence. As if reading his mind, he heard a few people shout, "Demons!"

"Is that what this is about," he called out, resisting the urge to reach back and draw the Sword of Dragons. The crowd edged inwards again, suddenly making him feel closed in. "They are not demons," he insisted, hoping to quell their advance.

"Then why did they attack one of us," someone pointed to the wounded man.

Cardin didn't know how to reply to that. He faltered for words, trying to figure out how he could placate the mob. However, much to his surprise, it was Reis who came to the rescue.

"This man attacked those three without provocation," he stood up, brandishing his bronze-dyed sword. "They defended themselves."

The other Warriors managed to finally push their way through the crowd and formed a circle around Cardin and the others. There was probably only ten feet of space from one end of the circle to the other, and with how many people were inside it now, that didn't leave much room. He was grateful for the Warriors, and even more grateful when Sira broke through and joined Cardin in the center.

"These are honored guests, not demons," he stated plainly.

"Guests of the King," Sira added. "Which means that man committed a crime by attacking them."

"Is it a crime to destroy demons," a voice shouted.

"To protect our children?" another added.

"They have brought only death!"

"The meteors were our punishment!"

The crowd pushed inwards again, and the Warriors had to use all of their strength to keep them back. It didn't matter, though, there were so many people that the Warriors' feet slid beneath them.

Cardin heard more shouts, people saying they would no longer tolerate demons, and that they had to take back their world before it was too late.

"They came to destroy us!" someone shouted.

"That's not true," Elaria called out. "We're here for peaceful reasons!"

Her words only incensed the mob further, and they pushed in closer, knocking one of the Warriors over. Suddenly a rock sailed over the line and barely missed Elaria. Then another hit Baenil in the back, catching him off guard.

They were losing control.

After another rock sailed past Cardin's head, he erected a magic shield around their group. The circle of Warriors suddenly found themselves pinned against that shield, but there was no way he could have safely separated the Warriors from the crowd. Rocks bounced harmlessly against his barrier, but Cardin was worried about the Warriors being crushed.

He had to get the visitors to safety! Could he create a portal? He'd done so once before, under extreme duress, but every time he tried it since then, dark magic interfered.

Cardin closed his eyes and tried to focus, drawing in as much power as he could. He tried to remember how he had done it back on Trinil, when the meteorite had come down right on top of him. But he had blacked out back then, and he remembered very little from that moment.

He couldn't do it. He didn't know how. With no other recourse that he could see, he turned to Elaria and was about to ask her to make one. However, the moment he looked at her, Endri's words echoed in his mind.

The Sword had already given him the knowledge he needed. He had to trust that the knowledge was there, and he had to let his instinct do the rest.

So he closed his eyes again, and thought about what he wanted to do with all of the magic he had drawn into himself. *I want to go to Archanon,* he thought.

The hairs on the back of his neck stood on end, and all of the energy built up inside discharged at once, to a point just ahead of him. It coalesced quickly, a wind inside of the shield stirring up dirt into a cloud. A bright, intense point of energy opened before him, and when he opened his eyes, he was face to face with a wall of energy.

He had done it!

But he couldn't keep the portal and the shield going for long. Magic continually flowed through him to power those points, but he was losing focus quickly. "Go now," he shouted. "Move!"

Grabbing Baenil and the newcomer, Elaria shoved them through the portal. She took a moment to look at Cardin in thanks, before she too passed through.

Cardin looked over at Reis, who stared emotionlessly at him. He wanted to say something to his friend, but they hadn't spoken to each other since the sentencing of the necromancers. Now wasn't the time for niceties anyway.

Sira knelt down next to the wounded man and ordered, "Reis, help me get him through!"

Reis glanced at the man, then at Cardin, before he slouched his shoulders. He sheathed his sword and bent down to gather up the man, insisting on doing so without Sira's help, and then he stepped between Cardin and the portal. He paused to look at Cardin, and then passed through the wall of light.

The crowd was pressing in more, and the Warriors were shouting threats now. Cardin hoped the mob would stop as soon as they saw that there were no 'demons' left to attack, so he dispelled the shield, and then grabbed Sira and hopped through his portal with her.

Just like stepping through a Wizard's portal, it was as if he had jumped through a door from one room to another. Except that here, in the foothills of the Ilari Mountains, it was still cold, and there were still piles of snow melting in the shadows.

He had brought them to the valley west of Archanon, known as the First City. The gates and walls stretched high into the sky before them, bridging between sheer cliffs on either side of the valley. The gates were open, as they often were during the day, but were well guarded on both the ground and in the towers. With all of the riots and the rise in crime in general, the King was being cautious.

The others had cleared away from Cardin's portal when they stepped through, but when it closed behind him, most gathered around him.

Except for Reis, who carried the injured man hurriedly towards the gates. If they were lucky, there would be a Wizard in the city with a talent for healing.

Looking to the others, Cardin asked, "Is everyone alright?"

There was a general consensus of nods, and he sighed gratefully. The short newcomer started to clean his short sword with a cloth he had produced from a pouch on his belt. In a brusque voice, he grumbled, "You humans certainly know how to show a visitor hospitality."

Cardin raised an eyebrow, and then looked to Elaria with a question in his eyes. She covered her face to hide a grin, but then caught Cardin's look and blushed.

"Who's your friend," Cardin asked.

"Ah, yes," she stepped closer to the short one. "This is Gilrin. He is a dwarf in service to the College of Serelik." Cardin vaguely remembered the name of that institution, the same institute that Baenil and Ventelis served. The last time the elves had visited, he remembered learning that the College was a place of education and research, and was highly respected.

Suddenly the gravity of what Elaria had said sunk in, and he felt a broad smile cross his face. "You're one of the dwarves of Darea?" Stepping closer to Gilrin, he extended a hand of friendship. "It's a pleasure to meet you!"

The dwarf stared at Cardin's hand, and then looked up at him with a frown. With uncertainty in his voice, he asked, "Am I supposed to give you something, human?"

Cardin frowned, but then retracted his hand, realizing suddenly that the shaking of hands might be unique to humans.

"Uh, no," he stuttered a moment. "I mean, it's just...it's nothing."

"Gilrin," Elaria said quietly, her tone that of a mother correcting her child.

Looking at her briefly, he seemed to catch himself, and then sighed. Holding his right hand to his stomach, he bowed deeply to Cardin. "It is an honor to meet you, Keeper of the Sword." When he stood upright again, he added, "I am afraid I am still shaken from our...welcome at Daruun. Please forgive my poor manners."

Smiling, Cardin returned the bow. "I understand. Let me be the first to welcome you to Halarite. This is Lieutenant Sira Reinar of the Warriors' Guild."

Sira stepped forward and met Gilrin's bow. Elaria looked at Sira in surprise, "Lieutenant? Congratulations on your promotion."

With a beaming smile, Sira nodded to Elaria, "Thank you."

Cardin then turned to Baenil, "And you, sir. I did not expect to see you back so soon."

Baenil's hair was neatly cut, his beard shaved off completely since the last time Cardin had seen him. He did not wear the nice robes that Ventelis had worn, but his trousers and tunic were the same earthy colors. They were far better kept than the soiled human clothes the Covenant had forced him to wear for so long. Baenil seemed to have learned to stand up straight again, yet his mannerisms still reminded Cardin of an abused animal, jumpy and uncertain.

"Um, Indeed," Baenil smiled awkwardly. "Though I wonder if I should have stayed home."

Before Cardin could say anything, Sira asked, "Why exactly have you returned?"

It was Elaria who replied, "We told Gilrin here about the ruins we found beneath Archanon. When Baenil told him some of the details, he grew excited."

With an eager nod, Baenil stepped closer, "Yes, yes, and I am quite excited to explore them further. We've come with Gilrin to ask permission to explore the ruins."

Cardin and Sira exchanged surprised looks. "Even with all of the kiklar down there?"

The kiklar were a giant, arachnid-like species that was attracted to magic, even though magic was exceptionally deadly to them. The creatures had swarmed around the King and Baenil after they had stumbled into the ruins while seeking shelter from the meteorites. They had barely escaped with their lives.

Sira asked, "Are you sure that's wise?"

"It is essential to the future of my people," Gilrin stated matter-of-factly. "It is history that has long been lost to us."

"Please," Baenil brought his hands together, as if pleading. "This is an opportunity we cannot ignore."

"And Gilrin thinks there's something down there that can drive the kiklar away," Elaria volunteered. "It'll be dangerous to get to it, but once we do, we'll be safe."

Looking again to Sira, Cardin let her answer. "I'm afraid it isn't up to us." She looked to the gates again, Reis having long-since disappeared into the city. "But we'll make sure you get an audience with the Allied Council." Nodding at the three visitors, she smiled. "Given their desire to smooth over diplomatic relations with the Dareann Elves, I'm sure they'll at least give you the opportunity to make your case."

Chapter 5

STOWAWAY

After the raid on the seaside warehouse, Kailar, Letan and the rest of the Warriors finished taking account of the criminals they had captured, which Kailar was pleased to discover was everyone else. Egil was the only one to escape.

The Warriors marched their prisoners back to the Guild complex and left them all in the dungeon, now over-populated with all of the criminals they had captured over the past few months. There was talk that the next raid would require using the city dungeon, but the Commander had resisted that notion for weeks now.

Even without being able to sense his essence, Kailar felt a brooding disquieted attitude from Letan. The Warriors went their separate ways to change out of their armor, including Kailar and Letan, but unlike the others, they would have to report in to the Commander as soon as he was ready to receive them.

Once they met up outside of their adjacent quarters, now in decidedly more casual clothing, Letan took the opportunity to lay into her. "What the hell were you thinking?"

"What do you mean," Kailar asked, playing dumb out of spite.

"You know damn well what I mean," he growled, his blue eyes impatient. "I've spent the last few months training you how to work as part of a unit again, and then you go and do something stupid like that."

Her cheeks burned, and she turned away from him. "If we'd waited any longer, the city's residents would have started waking up and would have compromised the mission just the same."

"So you should have brought that up," he planted his hands on his hips. "If you'd recommended moving in immediately, I'd have-"

"What," she glared at him. "You would have what? Heeded my advice and given the order?" He stopped short and didn't answer, but she already knew what it was. "Yeah, that's what I thought."

With a clenched jaw, he closed his eyes and drew in a deep breath. After a second, he looked at her and insisted, "We have to be more careful. *You* have to be more careful."

She scoffed and walked away from him, towards the Commander's office. He caught up to her and continued, "We can't just barge in and wreck every building we think the bad guys are squatting in. That warehouse belongs to honest people, and now the Guild will have to reimburse them for the damage *you* caused."

"*That's* what you're worried about," she gave him a disbelieving look. "You want to play it safe?" He started to reply, but she interrupted, "Devor has played it safe for decades, and look where it got you!"

"It got-"

"Criminals running rampant," she continued, flailing her arms out, "corrupt politicians, and Warriors capitulating to the criminals to the detriment of everyone."

"We did what we had to do," he growled. "Innocent people would get hurt!"

"Innocent people were already getting hurt," she glowered. "Or have you forgotten the slaves we rescued? Remember the conditions they lived in? The scars on their backs? All happening under your nose."

They had reached the Commander's office, the wooden door closed for the moment. They weren't sure if the Commander was awake and in there or not, so they stood outside and continued their argument.

"Yes, alright," he admitted, rubbing his temples. "We've made a positive difference since you came along. But without you and your powers, what chance did we have against them?"

"It is your duty as a Warrior to stand against those who harm the innocent," she growled. "Remember your oath? 'Honor and protect all whom you serve.'"

"I know the damn code," he growled. "And that's what I did, remember? We were disorganized, separated by wilderness, while the criminals were organized and had a vast network setup in every corner of civilized Devor. Moving against them before you showed up would have brought ruin to *everyone*. More than you realize even now."

"Right," she folded her arms. "Before I showed up. And since then, we've done things my way."

"Mostly," he pointed out. "I keep having to hold you back, remember?"

Once again, her face burned in embarrassment. Her line of thought was broken by that point, and she recalled the promise she had made to him, and to herself, yet again. She had to be better.

Suddenly the door opened, and the Commander stared at them expectantly. His dark face glowered at them in annoyance, and her face burned brighter, while Letan's cheeks likewise flushed. "Uh, good morning, sir," Letan stuttered.

Kent Querlin raised an eyebrow at him. "Are you two going to argue in front of my door all morning?"

Stammering a bit, Letan shook his head and stood at attention. "No, sir. Sorry, sir. We've come to give you a report on last night's raid."

"Good," he nodded and motioned them in. "I could use some good news."

Once they were inside and the Commander sat behind his desk, he listened, mostly patiently, as Letan detailed the events of the evening. Kent was less than thrilled about Kailar's destruction of the warehouse door or the destroyed crates caught in the crossfire. Thankfully, their actions weren't for naught - the other outlaws that they'd caught were some of the biggest names in organized crime. Furthermore, the Warriors had learned that those caught had gathered in the warehouse with the intent of boarding a ship bound for the colonies on Asirin.

The fact that the leaders were running scared from Devor was the best news they'd heard in months, and Kent attributed their success to Kailar's tenacity for a direct approach to all matters, and to her powers. She glanced smugly at Letan, but otherwise kept her mouth shut as Letan continued.

More concerning, however, were the assassins.

Kent listened intently as Kailar detailed her brief battle with them, and the powers they exhibited. Once she finished, she brought out a cloth that she had rolled the two darkened-steel daggers in and rolled them out onto his desk.

Gingerly, he picked one up, and his eyes lit up. Without access to normal magic, she couldn't feel the surge of power he no doubt felt from the enchanted weapons, but the fiery-orange gem in the pommel flashed brightly for a moment. Kent quickly set the weapon down and gaped at it.

"I've...never felt anything like that," he spoke quietly. "I've handled some enchanted weapons before, but nothing like that."

She nodded solemnly. "And while I wish that was the sole source of their incredible powers, I don't think it is, not entirely." Kent looked at her questioningly. "The only one left behind was able to incinerate themselves without their weapons."

Kent scratched his head and sat back in his chair, his brow furrowed deeply. "Any idea who sent them? Or where they came from?"

Rolling the blades back up into the cloth, unwilling to let them out of her sight, she shook her head. "None. I doubt they came from Devor, though."

Kent opened his mouth to ask a question, but immediately clamped it shut. "I doubt it as well," he said after a moment of thought. "Any suggestions on what we do about them?"

"For now," she glanced at Letan, "I don't have any suggestions other than to ask some of our contacts if they've heard anything. Barring that, it's likely they'll try again."

Kent nodded, and then stood up. "Alright. But that means you'll be looking over your shoulder for a while."

She smiled sardonically. "I'm used to it."

"Right. In any case, good job on the raid. At least there were no civilian casualties this time." Yet again, her face burned, memories from an early botched raid coming to the forefront. "I'm sure you two could use some rest. Dismissed."

With the Commander sated for the time being, Kailar and Letan left the Guild complex and went to the Inn at Water's Edge, one of many inns and taverns throughout Tieran. Tired, edgy, and hungry after a long night, the smell of the tavern's breakfast stew wafted tantalizingly past their noses. However, they hadn't come just for the inn's famous breakfast stew or cooked sausages.

The sun steadily marched across the sky, and the inn's breakfast rush was already over, leaving it empty, except for a few stragglers.

Kailar led Letan over to her usual spot in the far corner of the bar. Even though their civilian clothes helped them blend in, Kailar simply felt more comfortable out of her armor. In fact, these days she felt like armor had largely become unnecessary for her. It was rare that an opponent ever came close to touching her, and except for the assassins, none had penetrated her defenses since she'd gained her new powers. Unfortunately, as a Guild conscript, she was strongly encouraged to wear Guild-issued armor of some kind when doing anything officially sanctioned.

Except when she needed information.

"I thought you hated this cloak and dagger stuff," Letan remarked, looking around for the bartender, currently absent from his duties.

"I do," she grimaced. "But I stumbled onto Alric as an information source not long after the meteorites."

Raising an eyebrow, Letan asked, "In all of your free time away from me?"

She grinned mischievously. They'd spent almost every waking moment together since the burning skies, as much out of necessity as desire, since she was officially under his watch. However, Kailar had spent most of her life alone, and being with someone all of the time occasionally grated at her. Especially in that first month together, she often snuck away from Letan to find her alone time, until one day he simply said she didn't have to sneak away. He understood, and encouraged her to go out, so long as she didn't do anything that would get them both into trouble.

Sometimes she would just find an empty place to sit in darkness and just be by herself, but other times she would venture into the Water's Edge and sit alone at the bar. Alric, feeling that it was his duty as the proprietor, often tried to find out what bothered her. It annoyed her, but he had an uncanny ability to make people open up to him.

An ability that he volunteered when he found out she was a

Warrior intent on taking down the underground. Given that criminals seemed rampant in her early days on Devor, she was suspicious of his willingness to volunteer information. Until he confided in her about his little sister's involvement with organized crime, right up until she was found dead two years ago.

Which left Alric with some connections to organized crime, and a healthy desire for revenge. Most Warriors might not be willing to help him exact such revenge, and before Kailar came along, none of the Warriors were willing to stand up against the outlaws.

Kailar wanted to tear the very heart out of their organizations. That shared desire, and an ability to draw out information from people, made Alric valuable. At first she worried he risked his life, and she still worried about it to some extent, but he played the disparate elements against each other surprisingly skillfully. He also took the precaution of going to bed with a knife under his pillow every night, or so he assured her. At least once since they'd met, he had to ask her to help hide the body of a would-be assassin.

Which was part of why they were there today.

Alric came around from the kitchen with two bowls of stew. He was a tall and broad man, one who looked like he could break up a bar fight just by stepping in between a pair of sailors. As he took the bowls out to the only other patrons present, he caught sight of Kailar and Letan and acknowledged her with a nod. After serving the meal, he walked towards the kitchen again, asking, "Want the usual, love?"

Letan raised an eyebrow at the word 'love.' Kailar patted his hand, and nodded to Alric. "Two, please."

He disappeared into the back for a minute, and then returned with two bowls of breakfast stew. After setting them in front of Kailar and Letan and fetching utensils, he surveyed the inn before leaning against the back wall with a grin.

"You were the talk of the tavern this morning," he remarked. "Sounds like you had fun last night."

"Yeah," she shrugged before picking up the wooden spoon. She inhaled the savory smell of the stew, and quickly realized he had thrown in some extra seasoning, just the way she liked it. After years of living off of unseasoned game in the wilderness, she was getting spoiled. "At least, right up to the moment I was attacked by a bunch of assassins."

A dark look crossed over Alric's face, and he stroked at his full beard. "So that part was true, too."

Nodding once, she took a sip of the hot soup. It was strong and thick, and she loved it. Then Letan cleared his throat.

"Sorry," she wiped her mouth, "I should introduce you two. Alric this is Letan."

The dark look was quickly replaced by a look of absolute adoration. "Ah, so you're the one I've heard so much about!" He stepped forward to offer his hand, which Letan cautiously shook. "It's a right pleasure to meet you, sir."

With a half-grin on his face, Letan pumped the offered hand and nodded. "And you. I've heard nothing about you."

Squeezing Letan's hand before letting go, Alric replied, "Aye, that'd be our girl, wouldn't it?"

Letan raised his eyebrow again and looked at Kailar with a suspicious grin. "Our girl?"

She wanted to tell him 'don't worry,' but hoped he knew her well enough by now not to actually be concerned about Alric's shows of affection. Sooner or later, Letan would realize that Alric was that way with everyone.

Well, with everyone he liked.

Kailar took another sip of her soup, and then motioned to Letan's bowl to encourage him to try it. She watched his expression as he gingerly took a sip, and was pleased when a look of enjoyment came over his face.

Turning back to the barkeep, she asked, "So. You wouldn't by chance know anything about those assassins?"

Leaning back and folding his arms, he furrowed his brow in concern. "Unless I'm very much mistaken, they weren't hired by anyone I know."

Shaking her head, she replied, "I figured they wouldn't be. Not after one of them burned themselves alive to avoid capture."

"By the gods," Alric raised a hand up to cover his mouth. "They weren't exaggerating about that?"

She shook her head morosely. "No. They were powerful, too. Almost as powerful as I am, in their own way. They cast fire and lightning like a Wizard, and they escaped through individual portals." Resting her chin on one hand, she frowned and stared ahead absently. "Dark clothes, but no armor, so they're confident in their magic. Conceal every feature except their eyes. Only thing left behind was the burned one's daggers. The fire burned hot enough to melt anything metal."

"That's horrible," Alric let his arms fall to his sides.

They sat in silence for a while. She didn't mention that the blade of the daggers looked darker than normal steel. At first she had thought they were just like the darksteel weapons that Klaralin's orcs had wielded, but once she examined them in full light, she realized that they were a distinct shade lighter. Still, she felt like it was too big of a coincidence to ignore.

Kailar was so lost in thought that she didn't notice the slurping noises coming from Letan right away, but when she did, she looked to see him eagerly devouring his soup. When he realized Kailar and Alric stared at him, he stopped mid-sip, his eyes darting between them.

After a quick swallow, he asked, "What? It's good."

Snickering, she nodded and decided to enjoy her own breakfast. Alric took a few moments to tend to the other customers before he came back. "I take it you didn't just come here to ask me about the assassins," he nodded to her, resuming his position against the back wall.

In reality, she hadn't expected him to know much about them. Egil, on the other hand...

"One of our targets got away last night," Letan offered, wiping his mouth with the napkin. She smiled when she realized his bowl was empty.

Nodding, Kailar added, "A man named Egil. I don't know if he has a last name or not, but he used to run a group out of Neolas, collecting tolls."

Alric was already rolling his eyes. "Aye, I know of the bumpkin. Comes from a poor family on Edilas, but made himself rich as can be out here. He tries to hide his accent now, thinking he's better than everyone else."

Letan smirked, "Yeah that sounds like him."

"He was meant to be on that ship leaving port today," Kailar said. "Any idea where he'd go to ground after the warehouse?"

Chuckling, Alric nodded. "He's a coward running for his life. I'm betting he'll still be on that ship."

Letan and Kailar exchanged hopeful looks. "Any idea which ship," Letan asked. "The ones we arrested last night weren't as forthcoming with that detail, and there's half a dozen ships in port today, another half dozen anchored off shore, all due to depart sometime today."

As Kailar finished the last of her stew, she watched Alric as he stroked his beard thoughtfully. After another moment, he walked over to the window at the end of the bar and looked out into the port.

"That one," he pointed out. Kailar and Letan stood up and walked over to see which one he pointed at. "The Pranid. I know who the captain is, and if anyone would offer passage to Egil, it'd be him."

After trying to follow his finger, she saw which ship he pointed to, one moored to the largest pier, as it was one of the largest ships present. The ship's crew was busy loading up cargo, and from the looks of it, they still had plenty of time before the ship was ready to depart.

"We should get reinforcements," Letan turned to head out.

Kailar flipped a gold coin, far more than the meal would have cost, onto the counter and followed. "Thanks, Alric."

Before they went too far, Alric called out, "Oye, love." Letan again gave her a curious look. Ignoring it for the moment, she turned back to the barkeep. "About your assassins."

She looked for the other patrons of the inn, but they'd already departed some time ago and the inn was completely empty. Stepping closer to Alric, she nodded for him to continue.

"It just occurred to me," he frowned. "Why didn't they attack before last night? Because they didn't know how to find you before then."

"Yeah," she frowned. "Considering we've been everywhere *except* Tieran over the past month, that seems a big coincidence."

"Or not," Alric folded his arms. "Didn't the mayor return from Edilas yesterday?"

She opened her mouth to confirm his question, and then stopped short. Three months ago, when Letan had vouched for her, she recalled the Commander admonishing Mayor Warreck Evern, asking if rumors of his ties to the criminal underground were true. Ever since then, the Mayor had made it quite clear how much he despised Kailar.

Kailar also knew that there was a sizeable bounty on her head in

Falind. And ever since she had assassinated the Falind King, the Wizard Sal'fe had been king of Falind. Was Sal'fe responsible for the assassins? Had the Mayor given her up to Sal'fe?

After considering the possibility, she turned back to Letan wide-eyed and open-mouthed. His expression mirrored hers.

Giving their thanks to Alric, they departed quickly. When they were outside, she glanced around to make sure no one was in ear-shot, or at least weren't listening. The street was crowded with the usual daily traffic of the only major port city on Devor, and there was a din of constant noise that would help cover up their conversation.

"Do you think he's right," she hissed. "Could the Mayor be trying to eliminate me?"

Letan's hands were balled into fists, and he glared at the ground in thought. "If so, we still can't touch him." He looked into her eyes, the intensity of his anger apparent. "He's too big for us to act on suspicion alone."

"I know," she spoke through a clenched jaw. "We need to find evidence to present to the Commander." She thought about their situation for a moment, thought about the connection that Alric had just made.

Then she realized what they could do. Looking to her left, she walked along the inn's front until she could look around the corner at the docks, at the Pranid. Feeling the weight of her sword on her hip, a grin drew across her face and she looked at Letan, who had followed her over to look at the port.

A grimace drew down his features. "I hate when you get that look on your face."

Leaning over, she kissed him on the cheek. "You know you love me." And then her face grew warm, realizing what she'd just said, even though neither had actually said the word love to each other yet.

He stared at her, his face turning bright pink as he stammered out, "Umm, well, I mean…"

Fearing what he might say, or might not say, she grabbed his hand and pulled him along. "Come on," she smirked. "And don't worry about it."

He resisted her pull. "Wait, wait, wait, where are we going?"

"To the docks to interrogate Egil, of course," she flashed a grin back at him.

"But we need reinforcements!"

Shaking her head as she pulled him down one of the main cross streets for the docks, she shook her head. "No we don't! Just..." Stopping short, she looked at him again, realizing that while they were both armed, he wasn't wearing armor. "Maybe it'd be safer if I went in alone."

Clenching her hand, he shook his head adamantly. "I don't think so!"

Her heart leapt in her chest, and a smile blossomed on her face. If it had been anyone else, she would have been angry or annoyed. But it was Letan.

"Alright, then. Just stay close to me, okay?"

"Or we could get those reinforcements," he eyed her.

"It'd take too long," she shook her head. "And someone might notice marching Warriors and go warn them." She looked at him pleadingly. "You said last night that all I had to do was bring up my suggestion. I'm asking you to trust me, and to trust that I can handle this."

He stared at her hesitantly, but then sighed and nodded. "Alright. We'll try it your way."

Her heart felt light, and she beamed at him. Together, they rushed down the street, shoving through the crowd when necessary, until they came upon the docks.

A short distance later and they were at the specific pier that the Pranid was moored to. It was still a hive of activity, and briefly she wondered if Egil was actually aboard. However, recalling Alric's supposition, she realized he probably went on board the moment he escaped Kailar's grip.

With a confident stride, she walked down the pier side by side with Letan, spaced just enough that no one could get by them easily thanks to the various crates and barrels. She meant for them to be noticed, and noticed they were, as the crew on the actual pier one by one stopped working to gawk at them.

When the two of them finally reached the first worker, they came to a stop and Letan addressed the worker, a well-built woman that had the weathered look of someone who had spent a couple decades on the seas. "I'm Lieutenant Letan Velethar of the Warriors' Guild. We need to speak with your captain immediately."

Hesitant at first, the dock worker started to object, but then she eyed Kailar and nodded. "One second."

The worker turned towards the gangway, but Kailar grabbed her arm to stop her, eliciting a warning look that Kailar ignored. "You misunderstand. We're coming aboard to talk to your captain, now."

Anger flared in the woman's face. Through gritted teeth, she replied, "It's not my place to grant you permission to board."

Following along with Kailar's lead, Letan insisted, "We're not asking for permission. Escort us on board at once."

Kailar released her grip on the woman's arm, with the outward appearance of allowing the woman to lead them. However, Kailar suspected the woman would resist, as her eyes darted at her coworkers nervously, clearly unsure what to do.

With practiced ease, Kailar focused on creating the void within her that would allow dark magic to fill her being. She felt her body tingle with the strange emptiness that made her soul reverberate with power, and prepared to act.

Squaring off with them, the dock worker folded her arms and raised her chin. "And if I refuse?"

Deliberately slow, Kailar raised her left hand and faced her open palm at the dock worker. With a mental nudge, she released the pent-up power, unfocused without a weapon to channel it. The blast of purple-black energy sent the dock worker sprawling into several barrels behind her, and then she tumbled and rolled off between the dock and ship into the sea.

The rest of the dock workers reacted at once, all coming towards them menacingly, but Kailar and Letan drew their swords. "Easy, boys and girls," Letan cautioned, raising a Mage shield and stepping back into a combat stance. She glanced at him with a grin on her face, but the glower he gave her told her he didn't approve.

Her grin faltered, but they both knew that they were committed to her actions now. The crew of the Pranid looked ready to pounce on them, but Kailar imbued her weapon with enough dark magic to set it humming and made it glow a deep purple, and that stopped them in their tracks. Several crew members aboard the ship rushed to the side of the ship to see what was going on, including the captain.

"What's going on here," he demanded.

He was a typical privateer captain, without a dedicated uniform, but with far nicer clothes than his crew wore. His white tunic didn't have sweat stains and his trousers weren't worn by sliding down ropes or torn from getting caught. He also wore a gaudy tri-point hat.

If it came down to it, Kailar could easily defeat them all with minimal risk to herself. A part of her even reveled at the idea of fighting the entire crew off. But that might give Egil another chance to escape, or worse, lead to Letan being wounded.

So she opted for intimidation. Pulsing energy into her legs, she drew down, and then leapt up and over the captain and his crew, landing just to starboard of center. She was lucky, if she had jumped just a little further, she would have fallen into the open cargo bay.

Turning back to face the stunned-looking captain, she leveled her sword at him. "I know he's on board." Drawing her sword back and grasping the handle with both hands, she stared intently at him, keeping her weapon charged for effect. "You have one chance before I start tearing this ship apart to find him. Where is he?"

The captain's hand was on the hilt of his cutlass, and several of his crew had drawn whatever weapons they had, but none acted against her, not without the captain's order. The anger in his eyes might have intimidated someone else, but it had no effect on Kailar. She knew that she had won before the captain spoke.

Slowly taking his hand off of his sword, he glanced around at his crew, no doubt debating what effect it might have on their loyalty if he gave in to such aggressive posturing. Thankfully, he cared more about protecting his ship and crew than he did his reputation. "Down in the hold."

"Good," she smiled, lowering her sword. "Show me."

He started to object to being ordered around, but stopped short and nodded.

"And let the Lieutenant on board, too."

"Fine," he growled. "Let him up!"

Keeping a tight grip on her weapon, Kailar walked over to the nearest gangway and waited. Letan, unused to the movement of ships, struggled a little to come up, but made it unharmed. Both of them ignored the scowls the crew gave them.

Once he was safely aboard, the captain led them down into the hold. There were a few concerned crewmembers below that the captain ordered on deck after Kailar insisted, leaving just the three of them and a half-full cargo deck.

The captain hesitated one last time, before he pointed to a specific barrel. Kailar approached the barrel, but didn't discount Egil possibly having a weapon, and stopped several feet away.

After staring at the crate and perceiving the slightest hint of movement between strips of wood, she sighed and pointed her sword at it. "Have some dignity and come out on your own," she commanded.

A moment later, the lid of the barrel popped open, and Egil, dirtier than ever, slowly rose. "Easy, there, girly," he cautioned, raising his hands slowly, a rusted dagger held unthreateningly in his right. Kailar pointed her blade at the dagger, and he promptly dropped it.

Looking over her shoulder at the captain, she casually stated, "You may go."

With a frown, he replied, "Excuse me?"

Kailar was about to point her sword at him, but she didn't have to. With his free hand, Letan grabbed the captain by the back of his collar and hauled him over to the ladder. "Don't worry your little hat off," he smirked at the captain. "We'll be done shortly and you can leave dock only a little late."

As he tried to push the captain up the ladder, the captain stopped and turned to him. "Wait, you mean you're not arresting me or impounding my ship?"

Letan glanced at Kailar, and she nodded, grateful that he already knew what she intended to do. "Only if you continue to cooperate," he said, turning back to the captain. "I want your entire crew lined up on the pier and out of ear shot while we interrogate our prisoner for a minute." The captain appeared to start to object, but Letan interrupted, "If you cooperate without any objection, you're free to go once we're finished."

Clamping his mouth shut, the captain glanced at Kailar, then at Egil, and then he nodded and made haste up. "Clear the deck!" he shouted. "All hands to the pier, now!"

Kailar turned back to Egil, his face strained from trying to hide his fear and confusion. She waited patiently, allowing a grin to extend across her face as Egil's fear stretched into genuine terror. "What...what are you going to do?"

She didn't bother to reply right away, and allowed Egil to sweat. She didn't want to risk the crew finding out why she wanted to interrogate him. As the thunder of boots scrambling across the deck and down the gangways grew silent, Letan peaked his head above before nodding and joining Kailar.

"Now, then," she lowered her sword and stepped closer to Egil. "Now that we have a moment." She placed her hand on Egil's chest, and then gave a little shove.

"Hey!" he protested, trying to catch his balance but failing. He and the barrel crashed over and he smacked his head on the deck.

Straddling him, Kailar again placed the tip of her sword against his neck and smiled. "There, now, we're back where we were before. And this time no assassins are coming to interrupt us."

"Now, now, I didn't have nothing to do with those assassins," he waved his hands defensively. "Honest, that was just a lucky break for me!"

Kailar narrowed her eyes. She knew he was telling the truth, but she wanted him to help her make the connection to Warreck, if there was one to be made. So she moved the tip of her sword to place it against his left arm. She allowed the magical charge to vibrate the blade a little, and pushed the tip against his skin. The vibration drew blood, and he flinched. "Ouch, hey!"

"Lucky break," she asked. "Maybe a break is in order."

Letan's cautious hand rested on her back for a second, but she ignored it.

"I swear, I don't know nothing about them," Egil insisted. "I've never seen them before or heard of them."

"Who would?" she asked. "They came from Falind and knew exactly where I was, so who knew? Who are they working with?"

"I d-d-on't know," he stuttered, fear breaking down all pretense of proper speech. "I swear I don't!"

Pushing a little harder, she shouted, "It was someone in this city!" She wanted to release the magic in her sword, wanted to obliterate his arm. It would be so easy…

"The mayor," Egil cried out. "Evern, it might be Evern!"

She glowered. "Might be?"

"Yes, might be," he nodded emphatically. "Probably. No, it's gotta be him, it's gotta be!" Egil was hysterical, his eyes darting between his arm and her sword. "He was makin' a lotta money off of us, would take payments to convince the city guards to look the other way when we needed them to. Now he's losing everything cause 'o you."

Letan asked, "Because she's putting an end to organized crime?"

"Yeah, that," Egil nodded. "He just came back from Edilas, went there to ask them for relief after the falling stars, yeah? He probably wanted to cash in on your bounty himself."

Kailar looked at Letan, and he grimaced at her. "It's exactly what we thought. Maybe worse."

"Yeah," she drew her lips into a thin line. Then she turned her attention back to Egil and placed the tip of her sword against his forehead. "You'll testify to all of this, right?"

Pushing his head as hard against the deck as he could, he waved the sword away and replied, "Yes, yes, just...please, don't."

"Ease up, Kailar," Letan nudged at her arm with his free hand. "We've got him."

With a sigh of disappointment, more for show than anything, she pulled her sword away and held it loosely in her hand. "Fine. Get up."

Heaving a sigh of relief, Egil pulled himself up, wincing when he accidentally put pressure on his left arm. Once he stood, he grasped at his injury. "Come on," Letan motioned towards the ladder. "We're taking you to the Commander."

"Right, of course," he started forward. "Just...ease up, will ya?"

Chapter 6

THE DWARF OF SERELIK

When Cardin and Sira escorted the elves and dwarf into the city, they thought that another riot was going to start. During the course of the Orc War Campaigns, Cardin had grown used to traversing excited, cheering crowds in the Market District of Archanon, but this time they were met with silence.

It was not for a lack of attention, either. Everyone they passed stopped to stare at them, at the elves and dwarf. Some of the people showed obvious fear on their faces, others intense anger, but none spoke. Cardin shifted uncomfortably, but tried to put on a confident face.

Everything had changed in the wake of the cataclysmic winter events. Thousands had died, and even Sal'fe's staff couldn't resurrect all of the dead, especially not at the prices he demanded. Now there was no enthusiasm left from the commoners, there was only constant fear of the next disaster.

With growing regularity, mobs formed and protested, sometimes forcefully enough that Warriors and soldiers had to arrest them. He'd heard it was worse in some of the outlying cities, such as Valaras, where unrest had already been present even before the skies burned.

When they passed through the inner city gates, Cardin felt instant relief. Despite the occasional glare of a servant working in front of some of the wealthy houses, he felt far safer in here, especially with the large guard force posted at the gate.

Once they reached the castle, they were greeted by a morbid Governor Maral, who asked them to wait in the throne room for the King after Cardin explained the situation. If they were to meet the King in the throne room, then the council was not in session, which was a rare occurrence these days.

That changed when King Beredis met with them and listened as Elaria, Baenil, and Gilrin made an impassioned plea for access to the dwarven city beneath Archanon. As Cardin expected, the King was unwilling to say yes or no without the support of those left on the Allied Council.

With the assistance of the court Wizard, a meeting was quickly arranged for later that day, and within hours, they assembled.

If there was one thing that Cardin had learned about politics, it was that most politicians needed new information to be doled out to them carefully, and not suddenly or all at once. So he was not surprised when he and the others were asked to stay out of sight until called for.

At the moment, they were gathered in a waiting room just down the corridor from the council chambers, waiting impatiently for their turn before the Council. Cardin sat on a divan with Sira, his arm idly wrapped around her midsection while he stared at the marble floor in thought.

The others around him conversed quietly, but he scarcely heard anything they said. All he could think about was one of his latest dreams, of a tall figure clad in black armor. The figure was daunting, and yet they did not attack him in his dreams. Instead they tried to tell him something, but he couldn't understand them through their helmet.

Sira nudged him, startling him out of his reverie. "What," he looked at her, and then around at everyone else. Blushing, he realized the group stared at him. Had someone asked him a question? "Sorry, I was…"

"Somewhere else," Baenil asked.

Cardin nodded. "Essentially."

Nodding towards the elves, who were seated in individual chairs across from them, with Gilrin standing next to Elaria, Sira said, "Elaria asked how your training with Endri was going."

"Oh," he blushed, looking into Elaria's sunset-orange eyes. He started to tell her that the training was going well, but then stopped. It was an automatic response, but not a truthful one. "It's been…interesting," he amended. Then his head popped up. "Endri! He doesn't know we aren't in Daruun anymore."

Sira tilted her head to one side and asked, "Well, he's able to sense the power of the Sword, right?"

Cardin again looked to Elaria, recalling that she had been on another world when she first sensed the powers that the Sword of Dragons had given Kailar. Did that mean Endri could keep tabs on him at all times? He nodded, "Yeah, that's right. If he hasn't already, he'll figure it out and come find us when he needs to."

Elaria smiled, and was about to say something else, but was interrupted by a knock on the door. A moment later, Cardin's father Draegus opened the door. As the Captain of the King's personal guard, he wore the finest leather and steel armor, resplendent with a black and silver tabard with Tal's symbol on the front.

"Cardin, everyone," he nodded. "They're ready for you."

Glancing at the others, Cardin smiled encouragingly and everyone stood to follow Draegus out. He resisted the urge to give his father a hug when he walked next to him. He wanted to say something to Draegus, but he wasn't sure what, so he remained silent until they stood before the doors and walked in.

The chamber had once served as a war room for Tal during the Lesser Wars, but was hastily converted into a meeting hall when the threat of Kailar and Klaralin had necessitated an alliance between the four kingdoms and the Wizards' Guild.

Six wooden tables were set in a circle around the center of the room, each table serving each member of the Council. Immediately to his right as he entered the room was Tal, where King Beredis sat, along with the new Tal General, Idann Kale. Cardin tried not to show his distaste for the new General, and tried not to meet the former Daruun Commander's eyes. There were few people in the world that Cardin hated, but Idann was one of them. Seated in chairs against the wall behind the Tal table, he was surprised to see Prince Beredis also present. The last he'd heard was that the Prince was still touring the kingdom.

To the right of the Tal table was Falind's, Tal's greatest enemy before the alliance. The first and only Wizard King on Halarite, Sal'fe, sat by himself. He did not have nor need a court Wizard, and was still a bit of an enigma to Cardin. Surprisingly, Sal'fe no longer wore the dark grey or black robes that he often donned, and had opted instead for robes matching his Kingdom's colors, forest green with gold trim. He kept his gray goatee neat and trimmed, and his hair equally trimmed.

Next was the Wizards' Guild, where Cardin was pleased to see both Master Wizard Valkere and his friend and former mentor Dalin. Actually, he still looked to Dalin as a mentor, even though Endri had taken over training for Cardin. Dalin wore his usual dark blue robes, just as Master Valkere wore his customary white with gold-trimmed robes, and both smiled and nodded to Cardin as he made eye contact with them.

The next table in line was the Covenant's table, the central religious leadership of Halarite. They still had not elected a fourth member to replace the exiled Pevrin, and so were only three strong. Donning their usual black with red-trimmed robes, their hoods were down and they watched Cardin and the others enter with passive eyes. Once respected leaders of the communities of all four kingdoms, they had lost much of their clout with the Allied Council over the past year since they had been caught in too many lies and half-truths. Still, they tried desperately to calm the masses, and Cardin wondered if the riots would have turned into outright civil war by now if it hadn't been for their efforts.

The next table was empty. It had been empty ever since the meteorites fell, and the Dark Dragon Nuuldan had returned. The capitol city of Saran was completely wiped off the face of the planet, along with every man, woman and child. The entire political body of Saran was gone, including the King and all of his legitimate heirs. It had left Saran in disarray, and despite several claims of illegitimate heirs, it was a kingdom without leadership. No one on the Allied Council knew what to do about it, and some feared a civil war could erupt in Saran at any moment.

Finally there was Queen Sechel Leian of Erien. Their capitol city of Maradin was in ruins following a cataclysmic tsunami and subsequent battle against the invading necromancer army, and the destruction of the crystalline Navitas had left magical wounds near the city that no one was eager to go near. As a result, the Queen now ruled from her next biggest city, the port of Lassil far to the north. He noticed that she often dressed in far warmer clothes than she used to, often lined with furs of northern wildlife.

Cardin and the others reached the center, and Draegus joined the King at the Tal table. King Eirdin Beredis, a strong man with dark skin and a powerful voice, stood up and began, "Everyone here is familiar with Cardin, Sira, Elaria and Baenil. I would like to introduce our first dwarven guest, Gilrin of the College of Serelik."

Gilrin stepped forward to be closer to the Tal table and bowed to the King. "Thank you for your introduction, Your Majesty."

Nodding, Beredis then asked, "Would you like to present your request to the Council?"

That stopped Gilrin short, and his mouth fell open. Cardin almost chuckled at the sight of him looking so shocked. "Me, Your Majesty? It was my intent to allow either of my companions to present the request."

With a warm smile that Cardin recognized, the King encouraged, "You are the one with the most at stake, if I recall our initial conversation correctly. Furthermore, you seem to be at least as well spoken as your companions."

Gilrin looked back at Elaria, who smiled warmly and said, "Go on, Gilrin."

Memories of Cardin's first appearance before the Council flashed through his mind, and he felt for the poor dwarf. He hadn't taken the time to get to know Gilrin yet, so he didn't know what exactly the dwarf did for the elven College, but it probably didn't involve public speaking.

Clearing his throat rather noisily, Gilrin turned back to the King, and then looked around at the rest of the Council. Cardin decided that it was a good opportunity to try to get a better sense of the dwarf, magically speaking. He closed his eyes and extended his being outside of his body, an exercise he was well-practiced in. Something had felt strange when he first encountered Gilrin in Daruun, but he hadn't had time to figure it out.

Now he did. Gilrin was void of magic. In fact, it was as if he didn't exist at all, but for the tiniest hint that something living stood there. Cardin had only felt such a void twice since he'd become the Keeper of the Sword. The first time was when the Star Dragons had cut Kailar off from magic completely. The second was when he'd met Anila Kovin, one of the Covenant's trusted guardians. In the case of Anila, she was more powerful than anyone could have possibly known, but she used her powers to actively conceal herself so that no one knew what exactly she was – half human, half Wizard.

Focusing his mind tightly on Gilrin, Cardin attempted to determine if the dwarf likewise had hidden power. He'd managed to uncover Anila's secret by performing the exact same exercise. However, in this case, there was no hidden power underlying the void. There was just emptiness.

It felt unnatural.

"I am not actually much for words," Gilrin finally started. "So please forgive me as I try to think of how to phrase my request." He fell silent, his mouth half-open, as he continued to look around at each representative in turn, before his eyes fell upon King Beredis again.

Finally, he drew himself up and nodded. "I wish permission for my companions and I to explore the dwarven city beneath this grand city."

Just as Cardin had expected, the Council stirred in mild surprise. There were several whispers as individuals at their respective tables conversed quietly for a moment. This wave of reaction seemed to surprise Gilrin, who stammered for a moment, and then fell silent.

Once the din of conversation fell silent, King Beredis nodded again to Gilrin. "Please elaborate as to why you wish to explore the city."

Gilrin began to work his hands nervously, and he kept glancing back at Elaria. "It has to do with my people's history. We were once a powerful race, and by powerful I mean powerful in magic. Tens of thousands of years ago, all that changed. Every dwarf, everywhere, we lost our connection to magic."

"How can an entire species be cut off from magic," Master Valkere asked, his wizened voice curious but not incredulous. Realizing the implication that even the Master Wizard didn't understand how it was possible, Cardin grew even more interested in the situation.

"No one knows," Baenil replied for Gilrin. "It is an ancient mystery that has never been solved. While most of my research throughout my life has focused on humans, I've also studied the mystery of the dwarves, and so far I have not found any clues. No one has, as far as I know."

"Little is known from my people's time before the event," Gilrin added. "Just that we were powerful, and that following our loss of magic, our entire civilization across the Universe fell to attacks from countless others. Some wiped out dwarven kingdoms, others subjugated my people."

Cardin looked at Baenil and Elaria suspiciously. Did that include the Dareann Elves?

Silence fell upon the assembled Council. Cardin wondered why, until it occurred to him the implications of what they had just learned. In one cataclysmic event, the entire dwarf race had gone from a powerful, Universe-wide power, to a subjugated race.

Then something else occurred to Cardin, and he spoke without thinking, "This is the first intact dwarven ruin anyone has found."

Gilrin hesitated, and then amended, "The first in a long time, yes. Perhaps the most complete and unsullied ruins ever discovered."

Baenil added, "It is our hope that there might be some clue as to what happened to the dwarves in the city."

"Even if not," Gilrin added hastily, "it's a chance for us to study a well-preserved piece of my people's history."

The members of the Council glanced around at each other, as if wondering who would bring up the obvious issue with the request. It was Master Valkere who asked, "You are aware that the underground city is infested with a spider-like species?"

"A species known as the kiklar," Baenil nodded. "I told him all about them."

"As I have said," Gilrin continued, "my people were once powerful with magic. The kiklar are attracted to magic, and so were a common problem for my ancestors. Every dwarf city will have an enchanted device at the center that, once activated, will drive the kiklar out of the city."

Another low din of conversation fell upon the Council. "That is quite a powerful device," Valkere spoke in admiration. "How is it activated?"

That was where Gilrin and his companions hesitated. "We do not know, exactly," Baenil replied. "That is part of the risk we acknowledge. Once we find the device-"

"Which will not be difficult to find," Gilrin interrupted.

"We will have to figure out how to activate it," Baenil continued. "It could be as simple as throwing a lever, or it might require someone with magic to channel energy into it."

"Or it could be something else entirely," Queen Leian chimed in. "You really do not know, do you?"

"I'm willing to take the risk," Gilrin replied heatedly, not bothering to look at the queen.

"We all are," Elaria added hastily. "This is an important historical find."

"One which resides upon our world," King Beredis nodded. "Which is why you came to us to ask permission to venture into the city."

Gilrin and Baenil both nodded to the King. "Yes, Your Majesty," Baenil bowed, his voice turning meek. "Last time I ventured to Halarite, I, uh…I made the mistake of attempting to explore your sacred grounds without your permission. You see, we, that is…" Baenil's confidence vanished, and his usual nervousness returned. Cardin felt his heart go out to him, and wondered if he would ever fully recover from his captivity. As it was, Cardin was shocked that the elf was able to project confidence to the Council for as long as he had.

Elaria finished for him, "We wish to ensure future cooperation between our people, and feel that this venture would also represent an opportunity for our two worlds to work together and gain one another's trust."

"So your venture is officially sanctioned by your rulers," Queen Leian asked.

Elaria looked to her and seemed to hesitate for a moment, but then nodded. "Yes. We have the full support of the College of Serelik."

Cardin frowned, realizing that wasn't exactly what the Queen had asked. Were they there only on the College's initiative, and not actually representing the government of Darea?

A quiet din of conversation fell upon the chambers again, each table conversing amongst themselves, except of course King Sal'fe, who stared thoughtfully at the dwarf. Sal'fe had been suspiciously quiet during most of the meeting.

Then Cardin noticed something strange. Prince Beredis had stood up and was whispering quietly with the King. After a moment of conversation, the King looked at his son with mixed surprise and approval.

Finally, the King nodded and cleared his throat to get everyone's attention. "I would like to propose acceptance of their request, on the grounds of attempting to establish diplomatic relations with the Dareann civilization. Furthermore, as a representative of the combined Allied Council, I would suggest that the Keeper of the Sword and his companions escort the Dareann party into the ruins."

"I agree," Sal'fe nodded. Is this where he would play his hand? "Furthermore, if anyone could conduct them through the kiklar safely, it would be the Keeper of the Sword."

Cardin raised a curious eyebrow, and then nodded his thanks to Sal'fe. What was the old man playing at now?

Alaia was the first voice to object. "In order to reach the city, they will have to pass through the Tomb of the Ascended."

The Council members stared at Alaia silently, waiting for her to try to defend her position further. She and the Covenant had tried to use that as an excuse last time to prevent Elaria and Baenil's mentor, Ventelis, from searching for Baenil in the catacombs. They had been out-voted then, and without King Lorath to support the Covenant's position this time, the chances of winning a vote barring the Dareanns access were slim.

After looking around and finding no support, Alaia sighed and hung her head. "Very well, we will assent, but only if members of the Order are allowed to accompany."

"Anila would be a good choice," Cardin volunteered, and then felt his face grow warm. He had almost added that her powers would be useful against the kiklar. The arachnid-like creatures were attracted to magic, but were simultaneously susceptible to strong magic blasts. She was powerful, more so than a Mage, but Cardin had promised to keep her secret. He quickly added, "We've worked with her before. I trust her."

It wasn't entirely true, he still wasn't sure if he trusted her. On the other hand, they might be left with someone they didn't know and whom would interfere with their quest at every turn. Anila, especially considering her heritage, would most likely be interested in finding the truth, rather than suppressing it.

Alaia glanced at her companions, and then nodded. "That is acceptable."

"Erien supports this effort as well," Queen Leian nodded. "If needed, a contingent of Erien soldiers or marines will accompany the expedition."

Everyone then turned to the Wizards' table. Master Valkere glanced at Dalin, who simply nodded. With a grin, Valkere nodded his assent. "The Wizards agree. I propose that Sira Reinar command the expedition, and the rest of their normal team accompany them. Dalin can represent the Wizards' Guild in this matter."

Cardin smiled at Dalin, grateful to have his friend along, but the smile faltered when he saw his friend lower his eyes and look forlornly at the table. Was he uneasy about joining them for some reason?

Cardin then remembered Sira's promotion, and looked at the Tal table, at General Kale. Would he object? Or would he assent to the King's command that Sira and Reis accompany them?

Then the Prince stepped beside Idann and whispered into his ear. Idann looked to him in surprise, but then nodded and turned to Cardin. "Although we are short-handed in Daruun, I believe we could spare Lieutenant Reinar and Reis Kalind for this venture."

Reis. Cardin hadn't actually thought about it until just now, but this would mean that he and Reis would have to work side by side again. He still didn't know why, but his friend had avoided him like a plague ever since he'd started training with Endri. Was it because he was jealous of Cardin's time with the dragon? That seemed unlikely, but he really couldn't figure any other reason for it.

And why was the Prince encouraging both the King and the General to support Cardin's part in this venture? At least, that appeared to be what was going on.

"It is settled, then," King Beredis nodded. "Lieutenant Reinar, you will lead the expedition. Take whatever time you need to prepare, and depart at your convenience."

Cardin smiled at Sira, but she ignored his jubilance for the moment and nodded to the King. "As you command, Sire."

Then the King looked at Gilrin, Elaria, and Baenil. "On behalf of the Allied Council, I would like to extend an apology for the riot you encountered upon your arrival."

Elaria and Baenil exchanged glances, and then Elaria nodded to Baenil, who replied with his projection of confidence restored, "We accept your apology, Your Majesty. If I may make a suggestion in that regard?"

King Beredis and Cardin raised eyebrows at Baenil. "Please do," the King said.

"In order to ensure smoother diplomatic relations between our people," Baenil began, "I highly recommend we determine a neutral location where Dareann Elves and Dareann Dwarves would be welcome to arrive without harassment by your citizens."

The King frowned and began to reply tersely, but Master Valkere interrupted. "Your Majesty, if I may?"

Cardin almost smirked at the King's exasperated look. He was not used to being interrupted, even in Council sessions. "Of course, Master Wizard," he said with strained patience.

Valkere stood up to address the assembly, and began, "As the Council is aware, we have begun rebuilding the first Grand Wizard Hall in the north, with the intention of one day returning fully to Halarite."

Cardin felt his jaw drop open. That may not have been news to the Council, but it was news to him! Why hadn't Dalin told him about that decision? Is that why Dalin was away so often now?

"While our numbers are not what they once were," Valkere continued, "There are still enough Master Wizards present that we believe we can achieve something to help in this regard. It is possible that we could enchant the rebuilt Grand Hall such that it will create a field enveloping all of Halarite, or at least all of Edilas. With it, we could force all incoming portals to a central location at the Grand Hall. This would ensure that we would never have unexpected visitors again."

There was another outbreak of hurried whispers and surprised exclamations within the chambers, and Cardin stared at them slack-jawed.

"I did not think such a feat was possible," Beredis said cautiously.

Valkere visibly hesitated, glancing down at his hands for a moment before looking up. "Ever since the Keeper first reported his encounter with the orc shaman, ever since he learned that there was a grave threat attacking countless worlds, we have tried to find a way to help protect Halarite. I have heard of such abilities before in my travels to other worlds, and the enchantment that the necromancers used to block portals to Trinil convinced me that it was indeed possible. We still do not know exactly how to make it happen, but we are researching it diligently."

Beredis looked at the other council members in awe, and then nodded. "Given that we intend to relocate the Allied Council to the Grand Wizard Hall upon its completion, that seems to be the best location to direct incoming portals to. What of portal travel within Edilas?"

"It will remain largely unaffected," Valkere nodded. "However, we would also like to propose building static portals between all capital cities and the Grand Hall."

Cardin's head spun as he tried to soak in all of the new information he was incidentally being exposed to. It seemed as if a lot of things were changing that he hadn't been privy to.

"You wish to turn the Grand Wizard Hall into the hub of all activity on Halarite," Queen Leian opined.

Hesitantly, Valkere nodded. "Yes. That was not something we originally intended when we decided to rebuild the Grand Hall. However, the other Masters and I feel that it would be the most prudent option."

Cardin smirked. The Wizards had been isolated for three thousand years. Now they were about to become the central travel hub for the four kingdoms *and* for Halarite. He could imagine the discomfort some of the other Masters felt at this turn of events.

Glancing at the guests present, Beredis nodded. "I think this is wise. However I believe we should leave this decision for a future Council session."

"I agree," the Queen said with obvious relief. "I think we should all digest this proposal before making a decision."

Looking to Cardin, Beredis nodded. "Thank you all for coming today." Then in general, he said, "This Council session is now closed. Good evening."

Chapter 7

EVERN MANOR

"What do you mean it isn't enough?!" Kailar raised her voice more than she meant to at Commander Querlin. She and Letan had brought Egil before Kent in irons and made him confess all over again. It had taken a little insistence on Kailar's part to get him to talk, but when he finally did, the Commander listened intently.

With a frustrated sigh, Kent looked at Egil and asked, "Can you give us any specific details about the Mayor's involvement with your organization?"

Kailar looked intently at Egil, whose mouth had fallen open to talk, but then he stopped and furrowed his brow. "Me, personally? No, I never dealt with him. Tieran wasn't exactly my area of responsibility, if you know what I mean."

"Egil…" Kailar growled in warning.

Raising his bound hands defensively, he stepped back, only to bump into Letan. "Look, I'm serious, I never had direct dealings with that man! I only know that I was told if I ever needed to move people or, you know, things on or off Devor, all he needed was a bit of gold to arrange it!"

Turning back to Kent hopeful, Kailar felt her stomach sink when the Commander shook his head morosely. "The city council will not accept that as evidence of wrong-doing." Nodding at Egil, he added, "Especially coming from him."

She wanted to shout at Kent, *are you kidding me?!* But she managed to keep her temper in check. Next to Letan, Kent was her biggest ally in the Warriors' Guild, and she couldn't afford to alienate him. "So what do we do," she asked through clenched teeth. "What do we need?"

"Evidence of specific actions," Letan spoke before the Commander could. "Tieran is the biggest city, the most influential. A place this big thrives on bureaucracy, and I imagine the underground does too. Especially with how big their influence is, they'd need some sort of bureaucracy just to keep track of it all."

"Exactly," Kent nodded and walked around behind his desk. He then nodded at Egil and ordered, "Hand him off to the guards outside."

Kailar frowned suspiciously, but Letan moved without question and grabbed Egil gruffly by the shoulders to ferry him outside the open door. After giving the guards orders to find a place in the crowded dungeon for Egil, he came back and, at the Commander's order, closed the door and drew the lock.

Producing a key from seemingly nowhere, Kent went to the back of his office and unlocked a chest. He spent a few moments pulling items such as pieces of his personal leather armor out, before he finally pulled a few pieces of parchment out from the bottom.

Placing the documents on the desk, he nodded at them, and said, "This is the best I've been able to do so far."

Kailar and Letan glanced at the parchments, and she quickly recognized them as orders signed by Warreck. She scanned through the details in the orders, but Kent supplied, "I've been after Warreck for years, and I've tried to collect any sealed orders I can from him."

Unfortunately, the parchments were simply orders for city soldiers to change routine patrols, or for certain supplies to be bought from Edingard or from individuals visiting Tieran.

None of it was criminal.

"He's careful," Kent shook his head. "Nothing in these orders points to anything illegal, but I also happen to know that these coincide with times that the Warriors stumbled upon stolen goods being moved." With a heavy sigh, he added, "Back then, we let them all go." Kent looked directly at Kailar, his eyes alight. "We had to.

But now you're here."

The look in his eyes told her exactly what he meant, and she felt a grin stretch across her face. "You couldn't touch anyone or anything until I came along and stirred things up." She nodded. "You think we can get to him now."

"Maybe," Kent said cautiously. He gathered up the documents and placed them back in the chest. As he packed everything else in on top of them, he said, "But we have to be careful. Warreck has made the city council rich. Richer than anyone else on Devor."

Clenching her jaw, she nodded. "So that's why. Are any of them complicit?"

"Not that I know of," Kent shook his head. "They're aware of the rumors surrounding Warreck, but no one does anything about it."

"Not until now," she declared, looking at Letan. Kailar was surprised to see hesitance in his eyes. "Letan?"

His eyes darted between Kailar and Kent, before he sighed. "Correct me if I'm wrong," he shook his head, "But the Warriors of Tieran are funded by the city."

Kent grimaced and nodded. "The other reason I've had to be so careful. Before my time, a Guild Commander defied Warreck's orders. He cut Guild funding in half. We couldn't pay our Warriors a living wage, and some of them, realizing how lucrative crime was on Devor, left the Guild and turned criminals." He nodded at Kailar, "You've faced a few of those former Warriors already, I believe."

Thinking back, she thought about some of the crime rings she had broken up throughout Devor, especially the one failed raid that resulted in civilian casualties. It explained why some of them fought harder than others, or how they were able to readily outmaneuver the Warriors.

Kailar then realized how much Kent had risked when he'd allowed Kailar to join the Tieran Guild. Warreck hadn't been pleased in the least, and he could have easily cut funding again. As much as she would have liked to believe she could take on the underground by herself, she knew she needed help. If the Warriors lost more of their numbers, it could even now turn the tide back against her.

"The bastard needs to pay," she whispered, seething rage filling her heart.

"No argument from me," Kent nodded. "So do it."

Letan and Kailar exchanged surprised glances, and then looked at

Kent. "What exactly do you mean, sir," Letan asked.

"Do your thing," the Commander nodded at Kailar specifically. "You have a knack for stirring the pot and driving the rats from their nests. Find the evidence to present to the city council. Or catch Warreck in the act. Make him confess. Just…"

Kent hesitated, and then stepped around his desk to clasp them on the shoulders and give them a hardened, determined look. Kailar shifted a little uncomfortably at his touch, but remained still. Kent started to say something, stopped, and then shook his head. "Be careful. If you screw this up, everything we've accomplished will be undone. But if you can find the evidence to get him jailed, or at the very least removed from his station, we could finally be looking at the end of this long and bloody campaign."

Something welled up in Kailar's stomach at the Commander's words. Anticipation? Pride? Newfound respect for the Commander? She wasn't exactly sure what the feeling was, just that she wanted to act, now.

Letan reached up his hand to clasp the Commander's arm. "We'll do our best, sir."

Patting their shoulders, Kent nodded and turned away from them. He hesitated again, and then turned to them, his jaw set. "Kailar, I know you like to do things your own way, and that is exactly what has gotten us here. That said, Letan."

"Sir?"

"…Give her some leeway, but try to keep it within reason, okay? I don't want dead civilians or, gods forbid, a burning city on our hands. Report in as soon as you have something."

Taking that as a dismissal, Letan and Kailar turned and left the office. More than anything, she felt shocked by his final words. Yet it reaffirmed her belief that only through direct action could change be made.

The Commander's office was right in the center of the Guild complex, a mostly wooden structure like most buildings on Devor, and so very different from every Guild complex she had seen on Edilas. Their boots clomped loudly on the wooden floor as they headed for their rooms.

Neither she nor Letan had purchased a home in Tieran, and even if Letan's home in Corlas somehow survived the meteorites, the Crystalline Peaks were still bursting with dangerous bolts of green lightning. As such, she and Letan stayed in rooms in the Guild complex itself, whenever they happened to be in town.

Despite their growing relationship, Kailar refused to sleep in the same room with him, except on the couple of nights when they enjoyed one another's company. Usually even then, it was her going to his room, and sometime after, she would let him fall asleep, and then sneak out and back to her room, right next door to his.

The idea of forever being with someone made her uneasy, even though she felt herself falling for Letan. Even though he had stood up for her when no one else would. Even though he knew most of her dark secrets and still wanted to be with her.

Kailar extracted herself from her thoughts and sighed, forcing herself to turn her attention back to the Mayor. At least that was something that she knew how to handle.

"What is it," Letan asked.

"It's just..." She hesitated and looked at him with a frown. "Things are still so different here. No king or queen in their right mind would ever cut funding to the Warriors. All order would break down on Edilas."

"Whereas here, the criminals were already running free," Letan sighed. "So cutting funding really didn't change things." They reached Kailar's door first, and then stopped on either side of the door to talk. They glanced around to make sure no one was nearby, but typically there were few Warriors around during the day. "In fact organized crime kept petty crimes in check. If someone committed a petty crime without involving the underground, they'd make them pay up a dividend. Odd as it sounds, they made our jobs easier, when they weren't doing something inky themselves."

Kailar raised an eyebrow. "Is that why you would volunteer once a year to escort the supply runs?"

He smiled and nodded. "The biggest threat to people, at least the biggest that we could actually fight against, were animals, like those wolves."

Shuddering at the memory, Kailar replied, "Don't remind me."

They stood silently for a moment, Kailar wondering what she should say next. She wanted to focus on the task at hand, and not think about how they met, or everything that happened during that first month. She didn't want to think about the man in Edingard...

"So what do we do next," she asked quickly.

Letan raised an eyebrow at her. "We have to find someone who will point us in the right direction. The problem is, we captured some of the top lieutenants in the underground, and we still haven't found anything linking the Mayor. They must either fear him, or..."

"Or what," she asked, creasing her brow in a deep frown.

"Or he's promised to get them out somehow. And frankly, he's in a position to do just that. He could even go so far as to publicly condemn them to life imprisonment or death, and sneak them out of the city." Letan sighed in frustration. "We could try to interrogate the prisoners, but I don't think it'll do us any good."

Nodding absently, she considered their options, but then stopped when she thought about his words, and when she considered some of the things Kent had said to them. The Commander was right, she realized. Complacency was a problem on Devor, and she had a tendency to shake things up, especially ever since she had gained her new powers.

Her direct approach is what worked.

With a grin on her face, she motioned her head towards Letan's quarters. "Get your armor on and meet me out here. We're going to stir up a rat's nest."

Letan frowned cautiously, but she disappeared into her quarters and immediately set to work putting her leather armor on.

Her quarters were fairly sparse, since she had no personal effects beyond Guild-issued weapons and armor. She still had her travel cloak from when she'd first arrived on Devor, her one piece of sentiment, still muddy, bloody, and torn, draped over a largely unused chair in the corner. Otherwise, the quarters could have belonged to anyone, or no one.

With that less-than-cheerful thought, she finished donning her armor and newer, Guild-issued black cloak. After strapping her sword belt on, she stepped outside and waited impatiently for Letan. When he finally emerged from his quarters, he asked cautiously, "So, what's your plan?"

With a devilish grin, she shook her head and grabbed his hand, pulling him along as she headed out of the complex. "We're going to intimidate the Mayor."

He instantly tugged on her arm and drew them to a stop. "Hold on, Kailar. Please don't tell me you're going to break down the Mayor's door."

She felt her stomach flutter, a sensation of embarrassment and hurt. Truth be told, that *was* her plan, and the disapproving look on his face instantly changed her mind. So she looked down and shook her head. "No. That wouldn't help."

Staring silently, Letan drew in a deep breath and then let it out. "I know the Commander said to give you some latitude in the matter. So let's compromise. Let's go talk to him." She looked at him with surprise, but he raised a cautious finger up, "*Just* talk. You can intimidate through talk, can't you?"

A smile crept across her face, and she nodded. "Yes I can."

Nodding approvingly, Letan motioned for her to lead the way, and together they walked out the front door of the complex, nodding to the two guards out front as they went.

She wasn't completely familiar with Tieran yet, but there were a handful of buildings that she knew the locations of well. Warreck's home was one of them, especially since it was also where he ran the city from. There was a dedicated building for the city council to work from, small as it was, but he preferred the comfort of his own home.

Warreck's house was almost as big as the Guild complex itself, and overshadowed most other homes in Tieran. Given that only he and his servants lived there, she couldn't imagine what he needed such a big house for, but she didn't pretend to understand why people accumulated things, either.

With Letan side-by-side, she marched up to his front door and pounded on it without hesitation, ready to begin her intimidation from the moment Warreck opened the door.

"I'll follow your lead, since you have a knack for intimidation," Letan whispered. "But what do we ask him? I don't think outright accusing him of running a criminal empire will get us anywhere."

Impatient, Kailar pounded on the door again before she glanced at Letan. "I intend to accuse him of giving me up to Falind."

Before he could remark on her scheme, the latch clicked from inside, and the door opened quietly, a sign that it was well-maintained, like everything else on the house. A young woman wearing trousers and a white, neat tunic stood at the door.

Kailar was startled by her appearance. Somehow she had expected Warreck to answer, or at the very least, a stuffy, well-dressed servant, not a young woman with free-flowing blonde hair and a carefree face. After a moment of hesitance, the girl asked in a sweet, sing-song voice, "Can I help you?"

Recovering from her surprise, Kailar nodded and replied, "Yes. We're here to see the Mayor."

"Oh, of course," the girl smiled lightly. "It is a bit early for official business, but you are welcome to come inside and wait."

Frowning, Kailar glanced out at the shadows. "It's almost mid-day," she remarked quietly to Letan as they entered.

"Benefits of a cushy job," Letan whispered with a smirk.

"There's hardly anything cushy about my father's work," the girl admonished, closing the door behind them. "He's responsible for the entire city, after all."

Warreck had a family? Somehow Kailar hadn't considered that possibility. He didn't seem like the family type. Then again, a city mayor was the closest thing Devor had to a king or queen. She wondered if Warreck intended for his daughter or another child to someday take his place as mayor, assuming the city council agreed.

Kailar then realized that she knew very little about how politics worked on Devor.

Suddenly the size of the house made sense, when two children, far younger than Warreck's daughter, ran through the entryway screaming and chasing one another. They slid to a stop when they saw Kailar and Letan, visibly blushed, and quickly ran away.

The entrance was gaudy by Kailar's standards, though that wasn't hard to do. The wooden floors were finely-polished and adorned with multiple fancy rugs. The walls were decorated with countless paintings, some of which portrayed Warreck and his family, while others were of various landscapes, but each painting seemed to have been done by a different artist. And the wooden banister that ran up the stair case was detailed and exquisite.

Coming around to face them, Warreck's daughter bowed slightly and motioned to a cushioned bench against the front window. "Please feel free to have a seat. May I ask who is calling for my father?"

Kailar, stunned at everything she had just learned about their nemesis, deferred to Letan in this instance. "Lieutenant Letan Velethar and Kailar Adanna of the Warriors' Guild," he announced in his best business tone.

Appraising their armor, and perhaps lack of ceremonial Guild attire, the young lady frowned, but nodded easily. "Very well."

She disappeared into another room and left them to stare awkwardly at each other.

"How is it I never knew he had a family," Letan asked quietly.

"So it wasn't just me!" She shook her head and inwardly cursed at herself. "This isn't exactly how I intended for things to go."

Easing onto the bench, he asked, "No?"

She refused to sit, and instead folded her arms and stared at him in consternation. "No. I intended to confront him the moment that door opened, not wait for him like visiting politicians."

When he simply smiled and shrugged, she turned away in frustration to examine some of the paintings.

If they were any indication, he had five children ranging from the eldest that they had just met, all the way to the youngest son, which she realized was one of the children that had run in screaming.

After a few moments of awkward silence, Mayor Warreck Evern appeared from the same room that his daughter had disappeared into, a concerned frown on his face. Like his older daughter, he wore surprisingly informal clothing, clearly not ready to entertain official guests. The only thing that looked carefully prepared was his brown, but graying hair, kept short and neat and brushed back away from his gaunt face.

Letan immediately stood up, and Kailar turned to face the Mayor fully, placing her hands on her hips to flair her cloak out.

"Lieutenant," Warreck stared at Letan. "Why are you two here?"

Kailar was about to speak, but then stopped when she heard a giggle from behind her. She looked up the stairs, and found one of Warreck's kids sitting at the top of the stairs, watching them.

Suddenly intimidating their father in the open seemed like a bad idea.

She glanced at Letan, who had also noticed the kid, and then he looked at Warreck. "We should take this to a private room."

Raising his eyebrows in surprise, Warreck also looked up the stairs, and then nodded. "The study should suffice," he beckoned them to follow.

They followed him back the way he came, and he took them into a room with a great window and multiple book shelves, along with a big desk. One of his servants was inside cleaning, but Warreck casually dismissed them, and then closed the doors.

Making a show to stand behind his desk, with the window at his back, he frowned and looked at Letan, ignoring Kailar. "What in the Six are you doing here without your Commander?"

"We've come to ask you some questions," Letan stated, and then looked to Kailar expectantly.

Happy to be given the lead, she smiled sardonically and asked, "How was your trip?"

At first, Warreck ignored Kailar and stared at Letan expectantly. That set Kailar off.

"I take it Sal'fe is enjoying the throne?"

Warreck's eyes darted at Kailar before they settled back on Letan. "Lieutenant, do you intend to let your subordinate mock me further?"

Kailar's jaw clenched, and she almost shouted at him to make him pay attention to her, but that wasn't the kind of intimidation she needed to use.

When she looked at Letan, he simply folded his arms and ignored the Mayor's question, much as he ignored Kailar.

She decided to push the matter harder. "I don't suppose any of the gold he paid you is going to make it into the city coffers?"

Glaring at Kailar, Warreck shook his head and folded his arms. "Not that it is any of your business, but the four kingdoms did not give us any relief money or personnel."

"That's not what I meant," she stated, mirroring his actions by folding her arms. "How much did Sal'fe pay you? How high is the bounty on my head?"

Warreck hesitated just a little too long before he scoffed. "I did not directly speak to Wizard King Sal'fe while I was there."

Opening her eyes wide, Kailar replied, "Wow, you're really good at that!" The Mayor tilted his head to one side, so she added, "Lying with a straight face."

Warreck unfolded his arms and leaned forward, resting his hands on his desk to glower at her. "Be careful of your words, wench. You do not have the privilege to throw baseless accusations at me without repercussion." Turning away from her to look out the window, he continued with false bravado, "In fact, since the four kingdoms denied us relief money, I am sure the city council would support turning you in for the bounty on your head to fund our relief efforts. It is up to two thousand gold, by the way."

She wasn't sure how to feel about that. The last time anyone had heard, her bounty was still only five hundred gold, a royal sum already. Why had Sal'fe increased her bounty?

Another thought occurred to her, and she turned to Letan. "Isn't it true that the mayor's office is privy to any actions the Guild plans to take ahead of time?"

Letan stared at her, but then seemed to understand where she was going with the conversation, and so nodded. "Yes, that's true." He nodded to the mayor and amended, "During your absence, our plans of action were instead sent to the city council."

"But the Mayor was back in office yesterday," she said and looked pointedly at Warreck, his back still turned to her. "Wasn't he?"

"Yes, he was," Letan nodded again. "So he would have known about our plans to raid the warehouse last night."

"How interesting," she glared at Warreck's back, sarcasm dripping from her words. "So if someone outside of the Guild wanted to find out exactly where I'd be this morning…"

Reeling on her, he pointed a finger at her and barked, "How dare you accuse me…"

Her hand was on her sword hilt in that instant, the rage building inside of her now threatening to explode. "Don't point your grubby finger at me! I know you did it, you pretentious bastard, don't even try to deny it!"

"Kailar," Letan's warning fell on deaf ears.

"Sal'fe's assassins knew exactly where to find me, and I *know* they were his," she continued. Stepping closer, she added, "I've been wanted by Falind since the Alliance released me, but they had no idea how to find me until now, four months after I arrived on this continent. And just after you returned. Awful convenient, isn't it?"

Her sword was partially drawn now, and charged with dark magic. She stepped closer, and he stepped back, until he pressed up against the window. Letan's cautioning hand cinched down on her shoulder, but she scarcely was aware of it.

"Admit it!"

"I…how dare…you cannot just…" Warreck stuttered and stumbled over his words. Kailar slowly drew her sword, and Warreck's eyes grew wider.

"Kailar, don't," Letan warned. "This isn't why we came here."

"Yes, listen to your Lieutenant," Warreck nodded emphatically.

"You would be unwise to draw your weapon against me."

Tilting her head to one side, she nodded. "Maybe you're right." She slid the sword back into its sheath, the locking notch clicking reassuringly.

Then she turned her right hand to face up, and focused dark magic into her palm. It was something she had never done before, but she was confident it would work, and sure enough, a purple-black ball of fire grew into existence just above her hand.

"Then again, I don't need a sword, do I?"

All color drained from Warreck's face, and her gamble paid off. Seeing her cast a type of elemental power without the aid of a weapon to focus it drove him over the edge.

"Alright, I did it," he yelled. "I did it, I told Sal'fe you were here, and agreed to help his assassins find you! Now stop, put away your magic! Just don't burn my house down, don't hurt my family!"

Kailar caught herself in her blind rage, and felt the flow of dark magic draw down in her hand. She had never intended to harm his children. Never the less, the fact that he even suspected that she was capable of hurting them cooled her temper. The flames vanished, and she lowered her hand. Letan's iron grip on her shoulder lightened, but he hadn't let go yet.

Looking around at his study, at the hundreds of books that probably had cost him a fortune by themselves, she narrowed her eyes at Warreck. "You didn't need the bounty, you clearly have enough gold without it. And if you reported to the city council that you didn't bring any gold or supplies back from Edilas, you pocketed the bounty for yourself. So tell me, what's the real reason you want me gone?"

Warreck remained silent, his composure returning. Pulling down on his tunic to straighten it, he took one step away from the window and let out a shuddering sigh. "I've committed no crime," he stated, his voice shaky. "Someone would have told Falind where you were sooner or later, it might as well have been me. I might as well be the one to have earned the bounty."

Raising an eyebrow, she asked, "That's it? You think I'm going to believe that someone as rich as you did it for a couple thousand gold?"

Cautiously, Warreck asked, "What other possible reason could I have had to turn you in?"

"To remove me." She leaned against his desk, Letan's hand restraining her from getting too close to the Mayor's face. "So that things could return to the way they were around here."

In an attempt to look taken aback and innocent, Warreck brought a hand up to his chest and gave her an over-emphasized look of wounded innocence. "Are you implying that I had some involvement in the criminal organizations on Devor?"

"Everyone knows it," she nodded. "Everyone's just afraid to say it out loud. Except me. I'm not afraid to call you a dirty, cowardly, nasty…"

"Alright, Kailar," Letan's voice had a finality that she instantly recognized. "I think we should leave the Mayor in peace for now."

A smirk flashed across her face at his choice of words, and then she glared at Warreck. After a moment of meeting him eye for eye, she pushed up off of the desk and backed away. "Alright. Let's go."

Together she and Letan turned to leave, but just before they opened the door, she placed a restraining hand on Letan's, and looked over her shoulder at Warreck. "Do yourself a favor, *Lord* Mayor."

He was still clearly shaken, so his contorted reaction was comical to her.

"Resign now," she told him. "Resign before you end up in a dungeon cell." Glancing at another painting on the wall by the door, this one of Warreck's eldest daughter, she nodded at the painting and added, "Otherwise your family might have to learn to live without you around."

Without another word, they turned and left the study. The daughter and a servant stood outside of the study, concern on their faces since they no doubt heard the shouting. Kailar and Letan nodded to the two, and then showed themselves out.

It was a gamble, and one she wasn't sure would actually pay off. Warreck obviously valued his family, and based on the fact that they were largely kept out of the public eye, she figured he probably tried to keep them uninvolved in his criminal activities.

She naturally would have preferred arresting him, but if they could get him removed from office, he would be far less of a threat, and a more honest mayor could be chosen by the city council.

At least, that's what Kailar hoped.

Together Kailar and Letan headed back for the Guild complex, their pace a lot slower than it had been on their way to Warreck's house. She looked over at Letan, and suddenly felt her stomach sink. His eyes were bright and seething with anger, and she suspected it wasn't anger towards the mayor.

When he saw her staring at him, he clenched his jaw and stopped them. The streets were as busy as ever, but he shook with rage and looked ready to dress her down despite the audience they would have.

Shaking her head, Kailar sighed. "I'm sorry. The conversation didn't exactly go the way I wanted it to."

Letan was silent for a beat, but then he spoke quietly, which she found more unnerving than if he had yelled at her. "You mean when you conjured fire and threatened to burn the place down?"

Reeling on him, she defended, "I never intended to burn it down!"

"That's exactly what would have happened if you'd let that fire loose," he replied, glancing at a couple passing them by. "Even a few feet away, that fire was hot enough to make me sweat!"

Stopping short of a terse reply, she felt her jaw fall open. "It was?"

Nodding, he frowned and asked, "You didn't feel it?"

Kailar tried to think back to that moment, tried to remember what she felt, but all she could remember was the absolute rage, and the strange sensation of the void within her creating the power that fueled the fire.

"I didn't feel a thing," she half-lied.

"And that's what scares me," Letan's voice softened. He gently grasped her hands, "You have a power unlike any other, Kailar. And these hands *can* do so much good, if you let them. But they can also do some pretty damn terrible things." He raised them up between her and Letan and squeezed. "But only if you let them. I've vouched for you because I believe you can control your power, and your temper. Am I wrong about that?"

Her memory again flashed to the man in the alley in Edingard, and she felt her throat catch. The truthful answer was that no, she probably couldn't. But she couldn't tell him that. Not if she wanted to make up for her failures. He knew that, and he knew she needed to be called out on it. Even if it frustrated her.

There had to be a balance, she decided. A balance between her impulsiveness and caution. So she resolved to find it, and she nodded to Letan. "No, you're not. I'll keep working on it." She squeezed his hands. "I promise."

They stood like that in the street for several moments, before Letan released her hands just long enough to wrap his arms around her. His were the only arms in the world she felt comfortable being lost in, and she embraced him tightly, squeezing with all of her strength, trying to fill the void in her chest with his essence so that she didn't have to feel so cold or alone.

Several minutes passed by before she released him from her grip, and she pulled away just enough to look into his deep blue eyes. "Please don't ever let me go too far."

Raising his eyebrows, he asked, "You mean you'd actually let me hold you back?"

With a mischievous smile, she replied, "Depends on my mood."

"Yeah, that's what I thought," he laughed. "I mean, you can conjure elemental magic now. I don't think a Wizard could stop you if one wanted to."

That made her pause in thought, and a grin stretched across her face.

His smile turned into a grimace. "Oh no, not that look again."

Chapter 8

AN UNEXPECTED VISITOR

Wizard King Sal'fe passed through a portal from just outside of the walls of Archanon, taking him from the middle of Edilas directly into Falind Castle's throne room.

After he stepped through the wall of light, his connection to the origin was severed, and the portal closed of its own accord, allowing him to relax his concentration and leave behind the Allied Council.

The throne room was left largely unchanged since his coronation, with a gold-patterned polished marble floor, a high arched ceiling with iron reinforcements, and on one side of the long room were open archways that opened up onto a great balcony overlooking the city. Giant, heavy forest-green curtains adorned the archways and were closed to keep out the cold spring night air, the kingdom's bronze wolf head embroidered across the pairs of curtains in each archway.

Sal'fe stared at those emblems, his thoughts wandering to the Allied Council meeting. It wasn't the discussion about the dwarven city or the history of the dwarves that occupied his thoughts, but the idea that all portals originating outside of Halarite would be funneled through the rebuilt Grand Wizard Hall in the North.

Such a change would greatly curtail his ability to leave Halarite of his own volition in the future. It was something he had plans to do, especially after the power Klaralin had displayed. Unfortunately, the constant needs of managing Falind Kingdom and the incessant Allied Council meetings had kept him from leaving Halarite so far.

Not that he complained about the position he had gained. Now more than ever, he was in a position to do the right thing. To do what was necessary. And more. So long as the rest of the Allies didn't interfere.

Furthermore, with the staff he held in his right hand, the Staff of Aliz, he was still looked to by the other kingdoms to bring back to life those lost in battle, for a price.

Falind Kingdom was now the wealthiest of all countries on Halarite, thanks to him. He had funneled a significant portion of those funds into multiple projects throughout the kingdom, improving city life, improving infrastructure throughout, and funding projects needed to ensure that future threats to Falind would have little chance of success.

It would soon be time to look to increasing his powers further. But how could he convince the Council not to funnel off-world portals to the Grand Hall? How suspicious would the Wizards' Guild become if he regularly returned from other worlds without telling anyone why he had left in the first place?

A voice in the back of his head told him, *that's exactly why they want to do it. They want to control you.* Sal'fe dismissed the thought almost the moment he had it. He couldn't give into paranoia, not now. Not when he was closing in on fully securing his kingdom from any threat.

Then a thought occurred to him, a way to bypass the Wizard's machinations, but only if he acted quickly, and...

Suddenly he was aware of another presence in the throne room, and a woman's voice spoke from the throne itself, "Personally, I think the curtains are hideous."

Spinning towards the throne and readying his staff, he prepared to defend himself, and wondered where his guards were. Seated in the solid-oak throne, a lone woman in light leather armor sat with her back against one of the arm rests and her legs hanging over the other. Her face was pale, her long hair was black as night, and her eyes were deep and ominous.

"Kailar," Sal'fe spoke carefully, a deep frown carving crevasses into his face.

Flashing a wry smile, she nodded, and sat up straight in the chair, her hand grabbing a sheathed sword that she had set beside the throne. "It's about time you showed up," she sighed. "I've been waiting here for a couple of hours." Casting her eyes about with a concerned frown, she added, "Honestly I expected more guards. Not a single one inside the throne room?"

With a sly grin of his own, Sal'fe prepared himself for combat, drawing magic into himself. For months, the people of Falind had demanded her head. Not that he needed to solidify his claim to the throne, but any doubters that still remained amongst the nobles would be silenced if he presented her head to them.

"So tell me," she began again, standing so that she could secure the scabbard to her belt, "How long have you been training your assassins?"

Sal'fe's lieutenant had only just informed him of their failure to eliminate Kailar before the Wizard King was called to the emergency meeting in Archanon. He was displeased by their failure, but also surprised to learn that Kailar had somehow regained her powers.

That meant she was dangerous, but no magic that he knew of could contend with the life-draining power of the Staff of Aliz, not even a Mage's shield. He had tested that power on several of his assassins, and then brought them back to life, just to learn the limitations of his new powers.

"Apparently not long enough," he raised an eyebrow. Kailar appeared surprised by his willingness to confess. "However, considering you retain the powers of the Sword of Dragons despite the best efforts of the Star Dragons, I suppose I should not judge them too harshly for their failure."

Recovering from her shock, she moved away from the throne and walked around Sal'fe in a big circle, easily accommodated in the large throne room. He followed her by turning his head, but did not bother to turn his body. "Did they tell you the details? They didn't really try. I mean, the battle lasted seconds."

Sal'fe clenched his jaw, and decided he would have to remind them later why they should never leave out any details.

"Tell me," she continued to circle, coming around behind him and briefly out of sight. "Why would a Wizard train Mages to grow beyond their normal powers? I thought your people hated our kind."

When he turned his head the other way and she came into sight, he noticed that she had drawn her sword. Her face was contorted in a look of barely-contained rage.

"I see great potential in humans," he replied. "They are not the lower species that the other Wizards believe them to be. They can be useful," he added with a grin. "When properly tempered."

Stopping, she turned to face him fully, her grip on her sword tight enough that he could hear leather straining. "We aren't your pawns, you old bastard," she spat at him. "I'm tired of your kind thinking you can control and manipulate us."

"But we can," he smiled. Then he leveled the staff at her, and unleashed the life-draining magic upon her.

In an instant, the power connected with her shield in a great flash, blinding him for a moment. When the flash receded, she remained standing, her sword crossed in front of her.

That was when he realized that he hadn't felt the power of her shield. All he felt was his attack disappear, as if into a void of nothingness.

A satisfied smile drew across her face, and she leveled her sword towards him, the blade humming with energy. Sal'fe raised a shield just in time when a blast of purple-hued magic lanced out at him, and immediately felt his mind grow weary from the assault.

His shield held, but it didn't feel like something had tried to pass through it, but rather like something had stolen his power, and the effort needed to maintain the barrier was immense!

In an instant, the pieces clicked together, and he knew that she used dark magic against him. Knowing very little about such power, he feared that he could not contend with her.

Thankfully, despite not guarding the inside of the throne room, several of his assassins were just outside, and they felt the Wizard King's powers flare as he unleashed another assault upon her. Two assassins rushed in from the main entrance, while two more flanked Kailar by coming from the corridor opposite of the balcony.

Each unleashed an elemental attack upon Kailar, and each connected with her shield on-target. Their second strikes, however, missed, and the curtains suddenly were ablaze.

Panicking, he tried to track Kailar's movements, but she was faster than he could have imagined. She went toe to toe with the pair of assassins that had come from the corridor, her steel sword connecting with their darkened steel daggers.

Sal'fe tried to take her life again, but this time she dodged it, and his life-stealing magic ended one of his assassins. She was too fast and too powerful, and his only hope was to get close to her to directly touch her with the staff.

Old as he was, he could still run, and he closed the distance quickly. The other two assassins likewise drew in closer to her.

Kailar buried her sword into the survivor's chest, and then turned him around to put his body between her and the two oncoming assassins. Then she turned to Sal'fe, raised an open palm, and unleashed an unfocused blast not directly at him, but at his feet. The marble floor exploded in front of him, and he barely raised a shield in time to block chunks of marble from smashing his face in.

When he was clear again, he saw Kailar run into the corridor beyond, but then she stopped just inside and turned to him. He leveled the staff at her and prepared to unleash another assault, if only to keep her occupied until he could get closer, but suddenly a wind swept through the throne room, and a portal appeared between them and her. Though invisible from behind, he recognized the outer edges of it, harmless bolts of lightning dancing around it.

She was escaping!

He tried to disrupt the portal with his own power, but hers was made of dark magic, and he didn't know any way to stop her. Walking towards him, she disappeared from sight into the void of the portal, and a moment later, it too vanished.

Cursing, he lowered his staff and stared after her. The other assassins reached her departure point and checked inside the corridor to make sure she was really gone, and then they turned to him. Their eyes grew wide at the same time that he smelled smoke and felt heat from behind, and he turned back to the curtains, now completely ablaze.

Further enraged, Sal'fe quickly drew in energy for an elemental power, and he unleashed a torrent of water upon the curtains. While dousing the flames, the tattered curtains ripped apart and fell onto the large balcony, smoldering and smoking. Some wood framing on the castle had also started on fire, but he easily doused that as well.

Several castle guards, along with more assassins, came barreling into the throne room, weapons drawn.

"Stand down," he growled at them. "The danger has passed for the moment."

They stopped short, their eyes darting between the smoldering curtains, their King, and the two dead assassins. "Your Majesty? What happened?"

His temper flared, and so did the blood-red gem atop the staff as he leveled it at them threateningly. "Why were there no guards in the throne room?"

The guard he pointed directly at stuttered. Sal'fe didn't know the man's name, but he had seen him regularly in the castle. There were no officers for him to directly blame. "I, we, I mean, the Captain, she..."

"Get her," he roared, stepping closer while wrenching the staff back to his side. He allowed the power in the staff to remain, the gem glowing to remind the others of his power. "And you," he pointed at one of the other assassins. "Bring me Ardelle."

Bowing quickly, the assassin ran out to find the former captain of the guard, and now his most trusted assassin, Ardelle Adalain. The other remaining assassin looked at the two bodies, and then asked, "If I may, Your Majesty, shall I take these two away? Or..."

A part of Sal'fe wanted to let their bodies rot. Their failure was spectacular, and he wanted the others to know that there were consequences for failure.

However, the more he thought about it, the more he realized that they could not have anticipated Kailar's use of dark magic any more than he could have. Sighing, he refocused the latent power still in the staff and walked over to the bodies. Touching each with the blood-red gem, he allowed life to return to their bodies, healing the stab wound of the one that Kailar had impaled.

When they came to their senses, they both rose to their knees and lowered their heads in reverence and thankfulness.

A cold wind suddenly blew in from the night outside, and Sal'fe shivered. Looking again to the tattered ruins of the drapes, he sighed. Those had been his choice. For whatever reason, the former king of Falind had put up blue drapes, and Sal'fe had ordered them torn down and replaced with ones matching the kingdom's banner colors.

It would take weeks to make new ones, and the nights were still frigid, the wind bitter and strong since so much of Daruun Forest had burned down after the meteorite storm.

Even though neither Ardelle nor the guard captain had arrived, he told all around him, "I want the usual guard rotation doubled, especially at night. It seems our nemesis has grown powerful, indeed."

Someone, he wasn't sure who, acknowledged his command. He didn't care, as long as it was eventually done.

Drawing in a deep sigh, the Wizard King turned back to where Kailar had departed. Sending more assassins obviously would not work. He would have to find another way to deal with her.

The question remained, what had she hoped to gain by confronting him directly? Did she get what she needed, or had he succeeded in countering her objective? Why had she fled when she did?

Either she was a fool, or she was playing a smarter game than he realized.

She means to undermine you, the voice in his head suggested. *She has shown that she can invade your kingdom at will, and leave at will.*

Drawing in a deep breath, he looked out the balcony into the cold night. If that was true, then he had two real recourses. Either he would have to destroy her, on his own terms, or he would have to find a way to bend her to his will.

Sal'fe preferred the latter option.

Chapter 9

THE SYLARIC STONE

In all of Dalin's 288 years, the sight before him now was one that he never expected – the Great Library of the Grand Wizard Hall half-emptied of its books.

For much of his life, short as it was, he had spent many hours in the library, pouring over source materials, reading the journals of past Wizards, learning what he could when he was ready. Of course, as with any Wizard born in the Grand Hall, what he was and wasn't allowed to read had always been strictly controlled, at least up until he had graduated his apprenticeship from Master Aenar.

Stacks and stacks of books, piled high across multiple levels, lit by Wizard lamps and everlasting torches, and multiple skylights looking up to the false blue above, it was impressive, and even to one who had known it his whole life, the sight always filled his soul with awe. This, more than anything, was what had kept him in the Guild, even when he grew to detest the Guild's dogma.

Breathing in the air of old books, Dalin let it fill every bit of his body, and felt his muscles relax. Even now, half-empty, it was still home. Better still, all of the missing books were safe in their new home, in the Wizards' Guild complex in the North of Edilas, still being rebuilt.

As he passed through the enchanted steel arch that blocked most Wizards from entering the restricted area, that sense of warmth and welcome changed to a sense of foreboding. This was the room where he had first learned of the Sword of Dragons.

This is where his journey had truly begun.

Most of the restricted books had already been moved to Halarite, but there was still one shelf being emptied by a couple of Master Wizards, including Grand Master Valkere. He, Master Syrn, and Master Eira all turned towards him when he entered, and a light smile crossed the Grand Master's face.

"Ah, Dalin, thank you for seeing me," Valkere spoke lightly. He carefully set two dusty old books into a small crate on a marble table and then met Dalin halfway.

"Of course, Grand Master," Dalin bowed, his borrowed ash wood staff still feeling awkward in his right hand. His own oak staff was lost somewhere in the jungles of Trinil, taken by the necromancers and more than likely destroyed in the meteorite storm. The staff he held now was usually one given to apprentices so that they had one with which to explore their powers, so that when it came time to craft their own staff, they had something to model it on, both physically and magically.

While Dalin had chosen the wood of his new staff, he had little time to do more than that, and for now, he made do with the apprentice staff.

Glancing over his shoulder and nodding for the other masters to continue, Valkere gently pushed on Dalin's shoulder to guide him out of the restricted area. Next to the arched entrance were the Masters' staves leaning in the corner, and Master Valkere gracefully took his white staff as they entered the larger library.

Dalin had returned to the newer Wizards' Guild to gather a few of his belongings that he would need on his quest into the ancient dwarven city. Most of his belongings had already been moved to the rebuilt Guild complex, but there were still some items he had needed here.

The library was full of other Wizards actively packing up books, but Valkere found them a quiet corner to converse. When they were alone, he looked into Dalin's grey-blue eyes and allowed a frown to deepen the wrinkles on his face. "I wish to speak with you about the Keeper's mission into the dwarven city," Valkere began, catching

Dalin off guard. "Am I correct that you do not wish to go on this quest?"

Shifting his weight nervously, Dalin felt a flutter of uneasiness in his chest, and he averted his eyes for a moment. "That is correct, Master."

Tilting his head to one side to catch Dalin's attention, the Grand Master asked simply, "Why?"

Tightening his grip on the apprentice staff, Dalin looked the feeble thing up and down, and then stared at Valkere plainly. "Cardin no longer requires my services."

The Grand Master's eyes grew wide with surprise. "He does not? When did he tell you this?"

Shaking his head, Dalin corrected, "He never said so. However…" He looked down, trying to find the right words. "He has another to train him now, far more experienced in the matters of the Sword of Dragons than I ever could be."

The Grand Master was silent for a moment, and Dalin waited patiently for him to reply. Ideally, Valkere would assign another Wizard to the quest. Whether or not that was true, Dalin resigned himself to the fact that this would probably be the last time he would accompany Cardin on a mission.

Narrowing his eyes, Valkere said, "I believe that your accompanying the Keeper is vital to his future. Vital to everyone's future."

Looking up in surprise, Dalin's mouth opened to protest, but then he stopped and waited for the Grand Master to continue.

When he realized that Dalin would not interrupt him, Valkere pointed out, "You are more than just his teacher, Dalin. Surely you realize that."

Now it was Dalin's turn to frown. "What do you mean?"

Raising his eyebrows, the Grand Master nodded, "You are his friend. While you may look young by human…by *Halarite* standards," he amended, "you are older and wiser than he is."

A deep well opened up inside of Dalin, his heart aching with the knowledge of just how useless he had become. "With respect, Master, so is Endri."

Closing his eyes for a moment, Valkere nodded. "While that is true, he does not have history with Cardin." Opening his eyes and staring into Dalin's soul, he pressed on, "You believed in Cardin when few others did. You saw his potential before anyone else. That faith in him will be vital in the days to come."

The Grand Master's words sparked suspicion in Dalin. Did he know something about the future? Dalin had learned after their return to Edilas that Valkere had seen the coming apocalypse long before it arrived, and that was why he had restricted travel to Halarite. Was some other catastrophe on the horizon?

"Master, I…"

With a curt nod, Valkere added, "I am making this an order, Dalin. You must be with the Keeper through the coming days."

Dalin immediately wished to refuse, his rebellious spark surfacing. He almost vocalized his resistance to the order, but then he stopped himself. This was the will of the Grand Master, and while rank held little importance to him, Valkere had earned his respect. Particularly when he had ordered the Guild Hall on Halarite to be rebuilt, with the intent to bring all Wizards home at last. Valkere wished to ensure that Halarite would never again stand alone.

Was that what this was about? Protecting Halarite? There was no doubt that Cardin and the Sword of Dragons would continue to play a vital role in the coming days. Perhaps Master Valkere also believed that Dalin would shape the future somehow.

Reaching into one of his robe's pockets, the Grand Master pulled forth a silver gem half the size of a fist. "You will need this to better serve," he nodded, offering it to Dalin.

Immediately recognizing what it was, Dalin gawked at his master. "A sylaric stone?"

Raising an eyebrow, Valkere nodded insistently. "You need a new focusing stone for your staff, do you not? I believe this will be superior to any natural ones you might find."

That was an understatement. Sylaric stones were essentially magic in physical form, conjured by the most powerful Wizards over the course of weeks. It was written that they granted both a channeling of magic free of any resistance, and a source of power to draw from beyond the physical Universe. Any power a Wizard had would be magnified.

They were never given to younger Wizards because of the focus and control needed to wield them safely. Most Masters agreed that if a Wizard did not have the focus or talent to summon one themselves, they weren't ready to have one.

"I cannot accept this gift, Master," he half-bowed and backed away. "I could never control…"

"Dalin, I do not believe you understand," Valkere shook his head, stepping closer and pressing the stone against Dalin's chest, the dense, cold object sending a pulse of magic through his robes and into his soul. "You have studied hard, and you have learned control beyond your years because of your desire to find purpose beyond the Guild." With a light chuckle, the Grand Master added, "It is ironic that your resistance to our structured existence has allowed you to see the Universe and magic in a way that most of us cannot."

Dalin searched the other's face inquisitively. "Master?"

Lowering his head and shaking it, he looked intently into Dalin's eyes and said, "You saw the danger of the Sword, the danger of Kailar, and then you saw the potential in Cardin Kataar. You saw what no other Wizard alive today could have seen, save perhaps your own mentor. You saw it because you had not allowed our Guild's complacency to addle your imagination, your creativity, nor your intuitive senses. You reject the arrogant presumption of the rest of us as a matter of course. While this may irritate the rest, I believe it is a necessary paradigm shift in our culture, and it is perhaps your greatest strength."

A lump formed in Dalin's throat at the memory of his lost mentor Aenar. The one who had trained him, and then saw within Dalin such potential that he had insisted Dalin be granted access to the journals and books about the Sword of Dragons.

Valkere's implication actually made Dalin blush.

"This belongs to you, now," Valkere insisted, setting his staff aside long enough to use his other hand to open Dalin's, and then he planted the stone in it firmly. "While you may find it difficult at first, you must learn to control the powers that come with this."

Yet again, the Master's words sparked suspicion within Dalin. But then the Master released his grip, and Dalin grasped the stone. Holding it in his hand, a tingle ran up his arm and into his body, a feeling like a well of strength had just opened up into him.

It was exhilarating and frightening all at once! He held the stone up closer to his eyes, and saw the silver stone take on a new glow, and in that instant, he felt as if he stared into the Universe. Except it was cold…the Universe was cold, not warm like he would have thought. Even more unexpected was that the cold didn't disturb him or make him shiver.

It was a void that waited for him. So he did the only thing he could think of. He let his essence fill that void. And before his eyes, the silver faded to a deep, dark blue, almost matching his robes. The cold was gone, replaced with a piece of his soul.

Dalin understood what that meant, and he was in awe that it had happened so quickly. The stone and his soul were now permanently linked.

"You see," Valkere beamed. He picked up his staff and looked pointedly at Dalin. "I told you that you were ready." Very quickly, the Master's smile faded, quickly replaced by one of sadness and remorse. "It is done..."

Dalin's eyes grew wide. "Master? What is done?"

Before Valkere could answer, the floor beneath them shook violently, accompanied by a deep, loud rumbling. Dalin lost his footing and nearly crashed to the marble floor, had it not been for Valkere's quick reflexes.

All around them, books crashed down and stacks fell over in a great clatter. Cracks immediately formed in the marble floor, walls, and ceiling, and the light from the skylights dimmed.

An ear-splitting roar pierced the air like a spear, echoing throughout the entire realm, and within Dalin's thoughts. He tried to cover his ears, but all he could do was wait out the long, terrifying screech.

He knew that roar, and a great shock overwhelmed him. It was the same roar he'd felt and heard at the Battle for Maradin.

The entire Guild Hall shook again, more cracks formed, more books and shelves crashed, pinning or even crushing some of the Wizards. And the flash of a giant, black tail arched over the skylights.

"He is here," Valkere grimaced. "So the visions were accurate..."

There was a blast of red light, and the building jolted violently. Dalin grasped the apprentice staff and the sylaric stone, trying desperately to keep his balance and comprehend what was happening.

Valkere gripped Dalin's shoulder, and shouted above another roar, "You must go now!" There was a flurry of magic nearby, most likely in the Grand Hall itself. Magic that Dalin recognized as attacking spells and defensive shields. Another flash of red light, and many of the defensive spells were suddenly gone.

"Go where," Dalin asked, barely holding on to a crumbling wall.

The other Masters stumbled out of the restricted library. Valkere looked at them, and then at Dalin again. "I should have forced our evacuation sooner," he shook his head. "I am so sorry. I have to keep him distracted long enough."

Master Syrn stared at Valkere, wide-eyed. "Grand Master?"

The roars and the shaking had stopped, but only for a moment. Valkere looked at Syrn, and nodded. Then he turned and looked out into the library. Dalin felt power gather around Valkere, and before he could ask what was going on, the Grand Master suddenly lifted off of the ground, a gold-white glow surrounding his body.

Using magic to speak to everyone still in the Guild complex, the Grand Master ordered, "Everyone evacuate now! Go to Halarite immediately, and do not return!"

Then the terrifying voice that Dalin had heard in his head at Maradin spoke again. *"There you are!"*

It was Nuuldan's voice. The Dark Dragon.

Somehow, he had found their realm.

Suddenly half of the roof of the library was gone, ripped away and sent tumbling into the infinite void beyond the Grand Wizard Hall. A massive clawed black paw had torn it away, and a moment later, a giant black head with glowing red eyes peered into the library, at Valkere as he rose higher, closer to the dragon's terrifying gaze.

"Master!" Dalin shouted.

"I am the one you want," Valkere's voice echoed throughout the realm.

"Where is the Shadow Quartz?" Nuuldan's voice ripped through Dalin's thoughts. Cringing, he nearly dropped the stone and his staff. The voice was overwhelming! *"I know they gave it to you!"*

Intense points of power formed all throughout the realm, and Dalin knew that those few Wizards still left in the Guild Hall fled. They knew what had come for them, and that the only safe place now was Halarite, where the Sword of Dragons was.

Several of those points came from within the library, as the Wizards scattered throughout fled.

Nuuldan saw this and turned his head, a red glow forming within his mouth. Before he could unleash it, however, Valkere's glow grew strong, and suddenly a blast of pure magic slammed into the Dark Dragon's jaw, throwing his red blast wild into the void.

"Go now," Valkere turned to Dalin, his eyes glowing gold.

Suddenly Dalin knew exactly what the master was doing. That glow was something he had read about in books, about the very oldest and strongest of Wizards.

If they allowed their powers to grow beyond their control, it would overwhelm them. So much so that their bodies expelled magic violently, resulting in a catastrophic explosion. The only thing such masters could do was contain the destruction the only way they knew how to, by locking themselves in their studies and using their last bit of control to shield the rest of the Grand Wizard Hall.

The same thing had happened to the last Grand Master, when Dalin was a child.

Only Valkere wasn't going to shield anything.

As the Grand Master's glow became blinding, Dalin knew he had only moments. He turned to the other Masters, but they had already fled through portals. Planting the ash staff in the ground, Dalin focused his powers through the staff, only to have it suddenly redirect through his other hand, through the sylaric stone.

A portal exploded into existence, bolts of lightning larger than usual lancing out and gouging chunks out of the marble. The stone was infusing the portal with magic uncontrollably, but he had no choice!

With only one last glance back at his Master, he dove through the portal, and felt like something had just shoved him with the force of a hurricane. He flew out the other side and tumbled through the grassy field near the rebuilt Grand Wizard Hall on Halarite.

The world was a dizzying spectacle around him, and darkness edged at his vision, until he finally came to a skidding stop face-first.

"Dalin!" Master Syrn's stern voice came to him a moment later, and hands took hold of his arm, turning him onto his back.

Above him was the pristine blue sky, with only a few wisps of cloud. And Syrn's graying old face and blazing green eyes searching his eyes for answers.

He didn't look at her. All he could do was stare into the infinite blue. It was all over faster than it had begun.

Sitting up, he looked to where his portal had been, and was surprised to find scorched grass. Had he done that with an overpowered portal? Or had he barely caught the edge of the final moments of the Grand Master of the Wizards?

A pit formed in his stomach as the flurry of events suddenly coalesced in his head. It had all happened so fast, but now he understood.

Their home was gone. And so was the greatest Wizard.

Chapter 10

UNDER THE SHADOWS OF THE MOONS

When the knock came at Kailar's door, she had already pulled on a tunic and trousers, having heard a knock at Letan's door only a few minutes ago. This late into the evening, when most sensible people were ready for or in bed, she knew that whoever called on him would come for her next.

Taking an extra moment to quickly lash a belt on, complete with a sheathed dagger, she opened her door to find Letan waiting, accompanied by a young Guildswoman that she recognized but didn't know by name.

For a moment, Kailar thought about teasing Letan for bringing a woman with him to her room, but something told her that tonight was not the night for jokes.

Letan gave her a worried look. "We've been called to the Commander's office." He motioned for her to follow, and nodded to the young woman to lead the way.

Falling into step beside Letan, Kailar cringed. Was this about their visit to the Mayor? Did Warreck gain some level of courage to complain to the Commander?

A part of her didn't care if he did, but then she immediately thought of the conversation they'd had with Kent that morning, about what happened the last time someone challenged the Mayor. Would he cave into demands from Warreck?

The journey through the Guild complex took them down a set of stairs to the main floor, and then to Kent Querlin's office. As she feared, when the Guildswoman led them in, Kent was behind his desk, still in his duty outfit, and the Mayor hovered beside the desk.

She glowered at Warreck, and felt her insides boil.

"You wished to see us, sir," Letan said tepidly.

Holding his hands behind his back, Kent nodded to the Guildswoman and calmly said, "Wait outside, please. And close the door behind you."

The Guildswoman casually left the room and gently closed the door, belying the fact that she probably had no idea what the situation was.

Once the latch clicked securely, Kent looked first at Letan, and then Kailar in the eye. "Mayor Evern has leveled charges against you two. Apparently, you barged into his house and threatened him."

Kailar's temper flared, and even though she knew that Letan should have been the one to speak, she stated calmly, "We didn't barge in, sir."

"What do you call it, then," Warreck indignantly asked.

She scoffed, and replied, "Knocking at your front door."

Rushing to cut off any other responses, Letan nodded, "There was no barging in, Commander. We knocked, were let in by his daughter, and waited in the foyer to speak to him."

Kent looked to Warreck for a response, to which he sighed and said, "Fine, they were polite at first. Once they had me alone in my office, they leveled threats at me. Kailar nearly burned my house down!"

Almost letting her temper get the better of her, Kailar opened her mouth to speak, but stopped and allowed Letan to instead.

"Again, he does not speak the truth," Letan cut her off. "Kailar did show him one of her newest powers, but she was in full control of it at all times." Kailar gave him a sideways glance, surprised by his willingness to bend the truth in her defense.

At that, Kent raised a hand up to stop Letan. "And just why did you summon magic in the Mayor's presence?"

"To threaten me, of course," Warreck declared.

Looking carefully at the Mayor, Kent insisted, "With all due respect, I asked Kailar the question."

Thinking quickly, it took Kailar only moments to respond, "To show him why Sal'fe's assassin's failed." Warreck started to object to her partial lie, but she interrupted him, "After which he admitted to revealing to Sal'fe my presence here, and he admitted to helping Sal'fe's assassins find me."

That brought a raised eyebrow to Kent's face. They had not yet reported any of their findings to the Commander, since Kailar had gone straight to Falind after interrogating Warreck, and then she and Letan went straight to their rooms to discuss her encounter with the Wizard King.

Turning to the Mayor, Kent asked, "Is this true?"

Before Warreck could answer, Kailar insisted, "Don't forget the part where you never intended to share the bounty with the city."

Kent glanced at her with an unsaid 'be quiet,' and Letan placed a cautionary hand on her shoulder. When Kailar clamped her mouth shut, Kent turned back to Warreck and patiently waited for the Mayor's response.

She thought she had him, but Warreck was prepared. "Whether true or not is of no concern to you, Commander. You know that."

"I think it concerns me when you've brought a direct threat to one of my Warriors," Kent folded his arms and stared evenly at the Mayor. "Especially without consulting me, and especially after you agreed to let her remain under my supervision."

Narrowing his eyes at Kent, Warreck shook his head. "Do not test me in this matter, Commander. Your Warrior threatened me, no matter how she tries to spin it. Worse, she threatened me with magic that could have burned my house down, and killed or hurt my wife and children. My trip to Edilas has no bearing on this proceeding. Especially since there is no evidence of her claims."

Raising an eyebrow, Kent replied, "Nor is there evidence that she threatened you."

"My daughter and a servant witnessed it…"

Unable to control herself, Kailar spat out, "Another lie!"

"Do not interrupt me, you little whelp," Warreck glared at her.

"Commander, please," Letan stepped forward ahead of Kailar. "We were behind closed doors in the Mayor's office during the entire conversation, they could not have overheard."

"They heard shouting," Warreck defended.

Kent raised a hand and shouted, "Alright, enough!" Massaging his temple, he sighed in relief when they all did as he said. Kailar stared at the Commander anxiously, wondering how he would handle the situation. Would he be forced to have them arrested? It didn't matter that Kent supported them and asked them to 'do their thing,' not if an order from the civilian government that employed them forced his hand.

She weighed what she should do if it came to that. No one on Halarite could truly hold her in prison against her will, not anymore. But the idea of failing yet again to fix society and having to run and hide again didn't sit well with her.

"With respect, Mayor Evern," Kent finally spoke, "there is not enough evidence to convict Kailar." When Warreck began to protest, the Commander raised his hand again, and Kailar's heart leapt into her throat. "However, your accusations do require further investigation. During which time I will relieve them of Guild rank and duty."

"What?!" she burst out before she could stop herself. Letan fell back a step, and his hands fell to his sides with dead weight.

"Stop," Kent raised a finger at her. "Just stop, Kailar."

"That is not good enough, Commander," Warreck stated, planting his fists on his hips. "I demand you arrest them immediately."

"That is not your decision to make, Mayor Evern," Kent shook his head.

"Then I'll have soldiers arrest them," he said with a scowl, and started for the door.

"Warreck, you know what'll happen if you try that," Kent warned. "You've seen what happens when soldiers and Warriors fight each other."

Kailar's eyes grew wide, and Warreck stopped in his tracks. That was a story she hadn't heard yet.

With deliberate slowness, the Mayor turned back and stared at Kent. The Commander stared back, and then nodded. "I promise you, by your orders, I will investigate the matter personally, and if your accusations are true, I will arrest them myself."

A protest hung in Kailar's open mouth, but she managed not to say anything. Warreck glared at her, then at Letan, and then finally looked back at Kent. "Very well. However, I want this matter resolved quickly, or I cannot guarantee that your Guild will remain fully funded."

In a great huff, Warreck threw the door open and barged out. The Guildswoman glanced back inside, and then followed the Mayor to officially escort him out.

Once he was out of earshot, Kailar grumbled, "Sometimes I think it would be so much easier to just teleport him to the middle of nowhere."

Kent glared at her and stalked past her to close the door, while Letan lectured, "You're not helping."

Once the room was secure again, Kent wheeled on her and demanded, "What were you thinking?!"

Taken aback, Kailar glanced at Letan in puzzlement. "Sir?"

Kent rubbed his face and stalked past them to his desk. "I don't know what really happened, but you shouldn't have confronted him until you had solid evidence."

"I was trying to fish for information," she replied.

Letan nodded, "And I agreed with her suggestion to confront the mayor. We had no other viable leads."

Shaking his head, Kent walked around to his desk and sat in his chair, groaning as he went.

Kailar approached the desk and planted her hands on it to lean towards the Commander. "Sir, you asked me to stir things up, remember? To do what I do best. This isn't over yet."

Looking bewildered, Kent said, "Yeah, for the moment. But now the Mayor has a public reason to defund the Warriors, and that'll take us back to square one!" Looking at Letan, he emphatically motioned at the Lieutenant. "Now I have to relieve you both of your Guild status."

"Commander, please," Kailar objected, standing up straight. "We have him rattled, and now he'll make a mistake! That was the point of all of this."

"It doesn't matter!" Kent's balled fist slammed down onto the desk. "Don't you see that? Unless you can resolve this mess immediately, he's going to effectively shut us down. All he needs is a few days to convince the rest of the city council, and I'm sure he has dirt on most of them."

"Okay, then," Letan offered, his voice catching. Kailar wondered if he was hiding a deeper fear that he hadn't admitted to her. "That's our timeline, then. Bring him to justice in less than three days."

Kailar smiled and nodded, and when she looked at Kent again, the doubt on his face was palpable. "I've been working on him for years. You think you can do better?"

"I think we can," Kailar nodded emphatically. "If you'll give us just a little more leeway."

Stepping up beside her, Letan looked at her with a half-hidden smile. "You already have an idea, don't you?"

"I do." She looked at the Commander, and explained, "We don't have time anymore to wait for Warreck to make a mistake. I admit my original plan hasn't gone as well as I'd hoped. So we follow up on the only other potential lead we have. We go back to the only member of the underground who has actually cooperated with us, even if it was under duress."

"Egil," Letan asked her.

When she nodded, Kent eyed her suspiciously. "Him again? You know we need more than his word."

"Exactly," she folded her arms and looked at Letan confidently.

It took him a moment, but then his face lit up. Bringing his hand up to stroke his beard, Letan nodded slowly. "In order to have eluded us not just once, but twice like that…he still has contacts in the city."

"Exactly," she smiled. "And maybe even outside the city. There *must* be proof out there."

When she looked again at Kent, he was clearly hesitant. "That may be, but you're relieved of Guild status, and we were forced to send Egil to the city prison. City guards won't let him into your custody anymore."

Raising an eyebrow, Letan said slowly, "They don't know we've been relieved yet…"

"Oh they'll learn quickly," the Commander sighed. "I'm sure Warreck will ensure the entire city guard knows before he makes it home tonight. There's no way they'll knowingly release him to you two. The best I can do is delay telling the other Warriors, but that won't get you into the city dungeon, and anyone in the Guild who helps you becomes culpable."

Kailar's eyebrow shot up. "That's easy enough to circumvent," she said with a smile.

Letan and Kent exchanged glanced.

"No one else needs to know," she continued. "There usually isn't a guard actually watching all the cells, right? Especially at night."

With an uneasy nod, Letan said, "Right, they have a separate office for the on-duty guard to sit in."

"Stop right there," Kent said, raising a hand. They looked at him, and Kailar was about to push harder, but the Commander looked her square in the eye. "I don't want to know the details, that way I don't have to lie if this takes longer than you expect. But for the love of the Six, be quick about it. We're very short on time."

She knew that the Commander already had an idea of what her plan was, but as long as they didn't actually say it out loud, he was safe. Or as safe as he could be after defending her and Letan.

Nodding, she stood up straight and looked confidently at him. Letan joined her, and as he motioned towards the door, said, "With your permission, sir."

Kent's eyes darted between the two of them, his expression one of fear and hope rolled up together. After a moment's hesitation, he nodded. "Dismissed."

With that, they turned and quickly left, Kailar leading rapidly with Letan trailing along. She asked him to meet her in her quarters after he put on leather armor, and then went to her quarters to strap on her own gear.

She had just finished lashing her sword onto her left hip when there was another knock at the door. Kailar let Letan, now armed and resplendent in leather armor, into her room, and then locked the door shut. "Well, then," she drew in a breath. "Want to hear the plan?"

Letan nodded. "I think I have an idea what you want to do, but spell it out."

"I'll grab him from his cell with a portal," she explained, looking him straight in the eye. "But in this case, I think it's better if you stay here."

Raising a suspicious eyebrow, he asked, "And why's that?"

While she hadn't had an exact plan before now, it immediately unfolded in her mind in its entirety, and she knew what she had to do. Unfortunately, she didn't think Letan would fully approve. Which meant she had to keep some of her plan from him.

"I intend to offer him a deal, and won't let him out of his cell until then," she half-lied. "But if a guard comes around while I'm talking to him, it'll take too much time for both of us to escape through a portal. It's easier for me to either stay hidden or escape before a guard can identify me."

He looked down and scrunched his nose up. "If you portal out of there, they'll know it's you just by that fact."

"All the more reason for just me to go," she nodded. "But, I need you to stay here so that when I send him back, you can ensure he doesn't make a run for it. I still can't go through ahead of him, and I'm not sure yet what would happen if I went through at the same time as him." That last part was true. She suspected she could take someone through at the exact same time, but she also knew that the moment every bit of her stepped through, the portal would close, and if the other person were even a half-step behind her, it could end disastrously.

After thinking about it another moment, Letan sighed and nodded. "I don't exactly like it, but I think your plan is our best shot." Looking her in the eye earnestly, he added, "Be quick, okay?"

Something in her chest warmed, and she smiled affectionately at him. "I will."

After another moment of staring into his beautiful eyes, and feeling the lump of guilt at having only told him half of the truth, she turned and faced the only empty wall in her room. Focusing her will, she raised her hand at the wall, and coerced magic out of the dark, creating a violet portal.

Knowing that there was no time to hesitate, she rushed through, and found herself in a dark, smelly corridor carved beneath the city hall. Several cells lined the right side of the dungeon, all equally carved out of the rock and mud, held up by wooden beams and the iron frame of the cell bars.

When her portal closed behind her, darkness broken only by intermittent torchlight met her, but she could see easily enough. The first cell held one startled woman in rags, and her appearance and stench confirmed Kailar's theory that she had been imprisoned for weeks.

The next cell down, however, had both Egil and another man, both sitting on the floor, startled awake by her sudden appearance. Egil still wore his ragged, worn clothes from the ship they had found him in, but the other man looked and smelled like a long-time prisoner.

This was where her powers would be put to the test. Opening a portal was almost second nature to her now, even with dark magic. But this would be something else entirely.

"Hello, Egil," she smiled. "Would you mind standing up?"

"What," he asked, bleary-eyed. "What you doing here?"

"Let's just say I need to have a private chat with you," she said pleasantly, and then changed her expression to a menacing glower. "Now get up." Her demeanor, no doubt aided by the darkness, was enough to spring him into action and onto his feet.

Looking at the other man, she pointed to the cell wall to her right. "Get out of the way." He looked at her bleary-eyed, but like Egil, wisely decided to follow her orders.

Once the other prisoner was clear, she closed her eyes, and focused, backing up from the cell bars just enough. Within moments, another portal opened directly in front of her, the other end opening just inside of Egil's cell. She didn't want to give him time to get any ideas, so she stepped through.

Once face-to-face with him, she didn't waste any time and grabbed his arm to twist it and turn him to face away from her. "Ouch, easy there, girly!"

As the portal behind her closed, she focused again ahead of Egil's face, and with greater effort, managed to open another portal.

With just a small twist of Egil's arm, she forced him forward, and together they marched through the portal. Right into the middle of the Desert of Ca'aluun.

It was well past midnight this far to the east, and the moons were bright enough to light up the white sands, turning into a vast, blue-white sea. It was surprisingly cold, despite being spring in Edilas, but it was easy enough to see that they stood atop one of the tallest dunes in the western half of the desert. In fact, by intent, they were only a few dunes west of where she and Klaralin had faced the great scorpions.

Kailar shoved Egil down onto the shifting sands, and walked along the dune's ridge, staring up at the larger of the two moons.

"Welcome to Edilas," she turned to flash a dark smile at him. "This is where you wanted to go, right? I thought I'd help you get here."

It took him only moments to get his bearings, before he stood up and brushed sand off of his trousers. "I meant to go to Asirin," he grumbled. "And not in the middle of the bleeding desert!"

With a shrug, she said, "Isn't it better than a dungeon?"

She expected Egil to panic, to beg for his life, to agree to anything. He was a common thief, and he'd already shown his cowardice when they cornered him aboard the ship.

So when he folded his arms and stared at Kailar stoically, she felt her throat catch in surprise. "I see," he spoke calmly. "Taking a page out of my book, eh?"

At first, Kailar frowned at the implication, but then something grasped at her chest, a cold clench that drew her stomach down and turned her hands and face clammy.

Several months ago, she had faced off against him in the fields east of the Crystalline Peaks, furious that he would use fear to coerce innocents into giving him their hard-earned cash. While Egil was hardly innocent or hard working, she realized that she was stooping to his level, and he knew exactly what her intentions were.

Never the less, she knew there was no turning back now. Pushing her self-doubts into a deep, dark corner of her mind, she continued. "As you can see, I'm able to go anywhere I want, any time. I could leave you out here, in the middle of the desert. Surely you've heard the rumors about those who dwell beneath?"

He was unimpressed.

Changing tactics, she folded her arms to mirror him and faced him evenly. "Fine. The deal is simple. You help me find irrefutable proof that Warreck has colluded with the criminal underground, and we'll let you go."

Narrowing his eyes, Egil shook his head. "No."

Once again caught off guard, she felt her arms drop to her sides. "No? You'd rather be left to rot in jail? Or," she waved around them, "left out here to rot?"

"Come, now, girly," he shook his head. "I'm a business man, remember? You gotta sweeten the deal."

Frustration overcame her surprise, and she glowered at him. "At this point, you'll be lucky if I let you live."

Scoffing, Egil scratched his head. "No, see, not like that. Have you seriously never negotiated a thing in your life?"

Drawing her sword, she let dark magic flow into the blade, setting it humming with a hint of a glow, before she pointed the tip squarely between his eyes. "I'm not here for a haggling lesson, dimwit."

Still he looked unmoved, and she very nearly let loose a blast of magic. She wanted to see that smug look popped out of existence.

But she didn't. Before he said anything, she already knew why.

"You've broken into the dungeon to extract me," he shook his head. "Which means you're desperate. I'm all you've got, sweetheart. Kill me, and you've got nothing."

Even though he likely knew it was an empty threat, she sneered at him and said, "I'd have the satisfaction." When he didn't respond, she drew her sword back to her side and let the magic dissipate. "Alright. You want a sweeter deal? I'll take you wherever you want to go, personally."

A wide smile drew across his face, and he nodded with satisfaction. "See, now that's more like it."

"But *only* after you help me present the evidence to the Tieran city council."

That stopped him short, but only for a moment. He nodded once. "Fine. But how do I know you'll keep your word and not kill me, or drop me back off here, or deep in the Wastelands?"

"Or the Plains of Glass," she helpfully added. "You don't, exactly." Clenching her jaw, she sheathed her sword and glowered at him. "But you see, I've been spending more time around this honorable man, and he's starting to rub off on me."

"Literally?"

Impulsively, she let out a minor thump of energy that knocked him off of his feet. She hadn't meant to, but his remark was disturbingly close to the truth.

"Oye, watch it," he snarled at her.

Kailar turned around, partly to hide her face, and partly to summon another portal, stirring the sands into a vortex of energy. Turning her head just enough to watch him stand up and brush the sand off again, she motioned towards their exit. "Letan will be waiting for you on the other side, so don't try any funny business."

Grumbling, Egil tried to walk around her, a difficult task on the narrow sandy peak, until he was between her and the portal. "The things I do to survive," he complained, before stepping through ahead of her.

Chapter 11

SEPARATE PATHS

With all deliberate slowness, the sun rose over the Ilari Mountains to the east, finally casting its warmth upon Cardin's face as he waited patiently outside of the western Archanon gate. The tough mountain grasses around him were overflowing with yellow and white flowers, save for the roadway that stretched west towards the Great Road.

He, Sira, Elaria and the others were set to head underground soon, but he had yet to talk to Endri since the last council session. Granted they didn't have to leave immediately, but he knew that Gilrin and the elves were anxious to get started.

Which meant his training with Endri would come to an end for the time being. Would the emerald dragon understand, or demand that his training take precedent?

No sooner had that thought crossed his mind than did he feel a familiar presence, and as expected, Endri had sought Cardin out for their daily training. Gazing up to the west, he saw Endri's familiar form gliding gracefully towards him, the sun glinting off of his scales. As always, Cardin's heart beat faster and an exhilarated smile filled his face.

Whenever Endri went off on his own, it didn't matter where Cardin was in the world after that, the dragon always knew how to find him.

Crossing his arms, Cardin watched Endri gracefully touch down several hundred feet away. With great long strides, the dragon quickly reached Cardin, where he lowered his head in an attempt to look at Cardin eye to eye.

"Hello, my friend," Cardin smiled.

Tilting his head to one side, Endri asked, *"What has brought you to Archanon?"*

The smile on Cardin's face faded a little, and he let his hands fall to his side. "Well…something came up. Actually, we've had visitors to Halarite. Dareann Elves and a dwarf."

Raising his head a little to look towards the city, Endri nodded. *"I thought I felt an off-world portal open after I left you. I take it the elves are the ones you told me about?"*

"Yeah, Elaria and Baenil," Cardin nodded. "They wish to explore the ancient dwarven ruins beneath Archanon, and…" The dragon continued to stare at the city, not giving Cardin his full attention. Cardin was about to call him out for his wandering attention, but then noticed the dragon's face slowly turn to a troubled look. It was then that Cardin felt the approaching pulse of another person, and he turned to find a young squire running towards them, having just cleared the open gates.

Running squires weren't entirely uncommon, they were essentially the messengers of the kingdom. When one ran towards Cardin, however, that usually meant something was wrong.

As he turned fully to face the approaching squire, he stretched out his awareness to their surroundings to see if he could feel something out of place. Instantly he felt a collection of powerful presences up at the castle, and he knew that several Wizards had gathered. Given that he had been waiting for Endri for the past hour, they had to have arrived within Archanon earlier in the morning.

The squire reached him, and quickly bowed, only partly out of breath. "Keeper, please come quickly," he immediately spoke. "King Beredis has summoned you and your team to the Council chambers. The Grand Wizard Hall was attacked by a Dark Dragon!"

Cardin's heart skipped a beat and his stomach sank. There was only one known Dark Dragon left in the Universe, as far as they knew, which meant it could only have been Nuuldan. He began to follow the squire, but then stopped and glanced at Endri.

The one question he meant to ask him today anyway became ever more imperative. "I don't suppose you can shrink down to a smaller size?"

Endri shook his head slowly. *"I cannot. I have heard that the elder dragons learned to change their size, but it is not a skill I have learned."*

Finding that fact curious, Cardin would have normally asked why only elder dragons could do so, but now was not the time. "Should I ask the King and the Wizards to come outside, then," he asked instead.

Hesitating a moment, Endri nodded once. *"If they would be willing. Otherwise I would need to impose upon you to relay the meeting to me through your mind, and I am unsure if that is a skill you can learn quickly."*

Apparently that was another lesson he could look forward to. Nodding, he turned back to the impatient squire and fell into a run with him. Behind him, he heard and felt a wind kick up as Endri took to the skies.

Once they entered Archanon, the people of the Market District gazed up in awe as Endri flew overhead, headed for the Castle District. Suddenly Endri called down to Cardin, *"On second thought, I will ask them myself."*

Since the dragon only spoke through projection of a mental voice, Cardin knew that he could make his request directly to King Beredis and the Wizards.

His heart racing, and not just because he was running, Cardin feared the worst. Had Nuuldan returned to Halarite and attacked the Guild Hall being rebuilt in the north? Or had he somehow found the Wizards' special pocket dimension and attacked that Guild Hall? Was Dalin safe? How many Wizards were hurt? Was the attack still under way? Was Halarite under threat?

Passing through the inner gates, Cardin forced himself to stop thinking of all the worst scenarios, and focused only on what he could do to help if Nuuldan was still present. He hadn't figured out yet how to summon his avatar on command, but perhaps under the right stressors, he could do it again.

By the time they reached the wide courtyard in front of the castle, Endri had already landed and stepped to one side, dwarfing the houses around him and impressive in size even next to the castle. He and the squire slowed to a walk as they entered the courtyard, and then he sighed with relief when the large doors into the castle opened and one of the first faces he saw was Dalin's.

King Beredis, Prince Beredis, Dalin, Master Syrn, several other Master Wizards, and Cardin's entire party for the upcoming journey all stepped out into the courtyard, minus the marines promised from Erien. No other members of the Allied Council were present, but Cardin assumed that would probably change soon.

"Dalin!" Cardin called out his friend's name in relief and rushed to meet up with them.

"I am unharmed," Dalin nodded, his face grim.

"Nuuldan was here," Endri inquired.

"No," Master Syrn shook her head, gripping her staff firmly. "He came to our universe and attacked us there."

"It happened so fast," Dalin shook his head, grasping his ash wood staff firmly. The Wizard's power flared for a moment in an unusual burst of emotion, and in that instant, Cardin felt something different about his friend's presence. A strength of will and power he had never felt before. "He...the Grand Master." Dalin's voice wavered.

Color drained from Cardin's face as his extremities grew numb. "Master Valkere?"

That was when Cardin noticed the look on the other Wizards' faces, and on the King's. That was the moment he knew what had happened.

Looking to Endri, Master Syrn nodded stoically. "Grand Master Valkere sacrificed himself to protect the Grand Hall long enough for most of us to escape. If what Dalin has told us is true," she turned to look at Dalin, her face grim. "Then he also sacrificed himself to destroy the entire Guild Hall. By allowing his power to consume him."

Out of the corner of his eye, Cardin saw Endri's head rise up in surprise. *"I see,"* the emerald dragon spoke softly. *"It is possible he wounded Nuuldan in the process. Even the most powerful Dark Dragon would not be immune to such an outburst of magic."*

Cardin frowned and was about to ask, but Sira beat him to it. "I'm sorry, what do you mean he allowed his power to consume him?"

A scowl crossed Syrn's face as she looked at Sira with impatient eyes. "A Wizard grows ever more powerful throughout our years. Through trained control, we are able to contain the power constantly flowing within and through us, Master Wizards even more so. If a Master Wizard loses control, most often inadvertently, all of their power is unleashed at once. Without proper safeguards, it is quite destructive."

Suddenly Cardin's growing powers scared him more than ever. Could that happen to him someday?

For a long time, the group stood silently, contemplating the gravity of the situation, and mourning the loss of Valkere.

Looking to Syrn with sympathy, Cardin asked, "How many other Wizards lost their lives in the attack?"

Her face was long, but there was a hint of growing anger in her eyes. Drawing in a breath, she slowly shook her head and replied, "We do not know exactly yet, but there are at least forty three missing."

Given how many unrecoverable casualties the Wizards had already suffered over the past year, it was a devastating blow. At that thought, Cardin felt a sour taste in his mouth and he reminded himself that the loss of one life, no matter the circumstances, was always a blow. Had he grown so accustomed to war and casualties already?

Then Dalin looked at Endri intently. "I was there when Master Valkere faced the Dark Dragon. Nuuldan asked him where something called the Shadow Quartz was. Do you know what that is?"

The dragon's brow furrowed, and he looked quizzically at the assembled group. *"No, I do not."*

"He seemed very certain that the Wizards had it," Syrn added. "Why would he come to our Guild Hall in search of it?"

Thinking further on it, Cardin added to the question, "Especially since we know he's been out of touch since long before the Star Dragons ever encountered the Wizards."

"That is not entirely accurate," Endri corrected. *"We have encountered Wizards of Halarite on other worlds throughout the millennia, though the encounters were rare."* Cardin exchanged surprised looks with Dalin, and was even more surprised to find that Syrn appeared startled by that revelation. *"However, for him to believe the Wizards to have something vital to him means that he has learned more about Halarite since you drove him away."*

Speaking for the first time, King Beredis intoned, "Then someone must have told him about the Wizards. They must have led him to believe the Wizards had whatever this Shadow Quartz is."

"Exactly," Endri looked off into the distance, his eyes unfocused.

"But who," Cardin asked. "Unless he came back to Halarite sometime in the past few months, who would know anything about us?"

The thought that occurred to Cardin must have occurred to the King, Sira, and Master Syrn at the same time. Everyone turned to the elves, but when Elaria and Baenil noticed, they both raised their hands defensively. "He definitely hasn't been to Darea," Elaria defended. "I'm sure I would have heard about it, and I can't imagine any reason an elf would cooperate with a Dark Dragon."

Cardin believed them, and as everyone looked away from the elves, it seemed that so did everyone else. "So then how did he learn about the Wizards' Grand Hall," the King asked absently.

After a moment of silence, it was Gilrin who replied. "I think 'how' is the more difficult question to answer," he spoke, the frown on his face conveying annoyance at them all. "But the who can at least be partly answered – it must be someone else that knows about you, outside of the elves and the Star Dragons."

It was an obvious conclusion, and Cardin felt glad that the dwarf had pointed it out.

"Then the question remains, who would support Nuuldan and knows about Halarite," Endri nodded at Gilrin. *"Either way, if he is brazen enough to attack the Grand Wizard Hall, even knowing that the Keeper of the Sword might come to defend it, then he must have found a powerful ally in very little time."*

With a grimace, Cardin ran his fingers through his growing hair and nodded. "That is probably the most disquieting conclusion I've heard yet."

"Yes," Endri nodded. *"Which is why I must return to the other Star Dragons, to track down who might be involved, and find out what this Shadow Quartz is."*

Endri crouched down, ready to leap into the air to leave them, but Cardin reached out a halting hand. "Wait!"

Thankfully the dragon didn't leave them yet, and he looked back down at Cardin. Cardin gulped, looked at the King, and then at Sira, and then asked Endri, "Can I come with you?"

"What?" Sira's startled voice cinched Cardin's heart.

Stepping closer to her, he looked deep into her eyes and explained to everyone, "This is what I've been training for, right?" He looked at the Star Dragon and continued, "I mean, I may not be ready yet, but if there's even a chance that Endri could run into Nuuldan again, I should be there to help defeat him."

Endri considered the request for a moment, eyeing Cardin while tilting his head to the side. Cardin took that moment to again look to Sira, whose worried eyes sent daggers through his heart.

Noticing their exchange, Endri replied, *"I could be gone for a long time. Days, weeks, perhaps longer."*

Looking up into Endri's starry eyes, Cardin nodded. "Even more reason for me to come with. I can continue to train with you, and learn more about the Universe at the same time. Magic is all-encompassing, right? Wouldn't it help me to experience what other worlds are like?"

"Indeed it would," Endri nodded. He looked then to King Beredis and asked, *"Would you permit it, Your Majesty?"*

Beredis looked at Endri, and then at Cardin, the idea clearly one he was not comfortable with. "It would not entirely be up to me," he replied after some thought. "The Allied Council agreed that all matters concerning the Keeper of the Sword would be decided together." After another moment of hesitation, he looked up at Endri and asked, "Would you be willing to delay your departure for a few hours? I believe I can convince them of the wisdom of letting Cardin accompany you."

Once again, Endri looked at Cardin hesitantly. Cardin also grimaced, not looking forward to yet another boring Council meeting.

Then, much to his surprise, Prince Beredis added his own opinion. "Father, time may not be on our side." Everyone turned at once to stare at the Prince, who didn't appear to mind the extra attention. "If Nuuldan has indeed found allies, then finding out who they are, and discovering where Nuuldan is now, especially if he is wounded, is an immediate need. One of our allies has been brutally attacked. This is clearly an emergency."

Most often, Cardin hated the Prince's impulsiveness. In this case, however, it could work to his advantage. More than that, Cardin realized that the Prince was right. Maybe his father's lessons were actually wearing off on the kid.

The King considered the Prince's point for a moment, and then turned to Master Syrn. "I suppose we have not yet drafted emergency procedures yet, so there is nothing saying we could not decide, together, that the urgency required quick action."

Glancing at the King, then at Endri, then at Cardin, and finally back to the King, Syrn raised an eyebrow and remained silent for several moments. She then looked to the other Master Wizards present. Knowing what had just happened to them, he was rather surprised by how they considered the situation with so little emotion. And, for that matter, without saying a single word. Then again, with their age and experience, it was possible that they simply hid their emotions a bit better than he realized.

After each of the Masters nodded, Syrn in turn nodded. "We agree. The situation is unique, and I believe if there is a chance of stopping Nuuldan now, while he is vulnerable, we must allow it."

The King nodded, and said, "Very well. Cardin, you-"

"Your Majesty," Sira interrupted, suddenly stepping beside Cardin. "I respectfully ask permission to accompany Cardin."

The King's eyebrows were raised in a combination of surprise and displeasure, but after a moment of considering it, he nodded. "It might be wise to have all of you work together on this mission. Your record speaks for itself."

A broad smile stretched across Cardin's face, and he had to forcefully keep himself from reaching out to hold Sira's hand. It was no secret that they were together again, but it would be inappropriate to display their affection now.

However, Cardin's jubilation was short lived. Master Syrn interjected, "With respect, King Beredis, your implication would be that Sira, Reis, and Dalin accompany the Keeper." The King nodded in affirmation, to which Syrn replied, "I must decline."

"Master?!"

Syrn glared at Dalin, and then again addressed the King. "We have just endured a devastating blow. We must rally our people to the rebuilt complex and hurry to complete it, especially its defenses. If Nuuldan believes we have this Shadow Quartz, he may risk coming back to Halarite to search our rebuilt home."

"Master, I must object," Dalin began. "Master Valkere insisted that I-"

"Be silent!" Syrn's terse tone left no room for argument. "I will not allow another Wizard to be lost needlessly."

Dalin opened his mouth to object further, but he stopped himself and looked around at the others. His face turned a shade of red, but Cardin knew it was not out of embarrassment. Dalin often expressed his frustration with the Wizards' Guild and its rules and ranks. This would drive him to hate his Guild even more.

"I am sorry, Your Majesty," Syrn half-bowed. "That is my final decision."

Beredis drew in an apprehensive breath, but he nodded. "As you wish, Master Wizard. It is your decision to make. Lieutenant," he then addressed Sira, "How soon can you be ready to go?"

Shrugging easily, she replied, "We were already preparing for a long trip into the ruins, so just a few minutes to finish up."

Cardin was about to ask Endri if that was acceptable, but then Elaria cleared her throat. The group turned their attention to the elves, then, and Cardin realized that in their haste, they had actually forgotten about the elves and their quest.

"What about the dwarven ruins," Elaria asked.

"While we support your new mission," Baenil added, "I would prefer we be allowed to move forward with our own mission." He looked to the King and added politely, "With your permission, Your Majesty."

The King looked to the others, but the elves' quest had already been blessed by the Allied Council. Unfortunately with the proposed leader, Sira, now leaving with Cardin and Endri, they were without the bulk of their proposed team. Cardin knew that if they waited for the Allied Council to convene and discuss it, who knew who would be given command, so it was a decision the King would have to make on the spot.

Much to Cardin's surprise, Reis stepped forward. Having remained silent and in the back, out of view for the most part, Cardin was only mildly shocked when his old friend said, "With your permission, Your Majesty, I strongly request permission to take Elaria, Baenil, and Gilrin into the dwarven ruins."

The King looked surprised, and Sira looked at Cardin with concern and shock. "You don't want to go with us," she asked Reis.

He looked at her, glanced at Cardin, and then quickly averted his eyes. After a moment of searching the ground, he replied, "We promised them we'd help them. And I have come to know Elaria well."

With a smile on her face, Elaria nodded. "I trust him, and he's a competent leader, Your Majesty."

King Beredis considered the request for a moment, and then looked to Cardin and Sira for their support. Something began to boil in the back of Cardin's mind, and he wanted to ask Reis why he kept going to such lengths to avoid Cardin. But Cardin knew that now was not the time for such a conversation. He'd have to pull his friend aside before they left to ask about it.

Exchanging looks with Sira again, Cardin nodded and said, "If that is his desire, then it is your choice, Your Majesty." Suddenly he realized that meant that he and Sira would be alone with Endri. As much as he wanted Dalin with them, and as much as he wanted to resolve whatever was wrong between him and Reis, it still wouldn't be a horrible situation.

After considering the request for another moment, King Beredis nodded. "Very well. However, because of the contingent of Erien marines set to accompany you, I would like a higher-ranking Warrior to accompany you. I know that Lieutenant Kellis Morvan is in Archanon on an errand from Daruun. He will command the party."

A sour look crossed Reis's face, which further puzzled Cardin. Normally Reis and Kellis got along very well, the veteran Warrior having taken Reis under his wing years ago. Something was really wrong with Cardin's friend, and he wanted to get to the bottom of it.

When no one objected or said anything further, Beredis nodded at Sira. "Gather your gear and move out as soon as you can."

Bowing, Sira replied, "At once, Sire."

Chapter 12

FIRES OF JEALOUSY

When the impromptu meeting outside of the castle was over and Reis was no longer obligated to remain, he turned immediately and wove his way around the crowd to head for the Upper City's exit, bound for the Warriors' Guild complex where he had temporary quarters assigned to him. Someone may have called out his name, but he chose to ignore it.

As he left the courtyard, he heard the dragon leap into the air and fly away, his wings stirring up a sudden gale force wind, until he was high above. Reis glanced up at the dragon as it soared towards the western gate.

A part of him was angry over Cardin and Sira's reassignment, since they had already made promises to lead Elaria, Baenil and Gilrin into the ruins. On the other hand, he was glad that he didn't have to go with them to wherever they were going.

Reis heard his name again, but he didn't turn around to look. It was Cardin's voice, and he didn't want to have anything to do with him, not anymore. Not since Anila Kovin had revealed her secret to Reis, and then told him that Cardin knew all along. He'd done everything he could to stay away from Cardin since then.

When he was halfway through the Upper City, surrounded now by the manors of the kingdom's wealthiest, Cardin overtook him and stopped in his path. Reis didn't bother to look at Cardin's face, and instead tried to walk around, but Cardin moved to block him. "Reis, stop!"

"Out of my way, Cardin," he grumbled, feeling his heart racing. He balled his hands into fists and slowly looked up at Cardin, projecting as much of his anger as he could through his eyes.

"Not until you tell me what's going on," Cardin folded his arms defiantly.

"I don't owe you anything," Reis replied, trying to walk around the other again.

Cardin again blocked him. "I suppose twenty years of friendship counts for nothing?"

Glaring at Cardin, he spat back, "Apparently not! Apparently magic trumps friendship every time."

A quizzical look crossed Cardin's face, and he shook his head. "What are you talking about?"

Despite the growing pressure in his chest, Reis tried desperately to keep his voice down. "I'm talking about Mages, and Wizards, and everything in between."

It took only moments for realization to cross Cardin's face. Reis watched the other's expressions carefully, searching for any look of guilt or regret, though he didn't expect to see any. With a guarded tone, Cardin asked, "You know about her?"

"Yeah," Reis planted his hands on his hips. "No thanks to you, I found out on my own."

Stepping a little closer to Reis, Cardin asked, "That's what this is all about?"

Reis planted a finger into Cardin's chest. "You let me get close to her, you let me trust her, even though you knew she was lying to me."

"It wasn't my place," Cardin started to say.

"You were my best friend!" Reis shouted a lot louder than he intended, and he felt his cheeks turn bright red. He drew his arms back to himself. "But I've had time to think about it. To think about everything I've seen over the years. And it's always about the magic, isn't it?"

Another quizzical look overcame Cardin's face, and it was all Reis could do not to punch the look off of his face.

When Cardin didn't say anything, Reis explained, "You always afford those with magic more respect."

Cardin's eyes grew wide, and he scoffed. "You're joking, right?"

"I suppose it isn't entirely your fault," Reis growled. "It's our whole society. Mages live twice as long as the rest of us, but you get promoted twice as fast."

"Magic power has nothing…" Cardin stopped himself short. "Magic is part of combat prowess, it has nothing to do with leadership capability, let alone promotions."

"Name one Commander or General in the past decade that wasn't a Mage," Reis demanded. "I can't think of a single one. And leadership potential? That's because all of the leadership training is focused on your lot, and the rest of us have to figure it out on our own. That's why Sira was promoted before me. That's why Kellis was chosen to lead the expedition, not me."

Cardin's face had started to soften, but then he scrunched up his nose. "That was a political decision, and you know it!"

"And there's always extenuating circumstances," Reis countered. "Excuses. Special reasons. But it always comes down to Mages. And then Wizards get their own spot on the Allied Council while also acting as advisors to every member of the royalty, except for the one King who's already a Wizard."

"The Beredis family," Cardin pointed over Reis's shoulder. "They have no magic, but they've ruled Tal for centuries."

"Yeah, after a dictator of a Mage was deposed by them," Reis folded his hands. "A Mage took advantage of the people, used them, killed them at will, sat on the throne ordering the death of thousands on a whim. Most of their victims were powerless. So a powerless family gathered allies, rose up and deposed that Mage. No one gave the Beredis family power, they had to take it for themselves!"

Cardin started to retort, but then stopped himself and looked down, his jaw taut and his hands clenched. "This isn't the time or place for this debate, Reis," he finally looked up. "We've wandered way off topic."

"And that's the problem with you," Reis scowled. "All of you. You think I'm making it up. But I'll bet you anything if I had magic, I'd have been promoted at the same time as Sira, or before. They would have let me command the expedition. I could have-"

"That's what this is really about," Cardin pointed a finger at him.

"Jealousy."

Reis batted the finger away, and very nearly punched Cardin. He wanted to shove him, to curse him, to throw him down and walk all over him.

But there was a twinge in the back of his heart. A pang that came from decades of friendship. A glimmer of guilt and shame.

Cardin was right. Not about everything, but he was right about that. Reis was jealous. As far as he was concerned, however, it was righteous resentment.

"Things have happened the way they have," Cardin stated matter-of-factly, folding his arms. More smugness. "Since when has anything ever happened exactly the way we want them to, Reis? Since when has anything ever been fair? You didn't get the promotion, Sira did. That doesn't mean you won't get the next one."

"Yes it does," he grumbled.

"Well you certainly won't with that attitude," Cardin's hands flailed outward. "You've walked around with a bad attitude for months. Do you think just *maybe* that might have something to do with you being passed over? Before that, I recall you commanding patrols on more than one occasion, even though Idann didn't want you to, but others saw your potential and gave you those jobs, some of whom were Mages."

Reis tried to interrupt, but Cardin raised a hand to stop him. That by itself almost set Reis off again. "No, stop. You want to end our friendship over all of this?" He lowered his voice, and added, "Over Anila? Then fine, go ahead." Rage boiled up inside of Reis, and he was ready to walk away, but then Cardin added, "I'll miss you. I already do. But if you feel like I am such a horrible person because of my powers, then you need to do what's best for you."

The burning anger inside of Reis perished instantly, and he felt a void open up inside of him. The regret he'd felt over his jealousy magnified tenfold.

"But before we part ways, I want you to consider one thing," Cardin spoke quietly, glancing around. Reis was too stricken to also look around, but it was likely that others had drawn near because of their public argument. "You haven't told anyone her secret either, have you?" Reis averted his eyes from Cardin's. "I didn't think so. Because she asked you not to, am I right? And even though you might hate her now for keeping her secret from you, you're still honoring her request. Why is that?"

Considering the question for a moment, Reis replied, "Because she's afraid of how others will react if they find out what she is."

Cardin moved so that he stood in front of Reis's gaze, getting his attention. "Did you ever consider that's why she didn't want you to know? Because she was afraid of how you'd react to her?"

He wanted to look away from Cardin, but he locked his eyes on the other's, knowing that Cardin was right, which further fueled Reis's anger. Never-the-less, Cardin's point was valid. Reis might very well have done the same thing if he were in Anila's position.

Cardin again looked over Reis's shoulders, and then he finished, "I don't know how long we'll be gone, but I'm going to leave this in your hands. When we get back, you let me know where we go from here. Friends...or not." Cardin's voice wavered with his last statement. But then he walked around Reis towards the castle.

He didn't look back at Cardin. He didn't know what to do. Standing in the middle of the street, he stared ahead at the Upper City gates. Suddenly he was very much aware of eyes all around focused on him. He looked around, and noticed several of the nobles and their servants in their gardens, gawking at him. Some suddenly went back to work when his eyes fell on them, others stared at him reprovingly. How many of them were also Mages?

He banished the thought the moment he had it. Then his eyes fell upon someone else nearby.

Elaria.

Someone else with magic. Someone he had once wronged, just because of who and what she was.

Over the past few months, he'd had a lot of time to himself to think about everything. To see the patterns in the world, that those with magic were given more. That anyone without magic was given less opportunity just because of who and what they were.

Suddenly he realized that he was just as guilty of judging others based on magic. Anger boiled up inside of him again, anger at himself, and at society for being built the way it was.

Elaria approached him then, her face soft, her burning sunset eyes sympathetic. He almost told her to go away. But the closer she drew, the more he suddenly longed for her company.

She had been born into a society where everyone had magic. Except for the dwarves, he realized.

"Are you alright," she asked, stopping within a few feet. Memories of the dance at Maradin passed through his mind's eye, of getting to know her, waltzing with her, and seeing who she was beneath his preconceptions.

Not wanting to admit the turmoil and anger seething inside, he countered with his own question. "Why did you come back with Gilrin?" He needed to know, he realized, and he hoped for an answer that would give him hope for the Universe, for himself.

Tilting her head to one side, she replied, "Because he asked me to."

A rushing sensation accelerated his heartbeat. "You know him personally?"

She nodded with a warm smile. "We're friends. Every time I return to the College, I look for him and tell him all about the worlds I've explored, and he tells me what's happened at the College, and we just...talk."

Despite the darkness he felt in his heart, he felt a smile stretch across his face. "So the fact that he's a powerless dwarf doesn't bother you?"

This time it was Elaria's turn to give a sour look. "No," she said tersely. "But I should tell you, that's not exactly a common thing on my world." Reis's smile melted, giving way for the return of loathing. "Dwarves are considered..." She hesitated, looking around while searching for the right words. "Well, they're pretty much only servants on our world. It's only those like myself and Baenil that treat them differently."

Reis frowned curiously, and asked, "Why are you different?"

Shrugging easily, Elaria replied, "Because of what I've seen, out there, in the Universe. Because of what I've learned. And while Baenil always treated dwarves better than others, I suspect his time as a captive on Halarite helped him to appreciate them more."

Any response Reis might have had was lost in her last words. It was a reminder of the troubles within the Order of the Ages, of how lost they were. At how lost he felt because he was forced to question the very faith that had sustained him throughout his life.

How much of his current anger and frustration was because of that?

It occurred to him that despite how much time he'd had to think since the Battle for Maradin, he still needed to wrestle his demons.

"To be honest," Elaria suddenly added, stepping closer to him until their arms touched. "That's really why I'm here."

A frown creased his forehead. "What do you mean?"

"There are hardly any records from the time of the dwarves," she looked into his eyes. "They've pretty much lost all legitimacy as a culture, and they have no real identity other than as servants and workers for the Dareann Elves. This is the most concrete piece of their history that has been found in generations. Maybe these ruins can help them gain their identity again. Maybe even find out how they lost their connection to magic."

Raising an eyebrow, he asked, "Is their identity really so dependent upon magic?"

Grinning, Elaria shook her head. "I overheard some of your conversation with Cardin, and I'm sorry that your experiences with magic haven't been pleasant. I'm sure what I've told you hasn't helped. Still, magic was once vital to them. They were once a vast empire, or so legends have it. Losing their magic very likely contributed to losing their empire. I think they deserve to find out why that happened. And even if they can never get it back, maybe they can start to forge a new identity, based on who they were, and who they are now. I'm not saying they need to become what they were, I'm saying I want them to become more than they are."

She paused for a moment, and then added, "Besides which, even though it may be a pipe dream, I'd love to educate my own people too, and hopefully turn them away from treating anyone else like servants." She laughed ironically. "Yeah, saying it out loud like that sounds ridiculous, doesn't it?"

A grin creased at Reis's face, and he realized just how long it had been since he'd felt that characteristic grin. "No, I don't think it does."

Rolling her eyes, Elaria replied, "Well, you just don't know my people that well."

Chuckling, he looked back at the castle, and found that all of the others had either gone inside or had gone around them to leave the Upper City. "Maybe you can tell me all about them on this expedition."

"Sure," she smiled. "But only if you promise me one thing."

Suspicious, he asked, "What's that?"

"Tell me why you suddenly hate your best friend."

He stopped short of saying anything, and felt his grin fade. He wasn't sure he wanted to talk about it with anyone. But then, maybe he needed to.

So he nodded. "Alright. But I get the feeling we'll be moving out soon, and I need to get my gear."

She turned and faced the Upper City gates with him. "Then tell me along the way."

Warmth threatened to enter the recesses of his heart, and he realized it would be good to talk to her alone again. So he nodded, and together they headed out. "I can't tell you everything," he cautioned, realizing that he still didn't want to betray Anila's secret. "But I'll tell you what I can."

Chapter 13

TRAITORS

The sun crept over the horizon, lighting up the bay east of Tieran, and warming Kailar's pale face. She closed her eyes for a moment, trying to banish the worry in her heart as she waited impatiently.

After she had brought Egil back to the Guild Hall, they'd discussed their next move, and Egil insisted that the only way he could figure out how to help was by talking to one of his contacts. Of course, the catch was that if either Kailar or Letan accompanied him, they'd immediately recognize the two and his contacts would scatter.

She and Letan stood across the street from a shop on the western edge of town, partially hidden around the corner of another building. Egil had led them to a supply shop for adventurers that Kailar distinctly remembered visiting when she had first arrived on the continent. That had nearly induced a panic in both her and Letan, because the closer to the edge of town that Egil had led them, the more worried they were that they were bound for Dillarn's shop, the local map-maker and purveyor of unusual artifacts and curiosities on Devor.

Thankfully, Egil hadn't led them to Dillarn's. With a sardonic grin, Kailar recalled that this shop's owner was the one who had sent her to Dillarn.

Egil was still inside, and a lantern had been lit within upon his arrival, but they hadn't seen any other movement or activity in hours. Now that the sun rose, Kailar feared discovery by Egil's contact. Furthermore, if someone at city hall hadn't already noticed the missing prisoner, they soon would, and the mayor would no doubt suspect Kailar and Letan.

Which would mean city guards might already be looking for them.

"I don't like this," Letan grumbled, shifting his weight from one leg to another. Kailar noticed that his hand rested on his sword hilt, ready to unsheathe at a moment's notice.

"I know," she sighed impatiently, feeling herself reach for her weapon as well. She started to worry about another repeat of the raid on the warehouse. "I don't enjoy standing idle and waiting. I want to *do* something." Suddenly a yawn threatened to overtake her, and she tried in vain to suppress it. When was the last time she'd actually slept more than an hour or two?

Closing her eyes, Kailar tried to channel energy from dark magic into her, to revitalize her and keep sleepiness from dulling her senses. It wasn't as easy as it had been when she was a Mage – dark magic was so different that she sometimes had to remind herself that she had to perform the opposite act with magic to get it to work the way she wanted. Never-the-less, it helped momentarily, and her eyes opened wide again.

Just in time to watch the shop's front door open, and much to her relief, Egil strolled out. His face was long, and Kailar feared that he hadn't learned anything of value. He looked all around to make sure no one saw him, and then he made eye contact with them, before he turned and walked towards the outer edge of town.

Kailar immediately knew why, and assumed that Egil was under suspicion, and he didn't want to be seen walking straight over to them.

Glancing at one another, Kailar and Letan walked around the back side of the building they had been using to hide behind, and rushed ahead. After a few minutes, and at the very edge of town, they circled back around and intercepted the former bandit leader.

Egil made no attempt to evade them, but he was still very nervous.

"What'd you find out," Letan demanded, his hand on the hilt of his sword. Kailar knew why, and she extended her senses, trying to detect any danger nearby that might indicate an attempted ambush. Surely she had shown all of the criminal underground how dangerous she was, but that didn't mean they weren't above stupidity.

Shaking his head, Egil replied, "That I should have known how deeply seated we really were on this continent."

Kailar glanced at Letan, and then asked, "More than the Mayor's office?"

"The mayor, city soldiers across the continent..." Egil hesitated and looked at Letan. "The Warriors' Guild."

Letan's head snapped up. "Excuse me?"

Shifting nervously and wringing his hands, Egil said, "All those years on the western side of Devor, and no one thought I should know about it." His shifting turned into nervous pacing, and he waved his hands around as he spoke. "I mean, yeah, sure, I'm not the most important man in the business, but seriously, no one thought to tell me?"

"Tell you what?!" Kailar's voice wavered with impatience, and she grabbed Egil by the shoulder to make him stop. Clenching on a muscle group, she forced him to look her in the eyes.

Egil hesitated, but finally said, "I told them I couldn't make it out of Tieran, that you two were watching the docks, so I needed to find a new place to hide. They told me that with you two being based in Tieran, most of our business was moved west, to Edingard." Kailar felt a lump form in her throat. "To the Warriors' Guild."

Shock overcame Letan's face, and he stepped back as he shook his head. "You can't be serious."

Eying Letan fiercely, Egil replied, "I'm dead serious."

Kailar clenched his shoulder again, forcing his attention back to her. "Why were you so nervous to tell us this?"

With a puzzled look, he replied, "You have to ask? I'm supposed to get you evidence. Well, if evidence still exists, it's in that damned Guild house."

She realized what that meant a half second before Letan spoke, "We have to confront them. And we have to take Egil with us, because he may know what to look for."

Releasing her iron grip on him, Kailar stepped back. "I see." After a moment of thinking about it, she shrugged. "So what's the problem, Egil? You didn't really think this was going to be easy, did you?"

Glaring at her, he shot back, "I didn't think I'd have to openly betray the others! If word gets off of Devor of my involvement, there'll be nowhere for me to go."

She remarked casually, "That's not really my problem. You'll just have to figure something out after all of this is over with."

"Easy enough for you to say," Egil grumbled.

Shaking her head, she turned to Letan, noticing the unusual pale color of his face. "Are you okay?"

At first, he didn't reply. But then he drew his hands into fists and clenched his jaw. "No. No I'm not." He looked into her eyes, and she noticed a fire in his blue eyes that she had never seen before. "But I will be once we expose those bastards."

At first his words surprised her, but then she realized why he was so taken aback. He was good to his core, perhaps too good sometimes, and he truly believed in the mission of the Warriors. Turns out, some Warriors weren't so honest and honorable. She was hardly surprised about it, but she supposed that Letan had hoped for at least one incorruptible group in the world.

More than that, she realized, he had learned only yesterday that several Warriors, after the Guild had lost funding years ago, had turned to crime. It spoke volumes of the corruptibility of any organization on Devor, or anywhere else for that matter.

The world was even less pretty than he had probably ever realized, even having lived on Devor for so long.

Raising her eyebrows, she asked him, "So what do we do? Sneak in? I'm not sure how effective that'll be, but I'll help us do it if you want."

He thought about it for a moment, and then shook his head. "No. Not this time." He looked pointedly at Kailar.

"Uh, just a thought," Egil chimed in. "If you go in with swords drawn, they might have a chance to cover up or hide any documents."

Kailar grimaced, knowing that he was right. Then she looked at him curiously, an idea occurring to her. When Egil saw the grin on her face, he sighed. "I'm not going to like this, am I?"

With a wry smile, she asked Letan, "Still have those shackles?"

He must have had the same thought, as he mirrored her smile and produced the shackles before he forcibly put them on Egil, who cursed them both. "I can't believe I let you talk me into any of this."

"Shut up," she grabbed his arm and twisted it just enough to make him wince. "You're our prisoner now, and you're going to get us into the Edingard Guild house." *After all,* she thought to herself. *They don't know yet that Letan and I have been removed from our positions.*

A short portal hop later, and they stood in the middle of Edingard. Further southwest than Tieran, the city was nestled on the eastern side of the Barrier Mountains, a monumental range that stretched from the northern shores all the way to the southern and quite literally created a barrier between the small eastern nub of Devor and the vast western section. The sun hadn't quite risen this far west yet, there was only the predawn glow of the coming light to the northeast, and the air was considerably colder.

She couldn't see the peaks to the west, not yet, but she could almost feel them glowering over her. And she shivered. Not for the cold, but for the bitter taste that her memories of the city left in her mouth. It wasn't her first time back since joining the Devor Warriors, but every time she came, she remembered the face of the miner that had stalked her.

Driving her guilt deeper was that her actions had been in vain. Letan had found out Kailar's true identity less than a month later, and despite his initial anger, he came back to her anyway. And he was still with her.

She could never tell him, or anyone else.

Tearing her thoughts away from that horrible evening, she looked ahead at the Guild house. Unlike most of the Guild halls on Edilas, the halls on Devor, including Edingard, were akin to manors, converted to be used as bases of operations for the disconnected Guild. Edingard's manor was constructed from local wood, and it stood out from the rest of the city only in that it was one of the largest structures in the frontier town, and was well lit with everlasting torches, some of the only ones found on Devor. Also unlike Edilas Guild Halls, there were no obvious guards present outside.

Recalling how lax the Warriors had seemed during all of their previous visits, Kailar thought that they could have actually easily snuck in. But their course was set, and until they met the local Guild Commander, they would keep up the ruse.

Letan had preceded Kailar through the portal, pushing Egil along, so he approached the simple wooden door to the building. Kailar rushed ahead and opened the door for the others, the rusting iron hinges groaning as she did so. After Letan shoved Egil inside, Kailar followed, closing the door behind her.

The first room was a foyer designed to receive visitors, and there they finally found a guard, having been startled awake by the screeching door. He wasn't in any form of armor, and his tunic was half-untucked from his trousers, while his sword and scabbard lay uselessly across the table, which he used to prop his feet up on. Even from here, she could smell him, rank and suspiciously like alcohol.

"What in the name…" the Warrior slogged out groggily. "Who are you?" He looked around for his sword, despite it being right in front of him.

Drawing himself up to his full height, Letan replied, "I am Lieutenant Letan Velethar of the Tieran Warriors' Guild, and this is Kailar Adanna. We've apprehended this bandit on the mountain pass and need to throw him into your dungeon."

"You what?" the guard asked, his sword finally in hand, but he seemed not to realize that it was still in its scabbard. "Bandit? Wait, Kailar?" His eyes fell upon her, and that sobered him up quickly.

"That's right," she smirked. "Time to actually do your job."

The guard's face soured, but her reputation was well known, and he immediately lowered his sword, for what that was worth.

"I suggest you neaten yourself up and wake the Commander," Letan looked the Warrior up and down judgmentally. "I have it on good authority that there's a bandit camp north of here that we'll need to raid."

The guard eyed Letan, and then snorted out a laugh. "Really? That's interesting, 'cause we don't know anything 'bout it."

"Well then I know something that you don't," Letan glowered. "Now go get your Commander, or you'll be the next one in shackles."

Mockingly, the guard replied, "Ooh, yes sir, whatever you say, sir."

Kailar clenched her fists, and as the guard turned to leave, she couldn't help but reach out and grab his arm, spinning him around. "Hey, watch it, lady!"

"Show a little respect," she threatened.

"Or what?" he immediately replied, but then his face slackened with sudden realization and fear.

"Or I'll make you."

"Kailar," Letan warned her off.

She held on to the guard for another moment, just enough to make him wonder if she would actually hurt him, and then she let him go.

He stumbled backwards, trying desperately to get away, and then he composed himself. Or rather, he stopped panicking, and turned with a show of dignity and left the room, his tunic still a mess and his sheathed sword still unattached from his belt.

Once he was out of earshot, Letan cleared his throat. "Nice little show you put on," he remarked.

Looking at him with as sincere a frown as she could muster, she asked, "What show?"

Letan shook his head in response.

"This is insane, you know," Egil grumbled, straining his shackles.

Kailar stepped over to the others, folded her arms, and stared into Egil's eyes. "You have a better idea?"

With a defiant look, he replied, "No. That don't mean this isn't insane."

She was about to deny that, but then stopped and looked at Letan. He drew in a breath and nodded. "He's probably right."

With a droll smile, she turned to face the door that the guard had left through, and waited.

They didn't have to wait long. The morning's first light peaked through the windows just as the Commander, Lenned Callum, entered the waiting room, along with the guard, who had finally made himself semi-presentable.

Commander Callum was a burly man, very hairy, and accustomed to living in a frontier town. They had worked with him each time they had visited Edingard, and he was definitely not a strict enforcer of the rules of the Guild, but even now, she found it hard to believe that he was a traitor.

"Lieutenant Velethar," he spoke to Letan. "Welcome back to Edingard."

Nodding, Letan replied, "Thank you, Commander."

The Commander glanced at Egil, and then at Kailar, before he remarked, "I wasn't aware you were operating in the area."

Motioning his head at Egil, he replied, "We had a lead on Egil.

He was supposed to be in Tieran, but we found out he was doubling-back to the west."

Raising an eyebrow, Lenned nodded. "I see. Well then, we'd be happy to take him off your hands."

Letan tightened his grip on Egil's arms, and replied, "Before that, we'd like to talk privately in your office. He has a confession to make that I think you'd find interesting."

"Does he, now," Lenned smirked. "Something about a camp to the north?" Letan nodded, and Kailar had to look away to keep from smiling. "Very well. Follow me."

They left the front guard behind and ventured further into the manor. Everything was built from local wood, and Kailar realized they would have to be careful. If it turned into a fight, she would have to refrain from conjuring fire, or the entire complex could go up in flames, destroying any evidence contained within.

The Commander's office was actually only a short trek down the first floor corridor, and the office itself was something of a surprise. While it was indeed a frontier town, she didn't actually think of Lenned as a hunter, but the multitude of skins, antlers and skulls adorning his wall told her otherwise. She was also struck by the fact that most of the skins and skulls were of predators, specifically of Duzai wolves. She knew those wolves were sensitive to magic and generally stayed away from anyone with power, unless they were in very large packs.

Surprising her further was that there was no desk, but rather a long bench table attached to one wall, with a multitude of papers strewn about the left side, and tools and scraps of leather on the right. There was also a tanning rack and other tools against another wall, and a few wooden chairs adorned with the furs of his kills.

She also noticed a couple of chests in one corner, and she hoped that something connecting him, and Mayor Evern, to the criminal underground was within those chests or on the bench.

Once Lenned closed the door behind them, they all turned to face each other, and the Commander asked, "So what's this all about?"

She could tell by the look on his face and the smugness in his voice that he expected a ruse from Egil to get Kailar and Letan away from him, just long enough to 'escape' from the Edingard dungeon.

Kailar looked at Letan, giving him pleading eyes. He looked at her for a moment, and then said in a gravely serious tone, "You can start."

Turning, she took another quick assessment of the room, and then ambled towards his leatherworking bench. "Tell me, Commander, how much do you know about the criminal underground on Devor?"

She didn't turn to look at him, but she could tell from the tone of his voice that he was perplexed by her question. "Only what I read about in the reports, and what we've encountered here in Edingard."

Looking over the pieces of scraps and tools, she nodded. "I see. So you have no idea who Egil is?"

"Who," the Commander asked. She heard his heavy footsteps come closer to her, as she started to move down the bench towards the papers on the left side.

"Me," Egil spoke up. "Surely you've heard the name before, what with the work I used to do in the west."

She reached the papers and started to glance over them, looking for anything that might be useful to them, but in that instant, Lenned inserted himself between her and the bench and pushed her away. She was surprised by his forwardness, and had to consciously keep herself from retaliating.

"Those do not concern you," he glowered at her, drawing himself up to his full height, which was considerable. If she had encountered him when she was powerless, she would have found him very intimidating.

In mock innocence, she asked, "Oh, they don't? Nothing in there incriminating you?"

Any pleasantries were gone, and he glanced at Egil with venom in his eyes before he asked Kailar, "Just what do you think you know?"

"I know that you have something we need," she shrugged. "And if you don't give it to us willingly..."

She felt a warning in the back of her head, but before she could react, the Commander's giant hand shoved into her chest and pinned her against the wall, hard enough to shake the manor's frame.

Kailar gasped for air, and the room spun and grew dim. "Hey!" she heard Letan shout, and there was the clanging and thumping of Egil stumbling to the ground as Letan shoved him out of the way.

Lenned released her and she crumpled to the floor, breathless and trying desperately to force air back into her lungs. Out of her darkened peripheral, she saw the oversized Commander turn and cross the distance to Letan in a single giant step, and his burly fist slammed into Letan's head, sending him sprawling and his drawn sword clanging out of hand.

Only after they were both down did Lenned draw his weapon, and as Kailar worked to regain her ability to focus, breathe, and move of her own accord, he turned on her. Lenned's sword pulsed and vibrated with magic, and he pointed the tip at her.

It was a brilliant move. Incapacitate the biggest threat first, then the next biggest threat, and only after that, kill her before she could recover. No gloating, no dialogue, just swift and sure action.

Summoning every ounce of willpower into her that she could, she projected a barrier in front of her just in time, absorbing his arcane blast relatively easily. As strong as he was physically, his magic was still no match for hers. That was his first mistake.

He roared a challenge and moved to impale her, but even his strength and sword were no match for her shield. His sword glanced off so forcefully that she saw the metal bend a little, and he impaled the tip into the wall under the work bench. That was his second mistake.

A sudden spasm of coughing overcame her, and she saw stars in her vision, the edge of unconsciousness threatening her. His first blow must have broken ribs and possibly wounded her lungs, and she knew that if she didn't end the battle immediately, she'd pass out and be at his mercy.

Lenned was strong, and he managed to extract his sword from the wall in moments. The construction of the steel had allowed it to bend without permanently deforming, but the tip was broken off. She smiled inwardly at that victory.

His last mistake came when he decided to draw his sword back to swing at her more forcefully. In that moment of vulnerability, she willed as much dark magic into her hand as she could, and she thrust it out, letting loose a shard of blackened ice that surprised even her.

Without armor, and with his sword drawn back, he didn't stand a chance, and the inch-thick shard impaled his chest. His face contorted into a cacophony of pain, surprise, and admiration. He drew in a breath, and when he exhaled, it came out as a wheeze, while blood trickled out of his mouth.

His grip wavered, and then he dropped his sword, the heavy claymore clattering to the ground. Then he, too, fell, thumping onto his knees.

Darkness edged into her vision again, so she closed her eyes and focused on healing herself. It was a power she hadn't relearned with dark magic yet, but learning all of her other former powers, plus new ones, hadn't been too difficult. She just had to remember, and then figure out how to do the same with dark magic.

It was warm, she remembered. She drew in the dark energy, and tried to focus it inwards, into her chest. It had been so much easier when the Sword of Dragons had given her such power!

Somewhere in the back of her mind, she was aware that the Commander finally collapsed onto his side. Egil stirred noisily, and she thought she heard Letan as well.

Kailar focused harder, but then relaxed when it occurred to her that she already knew how to heal. She just had to gather the required dark energy. So she focused on that, and on the strange sensation of pushing power out, only to have it become available as a result.

The warmth came, then, and whatever was broken in her chest twinged in pain as it set itself, and then immediately she felt better. She could breathe!

Her eyes shot open, and her eyes darted about the place while she gasped in air. Egil was already up, and was helping a dazed Letan onto his feet.

She heard shouting in the hallway, and knew that they had only moments before the other local Warriors came bursting in. Fully refreshed, she quickly pushed herself up, and then drew her sword. A glance at the Commander, and she could see that he was still alive, but barely. Blood trickled out of his mouth, and since the ice shard was already melting, chilled blood oozed out of his wound. He probably didn't have long to live, so she considered healing him.

The door burst open, and three Warriors filed in, their weapons drawn, powered with magic and ready to strike.

Letan, recovering from the blow to his head, stumbled to his feet and tried to pick up his sword, and one of the offending Warriors moved to intercept him, but Kailar stopped him short with a blast of arcane magic just in front of him, blowing a hole through the wall into the hallway.

"Stop!" She stepped towards them, already projecting a shield in case they ignored her in the heat of the moment. One of the

Warriors released a blast of magic at her, but just as with the Commander's, her shield easily absorbed it. "I said stop!"

"You've killed our Commander," one of them protested.

"Not yet," she shook her head. "But he'll die soon if you don't stop."

All three looked ready to die fighting her, and she could hear several more clomping boot steps throughout the Guild house, the entire place coming alive with Warriors.

"He was a criminal," she pressed, not daring to step closer to them, for fear of enticing an attack. She didn't want to kill more, not if there was a risk that the proof she needed could be lost. "And I don't know if any of you were part of it or not, but I don't care. Right now, you have one chance to save your own lives!"

She heard other Warriors in the hallway, and one looked in through the fresh hole in the wall.

"Screw you," one of the Warriors replied, her voice filled with venom. Her hand shook, and Kailar decided that if any of them were to attack, it would be her. For a moment, Kailar even wondered if the woman was romantically involved with her Commander. "We should kill her now!"

"You can't," Egil cautioned, raising his shackled hands in a clatter. "Trust me, we tried, again and again."

Eyeing him skeptically, the woman replied, "We're a bit tougher than *your* common rabble."

Letan, his legs still shaky, added his support, "She has a power unlike anything you've ever seen before. Some of you have seen her in action," he nodded to the one who looked through the hole in the wall. "You won't stand a chance, I promise you. But if you sheath your swords now, you'll live. We can sort out who was involved with the underground later, or you can leave before then. Or even confess and help us end this now, before anyone else gets hurt. Frankly, I don't care. We came here for one reason, and if we get what we came for, we'll leave peacefully."

"But then you'll be back," the first man spoke up. "To arrest us."

Letan and Kailar exchanged glances. "Like I said," Letan replied, "you'll have time to decide what to do next. Run, make a deal, or spend the rest of your days in a dungeon. I'd say you'll have several days to make that decision."

It wasn't exactly ideal. Kailar didn't want to let anyone go when they could cause significant trouble later. However, Letan had a point, and she marveled at the fact that he was being pragmatic despite the situation. They'd come for one thing, and one thing only. To that end, she looked at Egil and said, "Look through the papers on his desk, see if there's anything we can use."

Egil glanced wearily at the other Warriors, and then nodded. He moved towards the papers, but then paused and looked at his hands. When he looked at Letan, the Warrior nodded, and withdrew the keys, handing them to Egil to extract himself. He set to work freeing himself, making quite a ruckus of it, but he was quick, and obviously knew how to get out of shackles fast.

"And what, exactly, are you looking for," the woman asked.

At first, Kailar wasn't going to tell them anything, fearing that the woman could get word ahead to Tieran, but then Kailar immediately dismissed that idea. No one could get back to Tieran faster than Kailar. And for all she knew, the woman might help. Kailar glanced at the Commander, saw that he was barely holding onto life, and decided it was worth a shot.

"Proof of Mayor Evern's involvement in the underground," she looked at the woman squarely. "Undeniable proof. Something with his seal on it."

The woman's face paled, and she allowed her sword to lower. "You're…you're kidding."

Her response piqued Kailar's interest, and she likewise lowered her weapon. "You know of something?"

"You're mad," the first man growled. "You're going after the most powerful man on Devor."

Kailar chuckled. "Maybe. But I'm the most powerful woman on Devor. I can handle it." Letan cleared his throat. Nodding towards him, she amended, "Especially with his help."

Looking again at the woman, Kailar added, "Your commander is still alive, and I might be able to heal him with magic. How important is Lenned to you?"

Lowering her gaze, she shook her head. "It's not that." Then, quite surprisingly, she looked up at Kailar with a cruel smile. "I'll tell you what. If I give you the proof you seek, will you let him die?"

In that instant, Kailar realized that she had read the woman completely wrong. Indeed, for the first time since the Warriors had entered the room, she noticed that the woman had a lieutenant's rank insignia.

She was the Commander's second in command, Kailar guessed. And she had ambitions to become more. Much more, if she was willing to give up Evern.

With a casual shrug, Kailar said, "That's easy enough." She could always hunt the Lieutenant down later, if there came a need to. Which, Kailar wagered, there would be.

Pointing her sword to one of the chests that Kailar had eyed earlier, the woman said, "That one." Then, she produced a ring of keys from her left pouch, and threw them towards the chest. "In fact, take them, I don't need anything in there, not after you're finished."

Glancing at Letan, she then looked at Egil, who stared at her open-mouthed. Kailar nodded, and Egil abandoned the bench to work on opening the chest.

Looking back at the woman, she asked, "What will we find in there?"

A wicked smile crossed her face. "Everything."

Chapter 14

EXILED

The emptiness of Dalin's quarters in the rebuilt Wizards' Guild complex echoed the emptiness he felt inside. His new home on Halarite should have filled him with joy, since he felt that the Wizards belonged on Halarite, and he should have been pleased that they had rejoined humanity.

Except that nothing was further from the truth. The Wizards hadn't rejoined society, they'd merely relocated to their home world. Isolated in the far north of Tal, where the cold had not yet fully given way to the warmth of spring, with no roads leading to or from it, they practically were no closer to civilization than before.

No, he thought to himself. *That was not the intent of coming back here.*

Valkere's intent was to bring the Guild back into the fold. To make the Grand Wizard Hall the hub of travel to and from Halarite, and the seat of the Allied Council.

Now, with their private universe compromised and their Grand Master dead, Dalin feared that the remaining leadership would return to their isolationist ways. Especially if Master Syrn was elected Grand Master. That decision was yet before the Council of Masters.

In fact, he suspected that there were minutes left before the Council of Masters would lock themselves away, for who knew how long, until a new Grand Master could be chosen. It was a process he had only ever heard of, performed usually only once every two or three thousand years, and usually involved the very eldest presenting their cases to the others, before deliberation commenced.

Somehow, he just knew it would be Syrn. On the one hand, she was the closest to an expert on the Star Dragons and the Sword of Dragons that the Council had, aside from Dalin. On the other hand, she was not an advocate of Valkere's most recent decisions. In fact, he suspected she was the most vocal opponent to Dalin being given special dispensation in the first place.

Dalin thought of his final conversation with Master Valkere, how he had insisted that Dalin accompany Cardin. That somehow, whether sooner or later, the Keeper of the Sword would rely upon Dalin. Maybe not for his magical prowess, but for his confidence in Cardin, and his unique view of the world.

The Masters, at Syrn's behest, had countermanded that final order. If Valkere was right, this act could potentially spell doom for all.

Dalin looked around his quarters, somewhat larger than his old place. Those old quarters were now destroyed, he realized, his private corner for over two hundred years disintegrated into the void. Would he miss it? Or would the larger quarters, with built-in book shelves and windows looking out onto a grassy courtyard, grow on him?

Could he do it? Could he follow the Masters' orders this time, stay away from Cardin, and watch from a distance? Study in the new library, try to recreate some of the lost texts, build a new staff with his new focusing stone?

Fumbling in a pocket in his robes, Dalin produced the sylaric stone and held it in his palm, letting the ambient light from outside dance throughout its inner azure facets. There had been little time for him to study it since Nuuldan's attack, but now that he examined it closely, he was fascinated as the inner surfaces seemed to move about of their own accord. It had turned a dark blue to match his own soul, or that was the legend of the sylaric stones – if a Wizard could connect to them, they in turn formed a permanent bond with the Wizard, and reflected the Wizard's spirit.

Blue was Dalin's color, deep dark blues like those of the ancient oceans or the clear skies high in the mountains. Blue had always called to him, something he learned very early in life when he was given the same test that all Wizards were given.

It was his first memory, from when he could barely walk. A great big circular room, surrounded with banners of every color. Infants were placed in the center, and whichever color they wandered to would determine their path for the rest of their lives.

There was some debate as to the actual meaning of the colors, and because of the uncertainty that existed even after ten thousand years, the standing rule was that no Wizard would train under a master whose color matched their own, in order to expose them to the various magics of the Universe.

Yet there was still so much that Dalin was not even allowed to learn. *That* frustrated him more than anything. There were secrets that the Council of Masters kept from all others – what the colors truly meant. There were theories, of course. Wizards couldn't help but notice that seers, for instance, were only ever light colored Wizards, silvers and whites and such. All Wizards could cast elemental magic, but the most gifted elementalists always seemed to be blues, reds, browns and greens.

However, Dalin had long suspected something else behind those tendencies. Did Wizards drawn to those colors have a natural gift with those types of magic? Or were they simply more talented because the Masters focused their training, despite the claim that they wished to expose them to a broader range?

He hated the Guild, now more than ever. All of his life, he'd seen through the artificial structures, the unnecessary restrictions, the hidden meanings, the mysteries, the controls…

Gripping the stone as tight as he could, the decision came to him at once, and he knew that there no longer was another way.

Dalin stood up and finished packing his travel pack, the one he had started packing before Valkere had summoned him back to the former Guild Hall. There wasn't much left to pack, and the last thing he put inside was the sylaric stone.

Then he looked at the gnarled piece of oak wood he had laid on the table next to the pack. It was a branch from a tree in the atrium in the former Guild Hall, one that had naturally fallen to the ground. Oak had always been his favorite wood, and he knew that his new staff would have been shaped out of it.

Would have been.

He left it on the table and headed for the exit, stopping just inside to look around at his new quarters one last time. Drawing in a breath for courage, he stepped outside.

Taking advantage of being on a planet's surface, the Wizards had decided to build the housing separately from the Grand Hall, with courtyards and fountains everywhere, and while the doors to all quarters in the old complex had been within a great hall, all Wizards' quarters on Halarite went straight outside.

He smiled, realizing just how much everyone had longed for a real world to call their home, even if they hadn't admitted it.

To the west was the Grand Hall itself, where he knew that the Council of Masters gathered even now. As he hustled along through the courtyards, he looked around at the other Wizards moving about, but there were few. Most were engaged in using their combined powers to continue construction in other parts of the complex, molding and forming and modifying stone, marble, steel and other elements to their will with careful and concerted effort.

Unfortunately, despite Syrn's speech to the King less than an hour ago, little effort would be focused on defenses, as the enchantments needed would require the most powerful Masters to work together, and their efforts would be spent elsewhere for the time being.

The Grand Hall itself was one of the first structures completed, in fact the *only* structure completed at the moment. At its core, it was still just a grand, long rectangular building, like their former hall had been, big enough to admit a dragon. However, the satellite buildings that the side doors would open up to were different, complementing the Grand Hall with their size and shapes, with spires rising high above the circular structures, showing that Wizards were still, at their core, vain.

However unlike the former complex, there were several entrances into the various outbuildings, and thus quicker access into the central corridor, and the Council Chambers.

When he finally made it through the side corridors to the Grand Hall itself, he found that he was almost too late. The Masters were all funneling through the wide open doors into the Council Chambers. Much to his relief, Syrn had not yet gone in. Instead, she stood outside the doors welcoming everyone, attempting to impress the others with geniality.

Dalin wasted little time making his way over to her. Two other Masters were at her side, conversing with her in between her

"Welcome!" statements.

That is, until they saw Dalin coming. Without even exchanging glances with each other, they stepped up into a line, as if to prevent Dalin from entering the new chambers. One of them was Master Eira, the same forest-green Wizard that was with Syrn and Valkere in the library before Nuuldan's attack. The other was Master Phaern, a violet-robed Wizard like Syrn.

"Dalin," Syrn eyed him dubiously. "What brings you to the Council of Masters?"

Stepping close to her, and feeling somewhat proud of having interrupted Syrn's campaign efforts, he bowed and courteously began with, "Masters. I have come to ask you to reconsider the decision to forbid me from accompanying the Keeper of the Sword and the Star Dragon."

Syrn closed her eyes tightly, frustration enhancing her crow's feet. "Dalin, we have all agreed that we need every Wizard here to defend, incase Nuuldan decides to attack us again."

Dalin almost didn't take it any further. He felt his heart leap into his throat and a strange tingling sensation coursed throughout his body while his heart raced faster and faster. He almost backed off.

But then he thought of the courage Cardin had shown, over and over again throughout the past year. He knew then that he couldn't let his friend down.

Standing tall and defiantly, he countered, "You know as well as I do that there is no defense we could hope to conjure to defend against a Dark Dragon."

"I beg your pardon," Master Eira gripped his staff tightly.

"Nuuldan found our Universe within months of his return," Dalin continued undaunted. "You know it as well as I do that we cannot hope to defend against him by ourselves. Your decision has nothing to do with our defenses."

"That is enough," Syrn hissed, stepping closer threateningly. "It is not your place to question our decision!"

"Nor is it your place to counter the Grand Master's final wishes," Dalin raised his voice, loud enough that two passing Wizards stopped to listen.

"We have only your word about his final request, Dalin," Phaern frowned at him. "I am sorry, but we must make a decision based on what is best for the Guild."

Dalin was about to respond, but Syrn stamped her staff on the ground. "Do not argue further! Our decision is final. Your propensity for disobedience may have been tolerated by Valkere, but you will find the rest of us less patient."

Raising his eyebrows, Dalin remarked, "Interesting, since one of the core lessons for all Wizards is to be patient, like the Masters."

Syrn's staff creaked under her surprisingly strong grip, her hand clenched around it in frustration. "Do not think that just because you are no longer an apprentice that you cannot be remanded to a lower status, or placed in detention until we decide what to do with you." She pointed over his shoulder, and said, "Walk away now, while I still allow it."

Screwing up his courage one more time, Dalin balled his hands into fists, and nodded. "I intend to do just that, Master. I intend to walk away from the Guild. And to never return."

Whatever frustration or anger she and the others might have felt, that statement changed their attitudes all at once. Eira and Phaern exchanged stunned glances, while Syrn gawked at him, aghast.

It was at that moment that Dalin realized the crowd that had gathered around their argument. The Masters within the Council Chambers, and several other Wizards that were waiting anxiously within the Grand Hall for the election, all crowded around them. Everyone was deathly silent, and all eyes were on Dalin.

Feeling his face grow warm, he wished for his staff back, to have something to grip anxiously. He found himself instead gripping the hem of his robes, hoping his nervousness wasn't completely obvious.

"You...you cannot," Master Eira exclaimed. "You must not! Wizards cannot just resign from the Guild, Dalin."

"It is not without precedent," he reminded Eira. "Three thousand years ago, we allowed Wizards to leave at their own behest."

"Those Wizards were exiled," Syrn corrected, a quiet edge in her voice that he had never heard before. "The same would happen to you."

"You would never be allowed back," Eira added. "You would never be allowed access to any resources here. And should you ever call for aid from us, your call would go unanswered."

That last bit surprised him. Would that be true even if his call for aid was for Cardin, or the four kingdoms? Or did they just mean if he personally needed help?

Deciding that now was not the time to ask such questions, he simply nodded curtly. "I understand."

"Dalin, think about this," Phaern cautioned. "You have been given chances that no other Wizard has been given. Opportunities at such a young age. You will be throwing it all away."

"All to help a human," Syrn looked at him scornfully.

And that sealed it for Dalin. Syrn still believed that Wizards were better than humans, a separate and superior species.

"Thank you," he bowed specifically to Phaern, the only one of the three that had shown him any respect. "However, I have made my decision."

Narrowing her eyes, Syrn grasped her staff with her other hand in a huff. "Very well. Normally we would take your staff away from you, but since you have already lost it, there is nothing else for us to do. You may leave, Dalin. And you will never again return."

Turning her back on him in a huff, she pushed her way into the Council Chambers, leaving a stunned collective to stare at Dalin. Her final statement had been a jab to humiliate him, and to make him regret leaving.

Master Eira stared at him a moment longer before he, too, turned his back, but Master Phaern merely stared at him forlornly.

Drawing in a deep breath, Dalin turned away from the Council Chambers, towards the main doors that led out to where the portal courtyard was to be constructed. A crowd of Wizards stood between him and the exit, but they very quickly parted, opening a path for him to walk down.

After taking in another deep breath, he began his long walk, slow and deliberate, with pride in his steps. Whatever the others thought, he had to make them understand. He had to be confident in his decision. Perhaps, if he was lucky, his example would turn the tide of opinion within the Guild.

The Grand Hall was bigger than even the former Grand Hall, and just as tall, designed to receive dragons as well as large delegations, so it took him a lot longer than he would have liked to leave. The others watched silently from the sides, their faces a collage of expressions, ranging from disgust and reproval to admiration and respect.

And then one Wizard stepped in front of him. A Wizard barely older than him, wearing emerald robes and clinging to a redwood staff.

"Teira," he whispered, realizing that he had not given her a second thought when he had decided to leave the Guild. They had only spoken a few times since the Battle for Maradin, when he had learned that she had confronted the Grand Master and convinced him to bring the Wizards back to Halarite. Their old flame had not rekindled, but their friendship had sparked again.

Now he would probably never see her again.

Was she angry? Disappointed? Devastated? It seemed to him as if her face were a blank slate, but perhaps that was only because of the emptiness and fear he hid inside of himself.

She opened her mouth to say something, but then stopped and closed her mouth. Without another word, she stepped up beside him, faced the exit, and nodded.

At first he feared that she meant to leave with him, that she meant to resign as well. But no, that would not be like her. Unlike Dalin, she respected the bureaucracy of the Wizards' Guild, the Masters, and the ranks.

In this instance, he realized that she merely meant to escort him out. Not that the others would do anything to hinder him. It was, he suspected, merely the only way she could show her respect for his actions without breaking any rules.

Feeling his heart flutter and his courage return, he trudged along the last section of the Grand Wizard Hall, Teira by his side.

The crowd was thinner at the far end, with only a couple of Wizards on either side of the exit. Once they were outside, Teira stepped ahead of him and turned to stop their march.

Dalin waited for her to say or do something more, though he wasn't sure if he was hopeful or afraid of what would come next. He searched her eyes, trying desperately to figure out her emotions.

And that was when he realized what it was he saw, hidden deep behind the stoic blue-green of her eyes. Heartbreak. Not the kind that comes from a lover betrayed, but a friend who realized they were saying goodbye for the last time.

She observed his robes and his hands, and then smiled. Turning on the spot, she stamped her staff into the ground, and her emerald focusing gem flashed brightly. Magic stirred, and a moment later, a blue-white portal formed ahead of her.

Turning back to him, she nodded. "It is the least I can do."

Feeling that the portal would take him back to the western gates of Archanon, he returned her smile. "Thank you, my friend," he nodded. "I…I am sorry."

She nodded, her smile growing. "No, you are not. However, I am not surprised."

He looked at her, startled, but then realized what she meant. "I suppose I am at least consistent."

"Frustratingly so," she nodded. "Now go. Before the Keeper leaves without you."

Drawing in yet another great breath, he looked at her one more time, and then passed by.

Just as he walked through the portal, he heard her call out, "I shall miss you."

Dalin stopped on the other side, the portal having brought him into the valley face to face with the western gates of Archanon, and turned, wanting to tell her that he would miss her too. But it was too late.

After staring into the bright portal for a second, it closed, giving him a full view of Endri's emerald head, lowered enough to stare into Dalin's soul with those intense, star-like eyes.

Endri's lips curled back and up in an imitation of a human smile. *"I take it, then, that you shall be joining us after all."*

Nodding solemnly, Dalin smiled despite the void in his stomach. "So it would seem. For as long as I am needed."

Chapter 15

THE CELESTIAL SPIRES

Pulling on his leather backpack, Cardin looked around his small guest quarters in Archanon Castle, realizing that it might as well be considered his own room. While he had spent several days lately in Daruun, training with Endri and finally having a chance to fix up his and his father's house, the truth was that he had spent more time in Archanon in the past year than in Daruun. Every time he came back, this same room was ready for him.

Looking then to Sira, who also slung her pack over her shoulder, he smiled, and thought to himself, *Not just for me. For us.*

When Sira caught him staring, she smiled warmly and took his hand in hers. "Ready for another adventure together?"

Excitement stirred in his chest, and he squeezed her hand. "Always."

Only this time wouldn't be just another mission, or just another quest. This time, they would leave Halarite to step foot on another world entirely.

Their backpacks had already been packed for the trip into the ruined dwarven city, so most of their preparations had been to switch into light leather armor, light enough that they could travel easily and comfortably, but strong enough to provide some protection against whatever they might encounter.

For Cardin, it was almost a useless gesture. His powers were more than adequate to protect him against almost any attack, and if they came up against Nuuldan, leather would prove useless. Sira, however, had insisted he wear it anyway.

She looked magnificent in her armor and grey-white travel cloak. Then again, he always thought she looked magnificent. He had almost gone back home to grab his own travel cloak, but then realized that he had never replaced it or repaired it from his days of wandering Daruun Forest. So, earlier in the day, before they had learned of the attack on the Wizards, he had gone out into the Market District to find a new one, a simple green cloak that, in the wilderness of Tal anyway, would perhaps help him blend in.

Suddenly he realized he had no idea what kind of world they would be visiting, so it was possible his cloak would actually make him stick out like a sore thumb. That was fine, though, as long as that drew attention away from Sira.

Squeezing her hand again, he nodded for the door, and she preceded him out into the corridor. At first, their journey out of the castle and towards the western gate was slow and leisurely, but they kept exchanging excited glances, and their pace quickened. He could see in her eyes that she was as excited to explore a new world as he was.

Before long, they had rushed down into the Market District, and flew by countless vendors and patrons. As they rushed along, however, Cardin grew aware of the looks the citizens of Archanon gave him, and it stymied his enthusiasm.

The disdain in their eyes as they glowered at Cardin was oppressive, and he suddenly felt closed in. And he realized that it was him specifically, not Sira, that they glowered at. Some wore necklaces bearing pendants of the Six, a circle containing the six expanding lines, and they clutched them tightly as he passed.

His excitement waned considerably, and he wondered now if he was leaving Halarite at the worst possible time.

If he and Sira hadn't stumbled onto the mob attacking Elaria and the others, what would have happened? Would things have gotten worse? For that matter, they still hadn't received a report on the outcome. He hoped the Warriors were able to dispel the mob without violence after he rescued the others, but he feared that wasn't possible.

Unfortunately, that thought also made him feel sick. All it would take was one misstep, and the citizens would have exploded, or the Warriors would have drawn blood. It might not take much more than that to start an outright rebellion.

Looking at Sira, feeling a sick, dark sensation within, he asked, "Do you think... Is Tal on the verge of civil war?"

She had likewise observed the looks on the vendors' faces, and when she looked at him, he saw anxiety etching nervous lines in her face. "Civil war? I..." She hesitated, looking down. "I don't know." She glanced at one particular shopkeeper, obvious hatred in his eyes as they passed him by. "I hope not. Maybe the people just need time. Time to adjust, time to get used to the way the world works now."

Cardin looked down, uncertainty working around in his thoughts. "That might be the case." Nodding, he added, "Perhaps this is a good time for me to be leaving Halarite. If I'm not here, that's one less thing they can focus their ire on."

They continued on silently after that. When they reached the gates, his spirits suddenly lifted. On the other side, a few hundred feet away, his vision was filled by Endri's massive form, and a single man sporting dark-blue robes.

"Dalin," he exclaimed, rushing to his friend. Cardin wanted to hug the Wizard, despite how formal their relationship had always been, but the strained smile on Dalin's face made him stop. "Is everything okay?"

Glancing up at Endri, Dalin hesitated, and then said, "If you would still welcome my presence, I would like to come along."

Cardin frowned and glanced at Sira, who looked as puzzled as him, and asked, "Master Syrn changed her mind?"

Drawing in a deep breath, Dalin shook his head. "Not exactly. In either case, it is my intent to fulfill my oath to you, Cardin Kataar. I shall remain at your side for as long as you require my services."

A mix of emotions welled up in Cardin, and he felt his throat catch. Now, despite everything, he stepped forward and wrapped his arms around Dalin, as awkward as it was with each other's backpacks. "You are most welcome, my friend," he said. "I'm glad to have you with us again."

Dalin hesitated, but then his tense shoulders slouched, and he returned Cardin's hug.

After a moment, Cardin pulled away and clasped his friend on the shoulder, before he let his hands drop to his side, and he looked up into the light of Endri's eyes. "Well, I think we're as ready as we'll ever be."

The green dragon had watched the reunion with respectful curiosity, but he very quickly turned to business. *The world we will be traveling to has long been a place for my people to gather and discuss important matters. I will need to send you ahead of me, as the location you shall arrive at will be too small for me.*

Looking to one another in puzzlement, Cardin voiced everyone's question. "Too small? Wait, where are we going?"

Endri tilted his head to one side, pausing for just a moment, and then he replied, *It is much easier to show than to explain.*

There was a powerful stir of magic behind them, and Cardin, Sira and Dalin turned back towards the city. A dozen feet away, he felt magic gather into a distinct point, much like a portal, but it felt different, stronger, more focused. The typical flash winked before them, and a moment later, an oval wall of light appeared, wide enough that all three of them could walk through at the same time.

It was a portal not just to another place, but to another world, further than Cardin had ever travelled, not counting the former Grand Wizard Hall.

He focused on that oval of light, fascinated by the fact that there were no tendrils of lightning lancing out like a Wizard's portal. Was it because it was a portal to another world? Or was the focused intensity of it a result of Endri's greater control and understanding of magic? It was a question he would have to ask when the opportunity arose.

Behind them, Endri leapt into the air and spread his wings, momentarily casting them in shadow, as he ascended into the skies above Archanon, apparently needing to be airborne to follow them.

Dalin and Sira stepped to either side of Cardin, and they looked to one another in excited anticipation. Then, together, the trio walked through the portal.

The sensation was a little different from all of the portals Cardin had traveled through previously, in so much as there was a hair-raising feeling that he only ever experienced when a lightning bolt struck nearby, and he swore that there was a split second delay between entering on one side and emerging on the other, but it was so brief that he couldn't be sure.

What he was sure of, however, was that they had stepped through onto another world. The moment they were through, his eyes grew wide to drink it all in.

They were surrounded by pillars of rock, each pillar layered with colors of earthy reds, yellows, browns, and grays, all of them higher than the ground that he, Sira and Dalin stood upon. In fact, as his eyes wandered around, he realized that the pillars were arranged in rings around where they stood, and that the inner-most ring was only a dozen feet higher, and the next ring out was a dozen taller than the first, not to mention more numerous. All in all, he could see at least six rings of spires, and each spire was flattened on top, with what he quickly deduced were claw marks dug into them.

In fact, he suddenly realized that each pillar was big enough on top that a dragon could land on them. He hadn't realized that he had started to wander from where the portal had closed only moments ago, but then Sira's hands jolted out and grabbed him, saving him from walking right off of the pillar that they now stood atop.

Gulping his heart back down, he looked at her wide-eyed. "Thanks…"

Then, holding on to one another, they both peaked over the edge to discover that they were hundreds of feet above a shadowed, sandy bottom. Somewhere nearby, they could hear crashing water, but the source was not visible through the interspersed columns of rock.

Cardin felt the spark of another portal open, and they looked up, expecting to find Endri following them from above, only to realize that the sky was nothing like home's.

The heavens were alight with cascades of pinks, purples, and blues clearly visible even in full daylight, and at the center of that cascade of cloudy, impossibly distant colors was a single star, like Halarite's sun. Just to the right of that star was Endri's blue-white portal, far above the highest pillar, and the emerald dragon zoomed out, his wings wide. There was a sudden updraft, filling Endri's wings, and filling Cardin's nose with the smell of sagebrush and salt water. It wasn't a river nearby, he postulated, but an ocean shoreline.

Watching Endri's flight, their eyes fell upon their next surprise – there was another world in the sky! Not just a small moon, but a crimson and blue world that filled half of the sky, even though it was only a crescent, and it was encircled by a sparkling pearlescent ring. The world didn't seem to have a rocky surface, but instead looked like it was made of clouds, the reds and blues swirling around each other in complex patterns that never quite intermixed.

Endri circled them once, his flight coming lower and lower, slower and slower, until he had to angle his body up and begin pumping his wings in great swings, blowing dust and sand off of his chosen landing pillar in the inner circle, directly beneath that massive, ringed world. With an unexpected grace and beauty, he gently landed, and then dug his claws into the edges before he folded his wings.

"Welcome," he said, a hint of pride in his voice, *"to the Celestial Spires."*

Cardin's heart welled up in his chest, and he realized that his mouth hung open. Endri, with a near-perfect imitation of a human smile on his snout, drew in a deep breath, and then let loose a deafening roar to the sky above. More than that, Cardin heard the roar in his mind, just like when Endri spoke.

Only this wasn't just an animalistic roar. In his mind, he somehow understood that it was a call.

Come forth.

When the roar ended, there was an eerie silence, with nothing but the wind and the distant ocean echoing, somehow quieter, as if they, too, were in awe.

The first portal opened above them after a prolonged pause. Followed by another. And another. A golden dragon zoomed through the first, a violet dragon through the next, followed by a massive red, and then another green, a slight shade lighter than Endri.

In moments, the sky above them was filled with circling dragons of all sizes, some smaller than Endri, many larger, with the largest being one of two red dragons in the mix. There were so many colors, and their circling motion made it almost impossible for Cardin to count.

They all remained high above at first, until one by one, starting with the largest red dragon, they descended, each finding a perch to rest upon, beginning with the inner circle, and then once that was full, filling out into the next.

As they did so, Cardin kept track – Seven inner pillars, twelve in the next, and though there were more pillars in the third track, only seven more dragons were left to fill in.

The larger red dragon had landed next to Endri. At first, that dragon regarded Cardin and the others curiously, the ardent red stars of his eyes penetrating their souls. After the last Star Dragon settled onto its perch, the red turned to Endri, and spoke through its thoughts for all to hear, *"Greetings, Endri. I assume that you have called us here for a matter of importance."*

With a solemn nod, Endri replied, *"Unfortunately, yes. Nuuldan has attacked the Grand Wizard Hall."*

A wave of shock rippled amongst the dragons, their wings fluttering and their necks bending so that they could exchange startled glances with one another. In that moment, the great red dragon's starlight eyes fell upon Dalin.

Endri took this as a cue. *"May I introduce Dalin, Sira Reinar, and Cardin Kataar, Keeper of the Sword of Dragons."* Endri then turned his gaze back to the red, and added, *"This is Firdal, the oldest and most powerful among us."*

Without having to be told, Cardin bowed low, as did the others. Then he realized he wasn't sure if he should be the one to speak, or if he should let Sira do so, since she had always acted as the leader of their group from the beginning.

He glanced at her, and she at him. Was she as uncertain as he was?

Knowing that someone had to say something quickly, he gave her a slight nod.

"We are honored to be granted an audience with you," she called out as they all straightened up. "This is…" She looked around at the spires and at the sky, "A wonderful experience for us all!"

Firdal nodded his head, *"We are pleased to meet you as well. I am particularly glad to finally meet you, Keeper of the Sword."* The red dragon's eyes turned to Dalin again, and he said, *"I sense that you are a Wizard. Were you present when Nuuldan attacked?"*

Dalin hesitated a moment, but then nodded. "I was, sir."

"Did your people suffer many casualties?"

Drawing in a breath, Dalin looked down, his eyes growing distant. "We were still assessing how many were missing before I left," he spoke at length. "However, I am afraid that our Grand Master, Valkere, sacrificed himself to allow us all to escape."

The spark in Firdal's eyes dimmed for a moment, and his head drooped low. *"I am so sorry to hear that."* Glancing to some of the other dragons, he added, *"I was one of the few to have met him, before he was Grand Master."*

Cardin felt surprised, knowing that the Star Dragons hadn't visited Halarite in three thousand years. To remember someone you met so long ago, he could only imagine the impression Valkere had made upon the dragons.

After a few moments of silence, Dalin looked up again and stepped forward. "We came seeking your guidance. When Nuuldan attacked, it was not a random action. He believed that we had in our possession an item known as the Shadow Quartz."

Even if Cardin hadn't seen Firdal's startled reaction, he easily felt the sudden stir of magic surrounding the elder Star Dragon. Curiously, none of the others appeared to recognize the term, but Cardin felt some relief that at least one of them knew it.

"The Shadow Quartz," Firdal's voice spoke in dead shock. *"You are certain that this was what he said?"*

Dalin nodded confidently. "I am."

Firdal gathered himself up, drawing his head high, and he replied, *"And he believed the Wizards possessed it? Considering I myself do not know where the Shadow Quartz is, it is curious that he would believe we would have given it to the Wizards."*

Cardin slumped, feeling the spark of hope already fading. Then another thought occurred to him, and he asked, "Where would he have learned about this? Who told him where to look, and for that matter," he frowned at Dalin, "How did he figure out how to get to the Grand Hall?"

"An excellent question," Dalin conceded. "There are few outside of the Guild who have ever been there. *Very* few."

"Right," Cardin nodded. "Anyone before King Beredis and I?"

After a moment of thinking about it, Dalin shook his head, "I do not know. I only know that in my two hundred and eighty eight years, you were the first outside visitor."

Sira pointed out, "But it was built almost three thousand years ago, right?"

"Indeed," Firdal replied for Dalin. *"I was present when the Wizards began their migration to it. Myself and two others."* He looked pointedly at Cardin. *"Including the former Keeper of the Sword."*

Cardin's face lit up for just a moment, the image of the violet dragon in the mountain caves passing through his thoughts. "You knew Avall?"

"We all did," Firdal looked around at the other gathered dragons. *"She volunteered to stay behind and guard the Sword of Dragons as the final part of the quest. As far as I know, however, that was the only thing we left behind. The Shadow Quartz has been lost since we recovered it."*

With his brow furrowed, Cardin asked, "What is it, exactly?" Somewhere in the back of his mind, he realized that should have been one of their first questions.

The red dragon looked to some of his peers, and then settled his gaze upon Endri. When the green dragon nodded, Firdal's mental voice sighed. *"It was Nuuldan's final tool against us. How much have you been taught about the Dark Dragons and their origin?"*

Shrugging, Cardin replied, "Not much, to be honest. It began with Nuuldan, and he turned others to darkness, eventually bringing an overwhelming number to his side."

After another moment of hesitation, Firdal began, *"Nuuldan was once a Star Dragon, a white dragon whose name has long since been lost. Thousands of years ago, he came across an ancient ruin on a world that we had never visited before. There stood a monument within the ruins that spoke of the two magics of the Universe; power from stars, which we are all familiar with, and that from darkness, from nothingness, from the void in between matter. Before then, we believed our power to be the only magic."* Firdal hung his head low again. *"We were wrong. There were enough details about Dark Magic within the ruins that Nuuldan learned how to tap into it."*

Cardin saw as much as felt the shudder that coursed through the great red dragon's body. *"We are beings of pure light, and the darkness infected his body like an illness, cutting him off from the light, turning his scales black and dousing the lights in his eyes. Little knowledge has survived from so long ago, but we all know what came next. Several of our kin felt his presence disappear and sought him out, and what they found was emptiness and madness. He was brought before the First Ones, the original Star Dragons."*

While Cardin ached to ask questions, he remained silent, absorbing the information with awe, wonder, and absolute terror.

Continuing, Firdal's mental tone dropped to a morbid one. *"They tried to use their powers to dig into his soul and infuse it with light again, but it caused him such great pain that he lashed out, destroying one of the First Ones. He fled, but that was how it began. The Civil War.*

"Nuuldan believed that darkness was our future, and converted as many other Star Dragons as he could. He conquered several worlds during the war, and enslaved their peoples so that he could force them to further excavate the ruins. Within a thousand years, they finally found the heart of the lost empire – the Shadow Quartz."

A shiver worked its way down Cardin's spine, and he felt himself grow cold. He thought of his own connection to dark magic, and how he'd felt so conflicted since his battle against Nuuldan. Frustration, anger, impatience…was it going to cut off his connection to the stars as well? Would he eventually become an agent of darkness, like Nuuldan?

What if he hurt others? What if he lashed out and hurt Sira, or Dalin, or Endri? Or worse?

"Nuuldan learned that with the Shadow Quartz, he could force the conversion to darkness onto others, and we fell to his influence by the thousands." Cardin wasn't sure when, but at some point, Firdal had focused his attention on him. His red eyes burned into Cardin's soul, and he felt the dragon's tentative probe, as if to make sure he was still connected to star magic. *"We knew there was only one chance, and we invaded his world. Only to find that we were too late. He had devised a plan in which he would turn a star to darkness using the Shadow Quartz. We do not know precisely why he did this, other than as a first step towards turning our entire Universe to darkness. Our battle raged across his world, but we knew we had to save the star, so we sent our eldest, including the last few First Ones still alive, to stop him."*

Drawing himself up again, Firdal sighed audibly. *"We defeated Nuuldan, at great cost, and the star he had begun to convert was destroyed."*

Cardin's mouth fell open. "Vestuul. The necromancer home world."

"Yes," Firdal replied. *"Destroyed five thousand years ago. We did not know that Nuuldan survived. It should not have been possible. Yet it would seem he is stronger than we ever realized."*

With that sobering realization, Cardin hung his head low. His stomach twisted inside out as he considered the implications of the history of the dragons. Was Cardin just another Nuuldan waiting to happen?

Suddenly warmth coursed through his body when Sira took hold of his hand and squeezed reassuringly. He looked into her eyes, and his fear of the darkness gave way to her light.

"What of the Shadow Quartz," Endri asked, looking first to Firdal, and then to the other dragons. *"What happened to it? Does anyone here know?"*

When no one else replied, Firdal said, *"The remaining First Ones were to keep it safe. By the end of the Civil War, when the Sword of Dragons was forged and the Dark Dragons defeated, only one of them yet lived."*

Endri tilted his head. *"Astaria."*

"Yes."

The two dragons seemed to nod to one another thoughtfully, but spoke no further. After several moments of impatient waiting, Cardin asked the obvious, "Where is this Astaria?"

Endri turned his verdant eyes at Cardin and replied, *"We do not know. After the war, the Star Dragons decided to scatter into the Universe. There was a time when we could communicate across the stars because there were so many of us that there was always another close enough to hear us. Now, however, our numbers are so few that in order to watch over the Universe, we must be isolated and act on our own."*

"Those who knew her," Firdal added, *"thought she went back to the first world from which the Star Dragons came from. She spoke of wishing to find the truths of our past, the reason for our existence, and believed it to be there."* Looking to a nearby golden dragon, Firdal continued, *"We sent one to contact her there, but she could not be located."*

The golden dragon, who's mental voice sounded neither male nor female, nodded their head. *"Those living on the planet were very cryptic when I asked them about her. She may have at least been there at one time, but they were very protective of her."*

Cardin and Sira looked at one another, and she suggested, "Maybe it's worth going back there to look again."

Firdal's eyes narrowed in a dragon's version of a frown. *"You believe they would tell you when they would not tell a Star Dragon?"*

Looking at the dragon, she asked, "Why not? We lose nothing by trying. We have the Keeper of the Sword with us, and the situation has grown more desperate."

Trying to suppress a grin, Cardin thought to himself, *Plus I wouldn't mind visiting another world before going back to Halarite.*

"It may be our only chance to find out where the Shadow Quartz was left," Dalin added, "and perhaps with whom Nuuldan has allied himself with."

With a thoughtful and impressed look in his eyes, Firdal nodded.

"Sound reasoning, young one."

Cardin smirked, and wondered how it felt for Dalin to be called young. Then he realized that even by Wizard standards, Dalin *was* still young.

"I will take them," Endri unfurled his wings for emphasis. *"With your permission,"* he added, looking to Firdal.

"Very well," Firdal replied. *"We will continue to seek out other Star Dragons, and try to find any trace of Nuuldan. Please let us know if you should learn anything."*

And with that, the gathering was concluded. Cardin wasn't sure if the dragons spoke to one another privately with their thoughts, or if they just knew how to leave in an orderly fashion, but one by one, they took to the skies, starting with the outer track. Portals swallowed each dragon after they reached a certain altitude, and before long, only Firdal and Endri were left atop the spires.

They looked to one another intently, and Cardin knew then that they were, indeed, conversing privately. Endri's face seemed to slacken, and his muzzle hung open, but then he clamped it shut. His eyes seemed to spark, but then he gave a curt nod.

With one last glance at Cardin, Firdal leapt into the sky and spread his wings, allowing the natural updrafts to take him aloft. In moments, he disappeared through his own great portal.

Chapter 16

INTO THE WEB

After chatting with Elaria that morning, Reis's mood was considerably improved, and he even looked forward to spending the next several days down in the darkness. For starters, it would give him and Elaria a chance to catch up, but after asking her about Gilrin, he felt an overwhelming curiosity about the dwarf and his culture.

They spoke idly near the entrance to the tunnels, the shattered rock cleared away only a week after the skies burned. While they waited, Reis tried to ask Gilrin a multitude of questions, but the dwarf wasn't very forthcoming. At one point, Elaria gently grabbed his arm and whispered to him that it might take Gilrin more time to warm up to him.

"I'm already warmed up to the lad," Gilrin objected, his hearing surprisingly good. "You forget, he saved us all when that mob tried to lynch us. But," he narrowed his eyes and pointed a finger at Reis, "I didn't come here to be interrogated by a human. So let's keep the questions to a minimum, eh?"

Reis smiled sheepishly and nodded respectfully. "Very well, sir. I'll do my best to contain my enthusiasm."

After a few more minutes of awkward silence, Lieutenant Kellis

Morvan arrived, and shortly after, their troupe assembled. Reis and Kellis were the two highest-ranking Warriors, while a contingent of eight Erien marines would follow their orders. The marines would be especially helpful, since they were trained for fighting on the open seas over vast distances and within tightly confined spaces aboard ships.

Plus as second in command of the mission, that meant that Reis could boss at least some magic casters around, and that further lightened his mood.

That put their party at thirteen, until Anila arrived.

Reis had forgotten she was coming, and in fact was their guide through the catacombs. His spirits darkened at first, but then Elaria pinched his arm and glowered at him, reminding him of their earlier conversation.

With everyone assembled, Kellis reminded the troupe not to touch anything in the catacombs, a sentiment that Anila echoed while avoiding eye contact with Reis, and then they moved out.

With Anila and Kellis in the lead, Reis was content to stay back with Elaria, while Gilrin and Baenil walked between them and the leaders. The highlight of the journey, at least at first, was when they entered the Tomb of the Ascended, and for the first time since Reis's teens, he gazed upon the stone faces of the first humans to ascend to become gods - Archos and Talus.

Then their journey through the tunnels began, a dizzying and uneventful journey, with countless twists and turns through narrow tunnels. He had no doubt that Anila knew the way by heart, but sometime between the winter's cataclysmic events and now, everlasting torches had been fixed to the walls leading the way, ensuring they were never without light.

Upon arriving at the city entrance, Kellis and Anila brought them to a jarring halt, and Reis quickly saw why. Thick, sticky webbing covered the entrance tunnel.

Anila drew her thin, curved sword and approached the dusty webbing. The marines drew their swords as well, but Reis and Kellis refrained from following suit, knowing that their longswords would be useless in the tight confines.

Which did nothing to soothe Reis's nerves. The hairs on the back of his neck rose up, and a bitter-cold shudder coursed from head to toe. He hadn't seen a kiklar yet, he'd only heard descriptions of them, but his imagination ran wild. Giant, spider-like creatures, as big or bigger than a person, great big pointy legs ready to stab his face and tear him apart limb from limb...

Elaria stepped to the lead to examine the webbing for herself, her exotic daggers drawn and humming softly with magic.

With a sour face, she said, "They've already taken advantage of the new entrance. Has anyone else been in the dwarven city?"

Anila shook her head. "No, we only setup torches to this spot. No one was allowed past it for fear of the kiklar."

Lowering her arms, Elaria nodded. "Then our encounter may be delayed. If they built the webbing but it has never been triggered, they may not be close by."

Gilrin stepped up behind them and countered, "The moment we touch that web, even to destroy it, they'll know." Another shudder passed through Reis.

On the far side of the entrance, Kellis folded his arms and frowned at the webbing. "So it's a race, then." Looking to Gilrin, he asked, "Where will we find this warding device?"

Gilrin and Baenil exchanged nervous looks. "In the center," Gilrin replied. "Most likely the capitol building."

Reis cursed under his breath, and thought he heard Kellis do the same. Keying in on the dwarf's word choice, Reis asked, "Most likely?"

Gilrin didn't reply, but Elaria pointed out, "The marines give us the advantage we need to hold them off. We can do it."

Sergeant Indira Tein, the marine leader, stepped up behind Reis, her demeanor fierce and commanding. "We're only effective at distance when standing still. I recommend we take it slow, no running."

Reis looked skeptically at her. "With hundreds of those things coming down on us? Are you kidding?"

Sergeant Tein gave Reis an icy stare, chilling every corner of his soul. "I know how to fight, Warrior, and I know how to command my marines. If we run, more of the enemy will get past us and pick you lot off. That'll quickly turn into a bloodbath. But if we take it slow, we can keep most of them off of us, and hopefully the rest of you can keep the strays off of us."

At first, he wanted to point out how crazy her plan sounded, but then he stopped himself and realized that he could no more question her tactics now than he could if they were at sea. This was why they were here, and he had to trust the marines.

"Alright," Kellis nodded, apparently thinking the same thing as Reis. "What formation would you recommend?"

"Once we're down the stairs, my marines will surround the rest of you," she began, brandishing her cutlass. "Baenil and Gilrin in the center, with the rest in between. If any of the bugs make it past our line of fire and get close, help keep them off of us, and away from the center. Any questions?"

For a moment, no one replied, but before any further orders could be given, Baenil raised up a hand. "Not a question," he said, his voice unusually meek, "just a correction. They aren't bugs. They're magical arachnids, or more properly classified as magirachnids."

Everyone else stared dumbly at the elf, while Reis hid an amused grin.

Baenil's face turned a shade of pink, and he looked down anxiously. "Well, I mean…it's a common mistake."

"Naturally," Indira replied with an annoyed frown, brushing a stray black hair out of her face. A few of her marines chuckled, and Reis glared back down the hall, trying to figure out who the offenders were.

"Alright," Kellis diverted everyone's attention. "Right now, we need to figure out how to get through this web. I assume it's strong enough to entangle even us?"

"Very much so," Elaria nodded. "But it's not too good against fire. Stand back, please."

Kellis and Anila moved further down the corridor past the webbed entrance, while Reis backed up close to Baenil and Gilrin, the latter of whom poked his head around Reis's elbow to watch. Elaria placed her back against the corridor opposite the entrance, and held her daggers in front of her, both blades pointing at the web.

The whispered hum from her daggers grew louder, and a distinct blue-white glow emanated from the blades. She closed her eyes and furrowed her brow, the effort of conjuring elemental flame clearly difficult for her, but the results spoke for themselves. A blast of blue fire streamed out of the tips of the blades and shot down the entrance tunnel, igniting the webbing like dead grass.

The blast of heat made Reis shy backwards, but he bumped into the others and had to endure, hoping he wouldn't lose his eyebrows.

The web burned so hot and so quickly that after only a couple blinks of his eyes, it was gone, reduced to ash that settled slowly, while smoke billowed up and crawled along the low ceiling, directly into Reis's face.

With eyes burning, he ducked down low and uncontrollably coughed against the stinging stench. "Sorry," Elaria called, "I didn't think of that!"

"Come on," Kellis coughed out. "Into the city!"

Elaria, bent beneath the smoke, led the way, followed closely by Anila and Kellis. Reis was about to follow, but at the last minute he remembered that there was no light inside the city, so he grabbed the nearest everlasting torch and then ran after the others.

Of course, he hadn't thought of Elaria, an experienced explorer. By the time he caught up, they had exited the corridor onto the high landing above the city, and Elaria had done something to make her blades glow white, turning everything pale and casting eerie shadows.

Kellis glanced at Reis and nodded at the torch. "Good idea."

Smoke poured out of corridor and ascended towards the high ceiling of the massive cavern, disappearing into the shadows. Baenil and Gilrin came barreling out and bumped into Reis, nearly sending him over the edge of the landing.

He remembered what the King had said of his adventure in the city, and knew that it was a long ways down. "Move along, quickly," he waved towards the stairs left of the entrance, and looked at Anila. "I'd rather take the slow way down, all things considered."

For a split second, her eyes connected with his, and when she chuckled at his joke, he felt his pulse quicken again. It could have been a moment or an eternity, but she held her gaze longer than he expected.

Turning away, she and Elaria led the group down, with Kellis and Reis right behind them. Though Elaria's daggers cast a brilliant light, it clearly wasn't bright enough for the vast emptiness of the dwarven city, and at first he couldn't even see the bottom of the stairs or the cavern floor. He anxiously watched the edge to ensure he didn't risk falling, and he wondered why the dwarves hadn't built in any sort of railing for something so perilously high.

But then he caught a glint of reflection off of tarnished metal down and to his right. He held his torch over the edge, and felt relief when he saw a dusty stone floor, and the fractured remnants of a shield.

For a moment, he was terrified that he would see a bony hand attached to the shield, or even a whole skeleton, but as they descended, he was relieved to see no skeletons anywhere around them.

Then he noticed all of the webs.

Lots of webs.

When they finally reached the bottom and spilled out onto the solid, flat, wide-open stone floor, he immediately stepped to the side and drew his bronze-dyed longsword, relieved to finally have a weapon in hand.

However, he was also now at a disadvantage. While he was certainly strong enough to wield his weapon with one hand, he was better when he could use both, and in the deep darkness of the city, he didn't want to be left without a light.

Thankfully, Indira and another marine had thought to grab the nearest torches before following them. Realizing that he was in a position of authority, Reis thrust the torch towards another marine, and ordered, "Take this."

The marine looked at Reis indignantly, but when he looked to Indira, she nodded.

With a frustrated sigh, the marine took the torch in his right hand. Reis turned away then, and let a satisfied smile cross his face. This was more like it.

Unfortunately his mood dampened when he tried to peer into the infinite black surrounding them. Even with three torches and Elaria's daggers, he couldn't see a thing beyond thirty feet or so. Skittering, scratching sounds set his arm hairs on end, and he swore the darkness pressed in on them, growing closer and closer, threatening to swallow them up whole.

It was going to be next to impossible to see incoming kiklar.

"Gilrin," he looked to the dwarf, who was side by side with Baenil. "I don't suppose your people had a means of lighting cities that might still work today?"

Indignantly, the dwarf replied, "How should I know?"

Raising an eyebrow, Reis asked, "What do you mean? I thought you knew all about your people's history."

It was Baenil who replied, "There's very little information available about the dwarves, and most of their oral history has been lost over the millennia. However..." Baenil moved away from the outer wall and staircase, with Gilrin all but latching onto his robes.

"Form up," Indira ordered. "Keep your eyes and ears sharp."

The eight marines quickly encircled them, with the Sergeant moving just ahead and to the side of Gilrin and Baenil. Reis took up position to their right, matching Baenil's excited pace, while Kellis remained on the opposite side of them, and Elaria stayed close behind.

When Baenil didn't finish his sentence, Elaria asked, "However?"

"What?" Baenil glanced at her. "Oh, sorry. The dwarves were known to be good at altering the magical properties of, well, anything. Not just enchanting, which can wear off over thousands of years, but permanently changing things. It would stand to reason that if we can enchant a torch to last thousands of years, they could do better."

When a ramshackle outbuilding covered in webs faded into their light, Baenil nodded towards it and took them closer. When they reached the building, the marines adjusted their positions to give the webbing a wide berth. Baenil stopped just short of stepping on one such web, and narrowed his eyes at the structure, which Reis guessed was a family home of some sort. Then again, dwarven architecture, which looked as if it had been carved out of solid stone, was strange to him. *How did they do that?*

"There," Baenil pointed to a spot next to a web-covered doorway. "Except, that doesn't look like a torch. It's just...a square inset into the wall?" He looked at Gilrin in puzzlement. "I don't understand."

A broad smile drew across Elaria's face. "I know what those are," she spoke in quiet excitement. She raised one of her daggers up to better see, and her eyes searched the area around the square. "I've seen them before, but only on a couple of worlds. Over there," she nodded in one direction, on the opposite side of the house. "Let's get to that pillar."

Rushing around the webbed house, the group quickly made their way over to a broad pillar that presumably reached from floor to ceiling, but disappeared into the blackness above. With every moment they spent inside, the hairs on Reis's neck rose up more, and his heart beat harder. For all he knew, they were already surrounded. In fact, he was sure they were.

Once they reached the column, Elaria had to cut some of the

webbing away. *Great,* Reis thought. *If they didn't know where we were before...*

Lowering her daggers and letting them dim, she brushed her knuckles across an inset rectangle on the pillar, and her smile grew larger. "They're called glow-panels, or that's what the Krenic called them. And if these work like theirs, they just need a magic charge..."

Stowing one dagger, she pressed her palm against the panel. It started as a glow in the shape of her hand, and grew outward, until suddenly the entire panel lit up with an orange-white light. And then a panel above it lit up as well.

Suddenly, panels all up and down and around the pillar lit up, all the way to the ceiling high above, bright enough that they could see the neighboring pillars.

They could also see the jungle-like webs meshed between the pillars. And the dozen kiklar crawling along them.

Reis felt the color drain from his face. "Oh." Every single one of the black magirachnids turned their bodies towards the pillar and Reis's group. Most of them straddled their webbing on their back six legs while their bodies curved up and allowed them free use of their front-most legs as if they were arms.

Suddenly a chatter of clicks and screeches echoed all around, raising the hairs on the back of his neck, and more kiklar entered the light. "Well, then," Reis stammered. "Umm..."

And then the first one fell upon them.

The marines were fast and accurate, and only the marine closest to the descending kiklar attacked, releasing a blast of magic from his cutlass. One kiklar's body absorbed the blast, and in a sudden convulsive pop, the monster exploded in a shower of carapace and sticky blue-green goo.

Elaria dashed away from the pillar as another kiklar came sliding down it, but before it came within ten feet of the ground, it too exploded. More of the arachnids descended, suspended by thin strands of webbing.

With Elaria clear of the pillar, the troupe reformed into Indira's formation, and the marines unleashed their fury. A flurry of blue-white blasts lanced upwards, picking off every kiklar that came towards them.

Reis clenched his jaw and held his sword ready, but he despaired at his uselessness. Kellis and Elaria added to the defense, but Reis,

Gilrin, Baenil, and Anila remained grounded, and watched.

Every single kiklar they killed was replaced by another, emerging from the shadows above like a ghost. Until they came skittering towards them across the ground as well. Despite rushing noisily towards them, the marines barely reacted in time, but they were nothing if not quick and efficient. The blasts lancing upwards suddenly lanced outwards, picking off every kiklar on the ground before they reached the inner circle. Which left mostly just Elaria and Kellis to deal with the ones from above, and Reis knew that they might be overwhelmed rapidly.

One of the kiklars' existing webs snapped from a blast of magic, sending two of them careening away from the lit-up pillar, and that gave Reis an idea. "Elaria, can you burn their webs above us?"

She paused to consider his request, but then shook her head and released another blast of arcane power. "No," she shouted above the thumps of magic and exploding arachnids. "No, if they all burn, it'll suffocate us!"

Reis cursed under his breath. She was right, the smoke had nowhere to go, and the fire would consume the air, and with only one known entrance, who knew if the air would be replenished fast enough.

But then he noticed a distinct lag in the blasts of magic, and realized that the onslaught of kiklar had slowed. Were they running out of numbers? Or were they merely regrouping?

Waiting around to find out was a bad idea, so he looked to Kellis and shouted, "Lieutenant, we need to move!"

Kellis also noticed the slower onslaught, and he nodded. "Right. Elaria, can you light up pillars as we go?"

"I'll do my best," she replied, her eyes focused upwards. She then glanced around, and then pointed in a direction just to the right of the pillar. "The capitol building should be that way!"

With the marines keeping in perfect formation around them, the company began a slow, methodical trek towards the center. The kiklar only seemed to attack once every few seconds now, and even that slowed over time. Every time they attacked, it was from a completely different direction, either from above or from the ground. If Reis was right and the arachnids were testing the marines' line, then the monsters were smarter than he realized.

Hopefully they wouldn't find a weakness.

Their group entered the shadows, having to rely once again on the three torches and Elaria's glowing daggers. That made for a few close calls, and the kiklar renewed their assault in force.

The moment they were close to the next pillar, Elaria rushed through the marine line and slapped her hand against a glow panel. This one seemed to light up more quickly, probably because she had a better idea of what she was doing.

As the light travelled up, Reis noticed three kiklar descending upon the elf. "Elaria!"

He rushed out of his position as one of the marines released an attack on the kiklar, destroying one but leaving the others untouched. Elaria rolled out of the way as they tried to pounce on her, and then Reis was there, ready to fight.

"Get out of the way," Indira shouted, but the nearest kiklar launched at him, and he deflected its jabbing arm to the side. His sword clanged off of its carapace, eliciting a screech of pain from his opponent, but his blade hadn't dismembered it like he hoped.

And then a blast from Elaria caught it in one of its legs, sending it sprawling away from him and disintegrating its leg. Another blast lanced out from a marine, now that Reis was no longer between it and their line, and it exploded into nothingness.

The last of the three kiklar was gone, destroyed by a marine or Elaria. Looking at his sword, he grumbled at it, feeling even more useless.

Then Indira grabbed his shoulder and spun him around. "What in the Six were you thinking? Get your butt back in the circle!"

His face burned in embarrassment, and he did as he was told, forgetting for a moment that he outranked her. Elaria accompanied him and gave him a sympathetic look, but then she focused upwards, catching another kiklar that tried skittering across the intricate network of webs above them.

They lit up five more pillars en route to the capitol, and Reis didn't dare break formation again the whole way. Every time they drew closer to a darkened pillar, the kiklar increased their attack rate, but every time, with only Elaria breaking formation, they staved them off.

Until the fifth pillar. That was when the kiklar stopped attacking altogether. An eerie silence fell upon the troupe, and Reis exchanged nervous glances with Elaria and Kellis. Had they simply destroyed every single arachnid? Or was something else going on?

He feared it was the latter, and tightened his grip on his sword. Reis's mind raced, trying to figure out some way to get in past their carapace since his sword was otherwise useless against them. Then again, he realized that he never relied on brute strength when he faced off against a Mage. Just like in those battles, he'd have to figure out a way to be clever.

Their carapaces were like armor, he realized, and even the best armor had weak points. Usually beneath the arms and at the necks. Wherever there was a joint. And the kiklar had a lot of joints.

Resolved not to fail so miserably at the next encounter, Reis clenched his jaw and watched Elaria carefully. She momentarily stowed one of her daggers and pressed her hand against the panel, almost instantly lighting it up.

Reis's breath caught, but nothing happened. No screeches, no clicking, no sign of kiklar anywhere.

Was it over?

Elaria rushed back into formation, drawing her second dagger again.

Still nothing happened. A creepy silence fell upon the long-dead city, with only the breathing of their troupe violating the stillness.

It was then that Reis realized how different their surroundings were now. The outermost ring of the city was composed of single-story, small homes, but now that they were closer to the center, they stood in a wide avenue between three- and four-story buildings. The architecture was very square or rectangular, but all edges were beveled in this part of the city, unlike the simpler outer structures, and some of the taller buildings had one or two towers that reached towards the high ceiling above. Many of the kiklar webs used those towers as anchor points, making for a much denser network.

Yet there wasn't a single kiklar in sight.

"I don't like this," Kellis grumbled. "Where'd they go?"

"We've killed over a hundred of them," Anila commented, forcing Reis's jaw to clench.

"One hundred thirteen," Indira clarified.

"Right," Anila eyed the Sergeant curiously. "Maybe they gave up, realizing they were better off leaving us alone?"

"Not likely," Elaria shook her head. "Even the most primitive kiklar are tenacious, and they're territorial. We're in or approaching the heart of their network, so they're going to attack again. I guarantee it."

Looking towards the city center, Reis noticed that they were about to cross under a tall archway, covered from top to bottom in webs. "Or do they think we're dumb enough to get caught in that?"

Elaria and the others glanced at the arch, and she shrugged. "Maybe, but that's easily overcome. Let's get closer and I'll burn through it."

"Can't we just go around," Anila asked.

"No," Baenil replied. "Most likely this is more than just an archway, it's a wall surrounding the inner city. And I would be willing to bet that the kiklar have each archway closed off."

With a frown, Reis looked harder at the archway. "There's no portcullis or anything, how did the dwarves defend it?"

"It's not meant for defense," Baenil replied, fear edging into his voice and bringing out a slight stutter. "I, um, I believe that it, it's meant to, uh, to separate the inner sanctum from the rest. Living within the center was a symbol of status and power."

"Ah," Reis nodded, understanding completely. He realized that the inner wall of Archanon was used for much the same reason.

"That's still a prime spot for an ambush," Indira pointed out, leading the group closer to the arch. "The web is too thick to see how deep the archway is, but they might try to trap us inside."

Reis nodded, realizing that when the King and the others trapped beneath Archanon had come this way, they must have gone around the wall. Either that or the kiklar had only recently setup the web trap. How fast could they build those things?

"But at least that means we'd only have to focus our defense in two directions," Kellis pointed out. "We should be okay."

Hopefully, Reis thought to himself. *And hopefully these things aren't very clever.*

Indira stopped their advance about thirty feet away from the archway, and Elaria broke formation again, moving just ahead and to the right of the Sergeant. Then, just as she had before, she pointed her daggers straight at the webs and lowered her head, her brow furrowing in concentration.

Blue-white flames leapt forth from her blades, instantly igniting the webs in a brilliant flash and sending a massive billow of smoke up towards the ceiling.

Then the kiklar came!

They charged through the smoke with ear-splitting screeches, surprising Reis. But not Indira, who shoved Elaria aside and attacked the lead kiklar. The assault was so sudden and startling that the marines broke formation to go to the aid of their Sergeant, who was only able to take out two kiklar before she was tackled by one.

And then the rest of the kiklar came. All at once, the magirachnids streamed in overhead and descended on webs while dozens more skittered in on the ground, many of them attacking the rear flanks. So Reis turned his attention there, and called out, "Lieutenant!"

Reacting instantly, Kellis turned his attention behind them while two of the marines also turned back to help, and a torrent of magic attacks were unleashed behind and above them. But it wasn't enough, and one of the enemy came at Reis.

With no time to think, he feinted right, then attacked left, aiming for a leg joint, and striking true! The leg separated, and a sickly green-blue liquid erupted out of the severed appendage. The kiklar screeched and swung violently at him, but with ample lighting, Reis saw the attack coming and ducked just in time. He caught sight of a joint between their thorax and abdomen, and he stabbed with all of this strength, the length of his longsword working to his advantage.

The kiklar screamed when the blade sank halfway, and then Reis pulled it out and darted back. The arachnid thrashed about on its remaining legs, tripping backwards and tangling with its closest companions. The screech caught everyone's attention, and several blasts of magic sailed past Reis and destroyed all of the distracted kiklar in rapid succession.

Something slammed into Reis's right side and sent him flailing to the ground, knocking the wind out of him and blinding him with stars in his vision. Someone shouted, "Reis!"

He blinked away the stars and looked up to find a kiklar standing over him, the fang-like mandibles around its mouth dripping with some substance he guessed was venom. How much was it going to hurt? How quickly would it kill him? He realized he'd dropped his sword and had no hope of defending himself.

This was how he was going to die. Deep underground, by the fangs of a terrifying spider!

A flash of metal, and the kiklar screeched in agony, all three of its left legs cleaved apart. It fell on Reis, again knocking the wind out of him, while its sticky, rancid-smelling blood spewed all over his armor and hands. It thrashed about, threatening to crush him, but he scrambled out from under it just in time to watch Anila pierce its thorax with her long, impossibly sharp sword. It screeched and tried to bat her away, but she pulled her sword out and stabbed again, closer to its eyes and mouth. That was enough to kill it.

Pulling out again, she huffed at the creature, and then looked at Reis. She was the one who had called out his name, he realized, and she had come to his rescue. Staring dumbly, he realized that she had risked her life and saved him, all while continuing to hide her magic abilities.

Rushing over to him, she pulled on his arm. "Get up!"

The kiklar were still coming, Reis realized, and the marines struggled to hold them back at this point. He looked at the arch to see that Indira was alive, but her right arm hung down loosely, wounded even though no blood was visible.

Elaria had made it to the archway and slapped her palm against a panel in it. The glow flickered for a brief moment, and her frown deepened, until suddenly the entire area lit up! Not just the archway, but from the ambient glow that sprung to life in the city when every panel on the wall lit up.

"We need to get to that device," Kellis shouted.

"Baenil," Elaria waved the other elf over to her. Pointing through the archway at a fortress-like building at the top of stairs a half mile further into the center, she asked, "Is that it?"

"Yes, that's the capitol!"

Once Reis was secure on his feet, Anila dragged him back behind the line of marines, which had finally reformed into a circle, and were managing to keep the waves of monsters back, if just barely. He knew that all Mages eventually grew fatigued from overuse of magic, so he wondered just how long the marines could last.

"There's no way we can get there fast enough," Indira shouted. "We won't last long enough against this!"

Reis looked at Anila, and then at Elaria. He was surprised to find that the elf was already looking at him, a look of resignation on her face. Not resignation for their fate, but for hers.

Before she even asked Baenil her next question, Reis tugged on Anila's hand, which he only just realized he was still holding, and headed for the archway.

"How fast can you run," Elaria asked Baenil.

"How fast," he frowned. "I don't know! You've seen me run, how fast is fast?"

Just as Reis and Anila reached their side, Elaria looked at Reis, and then grabbed Baenil's arm. "Well, run as fast as you can!" And she pulled him out of the protection of the marines, both bolting for the capitol building. Reis let go of Anila's hand, realizing that he couldn't compel her to follow, and he took off after them.

Either the kiklar were too focused on the marines, or they were surprised by the sudden breakaway, and they didn't come after the elves or Reis. Not at first, anyway. Not until they made it to the stairs and bounded up them.

The stairs, made of the same gray-white stone as the floor, were deep but not very tall, and it made running up them awkward at first, but Reis quickly found his stride.

They reached the top in moments and came into a small plaza just in front of the capitol building, the entrance doors open but covered in webs. Elaria wasted no time burning them away, sending another plum of smoke up, but this time she watched for any kiklar that might ambush them from inside.

As they waited for the smoke to clear, Anila came up next to Reis, barely breathing hard despite having just run up two stories worth of stairs.

The smoke cleared, and the elves rushed in with Reis and Anila right behind them. He glanced back just long enough to see that the marine formation had made it through the arch, but were moving much slower and would not be able to get to them in time to help.

And then a kiklar landed on the steps only a hundred feet from Reis, so he jumped inside, and then looked at the doors, wide stone doors with metal frames that looked extremely heavy and probably impossible to close after thousands of years.

The entrance led into a dark antechamber that was wide and tall, with plenty of room to fight. Elaria hadn't yet powered up any of the light panels inside, but her daggers were bright enough that he could see a large humanoid statue in the center of the room.

Hoping to keep the kiklar out, Reis shouted, "Elaria, behind us," and darted out of the way just as the creature stopped at the entrance to get its bearings.

Elaria turned, and then unleashed a blast of magic that send the arachnid flying back down the stairs, where it exploded a moment later, coating the steps with its ichor.

"Alright, Baenil," Elaria turned back to the scholar. "You've been in a dwarven ruin before, where do we go?"

Baenil thought for a moment, and then replied, "Well if it's anywhere, it'll be atop the central tower." He pointed above them, "We just need to get up there, and hope that the stairs are in good shape."

Frowning, Reis looked up at the high ceiling, and realized that he hadn't noticed a tower as they'd rushed into the capitol. The antechamber was already twenty or twenty five feet tall, so how high up did the tower go?

"This way," Baenil rushed off to the left, "there should be stairs up to the top floor on either side."

Following the elf, Reis grimaced. If they took too long, like if Baenil led them in the wrong direction, the marines wouldn't make it, and they'd be trapped beneath Archanon with who knew how many kiklar bearing down on them.

Thankfully, Baenil was correct, and the moment they passed into a hallway off to the side, they found a stairwell, made of stone like everything else in the city, that led up. At every floor, the staircase doubled back on itself, and in the windowless, lightless building, that made coordinating their rushing pace harder. There were glow panels all along the corridor, but they didn't bother to stop to light them, and instead relied on Elaria's daggers for illumination.

When they reached the top of the fourth flight of stairs, Reis caught a glimpse of light through the door, and they burst out onto the roof of the capitol building. Right where several kiklar waited for them.

Elaria was ready for them and released arcane attacks from each dagger, destroying two kiklar in a heartbeat. As Baenil dove to the side, Anila leapt past him and sliced several limbs off of another one.

Reis looked above the door they had just come through, expecting a kiklar to be ready to pounce on them, and he wasn't disappointed. Just as it leapt down on him, he stabbed upwards, right into a weak spot in its abdomen. With the help of the kiklar's weight, his sword pierced through right up to the hilt, and together they toppled over, more rancid ichor splattering his armor and face.

A little got in his mouth, and the taste was worse than the smell! Reis barely held back a gag, and he shoved the squirming monsters aside, pulling his sword out while dry-heaving.

Thankfully there were only a few more waiting for them on the roof, and Elaria finished them off in short order. Then he noticed the tower that Baenil had mentioned, reaching at least three more stories up, more than halfway between the ground and the high ceiling.

He realized that was why the device would be up there! In the center of the ruins, literally in the center of everything, its magic field would more easily reach every corner of the dwarven city.

Reis stood up and looked over the lip of the roof to see that the kiklar assault on the marines hadn't let up. And the marines looked exhausted.

Then he noticed that the tower wasn't very big, the stairs likely only able to fit one person at a time. If they all went, they'd be a burden.

"Elaria, go," he shouted. "Get up there and turn that thing on!"

She glanced at him, and then ran towards the tower, leaving them to fend for themselves without any magic. The moment she disappeared into the door, three more kiklar fell upon them, one landing practically on top of Reis and knocking into him. He stumbled backwards, and tried to anticipate the kiklar's attack, using his sword to bat its arms away. Reis tried to cut at its joints, but the kiklar was too fast, too ferocious, and he barely had time to block its attacks.

He realized for the first time that their legs didn't end in spikes, like he originally thought, but in two tiny little clawed toes. Still, those claws could easily rend his flesh.

Backing around the corner of part of the roof's structure, he glanced behind him to make sure the way was clear, only to realize that it wasn't. A network of webs was right behind him, and before he could think of how he could get away from it, the kiklar shoved him right into its trap.

The strands were impossibly strong for how thin they were, and incredibly sticky. His sword and sword arm were completely immobilized! The kiklar paused and stared at him, and he felt terror drain all color from his face.

For the second time that day, he thought he was dead.

His enemy exploded in a shower of carapace splinters and fluid, yet again covering him head to toe in the rancid blood. And behind his former opponent stood Anila, her curved sword glowing with magic.

The blade cooled off, and the blue-white glow faded as she stepped up and expertly cut the web around his limbs and sword, freeing him.

Stepping away from the web, having to pull one last sticky strand from his shoulder, he looked at her wide-eyed, and then glanced behind her. The marines weren't in view from their vantage, but Baenil was, who stood staring at her slack-jawed.

Anila glanced at the elf and sighed, her shoulders slouched in defeat.

Her secret was out.

More screeches echoed from above, and they looked up to see four more kiklar skittering towards them, suspended by their webs and ready to pounce. Anila brought her sword up and recharged it with magic, ready to fend them off and likely expose her secret to the marines as well.

She didn't have to. From the top of the tower, there was a sudden grinding noise, like stone sliding on stone, and a brilliant flash of light. A luminous sphere of energy expanded rapidly from the tower, creating a beacon of violet light. All of the kiklar, everywhere, screamed. They weren't screams of surprise or worry, he realized, but screams of pain, of absolute agony.

In a great wave, the kiklar ran from the tower, as fast as they could atop their webs. He heard screeches from below, and they ran over to the edge of the roof, Anila making sure to release the magic in her sword so that the marines wouldn't see it glowing. The waves of kiklar surrounding the marines ran in great waves, crawling over one another in a desperate attempt to get away.

"She did it!" he shouted.

They were finally safe!

Chapter 17

DEPOSED

Despite how things had started out, Kailar decided that today was a good day. And it was about to get a whole lot better.

The Lieutenant from Edingard was right. They found everything they needed in Commander Lenned's storage chest, and more. Much more.

She, Letan, and Egil watched Commander Kent's expressions as he examined one of the papers that they had brought to him. It, like all of the others, bore broken wax seals, some stamped with Mayor Evern's personal signet, but some of the other papers were stamped by four other members of the city council.

The sheer arrogance of openly using personal signets on blatantly criminal orders shocked Kailar. At first, upon discovering the papers, she had wondered how they could have possibly kept Kent or any other honest people from finding incriminating evidence before now. However, Egil handily reminded her that the underground was everywhere, and keeping even misplaced documents out of the hands of the 'righteous do-gooders,' as Egil called them, was usually easy.

Letan still looked stunned, his eyes looking in Kent's direction, but mostly they were blank and unfocused. She sympathized, realizing that in one day, he had learned that not only were multiple politicians involved in the underground, but so was at least one detachment of the Warriors' Guild.

Still, only the Mayor and four council members were implicated in the recovered documents. That meant that there was still an overwhelming number on the council who were not complicit. At least, she hoped they weren't.

Every document that Kent read through, he looked at the signature, and then checked and rechecked the seal.

The broken seals might have been a problem, opening the possibility that the documents might have been altered or faked somehow. Thankfully, Lenned had apparently considered the same problem, and had apparently left a couple of the documents unopened, the seals intact and Warreck's impression clear. While they didn't know what was in them, hopefully Lenned had left them unopened with good reason. Kailar hoped they were 'formalities,' orders that Lenned already knew to carry out even without having to read the orders.

Then again, she worried, *they could merely be un-incriminating minutia.*

"This is incredible," Kent set the last opened paper down and stared at the array upon his desk, his jaw taut. "It's…unbelievable."

Kailar frowned, realizing that he was being literal. "Sir?"

"It's almost too good," he shook his head. "But, I don't know. I think I'm just trying to wrap my head around this. Last night you left to find even a shred of evidence. Now you bring me proof that it goes far beyond the Mayor. It will shatter the council."

"Maybe," Letan replied, stirring out of his reverie, "but I doubt it. And if they doubt the truth…"

Letan looked to Egil, who stepped forward. "I'll swear in front of the entire council that it's all true. Yeah, I know they wouldn't think my word was worth a horse's arse, and they might question those papers alone, but both together? Even politicians don't have their heads stuck that far up their rears."

Kent raised his eyebrows. "You'd be surprised what they can ignore if it's too inconvenient."

Kailar stepped forward and placed her fingertips on the Commander's desk. "Come on, Commander. This is what we've been looking for, what *you've* been looking for, all these years. We can finally take him down, and deal a crippling blow to the underground."

Staring at the papers, Kent drew in a deep breath, and looked at Kailar. She stared back evenly, confidently, willing the Commander to find his courage.

"Alright," he nodded, a smile finally cracking his face. She let out a relieved sigh. "Alright, let's do this."

As she backed away, Letan asked, "When and where do we arrest him?"

Kent glanced at the documents again, and his smile grew wider. He neatly gathered up the documents and handed Kailar and Letan the two unopened letters bearing the Mayor's seal. "I think it's time I take a page from your book," the Commander nodded at Kailar. "Let's do it right now. The Mayor is in session with the city council, no doubt telling them about last night's conversation. Let's show them his true colors."

Kailar's heart leapt in excitement. "Alright!"

Together, the four of them left the Commander's office. As they passed through the Guild manor, Kent ordered every Warrior they encountered to accompany them, until when they strode out onto the street, they had a column of twelve Warriors behind them, some in duty armor, some not, but all of them armed.

At first Kailar wondered about such an aggressive stance, but then she realized that the Mayor had likely told the city soldiers of her and Letan's demotion, and warned them to watch out for any problems. If any of the soldiers were part of the underground, they might try to arrange an incident as an excuse to attack.

The march from the Guild Hall to the city capitol was short, both having been constructed in the early days of the colony, and before long, the platoon faced off against two uneasy-looking city guards bracketing the double wooden doors.

Thankfully, the guards wisely didn't resist beyond an initial command for the Warriors to stop, and at the Commander's orders, the guards surrendered their weapons to two Warriors, who remained outside to stand guard with the soldiers.

Thankfully the foyer itself was unguarded, with only a concierge to direct visitors. He was completely taken aback by the show of force, and stumbled over his words, "Uh, well, yes, how might I help you?"

Kent briskly replied, "I'm afraid you can't, but thank you, sir."

As the Warriors tried to step past the concierge, he pushed his way in front to try to stop them. "I apologize, Commander, but the council is in session behind closed doors."

Glowering at the concierge, Kent replied, "I know. That's why I'm here. Now, step aside." He paused, and then added, "Please."

Kent's hand rested on his sword hilt, and the concierge took the hint. He stepped to the very edge of the room, as far out of the way as he could get, and watched the Warriors with trepidation.

Without further hesitation, Kent marched up to the double doors leading into the council chambers and shoved them open. Kailar, Letan, and Egil followed, and she tried her best not to crack a smile at the startled protestations from the Mayor.

Thirteen people presided over the council, a sharp departure from the political structures in the four kingdoms. While the mayors in Edilas were essentially lords of their respective lands, on Devor a mayor led an assembly of those who had been chosen by the four kingdoms to organize colonial efforts. They weren't vassals of the lord mayor, they were the wealthy and powerful elite of the city and, while technically subservient to a mayor, they held great sway on the politics of the region.

Knowing what she did now, however, Kailar realized that Warreck was never comfortable with that arrangement, and that was likely why he had involved himself in the underground. To secure real power over the council.

The thirteen sat facing one another at a long table, made of ironwood and stone brought across the seas from Edilas decades ago by who knew which wealthy lord, and while there were no windows in the council chambers, there was ample light from several everlasting torches, one of the few places that Kailar had seen such a prolific use of them on Devor.

"What do you think you are doing," Warreck, the only person standing, demanded, planting his fists on his hips. "You have no business barging in here!"

As Kent, Kailar, and Letan took up position close to the chair on the opposite end of the long table, the councilwoman who sat there immediately abandoned her seat. Egil stood off to one side, while the rest of the Warriors filled in behind them.

With a hint of genuine fear, Warreck's eyes darted from Warrior to Warrior. "I knew it," he muttered. "You have planned a coup."

Kent had drawn in a breath to speak, but at Warreck's words, he held it and then let out an exasperated sigh. "Nothing so dramatic,

Lord Mayor."

Another councilwoman, a surprisingly young woman with only some silver in her black hair, raised her eyebrow at Kent. "Then I suggest you explain yourself, Commander."

"And explain what *he* is doing here," Warreck pointed at Egil. "I take it you had something to do with his escape last night?"

Ignoring Warreck's attempt to turn the tables, Kent stood up straight and threw the papers down onto the table, spreading them out along half of its length. "Mayor Warreck Evern, I am here to officially place you under arrest, under charges of criminal conspiracy and corruption."

The look of shock on the mayor's face almost made Kailar laugh, his eyes and mouth agape as the council members grabbed some of the papers to read through them. Or rather, all but four of the members.

"What…what is that," the Mayor asked. "What exactly do you have there?"

Letan stepped up next to the Commander. "Orders and assignments to the Edingard Commander," he spoke tersely. "All of them illegal. Demands for protection payments from businesses. Arrangements for slave trading. Arrangements to release criminals from the Guild and city holding cells. And there are names in all of them; names of who the letters are for, who the targets are, who supports or will be making payments to the Guild for these activities…"

"And most of these letters bearing your seal, Lord Mayor," Kent raised his chin. "It seems you've been very busy. You and, let's see," Kent looked around the room, "Pamrin, Zeik, Eila, and Denorith."

The other nine council members turned their eyes on the named members in turn, staring silently, then scouring over the papers to confirm.

"This is outrageous," Eila, a woman well worn with age and with a colorful sense of style favoring multiple thin layers of cloth, slapped her hand on the table. "These are unsealed letters, Commander, you could easily have forged them."

Before Kent or Letan could reply, Egil stepped forward. "I can vouch for their authenticity, ma'am," he raised a hand.

"And who might you be," the first councilwoman asked. She was softly spoken, but somehow commanded everyone's attention each time she spoke. Kailar decided she needed to find out more about that woman after this was over.

Giving a flourished bow, Egil replied, "My name is Egil Atten." Kailar rolled her eyes at his unpracticed and exaggerated mannerism. "You might recognize the name."

Nodding, the councilwoman replied, "Yes, I saw your name on an arrest order recently. You realize that we cannot exactly take your word as honorable."

"Of course not, ma'am," Egil replied. "Especially since I'm saying what I'm saying because I made a deal, a get out of jail type of deal, if you know what I mean." The councilwoman raised an eyebrow at the Commander, but she allowed Egil to speak. "But that don't mean it isn't true. Thanks to this young lady here," he motioned to Kailar, "I was trying to run away to a whole other continent, and was told by my contacts that Mayor Evern was the man to see about that."

"Lies," Warreck slammed his fists on the table. "All bloody lies!"

"Be silent," the councilwoman demanded, snapping her head to glare at him. "If they are lies, we shall determine that as a council."

"There's more," Kailar offered, stepping to Kent's other side and presenting one of the sealed letters. Letan likewise presented the sealed letter that he held. "We don't know exactly what's written on these, but they bear the Mayor's seal and were with the rest of the letters."

One of the complicit council members, Denorith if Kailar remembered his name right, tried to snatch the letter out of her hand, but she yanked it back and stepped away, keeping the document as far from reach as possible while holding her other hand out, open-palm facing the councilman. "Don't even think about it!"

She didn't cast any magic, but she saw the look of horror on Warreck's face. With a roguish grin, she winked at him, but otherwise kept her attention on the councilman.

"Something to hide, Denorith," the first councilwoman asked.

One of the other council members took the letter from Letan. They carefully broke the seal and opened and read the letter. Kailar kept her letter back, waiting impatiently as Denorith slowly eased back into his chair.

The councilman reading Letan's letter frowned. "I am afraid this letter does nothing to prove your case," he glanced at Kent, turning

Kailar's stomach into an icy knot. "It is a letter detailing payment to the Guild for, and I quote, 'services rendered.' Nothing damning beyond that."

The councilwoman turned her eyes on Kailar, while Denorith, the Mayor, and the other three implicated council members relaxed.

Standing up, the councilwoman walked around the table and came up beside Kailar, holding her hand out patiently. Kailar looked her up and down, and found that she admired the woman's simple sense of style, especially for a city leader. She wore a simple tan skirt and a light-blue tunic over a white shirt, and her hair style was simple, pulled back in a neat and clean pony tail.

Kailar glanced at the letter, at the Mayor's seal on it, and hesitated only a moment longer. Finally, she handed the letter over, and hoped for the best.

Breaking the seal in full view of the assembly, the councilwoman turned her eyes down and read carefully. Within moments, her eyes grew wide, and Kailar's heart paused along with her breath.

The councilwoman looked at Kailar, and then turned to the assembly and lowered the paper to her side, careful to keep it away from Denorith. "It seems that our esteemed mayor demanded that Commander Lenned find a way to eliminate Lieutenant Velethar during his campaign in Edingard," she nodded at Letan, "in a way that would not arouse suspicion of the Guild. Furthermore," she glanced at the paper, "it assures the Edingard commander that Kailar would be dealt with after the mayor's trip to Edilas, where he would collect Falind's bounty on her head."

The room erupted in conversation and accusing shouts, as everyone stood up and separated, the implicated members moving towards Warreck while the others stepped closer to the Warriors. Warreck folded his arms and glared at Kent, but it was obvious that he was defeated.

That didn't stop two of the council members, Denorith and Eila, from pulling long, expensive looking daggers from hidden sheaths, but it was a useless gesture, as all ten of the accompanying Warriors drew their swords.

If that hadn't convinced the criminals to back down, Kailar opened her palm and lit a magical blue flame in it. Denorith and Eila stared in awe, and then quickly dropped their weapons and backed away.

"Shackle them," the Commander ordered. The ten Warriors walked by them to comply, while Kailar closed her fist over the flame to snuff it out. "And take them to the Guild holding cells. I don't trust them in the city jail, not until we can figure out who else the Mayor has in his pocket."

As the Warriors got to work, the councilwoman set the kill order down and rubbed her forehead. No one spoke until the arrests were made, and the implicated council members were marched out. The mayor, the last in line, pushed back and looked at Kent, ready to say something.

"Don't," Kailar ordered, shoving him back into the guards. "No claims that we'll pay for this, or that we won't get away with this. *Please* don't bore us with that tirade."

"I own this city," he growled. "The soldiers will mount a rescue, it'll be civil war!"

Giving the mayor a bored look, Kailar shook her head. "Not as long as I'm here. You really think they'll fight me, after all of the cleanup I've already done on this continent, in this city?"

"You're not invincible," he countered. "You can't stop them all!"

Kailar knew that he was right, but she wasn't about to admit that, so she replied, "Maybe, maybe not, but most of them won't survive the encounter. If they know what's good for them, they'll back off and claim loyalty to the Warriors and the council."

Turning to Letan, she smiled warmly at him. He focused on the Mayor, but Kailar didn't bother to look at him again. She heard the Warriors drag him away, while he cursed at Egil and warned that he would never leave the city alive.

Egil looked pointedly at Kailar, but she gave him a reassuring nod. It didn't matter that she didn't like him, he had held up his end of the bargain. As soon as the council was satisfied with his testimony, she'd take him wherever he wanted. The Mayor would never touch him.

The Mayor. Suddenly she realized that Warreck wasn't mayor anymore.

"We did it," Kent whispered, turning around and leaning against the table. "By the gods, we finally did it."

Even though the rest of the council stayed, the chambers were far less crowded now. The councilwoman, who had gone over to the other members to converse quietly for a moment, turned to Kent.

"You imply that you have been working towards this goal for some time?"

Smiling, Kent replied, "Yes, Councilwoman Aurin." So that was her name! Kailar knew all of their names, just not their faces. This was Reyla Aurin, and suddenly she stared at the councilwoman with a start. Reyla was the wealthiest council member, aside from Warreck. Kailar would never have guessed it, given Reyla's simple clothes. "A very long time," Kent added quietly.

Reyla approached them, and the other council members followed closely. "Then perhaps you already have a plan for what we should do next?"

With a frown, Letan asked, "You mean the council doesn't have a contingency plan for if something happens to the mayor?"

"Of course we do," she replied. "However, this is more than a simple matter of succession. Members of the council *and* top leadership in the Warriors' Guild have all been implicated in a vast network of the criminal underground. Which, based on your reports over the past few months, we might never have learned without this woman's help," she nodded at Kailar. "Thank you, Miss Adanna. I must admit, I am surprised with just how much you have done for us."

Kailar stared dumbly at Reyla, and felt herself at a complete loss for words. She couldn't account for why at first, but then she realized, this was the first time that anyone had actually thanked her for her efforts. Sure, Letan had complimented her on her skills, or her dedication, but everyone else criticized her, and not one person had thanked her before now.

A lump welled up in her chest, and it felt like it blocked her voice. She tried to stumble over her words, but then the other shoe dropped, when another councilor remarked, "There's also been a lot of unrest because of her."

The well turned into a kettle of rage, and Kailar nearly snapped at him, but Reyla interceded. "Perhaps that was exactly what we needed, Menil." Reyla beamed at Kailar. "Someone to stir up the pot and force us out of our complacency." Kailar smiled at the councilwoman's word choice.

Reyla looked again to Kent. "However, with everything that has happened, I fear that we cannot maintain our status quo. Refugees from Corlas are still displaced, and there is no telling when they can return home, if ever. We have no mayor, and it sounds as though the Warriors' Guild in Edingard are in need of new leadership."

She glanced at the other councilors, and continued, "Something must change if we are to prevent this from happening all over again."

"I agree," Kailar voiced her opinion before she could stop herself. "You're all disjointed, disorganized. Having independent cities left to fend for themselves leaves you all open and vulnerable, easy targets not just for criminals, but for anyone who wants to take advantage of you. Including the four kingdoms."

Reyla's eyes grew wide at Kailar's implication, and Letan rested a cautioning hand on Kailar's shoulder. "Kailar, this isn't the time…"

"Please," Reyla raised a hand, her voice patient. "Let her speak."

Suddenly Kailar's extremities tingled, and her face turned pink. She had spoken without thinking, but now they actually wanted to hear her out.

"Well," she started slowly and considered her phrasing. She thought of everything that had come to mind over the past few months, and tried to lay them out simply. "Look, you've already seen that you can't count on the Alliance to help you out. From what I've heard from sailors, the kingdoms can barely take care of themselves. And to be frank, the way they handled Devor from the moment it was discovered was a setup for failure. Sure, few people here seem to care about which country they came from, and the animosity between Tal and Falind is pretty much non-existent here, but part of that is because the towns and villages feel alone, like they can only count on themselves. Maybe it's time you all united."

At first, no one reacted. However, as she expected, it was Reyla who realized her implication first, and the Councilwoman smiled at her appreciatively. "Are you implying that we should create our own kingdom, young lady?"

"Kingdom, empire, country, call it what you want," Kailar replied. "But yes. You're on your own, so you might as well *be* your own. More than that, you need to work together, as one." Waving her hand generally towards Edilas, she continued emphatically, "Even as an alliance, the four kingdoms still bicker and fight over scraps of land and resources, instead of working on a united front. Unifying them is probably a hopeless cause." She paused and grimaced. "Believe me, I know. However, here you don't have flags and borders dividing you. Only the vast open wilderness separates you, and while that was a barrier to unification before…"

Kailar looked at Letan, who watched her with interest. She realized that what she was about to offer was all his fault, and she inwardly smiled at the thought of teasing him about it later.

Focusing back on Reyla, Kailar nodded. "You have me to help with the distance problem. I can make portals, I can help all of the towns' leaders work together."

"I see," Reyla creased her brow thoughtfully. She remained silent for several beats, her eyes growing distant as she considered Kailar's words. "You make a good point about why we could never unite in the past," she spoke slowly, carefully. "And I admit, the idea of unification is enticing."

The councilwoman turned to the other councilors, all of them likewise in deep thought. "There are many resources on Devor that, if we worked together, we could use to become a relatively independent nation. Instead of being forced to give our resources away and beg for the ones we can't get here, we could become trading partners with Edilas."

The councilors looked to one another cautiously. The one that had spoken before, Menil, was of course the voice of caution. "While I appreciate your idealistic view of the possibilities, Edilas might not let us declare independence." He looked at Kailar, at Letan and Kent, before turning again to Reyla. "They could cut off all supplies…" His voice trailed off when he no doubt realized that supplies were no longer coming from Edilas. "It could lead to war, if they wish to enforce their claim upon us."

Reyla nodded thoughtfully, and considered that statement for a moment. But it was Kent who had an idea about that. "Then we need to convince them that the benefits of our independence far outweigh any benefit of us remaining a colony." Everyone turned to him, and he smiled. "Considering the state of affairs on Edilas, that shouldn't be too hard. All we have to do is remind them that governing us requires resources that they could otherwise spend on rebuilding their own lands."

"Intriguing," Reyla tilted her head to one side. "Perhaps this could work after all."

The other councilors nodded, though some of them did so with obvious caution and worry on their faces. Kailar knew that doing something like this wouldn't exactly be easy, and more importantly, she understood that it couldn't be forced. Not like she had tried to do to Edilas.

It would only work if the leaders of the towns and villages of Devor agreed to it.

Suddenly Kailar noticed Reyla smiling at her. She frowned at the councilwoman, who drew in a slow breath before saying, "You do realize that you will have to stop referring to this as 'our land' and 'our people.'" She placed a supportive hand on Kailar's arm and looked into her eyes. "This is your land, now. These are your people."

Trying to find words, Kailar felt her mouth drop open. "I, uh…"

"She's right," Letan added. "You've more than earned your place here."

Something caught in her throat, and Kailar had to gulp it away. She tried to push back the stinging she suddenly felt in her eyes.

"I don't know what to say," she said, her voice breaking a little.

With a shrug, Reyla withdrew her hand and simply smiled. "From what I hear, that's unusual for you."

A chuckle escaped Kailar, and then before she could stop herself, she laughed. A sensation she had completely forgotten.

Genuine laughter.

Chapter 18

SEA OF MAGIC

With barely contained excitement, Cardin stepped through Endri's portal from the Celestial Spires to the dragons' origin world of Stella, and he was not disappointed.

The first sensation he felt was a change from dry warmth to a humid cool air. As his vision cleared from the transition, he beheld a great, rolling grassy landscape. Spread across the green of the grass were carpets of violet, blue, and red flowers. Strange-looking trees were spread across the landscape, far enough apart from one another that even the largest dragon could walk amongst them with room to spare.

Cardin had to blink twice, trying to clear his eyes of what he thought was an after-image of the portal distorting colors. However, try as he might, the pigment of the tree trunks remained the same, a distinct shade of lavender. Furthermore, their leaves were a blue-green color, creating a vista that was simultaneously enchanting and unusual.

Wandering away from the portal, his feet kicked up the scents from the flowers, familiar but with a strange, pecan-like smell mixed in. Stopping, he closed his eyes and drew in a deep breath, savoring the aroma while feeling the stirrings of hunger.

Sira and Dalin had both come through with him, but for the moment, each had wandered in their own direction, drinking in the vista with eyes wide open. "This is amazing," Sira exclaimed, gazing up at the sky.

When Cardin followed her lead and looked up, another portal opened high in the sky, and Endri soared through, his familiar presence suddenly resonating with their surroundings.

Cardin focused on the magic surrounding them when he realized how similar it felt to Endri's presence. Closing his eyes, he could feel and *see* the life around him, teeming with magic in a way he had never felt before. The ethereal vision looked as if the essence of magic was a dense fog lifting off of a warm river in winter, betraying the abundance of life on and beneath the surface. Every blade of grass, every insect, every flying creature, and each leaf radiated great swatches of magic, all of it stirring and rolling together and creating a dizzying mental image.

It was overpowering! Cardin had to shut himself off from the stream, and he nearly fell back from exhaustion and disorientation. Sira was at his side in moments, her arm wrapped around his torso.

"Cardin! Are you okay?"

Opening his eyes, he forced a smile. "No. I mean yes, it's nothing. It's just…this place." He looked again at the vista, just in time to watch Endri land a hundred feet away. "It's…"

"Overwhelming," Dalin finished, coming up beside Sira. "There is more energy, more magic here than anything I have ever felt before. We could swim in it."

Endri's version of a smile stretched across his muzzle, and he looked to his left, towards the closest tree, which Cardin realized was almost as tall as Endri, and created a great dome with its crown.

It wasn't the tree that truly caught his attention, but rather a creature that looked like one of the eels that Cardin had tasted at their reception in Maradin during the last winter. Unlike those sea creatures, however, this one gracefully swam through the air, it's grey and blue skin shimmering with light.

"In fact, some creatures on Stella do just that," Endri spoke. *"This is a world of magic unlike any other, and is one I have wished to visit for some time."*

Wide-eyed, the three of them gawked at Endri. Sira asked, "You've never been to your own home world?"

Turning back to them, the dragon shook his head slowly. *"No, nor was I born here. The Star Dragons left Stella long ago.*"

Cardin glanced at the others, and then asked, "Why?"

Endri considered his question for a moment, looking down at him with blazing eyes. His answer was deceptively simple, *"We moved on. Now, if you will allow me a few minutes, I will try to detect the presence of another dragon.*"

Though his answer garnered more questions, Endri did not allow the trio to ask, and he sat on his haunches and closed his eyes.

Cardin knew that he could not remain closed off from magic the entire time they were on Stella, not when he wanted to experience every aspect of the new world that he could, so he eased his senses open, letting some of the magic seep in and flow through him. In fact, he realized that was the key. From what he could tell over the last year, Wizards did the same thing, allowing magic to flow through them, rather than pool inside of their spirits. So Cardin did his best to emulate them.

His effort paid off, and he discovered that he could control the flow like a water faucet in an Archanon home. When it felt overwhelming again, he cinched off the flow just a bit more, and this allowed him to experience everything in manageable doses.

Realizing that he had also closed his eyes, he opened them to see Sira staring at him with a raised eyebrow. "Your aura keeps changing strength," she pointed out, frowning. "Is that on purpose?"

With a genuine smile, he nodded. "It is. I'm trying hard not to get overwhelmed again."

"Indeed," Dalin nodded. "You did well just now, picking up on a method that Wizards discovered millennia ago."

"Naturally," Cardin grinned at his friend.

Before Dalin could say anything, Sira looked at the Wizard and said, "His ability both amazes and concerns you, right?"

Dalin paused mid-breath, and then laughed. "Yes, I was indeed about to make that comment."

Cardin smiled at his friends, and then looked again upon Endri. There was a distinct pulse from the dragon, powers flexing to reach out into the world. Not knowing how far a dragon's senses could reach, he reasoned that it might be a while before they were ready to move on.

This meant that they had time to explore a little. Taking Sira's hand, he nodded towards the closest tree. "Let's look around."

Sira glanced at Endri hesitantly, but seeing that he did not respond to Cardin's suggestion, she allowed a broad smile to light up her face, and they set off with Dalin beside them.

The grasses were varied, but most were short enough to walk directly on. Cardin tried to avoid stepping on any flowers, but there were so many, especially of the blues and reds, that he soon had to give up. At least a pleasant side effect was that with each flower he stepped on, the smell of pecans grew stronger. Cardin glanced behind to make sure Endri hadn't moved, but then was shocked when he discovered that the flowers he'd stepped on had all popped right back up, apparently undamaged.

It seemed as though life on Stella was hearty. *I just hope that doesn't mean there are equally hearty predators about,* he thought. Then he gulped when he realized that dragons, perhaps the greatest of all predators, were born here. Hopefully other predators were just as peaceful, and would leave them alone in favor of their regular prey.

Sira squeezed his hand. "How can a world so utterly strange be so beautiful?" She slowly shook her head.

The crown of the tree they approached hung down low enough that the lowest branches would just barely be out of their reach, but the branches spread out wide, and the top ones reached high into the sky, creating a beautiful blue-green half-circle. The tree swayed lazily with a light breeze, and while the outer edge of the crown was packed with leaves, as they walked underneath, Cardin saw that the inner part was mostly bare, with countless branches creating a playground for dozens of the eel-like creatures to swim around.

Stranger still, Cardin realized that there was no apparent bark to the branches, and as they approached the trunk, it too lacked any appearance of bark. It was textured, but more like the stem of a flower, only far larger, and as they drew closer, he noticed a tinge of green in the otherwise lavender trunk.

The ground was almost perfectly flat surrounding the trunk, and there was no evidence of roots branching out, suggesting the roots grew deep. The trio stopped within touching distance, but none were brave enough to reach for it.

"It doesn't look like wood," Sira commented. "How is that possible? Is it actually a tree?"

Frowning, Cardin looked up into the crown, at the outer branches, at the leaves and how they swayed even when there was no breeze.

At the creatures whisking about effortlessly. One came down from the closest branch to investigate the interlopers, and focused on Sira. It stopped a few feet away from her, then inched closer, stopped, and inched closer again. She cautiously held out her open hand, with eyes wide open.

It drew a little closer, sniffed at her finger tips, and then whisked around her hand like it was another branch, its fins brushing against her fingers and arm. She giggled and looked at Cardin with the most beautiful smile. "It's adorable!"

"Magic," he blurted, eliciting confused stares from the others. "I mean, the energy around here, it's keeping the tree upright just like the creatures are swimming through it." Looking at the trunk, he closed his eyes and saw the magic flowing through the tree, starting beneath the ground and flowing out towards the branches, creating a field that he noticed the creatures were streaming across, making little eddies and waves.

"Incredible," Dalin whispered.

As the eel-like creature continued to play all around Sira's arm, she tilted her head to one side. "You mean, like a floating plant in a pond? Like a lily pad?"

Opening his eyes and watching the creature move further up her arm, and then start to whisk around her shoulders, he nodded. "Yeah, exactly."

Cardin turned to Dalin to see what the Wizard thought, but rather than watching Sira, his eyes were fixed upon the tree trunk. He reached out to touch it, but then noticed Cardin watching him.

Grimacing, Dalin sighed forlornly. "I was hoping…that is, without a staff, I needed a source of wood with which to craft a new one." He hung his head low. "This would be a magnificent world from which to craft a staff, but I do not believe that will be possible."

Feeling his heart go out to his friend, Cardin lightly touched Dalin's shoulder. So much had had happened over the past year, and now Dalin had lost so much. More than that, his words before they left Halarite resonated in Cardin's mind, and he was about to ask how Dalin was able to come with them.

Before he could, he felt Endri's presence approach. The dragon bent down low to stick his head under the tree's crown. *"Do not worry, my young friend,"* he spoke to Dalin. *"This is but one biome on this world, and I understand that Stella is as varied as any other world. Surely there are wooden trees elsewhere that we may find."*

Melting in relief, Dalin nodded. "I am relieved to hear that."

Moving closer to Endri, Cardin asked, "Did you find something?"

The usual tightness in Endri's face slackened. *"No, I do not sense the presence of another dragon. However, it is difficult to discern individuals here. It would be a good place for a Star Dragon to hide. In any case, I brought us to this general location because this is where Firdal said we could find a settlement."*

Sira walked next to Cardin, and said, "Then that's where we should go next."

"I agree." Endri nodded in one direction, which Cardin sensed was Stella's east. *"The settlement is at the base of those mountains."*

Frowning, Cardin turned and realized that the tree's crown had blocked their view earlier of a mountain range in the distance. In fact, it would probably be half a day's walk to get where they were going. "We couldn't have arrived closer," he asked.

"I did not wish to alarm them," Endri replied, pulling his head out and standing up tall. *"Besides, I sense that Dalin wishes to tell you something more. A hike to the village will be a good opportunity for him to do so."*

Cardin looked to his Wizard friend, and Dalin met his gaze for a moment before he averted his eyes. Now more than ever he wanted to know what happened between his friend and the Wizards' Guild.

Endri walked around the tree towards the mountains, so Cardin and the others met him on the other side of the crown, and together the four of them set out. Resisting the urge to press Dalin, he allowed the Wizard to gather his wits and begin when he was ready.

While they trudged along beside the great dragon, Cardin drew closer to Sira and took her hand in his. If nothing else, he was ecstatic to have this new experience with her.

Smiling warmly at him, she then gazed out upon the world ahead of them. "To think, only a decade ago, we were concerned with graduating as Warriors, and we debated how fast each of us would rise through the ranks." She shook her head in wonder, but then her expression darkened a little. "I just wish change didn't bring so much…"

Feeling his own stomach twist in uneasiness, he squeezed her hand. "Hardship," he suggested.

"Yeah," she grimaced. "And worse."

Endri glanced down at them, and commented, *"It is an unfortunate consequence when a society is forced to adapt to such paradigm-changing circumstances."*

Sira's expression darkened further, and she looked down at the grass and flowers, her eyes distant. "Society," she commented sourly. "Apparently ours is incapable of adapting."

The troupe remained silent for a long while, and Cardin searched for some reassuring words to give her, but none came to mind. Rather, as much as he wanted to believe in people, some of the actions people had taken lately reminded him why laws and guards were necessary.

"I'm not usually one for doom and gloom," he shook his head, "but I'm really starting to wonder if the kingdoms can survive much more."

Endri shook his head. *"You underestimate your own people, Cardin."* He and Sira looked up at the dragon in surprise. *"I have seen entire civilizations collapse under far less duress,"* he looked down upon them. *"And I have seen others endure far worse and survive, though not without their societies having to adapt. Your people are very capable of adapting to what has happened, and what is yet to come."*

Cardin tried to smile at Endri, but despite the dragon's encouraging words, he still felt worried about the days ahead. Sometimes he wished there was more that he could do, but then he realized that he wasn't exactly in the best position to guide the people of Tal. How could he lead when there was so much conflict within himself?

As the sun continued its trek along the sky, they fell silent and continued their journey east. Even though it had felt cool at first, Cardin realized that the sun had risen probably only a couple of hours ago, and the air quickly grew warmer. The tall mountains before them looked heavily forested, and he noticed that the trees around the group were getting closer together as they journeyed, so he wondered if Endri would stay on the ground or if he would eventually need to take to the skies.

After about an hour of walking in silence, Dalin suddenly blurted, "I left the Wizards' Guild."

"What?!" Sira gawked at him, and Cardin likewise gaped wide-eyed and open-mouthed.

"It was the only way I could accompany you," he added, glancing at them but mostly keeping his eyes ahead. "For one thing, I swore an oath to help you bear your burden," he nodded at Cardin. "And it was Master Valkere's final wish that I should remain with you through the days ahead."

Cardin considered his friend's words carefully, and wondered why the Grand Master believed it so important that Dalin be at his side. With an encouraging nod, Cardin said, "Tell us everything."

Dalin hesitated for only a moment, but then he launched into the tale, beginning with his meeting with Valkere in the library. He showed them the sylaric stone and explained to them the importance of it. Then he told them more of Nuuldan's attack and Valkere's sacrifice.

Finally, he told them of his confrontation with Master Syrn in the rebuilt Grand Wizard Hall, and his subsequent resignation. That was why he no longer carried a staff, not even the borrowed training staff – it was Guild property. For that same reason, he would not have been allowed to take the new staff that he had already begun to construct. He explained that more than likely, Master Syrn would order its destruction, very similar to how a Warrior's sword was ceremoniously broken when a Warrior was disgraced and banished from the Guild.

"So now I am here," he said, his voice wavering at the finality of his statement. A dark look came over his face, and he rubbed at his mouth. "I just realized, that means that I am officially homeless."

Cardin's face slackened. Wizards always lived in the Guild complex, he realized, and so Dalin was right, he no longer had a home, nor any sort of money with which to buy one or lease a room to stay at an inn.

Cardin hesitated to invite his friend to live with him, since after a decade of being alone, he and Sira were finally together again, and he cherished their time together. However, when his eyes met hers, he saw the sympathetic look in them, and her eyes darted to Dalin and back again.

"No, you're not homeless," he said to Dalin, tearing his eyes from Sira to look into the Wizard's eyes. "I happen to have a spare bedroom in Daruun, and it's all yours."

Looking bewildered, Dalin shook his head. "I could not possibly impose upon you." He glanced at Sira, and Cardin knew that his thoughts were the same as Cardin's earlier. "I will find another way."

"Please, I insist," Cardin reached behind Sira to place a reassuring hand on Dalin's shoulder. "You've already sacrificed so much for us, for *me,* and it's the least I can do, my friend."

After another moment of hesitation, the Wizard smiled and let out a great sigh of relief. "Thank you." He looked at Sira and added, "Both of you."

"Of course," she smiled.

With the issue resolved, conversation turned to idle banter interspersed by long strides of silence. The mood was notably lighter after that, as they discussed living arrangements, and the possibility of Dalin finding a trade with which to earn money and someday buy or build a home. Endri listened with apt fascination.

They marched deeper into the forest, and the trees grew taller, their crowns now high enough that Endri could pass beneath them if he slouched ever so slightly.

When there was no more room for Endri to maneuver around the trees, Cardin watched in awe as the branches swayed and moved away from the great dragon. Not in a way that suggested fear, but like a crowd parts in reverence to their king or queen passing by.

As the forest grew denser through the remainder of their hike, the carpets of flowers beneath the trees gave way to just grass with occasional small patches of flowers where the sunlight broke through the forest canopy.

At some point, several of the eel-like creatures, which Endri finally told them were called kaetz, trailed along behind them for several miles. After the first mile, however, Cardin realized that they weren't following the group as a whole, but instead they followed Sira. At first, they kept their distance, but slowly they grew braver, until the little whisker-like protrusions on their mouths tickled her neck and ears, and she giggled and ducked. This only made the kaetz excited, and they swirled around her elatedly. She finally had to shoo them away, and they scattered back into the forest canopy.

As they drew closer to the mountains, Cardin sensed something unusual, a concentration of power stronger than any of the trees or creatures they saw around them. Something, he realized, that was at least as powerful as Endri.

His hands tingled, whether because of the magic flowing around them or because of his excited anticipation, he didn't know which, but he was certain that there was another dragon nearby, and he told the others as much.

"Are you sure," Endri asked, his face scrunching into a frown. *"I*

sense no such power ahead."

Dalin's eyes shot up at the dragon, and then looked to Cardin suspiciously. He heard the Wizard mutter something about it finally happening to someone other than him, but Cardin ignored the remark and closed his eyes just long enough to focus on the sensation.

Except that it was gone, now. Disappeared as a lantern might do when covered by a cloak. Drawing on his experience in finding Anila's secret, he tried to find a suspicious emptiness, but he had to open his eyes to keep from tripping.

"I don't know now," he shook his head, frowning at Endri. "I swear I felt something."

"Look," Sira interrupted, pointing ahead as they navigated around a tree trunk as wide as one of Maradin's white towers. Just around the bend was a small village of several dozen huts. Huts made of wood, he noticed, glancing at Dalin.

Some of the buildings were square, some circular, and he noticed that none of them seemed to follow any specific design aesthetic, and they were not aligned in any specific grid pattern.

However, what drew his eyes were several structures in the center of the village that stood out even amongst the diverse huts. Whereas the rooftops of most of the village were made out of thatched together branches, leaves, and mud, the three in the center were much larger with roofs of solid wood, carefully shaped into narrow domes and arches. There was no way of knowing how rigid the wood was, but he reasoned that this was not an easy feat of engineering.

As they drew closer, several of the village's residents came into view, either walking towards them along well-worn paths, or emerging from huts, and instantly Cardin knew that this was no ordinary village.

For one thing, the residents were not all of the same species. Some were taller than Cardin, some far shorter, and their skin, for those whose skin he could see, were varied in shade and color. One villager in particular caught his attention, their face covered in gray and black fur that reminded him of a forest wolf. Another villager caught his attention just by his sheer size, at least eight feet tall, and his bare arms as big around as logs!

Perhaps the only unifying features were their clothes, mostly simple and unassuming, loose fitting, and bright with the blues, reds, and purples of the flowers from the nearby fields.

Cardin and the others had stopped the moment they saw villagers, and the two groups stared at each other in stunned silence across hundreds of feet of open space.

After several moments passed, the villager who looked like a humanoid wolf stepped out from amongst the others and approached, focusing mostly on the dragon. The wolf stopped halfway between the groups and gave a deep, respectful bow, his ears twitching this way and that, as if listening for the slightest sound that might indicate trouble.

"Greetings," he spoke, a feat that Cardin suddenly realized was rather impressive given the shape of his snout. However, as the wolf stood up straight, he caught sight of a pendant around the wolf's neck, and suspected that it was probably a translation pendant similar to Elaria's. "I am Ulpex, and you are most welcome to our village."

Endri bowed his head low to the ground, and Cardin and the others followed suit. He suddenly felt very out of his element, and wasn't sure what to expect. Were these people war-like? Peaceful? Xenophobic or welcoming?

Standing up straight, he decided that they were more welcoming than anything, given Ulpex's open arms and peaceful greeting.

Endri took the lead and replied, *"I am Endri of the Star Dragons, and these are my companions, Sira Reinar, Dalin, and Cardin Kataar."*

Ulpex's eyes focused on Cardin, on the hilt of the Sword sticking over his right shoulder, and then he focused on Cardin's eyes for the briefest of moments. Then his attention was back to Endri. "Meeting one Star Dragon was an unexpected honor, but now a second? Surely you do not come here seeking the same as the other."

Cardin felt another flare of energy, and immediately closed his eyes, focusing towards the center of the village. Somewhere towards the cluster of three buildings, someone or something with great power waited. Frowning, he realized that the sense of waiting was directed at him.

Someone in the center of the village wanted to speak to Cardin.

He felt a hand touch his shoulder, and opened his eyes to see Sira staring at him, concern edged by alertness in her eyes. Then he realized that Dalin and Endri likewise gawked at him. "What's wrong," he asked.

"Ulpex asked you a question," Sira stated, staring into his eyes.

Cardin's head snapped back, and he looked at the humanoid wolf, whom he realized had stepped closer. However, unlike Cardin's companions, Ulpex didn't appear concerned.

"I...don't know what happened," he frowned, feeling embarrassed and even frightened. "I felt that presence again, and I tried to focus on it, but I swear it was only for a moment. I think it..." He narrowed his eyes at Ulpex, who nodded to him. "I think someone wishes to speak with me."

"Your senses do not betray you this day," Ulpex stated. "Please, follow me." He gestured to the others, "All of you. As you can see, our village is spread out enough that even a dragon may walk amongst our homes."

Endri nodded his head slowly. *"Thank you, Ulpex. I promise to tread carefully."*

To say that the village was spread out enough to allow for Endri was barely truth, and as the other villagers parted to allow Ulpex to lead them in, Endri had to follow from behind.

They walked in silence, but somehow that didn't unnerve Cardin in the least. He felt at peace here, and while the magic was stronger than ever in the village, it felt serene, not at all like the drowning ocean he had felt in the field.

Yet there was a definite current, he realized, and they were following it. Right into a plaza surrounded by the three largest buildings, where in the exact center stood the most beautiful crystal he had ever seen. It jutted up out of the ground almost five feet, a lone purple, faceted stone glowing with magic, and as Cardin closed his eyes, he realized that all of the power in the area flowed towards and into the crystal.

Whatever it was, he believed that it was the reason for the village's existence. These people, whomever they were, had to be here for that. It enchanted him, drew him closer, until he stood face to face with it, with his reflection. Looking to his left, he realized that Sira had likewise been drawn to it, her deep blue eyes gazing into the facets.

He turned back to Ulpex, who stood behind them patiently, gazing upon the crystal as well. When he looked at Cardin, the back of his lips edged up in an approximation of a warm smile. "She will see you now."

Until that moment, Cardin thought that it was the crystal that had called to him, since he was sure it was alive, like the Navitas from Devor. But then Ulpex motioned to Cardin's left, and from one of the three large buildings emerged an elderly woman in red and black robes. Though she looked human, Cardin immediately realized that she was not by the sharp red color of her eyes. She had a full head of silver hair under her red hood. Despite the obvious years etched into her face, she looked beautiful, and walked with a confident grace that immediately reminded Cardin of royalty.

"Welcome, Cardin Kataar," she spoke, her voice as graceful as her mannerism, soft and yet commanding.

Not knowing what else to do, he bowed deeply to her, suddenly conscious of the Sword's handle now pointing towards the old woman. She reached past the Sword's handle and gently lifted his shoulder, urging him to stand straight. When he could look into her eyes again, she smiled warmly, and he realized in that moment that she was older than any Wizard he had ever met, and wiser, and most definitely the source of power he had felt earlier.

"I...who are you?"

"My name is Naerala," she nodded her head once, closing her eyes for a moment. Suddenly her smile was gone, fading into a deep frown that belied great concern. "There is something different about you," she said, her voice strained. "As if a great conflict lies within you."

Cardin glanced at Endri, who stood at the edge of the square and stared at Cardin and the woman, his penetrating starry eyes flaring for a moment.

Did Naerala know? Could she sense the dark magic within him? Could she feel the turmoil it caused, and the uncertainty in his heart?

Slowly opening her eyes, her brow still creased in a deep frown that accented her wrinkles, she said, "I thought I knew why you were here, but now I sense there is more to your visit."

"I..." He hesitated. "We come seeking help from another Star Dragon."

"You come seeking information," she corrected him. "This much I know."

"*Yes,*" Endri spoke. "*We wish to find Astaria.*"

She didn't look at Endri, but she nodded. "Yes, and more. You wish to know about Nuuldan."

Cardin felt his mouth fall open. "Yes," he nodded. "And about the Shadow Quartz."

"We assumed that only Astaria could tell us," Endri added, a tinge of anticipation in his mental voice.

Nodding thoughtfully, Naerala replied, "That may be." Narrowing her eyes at Cardin, she smiled. "I will help you find the answers that you seek."

For a moment, he wasn't sure what she meant. Help them find Astaria? Or find out more about Nuuldan's plans and allies? *Or,* Cardin thought with a grimace, *will she help me find answers about my dual powers?*

"What can you tell us," he probed.

She raised her eyebrows, and then shook her head. "Come now, young one. Surely you know that everything comes with a price, yes?"

Sira's eyebrows raised in surprise. "And what price might that be," she asked skeptically.

For the first time since she had emerged, Naerala looked to someone other than Cardin, her blazing red eyes focusing on Sira. "I do not speak of a monetary price. We require assistance with a problem, one which I believe you," she looked again to Cardin, "may be able to assist us with."

Exchanging a startled glance with Sira, he asked, "Me? Why me?"

Cardin watched Naerala's unwavering eyes, trying to catch any hint that she was interested in the Sword of Dragons, but they never flickered. "There is a copse in the mountains that is vitally important to us. However, a terrible monster has blocked the only entrance to it for several weeks. Would you be willing to help us drive it away?"

Cardin looked at her suspiciously, while his mind raced through possibilities. Was it a test? What sort of monster could keep these people, especially Naerala, from getting past it?

Cautiously, he asked, "Why me?"

A grin stretched across her face, and she shook her head. "It is not my place to say."

Sira looked at Naerala suspiciously, and asked, "And if we don't help you?" She feared for Cardin, he realized, and for the safety of the Sword.

Naerala again looked at her with trained patience. "I understand your concern, young one. Please be at ease. I have no desire to take the Sword of Dragons."

Cardin, Sira, and Dalin exchanged shocked looks. "How do you know what that is," Sira asked, motioning towards the Sword's handle.

"That is a question best kept for later," Naerala replied. Sira obviously didn't like that answer, her face scrunching in an annoyed glower.

Their host's grin widened as she stared at Cardin, and suddenly he felt his own face stretch into a skeptical smile. "You already know I'll help."

"Of course," she replied casually. "When you have lived as long as I have, you learn how to read people. Especially a species as predictable as humans."

It was like she knew exactly what to say to pique Cardin's curiosity. In a way, he felt like she was manipulating him to say and do exactly what she wanted. He also thought that, for whatever reason, she meant to aggravate Sira.

Before Sira could protest, Endri pointed out, *"You mean to test us. Particularly, the Keeper of the Sword."*

Naerala did not look towards Endri, but she did smile and nod.

"And why do you need to test us," Sira asked, stepping closer to Cardin. "Who exactly are you?"

"I am the spiritual leader of this village," she replied.

It wasn't really the answer they sought, and it was an answer that Cardin felt was obvious. She was tricky.

Sira opened her mouth to press Naerala further, but then stopped, and sighed. "I guess that's a fair answer," she nodded.

Drawing in a deep breath, Cardin glanced at Endri, who gave an assenting nod. "Alright," he said, letting out his breath slowly. "How do we defeat this monster you mentioned?"

Naerala shook her head, and replied, "For now, we rest. It is a long and arduous hike, and we only have a few hours of daylight left." She looked at Ulpex. "Please make arrangements for them to stay the night."

With a deep bow, Ulpex replied, "As you wish."

Smiling again at Cardin, Naerala turned and headed back into the building, which Cardin suspected was a temple, though he only believed as much because its dome stood taller than any other building's.

Ulpex came closer to Cardin and Sira, and Dalin followed him. "Please feel free to explore our village. We will prepare an evening meal soon, and you are welcome to join us. If you have any questions, all of the villagers here are at your disposal."

As the wolf-man smiled warmly, or as warmly as he could given his features, Cardin bowed to him. "Thank you.

Ulpex walked away after that, Cardin staring at his padded feet with interest, wondering how Ulpex's legs were shaped or worked, given that he stood upright and walked lightly, making almost no sound.

Then Cardin's eyes fell upon Sira, her face betraying her annoyance and suspicion of Naerala.

"Do you think she practices being cryptic," she remarked sardonically. "Or does it come naturally to her?"

Glancing back towards Naerala, who had disappeared into the building, Cardin shrugged. "I don't know. I suppose we'll find out."

Chapter 19

THE DEEP CITY

Reis, Anila, and Baenil watched in stunned relief as the last of the kiklar disappeared into the shadows, their screeches of pain fading. As suddenly as the battle had begun, it was over.

Reis stood by the others, watching as the rest of the company down in the square cheered. He wanted to cheer with them, he wanted to be elated that the battle was over, but he was afraid for Anila, for the secret she had just revealed to Baenil.

Elaria came down from the tower a few minutes later, and though she was visibly drained from activating the beacon, she was otherwise unscathed.

After they were sure that the kiklar were really gone, everyone gathered in front of the capitol building.

While Kellis and Indira accounted for everyone, Reis looked to Anila appreciatively. After the way he had acted, after how he had treated her, she still risked her secret to save his life. Since Baenil didn't know it was meant to be a secret, would he tell his companions or not? Let alone everyone else?

Reis didn't dare broach the subject around others, and instead listened as Elaria assured the marines and Kellis that the beacon would not stop for several weeks without being recharged. Never-the-less, Reis and Kellis agreed that it would be better to setup camp inside of a building rather than out on the streets, even if there was no other known threat.

At some point during the battle, Sergeant Tein had commanded her marines to drop their packs in the mad dash for the capitol, left behind somewhere halfway between the wall and the plaza. At Indira's command, half of the marine detachment split off to retrieve the packs, while the other half stayed to protect the rest of the party.

Reis and Elaria led the remaining party members into the antechamber of the capitol, still completely dark except for their everlasting torches. Elaria hadn't relit her daggers, and she looked too exhausted to even try.

Kellis saw it too, and asked, "Are you well enough to activate the glow panels in here?"

She heaved a sigh and peered into the darkness. "Maybe," she said. "But I think it'd be better if I taught you how to do it."

Kellis looked at her dubiously. "I appreciate your vote of confidence, but I'm nothing more than a Mage. I don't think I have the skills required."

Shaking her head, Elaria grabbed the Lieutenant's hand and dragged him over to a glow panel right next to the entrance, and planted his palm squarely in the middle of the light. "It's exceedingly simple," she assured him, fatigue giving her voice an annoyed edge. "It's pure magic, nothing special." She glanced at his sword, and nodded. "In fact, it's exactly like when you channel magic into your weapons. Just focus on gathering the energy into you, and then let it flow into the panel."

While his doubtful face never slackened, Kellis complied and closed his eyes. Reis watched with some awe and no small amount of jealousy as the panel flickered, flashing the pale blue-yellow light on them all, and then suddenly every glow panel in the antechamber blinked on simultaneously.

Drawing his hand back, Kellis stared in awe at the panel, and then at Elaria. "It was so simple..."

Turning away, Reis clenched his jaw, wishing he had the power to do something more to help out. In fact, he realized that he and Gilrin were the only powerless people present, and he wondered if the dwarf felt just as useless as Reis did.

Was that why Gilrin hung around him now? He hadn't noticed it before, but now that the threat was over and they had gathered in the antechamber, the dwarf stood right next to him, while Baenil inspected the perimeter of the chamber. And Anila, he noticed, was heading for Baenil.

The glow panels in the room all started in the center of each of the six walls and extended up into the high ceilings, meeting at a golden diamond shaped piece in the ceiling, and providing ample light on the strange statue in the middle.

In the shadows earlier, Reis had assumed that it had been a statue of a dwarf, but now he noticed that it didn't really look like a dwarf. Or if it was a dwarf, it was a heavily armored one. The best description he could think of for it was roughly humanoid.

Peering at the statue, he realized that the surface actually looked metallic, the color and polish of fine steel, but there wasn't any apparent rust or other blemishes on its surface. It was very dusty and had several cob webs hanging off of it, yet not a hint of decay. The armor was segmented with sharp, pointed edges on each segment, and the helmet provided only a small slit for eyes to peer through, if anything could have ever donned it.

He shuddered at the thought of something that large barreling down on him wearing a full suit of armor, since the statue easily stood fifteen feet tall, almost reaching the golden diamond set in the ceiling.

"That statue is unlike anything I've seen before," Gilrin commented, his brow deeply furrowed. He drew closer to the statue to get a better look. "Not in books or any of the drawings that Baenil and Elaria ever showed me."

Without thinking about it, Reis followed the dwarf and nodded his head thoughtfully, though his eyes were already drifting towards Baenil and Anila. They were in deep conversation, or rather Anila spoke rapidly while Baenil patiently listened.

Of course it had to be Baenil, Reis suddenly realized. The very elf that Anila had captured and guarded for nearly ten years. Perhaps she had even helped torture him.

Just like Reis had done to Elaria.

His stomach dropped out from under him and his hands grew cold and numb when he realized the similarity. He nearly jumped out of his skin when Elaria suddenly stood right next to him, her eyes fixated on the statue.

Staring at her, he remembered that night before the Battle of Archanon. He remembered the Prince commanding him to help them capture and interrogate Elaria. He was the one who had bound her hands to the chair when they had found an evacuated house to use. He had stood guard over her while the Covenant member, Pevrin, hit her over and over again.

Elaria looked at him and frowned. Startled, he looked down and felt his face warm. Not from embarrassment, but from shame.

"Are you okay?" She placed a hand on his shoulder, and he almost shrugged it away, feeling suddenly uncomfortable around her.

"I'm fine," he shook his head, and then he looked at Anila and Baenil again. Her back was to him, but he could tell that she had finished talking, and Baenil was considering whatever she had said. Finally, Baenil nodded once and said something to her, but Reis couldn't see or hear what.

A squeeze on Reis's shoulder reminded him of Elaria, and he turned back to her, a forced smile on his face. "Really, I'm fine. What about you?" He glanced up at the ceiling towards the beacon. "That seemed to do a number on you."

Raising her eyebrows, she nodded solemnly. "It wasn't exactly as easy as lighting up a glow panel. That thing took every ounce of strength I had to start it, and I barely managed it." Elaria looked again at the statue and sighed. "Whatever power the dwarves once possessed, I'd say it outweighs even what the most powerful of your Wizards have."

Reis shuddered at that thought, but somehow it wasn't really surprising after everything he'd learned about the dwarves today.

"This isn't dwarven," Gilrin declared, his abnormally large nose mere inches away from the foot of the statue.

Everyone turned their head towards him in surprise, including Baenil and Anila. Reis squinted and didn't see any writing, not even on the foot-tall stone pedestal that the statue stood upon. However, as he and Elaria drew closer, he realized that Gilrin wasn't looking at the pedestal, but instead was squinting closely at what Reis had assumed was decorative blue trim on each plate of metal.

Baenil and Anila also came back towards them, and everyone inched in around the statue to get a closer look. Indeed, there was very tiny blue writing inscribed in the trim, so tiny that Reis almost couldn't make out the shapes. It didn't help that the writing was completely alien to him.

He glanced at Elaria and wondered if her translation necklace would work on written words, but he somehow doubted it.

"I don't recognize this language," Gilrin stated. "But it is definitely nothing like any form of dwarven writing I've seen."

"Same here," Elaria added.

Feeling useless again, Reis supplied, "Me neither." A handful of the group stared at him dumbly, but for the most part, everyone, even Indira, was focused on the statue.

After a moment of protracted silence, everyone turned their eyes on Baenil. And he looked shocked, not baffled.

"It's elvish," he spoke quietly, as if afraid to say it. Reis's eyes grew wide, and he looked to Elaria for confirmation, but she looked as shocked as him.

"Which form," she asked Baenil.

"Ancient," he replied. "I mean, beyond ancient." With each word, his voice grew more and more excited. "I recognize some of this as contributing to root words in our language as well as three other elvish languages! This..." He shook his head. "This could be our common root language."

Once again, Reis looked to Elaria for help, as did several others. "There are multiple offshoots of elves throughout the Universe," she explained. "Actually, that's an understatement. There's probably at least as many elven worlds out there as there are human, but our species has diverged in more various ways." She shrugged. "We're fair skinned with pretty wild eyes and hair color by human standards, but some elves look almost human, while others look almost inhuman, both in color and in shape. Skin colors across the whole spectrum, hair colors, and, um..." She hesitated and glanced at Reis. "Some hairier than others." Shaking her head, she continued, "More importantly, with each world occupied by elves, their cultures are vastly different. Some are peaceful, some are pacifists. Some are war-like.

"However, as different as we all are, there's a growing belief, at least on Darea, that we all came from a root species. One species of elf, and one language, believe it or not."

"Wait," Kellis frowned, glancing at the statue. "If this is your root language, and it is ancient history, then how old are these ruins?"

Elaria looked at Baenil, and he stared blankly into nothingness, his face a contortion of excitement and awe. "Well it is difficult to say exactly," he said. "However, if I had to guess, at least fifty thousand years old."

There was a stunned pause amongst the group, while Reis struggled to wrap his mind around the number. Until recently, the people of Halarite believed history to be just over ten thousand years. For him, that had only ever been a number, one beyond reckoning. Even at almost thirty years old, the idea of a hundred, let alone a thousand, *let alone* fifty thousand seemed impossible.

Gilrin stepped back from the statue and stared up at it in a type of reverence that Reis had never seen in someone before, not even in the Order of the Ages. "Making this the oldest ruins ever found," he whispered. "This city could be old enough to give us the clues we need about my people's loss of magic."

Feeling left out of the conversation, Reis tried to think of an intelligent comment to make or a question to ask. Then he realized that the question was almost literally staring him in the face.

"But what is an elven statue doing in the middle of a dwarven capitol building?"

"That," Baenil began, but then hesitated. "Is a good question."

"It would suggest a deep level of cooperation between our two cultures," Gilrin said, his voice considerably less excited or reverent.

"It might mean that the elves and dwarves collaborated on some pretty impressive projects," Elaria commented. "It could also be a sign that the elves and dwarves once stood as equals. Maybe there's an ancient elven city hidden somewhere with a dwarven statue in its capitol building."

Gilrin snorted out a laugh. "I doubt that." He hung his head low and shook it.

Elaria walked around Reis to stand by Gilrin, resting a reassuring hand on his shoulder. Then, much to his surprise, she knelt down and wrapped her arms around him tightly. He leaned his head into the nook of her shoulder and let her hold him.

Reis never would have expected such a show of emotion from the dwarf, nor did he expect such familiarity between Gilrin and Elaria. Suddenly he had to completely re-evaluate Gilrin.

Baenil glanced around expectantly. "There must be more," he said. "We must find more evidence, more information, something."

Kellis drew in a breath and nodded. "Well, then, we should get to it. Reis, Sergeant Tein, help me with getting camp set up."

"There might be quarters in the ruins somewhere that we could use instead," Gilrin suggested, raising his head off of Elaria's shoulder. She took that as a sign to let him go and stand up.

"No," Kellis shook his head. "When we're not exploring, I want us all somewhere where we can see each other. Baenil," he called to the elf, who was already halfway towards one of the other doors. "I don't want anyone exploring by themselves. Two marines with each search party, minimum."

"Oh," Baenil stopped, looking confounded. "Sure. I mean, of course, Lieutenant."

Indira looked over at the half-dozen marines still present. "Gaelin, Lilla, go with him."

The two marines, one of whom held a torch, acknowledged her order and joined Baenil, who quickly disappeared through the door.

Reis turned to start setting up camp, only to realize that most of the packs containing supplies still weren't present. However at that moment, the rest of the marines returned carrying the packs.

Setting up camp was a quick effort, especially with how many of them helped. There was no need to setup a tent or tarp, and the temperature deep below ground, though cool, was relatively comfortable, the air somewhat damp but nothing like the hot, humid summers of Daruun. As such, there was no need to start a fire for warmth, even if there had been wood to use. The group had brought mostly dried bread and dried meats, anticipating the lack of wood and the fact that there was no game to hunt down in the deep city.

Gilrin and Elaria stayed close to Reis, which suited him just fine. He felt more comfortable around them than any of the marines. However, it also meant that Anila stayed far away, and at one point, he saw her duck out the front doors by herself.

Reis stared after her, barely hearing Gilrin and Elaria's idle chatter with each other while they finished setting out the last of the skins and blankets for makeshift bedding. He wondered why Anila would leave by herself, and why she had done so at a moment when no one else was looking.

Or so he had assumed. "You should go talk to her, lad," Gilrin spoke, suddenly at his side and nearly making him jump out of his skin.

Grasping his chest with his hand, he gave the dwarf a mock-glare for startling him. "Go after who," he feigned.

"That Covenant girl, of course." Gilrin nodded at the doors. "You keep glancing at her like you want to tackle her."

"What?!" Reis backed away from the dwarf, shaking his head. "No, I'm just concerned. She..." Gilrin looked at him expectantly, his hands on his hips and his head tilted to the side. "She saved my life on the roof, and risked herself doing so."

Elaria came up next to Gilrin and rested a hand on the dwarf's shoulder before he could antagonize Reis anymore. Looking sympathetically at him, she asked, "She risked herself? You mentioned this morning something about a big secret, is that what you mean?"

Hesitating, he frowned and looked up at the glow panels in the ceiling. "Morning. What time is it, anyway? How long have we been down here?"

"It's getting close to evening," Elaria replied. Narrowing her eyes, she added, "And don't avoid the question."

His face turned pink, and he sighed, nodding. "Yeah. She risked everything to save my life. Everything."

Raising her eyebrow, Elaria came closer to him, and then pushed him towards the door. "Even if you still hate her, go at least thank her for that."

"Hey!" Reis took a tentative step towards the door, but hesitated. "I never said I hate her."

Pointing at the door, Elaria insisted, "Go!"

Narrowing his eyes, he sighed and joked, "Yes, sir!"

Echoing Gilrin's motion, she planted her hands on her hips, but didn't say anything else.

His chest tingled with a combination of embarrassment and fear, but he turned and headed out. Only he wasn't as sneaky as Anila, and Kellis called out, "Reis!"

Giving the Lieutenant a mock salute, he said, "Don't worry, sir, Anila's ahead of me. We'll watch out for each other."

Not giving Kellis a chance to rebut, even though he knew he'd get in trouble for it, he ducked outside, and realized what he had just said. They would watch out for each other.

Just like they had done at Maradin.

I'm such an ass, he thought to himself, wiping his face in disgrace. Back then, she had risked it all revealing her secret to protect him.

Today, she had done it again.

Elaria was right, he at least owed her a thank you.

He didn't have far to go. Anila had only walked a short distance away from the door, and she waited for him expectantly. Feeling foolish, he realized that she had intentionally made sure he saw her duck out, so that he would follow.

Rubbing the back of his neck, he sauntered up to her while avoiding eye contact. Stammering a bit, he started to thank her, but then stopped and mentally lectured himself. *This is stupid,* he thought, *Say something to her!*

So he looked her square in her eyes, dimly lit as they were in the deep city, and he drew up his courage and swallowed his pride. "Thank you." He nodded and continued, "Thank you for saving me up there. For exposing yourself to do so."

For a long time, she stared at him, her eyes unemotional, her lips pressed thin. Reis braced himself for a snide remark or a quick, heartless acknowledgement of his gratitude. Maybe she had only come out to ask him again for his discretion about her powers. Maybe she wanted to hold saving his life over his head, leverage to keep him quiet.

"Thank you," she finally replied, her eyes dropping for a moment before looking into his again. "For keeping my secret when you had no reason to."

He was stunned, never having expected her to say that. Then, suspicious of what Baenil had said to her, he asked, "Is everything okay? Is Baenil going to…"

Shaking her head and drawing a light smile, she replied, "No, he'll keep my secret. He doesn't understand the stigma surrounding a half-Wizard, but he'll respect my wishes." The smile vanished, and she lowered her eyes again. "Despite what I did to him."

He wanted to console her about that, to tell her about his earlier revelation, but he didn't know how to say it without sounding pathetic.

Thankfully, she quickly filled the awkward silence. "I realized as I spoke to him, that I had no business asking anything of him. I was worried that he would use it to get revenge against me. But he didn't. He just acknowledged it, said he'd keep my secret, and went back to looking for clues."

"Yeah," Reis laughed uncomfortably. "He kind of has his head in the clouds."

Anila grinned. "More like buried deep underground."

Glancing behind him, Reis sighed and shook his head. "Look, I…" He hesitated, not sure how to say what he wanted to say. "I think I projected onto you. A lot." He rolled his eyes at himself, realizing how stupid he sounded. "I hate the way the world is, and I thought that you keeping your secret from me was another part of that. Actually I still thought that right up until a minute ago, and then I realized how stupid I was." She raised a curious eyebrow at him and smiled, and his face grew warm. "But the thing is, what I hate about this world is kind of in the same vein as why you have to hide who you really are."

She looked surprised. "Wow, that's quite an intuitive connection you just made." They stood awkwardly silent together for a moment before she asked, "Did that just occur to you as you said it?"

"Yeah," he grinned. "I guess it did."

With a warm smile, she sighed at him. "I guess there's hope for you after all."

Drawing in a deep breath, he chuckled. "Maybe, but I'm pretty damn stubborn, you know." Her smile grew deeper and she nodded emphatically. A day ago, her agreement would have insulted him. Now, however, he forced himself to acknowledge the truth, and promised himself he'd be better.

"We should get back inside," she motioned back towards the capitol building. "Before the Lieutenant sends out a search party."

Motioning for her to precede him, Reis followed her in, and let a wide smile blossom across his face. This was turning into a pretty good trip after all.

Chapter 20

SUFFOCATING SHADOWS

When the villagers said they would prepare an evening meal, Cardin had expected mostly fruits and vegetables, since they reminded him of some of the vegetarian monks on Halarite. The idea of trying another world's greens, or whatever color they might be, terrified and excited him, since he had no idea what fruits to expect from another world.

However, the assumption that everyone on Stella was vegetarian proved false. Spread around the town square were multiple serving tables, many of which bore simple platters of cooked or raw meat. Cardin wondered about the raw meat at first, but then watched as several of the villagers, who looked decidedly carnivorous, chose them over anything else.

Cardin was also relieved to discover that whatever creatures the meat came from, it wasn't the eel-like kaetz. There was something special about them, and it wouldn't have felt right. Rather it looked like the skins of some form of rodent, but the meat was surprisingly sweet and succulent, and cooked to perfection with a hint of a pecan flavor. When he asked, one of the monks confirmed that the they were seasoned with some of the flowers from the fields to the west.

Despite the serving tables, there weren't any dining tables or chairs, and the villagers found places in the grass around the square to enjoy their meals. Cardin, Dalin and Sira sat with Ulpex, who silently devoured his raw meal and allowed them to take in their surroundings, answering cursory questions about their food. Once Endri was certain that they would be safe, the dragon left to hunt for his own dinner.

After everyone finished eating, Cardin, Sira and Dalin roamed the village while Ulpex excused himself. They meant to wander quietly so as not to disturb the monk-like villagers, but every time they came close to someone, he or she would stop what they were doing to greet Cardin and the others.

The village was filled with people of all shapes and sizes, all of them overly friendly and just as curious about Cardin and the others as they were about the villagers. In fact this became somewhat of a hindrance, as everyone was eager to share their life story, how they came to Stella, and in some cases, why they had built their homes the way they had.

They also learned that all of the villagers held a deep respect for Naerala. Most explained that she had guided them better than any mentor they had previously followed on their disparate home worlds, and when Sira asked about Naerala's cryptic nature, most of them chuckled and looked at her as if she were a child struggling to understand basic concepts of nature.

The answer to Sira's question, however, was always the same – Naerala always knew the right thing to say.

After the latest villager excused herself to prepare for the evening, Sira stared after them with a sour face.

"Is it just me, or are the lot of them arrogant," she grumbled.

"Kind of, yeah," Cardin nodded. "They seem to have absolute faith in Naerala, though."

"And thus scoff at the idea of questioning her," Dalin nodded.

"Yeah, well, that sounds dangerous to me," she looked at them, her eyes set with concern. "It sounds like they would blindly follow her anywhere."

Dalin looked at her hesitantly, and corrected, "I do not believe it is blind faith. She has earned their trust and respect, if their various stories are any indication."

"Well she hasn't earned mine," Sira replied curtly. "I'm more apt to trust Ulpex than her at this time, and that's only because he was at least courteous to each of us."

"Either way," Cardin interjected, "she's our best bet at finding Astaria, and..." He hesitated, thinking back to their brief conversation with the village leader. "Maybe more."

Sira looked at him curiously, but then something else caught her eye. They looked towards another small hut near the village's perimeter, and there they caught sight of another monk, this one tending to his garden.

Or rather, he had been tending to his garden, until he saw them. The man was slender, his knees covered in dirt, but his most striking features were pointed ears and blazing red-orange eyes. Though his ears were big enough that they could see them even under his royal blue hood, they couldn't see his hair, but Cardin grew excited when he suspected the man was a Dareann Elf. It was, in a way, a familiar face, or rather a familiar race.

The trio approached him, but unlike all of the other villagers, he shied away from them at first. "We mean you know harm, sir," Cardin raised his hands up. "We were just curious about you."

The man considered Cardin's statement for a moment, but then set his hand spade down and brushed his robes off. "I see. May I help you with something?"

Glancing at the others, Sira was the one to ask the question, "Are you an elf, sir?"

"Indeed I am," he spoke, his voice soft and disarming. "I hail from the world of Ein."

Cardin's eyes opened wide, and he stammered for a second. "Oh, I see. Because of your eyes, I thought you might be a Dareann Elf."

The man hesitated for a moment and looked thoughtfully at Cardin. "You have had dealings with Darea before?"

Cardin grinned and looked to his companions. Sira smiled and answered, "A bit. Granted it was a rocky beginning, but..." She hesitated and exchanged a knowing look with Cardin. "Well, I think we're off to a better start now." Muttering, she added, "I hope."

When Cardin looked back, the elf gave a simple nod with no emotion. "I see. I myself only know of Darea by reputation." He thought for a moment, and then added, "Forgive me, I did not mention my name. I am Pelick."

Cardin gave a curt bow and introduced himself and the others. "I don't suppose you've heard of a world called Halarite," he asked.

Pelick frowned for a moment, but the frown quickly disappeared. "No, that is not a world I have heard of." The monk seemed to consider the name further, and shrugged. "There was a time when I thought I knew every world that existed. My time here has taught me how wrong I was."

An unintentional chuckle escaped Cardin, and he hastily said, "Oh don't worry. Until last year, my people thought that our world was the only inhabited one."

"I see," Pelick nodded thoughtfully. His eyes darted somewhere behind Cardin, and then focused back on Cardin's eyes. "Please forgive me, I must leave your company." He bowed deeply and added, "Enjoy your stay in our village."

After that, Pelick hurried around them, leaving his spade behind and his gardening incomplete. They watched him bustle away, until he walked around one of the many large trees scattered throughout the village and disappeared.

"What an odd sort of fellow," Dalin remarked with a raised eyebrow.

No sooner had Dalin said that then did one of the larger residents, the eight foot tall person they had seen upon first arriving, passed in front of them. The giant smiled and waved awkwardly, and apologized for blocking their view. Sira mumbled, "That seems to be the standard around here."

After their awkward conversation with the elf, the trio continued to explore the village, finding that the buildings throughout seemed to vary in design based on who occupied them or what purpose they served. Most, Cardin noted, had nothing covering their windows, and some even had patios with no wall between them and the interior. He wondered if the temperature in this part of Stella never grew too hot or cold. He also wondered if insects weren't a problem.

When the sun dipped below the horizon, they found their way back to the square. Then, as the sky grew dim, they were treated to a new sight – the leaves of the trees glowed! The entire village was illuminated in their blue-green glow, and as a pleasant surprise, the kaetz ventured further away from the trees, and they, too glowed brightly.

Even more shocking was when several other creatures emerged from the foliage surrounding the village. Small and fox-like, they had dark-grey fur except for glowing red-tipped tails and ears, and they wandered about the village like it was their home.

The villagers took no notice of this, but now that evening had come, most of the residents gathered in the square again. Three villagers that Cardin had not noticed before came along carrying large bundles of wood, and set about making fires in stone fire pits around the square.

Cardin and the others approached one of the first fires lit, unsure if they were intruding or not, but the villagers welcomed them and encouraged them to join in around the fire.

Dalin sat by himself cross-legged, as he often did when they were out in the field. Cardin pulled the Sword's scabbard off and set it on the ground before he and Sira sat and snuggled up against one another. The trio stared absently into the fire for a long time, watching as a villager tended to it and added another quarter of a log.

At some point, Ulpex sat down beside them and drew his legs up against his chest. Cardin glanced at their host, and tried not to stare at his legs, which were structured more like a canine's than a human's. *Don't stare,* he lectured himself.

"This is a beautiful world," Sira remarked, her eyes drawn to the crystal again. It pulsed softly with light, and Cardin could hear a soft hum coming from it, one which echoed through magic.

"Indeed it is," Ulpex replied. "I have lived here for many years now, but I never take it for granted." One of the fox-like creatures approached Ulpex and sniffed at his hand. After a moment, it nuzzled his palm, and then curled up next to him. Ulpex smiled warmly, and he looked at Cardin. "For many obvious reasons."

Nodding, Cardin reached for Sira's hand, and then looked at her, but her eyes were still focused on the crystal. "Hey," he nudged her, frowning. When she didn't reply, he prodded again. "Sira?"

That seemed to snap her out of it, and she looked at him suddenly as if he hadn't been there a moment ago. "Uh, what," she uttered. "Sorry. I…" Glancing again at the crystal, she shook her head.

"What's going on," he asked. "Why are you so fixated on that?"

"I'm not sure," she replied, her tone distant. "It's like something inside of it is drawing me in."

"That crystal," Ulpex supplied, "is why we are all here." Cardin had suspected as much earlier, and was glad to have his suspicions confirmed.

With a curious frown on her face, Sira asked, "What do you

mean?"

Absently, their host reached down and stroked the fox's mane while he explained, "We all come from different worlds, but we were all drawn here inexplicably." The story was familiar to them, but they settled in to listen to Ulpex's version. "Mind you, getting here was not easy for everyone, since not everyone here can make portals on their own. But the journey always leads to this world, to that crystal. It calls to us, in our dreams, in waking moments. Actually," he hesitated and glanced at Sira. "I am somewhat surprised by how strongly you have connected with it, Sira. My assumption was that you came here with the others to find the dragon, not the crystal."

Sira nodded. "That's right. I don't remember ever dreaming about it, or about this world. Those kinds of dreams were usually Cardin's thing." He smiled, remembering his childhood dreams of the dragon that would one day be his avatar. "Yet, there's something about it…"

When she didn't speak further, Cardin asked, "What is it, exactly?"

With an ironic smile, Ulpex replied, "I believe only Naerala knows the answer to that question. Unfortunately, she never tells us. She simply leads us through meditation and helps us to understand ourselves and the Universe. It is up to each of us to discover the truth of the crystal."

Drawing in a deep breath and adjusting his posture, Ulpex continued, "What I can tell you is that it seems to be a conduit for the power of the stars." That didn't clear up anything for Cardin, and the look on his face must have told Ulpex as much. "I mean, literally. I know that you can see and feel it for yourself. It endlessly draws in power, and yet power never flows out of it, so it must be a conduit to…something. Or somewhere. I honestly do not know."

Thinking of how the conflicting dark and light magic inside of him felt, Cardin asked, "Perhaps it is to a void?"

Ulpex shook his head. "No, that would imply dark magic, and it most certainly is not. In fact, you, Cardin, are quite an anomaly here."

Cardin's face grew warm and he shifted uncomfortably. "What do you mean?"

It was Naerala who answered from behind Cardin. "Dark magic has never been present upon this world before today." Approaching from the monastery with silent footsteps, her voice startled them.

She walked up beside the others, but did not sit down. Cardin asked, "Is that unusual? I didn't think dark magic was common anywhere."

After considering his question, she eased down and sat on her heels. "Star magic and dark magic are two sides of a coin, if you will forgive the parlance. Star magic derives its name from the source of its power, the stars themselves. It is also the reason for the name of Star Dragons, as they are beings of pure star magic.

"Dark magic," she continued, "is quite literally the opposite. It is absence. It comes from the space between the stars. I suspect that just as all of us here were born bathed in the magic of the stars, there are beings born in darkness and thrive in dark magic."

She looked at Cardin thoughtfully, her eyes focused on him, and it seemed as if she intentionally avoided looking at the Sword of Dragons. "The Universe is a natural balance between the two, but they always exist separate from one another. For light and darkness to coexist within a single entity is difficult to understand. By their very nature, they should cancel one another out, and you should be powerless. Yet I sense that this is not so."

Cardin blushed, memories of his recent failures racing through his mind, and he glanced at Sira and Dalin, both of whom listened intently. "Actually, sometimes that's exactly what happens," he admitted. "Every time I think I've crossed a threshold with my powers, dark magic asserts itself, and I'm suddenly powerless." He winced at the memory of breaking bones.

Naerala winced as well, and he wondered if she'd somehow felt his pain. For a long time, Cardin stared into the fire, lost in the dancing flames, while Naerala and the others remained quiet. He wondered about those flames, and reached out with his essence to feel the point of energy. It wasn't magic, but he could still feel it.

In his mind, he tried to imagine what it was like beyond the reach of the stars, way out in the void between them. Was there a dark equivalent to fire? Or did nothing work the same out there? Somehow there was power in dark magic, Nuuldan had proven that.

If it hadn't been for the Navitas, the Dark Dragon would have destroyed Cardin, taken the Sword, and probably killed everyone in Maradin out of spite. Those beings of light had sacrificed so many to stop Nuuldan, to protect Halarite, and it had given Cardin precious moments to figure out how to fight back.

He remembered the sensation of the blast hitting his shield, and how he felt as if every bit of magic and warmth had been drained out of him.

Shuddering, he closed his eyes and pictured Nuuldan, whose red eyes pierced into him like ice cold daggers. And then he felt the cold within his soul. The darkness took hold again, and his heart leapt in terror. *No!*

In an instant, he pushed away the power, and just like it always did, his connection to star magic was broken. He couldn't feel the fire, nor Sira or Naerala. The Universe was gone.

Somewhere in the distance of his mind, he heard a voice, *"Breathe! You must breathe! Let the magic flow back into you like air, let it bring you back from the brink!"*

His chest burned, and he realized he had actually stopped breathing! Gasping for air, he fell backwards awkwardly, barely catching himself on his elbows before slamming his head onto the ground. Naerala stood over him, her eyes gazing into his, and he felt for just a moment the warmth of her soul reaching out to him.

She retracted, but his connection to star magic remained, and he gasped for air. Sira held on to him, trying to keep him from falling completely over. The worry on her face was heart wrenching.

Clasping her hands behind her back, Naerala nodded. "It happened again."

Cardin pulled himself back up into a sitting posture with Sira's help, and he drew in a deep breath in an effort to settle his nerves. "Yeah, I…I don't know how or why."

Endri must have sensed his sudden disappearance, since the dragon's voice suddenly filled his head, *"Cardin! Are you okay?"*

Clenching his eyes shut, he sent a reassuring mental nod to the distant emerald dragon, and promised to explain whenever Endri returned. It didn't occur to him until much later that it was the first time that he had successfully communicated mentally, and yet he had done so as casually as if he had spoken directly to the emerald dragon.

Suddenly Cardin felt very self-aware when he realized the eyes of every villager were on him.

He looked at Sira questioningly. "You disappeared from magic," she explained uneasily. "Where you sat was an emptiness that felt so cold, so…"

"Even Nuuldan did not feel so empty," Dalin added, his face also scrunched up in worry. "Never in my life have I seen or felt something like that."

Easing back on her haunches again, Naerala looked at Cardin curiously. "Tell me exactly what happened."

Cardin shook his head, trying to clear his mind and recall what had led up to that moment of terror, but also afraid that it would happen again if he thought too much about it. "I...don't know. I mean, I was thinking about Nuuldan, and what it felt like to fight him. Suddenly I felt the darkness again. And then nothing."

Naerala's eyes grew narrow, and she shook her head. "There is something else that you are not telling us."

Shaking his head adamantly, he replied, "No! Not that I can think of."

He stared at the old woman, searching her surprisingly bright eyes for answers. Was he forgetting something? Did he cause it to happen? Had he failed to keep the darkness back?

Then, she asked a more specific question. "How did *you* feel?"

"Terrified," he replied without thinking. "I was afraid of becoming like Nuuldan." His voice shook when he added, "I'm still afraid that'll happen."

With a thoughtful nod, Naerala turned and stared into the fire. It seemed to flare at her gaze, and Cardin likewise stared into it. Sira drew closer to him and wrapped her arms around him, her head easing onto his shoulder and nuzzling the crook of his neck. He realized he was very cold after that experience, and her warmth was a welcome reprieve.

After a long time of silence, Naerala spoke again, "You are not a Star Dragon, Cardin Kataar." He looked at Naerala, but her gaze remained on the fire. "Star Dragons are beings of pure star magic. Touching the darkness infects them. It takes them over, closing in around the light within and cutting them off from the very essence of their being. It drives them to insanity."

Finally, she looked directly into his eyes to drive home her next words. "However, dark magic is not evil. It, by itself, cannot turn a human to evil. Your magic does not define you."

With that statement, Naerala stood up and bowed to them, before she retreated into the village.

Cardin thought about what she said, his eyes turning back to the fire. The logs collapsed and sent up a flurry of sparks, and he followed one with his eyes until its glow died out.

If magic didn't define them, then what did?

Chapter 21

SUCCESSION

The pieces were set.

Prince Idrill Beredis thought of that line, an old saying from a game that he never had the patience for. Something about positioning your pieces, manipulating the other side's pieces to where you wanted them to be, and then executing a swift and decisive strike.

He was a man with more patience than most realized. It had served him well, up until that blasted Wizard had shown up in his throne room. Ever since that day, all of his plans were ruined.

This time, however, a god was on his side.

With practiced patience, he walked along side his father through the castle corridors, their destination the front gates, where a crowd had gathered. That was how Draegus Kataar, who walked ahead of them, had described it, just a crowd demanding to speak to the King.

But when they entered the castle antechamber, it was clear that it was more than just a crowd. Angered shouts stabbed into the castle, and they grew louder the moment he and the King came into view. Not anger towards him, but specifically towards his father.

At the man that, as far as they were concerned, had brought them to ruin. All because word had slipped out that the castle coffers were practically empty, and that all of the letters of mark that Tal had issued in the past year were worthless.

It wasn't the only thing they were angry about. They had so many reasons to fear and hate, thanks largely to the catastrophes that his father had led the kingdom to. Allowing the elves and dwarf back into the city, back into the catacombs and the ruins deep underground was almost enough to incense another riot, but he and Zairel knew that more was needed. That was why Idrill had let it slip to castle servants how empty their gold reserves were.

The Prince smiled at his own cleverness.

As they stepped out onto the terrace, Idrill was impressed. Through careful manipulation, messages, and payments, he had ensured that the gates to the upper city would not be closed too quickly, and a crowd of forty or fifty angry peasants filled the courtyard. The castle guards had quickly summoned reinforcements, and a line of soldiers now stood between them and the mob.

Draegus took three steps down from the terrace and then stopped, while Idrill and his father remained at the top of the stairs. The King raised his arms for silence, but when the inane shouts and demands did not stop, he used his powerful voice. "Silence!"

The tone and how he stretched the word usually worked in his favor, but this time, the mob's anger was beyond reasoning. They did not quiet down, but rather Idrill swore their rage grew stronger. He noted a few more of them marching towards the castle, scattered in a line with rage fueling their quick pace.

Idrill scanned the crowd for a familiar hooded figure, wondering if Zairel was among them. While the god had agreed that Idrill's plan would help, he insisted that the only real way to achieve their goal today was that he would use his powers to influence the thoughts and emotions of everyone in Tal. Zairel claimed that his power of persuasion was unparalleled, and at the moment, the Prince believed him.

There was no sign of the god, which relieved the Prince. His presence out here was not part of the plan.

The mob's anger was palpable, and while Idrill had no magic sense, he could feel it in the air, an oppressive closeness that made him glad that none of it was directed towards him.

He hoped.

The crowd surged, and from somewhere in the middle, a rock sailed towards the King. It missed, and the King foolishly did not try to duck, but the attack elicited a cheer from the mass, and another rock was let loose.

Fearing his own safety, the Prince backed away from his father, who finally ducked. However, this time Draegus had stepped back up the steps and used magic to shield him.

"You're Majesty, get back," Draegus ordered. "You're not safe, you must go inside!"

Defiant, the King demanded of the mob, "What do you think you are doing?" But even his voice was lost in the mass of shouts. More rocks flew towards them, bouncing harmlessly off of Draegus's shield or missing entirely, one nearly hitting Idrill's shin. Realizing that he could easily become collateral damage, he retreated through the castle doors, and there awaited his father.

Wouldn't it be ironic if an errant stone killed the King now?

But no, that was not the plan.

Realizing that words would not calm the crowd, the King finally retreated inside. Draegus stopped at the door and glanced back, watching as a rock pelted the steel helmet of one of the other guards. That guard drew his sword and shouted a threat into the crowd.

The King's eyes grew wide, and he grasped Draegus's shoulder firmly. "You must take control, Captain! Make sure your soldiers do not resort to violence unless absolutely necessary."

The worry in the guard Captain's eyes might have been enough to reach his father's heart, but Idrill smiled. They had planned for Draegus to be in the throne room, but this would be even better.

After considering the King's orders, Draegus let out a frustrated sigh. "As you command. Get to safety, Sire, we'll try to disperse them." Then he looked at two castle guards who came racing through the halls. "Get these doors sealed," he ordered, "and get reinforcements out here!"

Just then, the mob somehow broke through the line of guards and rushed the castle. The two guards that had just joined them immediately pushed the heavy wooden doors closed, and rushed to settle the bar in place. Draegus remained outside, and Idrill swore he heard the sickening thud of people running madly into a magic shield.

Zairel's influence was, indeed, effective.

"By the gods," the King turned away from the door, his eyes staring in horror at Idrill. "What in hellfire are they thinking?"

Raising an eyebrow, the Prince replied, "They aren't, Father."

His father's jaw clenched, and he looked down. "I did not believe that our own people were this far gone. I knew there was unrest, but..."

Draegus must have moved away from the door, allowing heavy rocks to thud against it.

The guards looked to one another, and then at the King. "Your Majesty, you must get to safety!"

Seizing the opportunity, the Prince looked at his father and said, "We'll lock ourselves in the throne room." It was the safest place in the castle, once serving as the mead hall where all would come to find safety, long before the rest of the castle was built.

His father looked at him hesitantly, but then nodded appreciatively. "That may be the wisest course of action." Looking to the guards, he nodded, "Go find reinforcements. Do what you must to settle the mob, but I do not want this to turn into a slaughter! Is that understood?"

"Yes, your majesty," one of the guards nodded, and then the two ran down a side corridor.

Raising his hand up to hover just next to his father's shoulder, Idrill motioned towards the double-doors leading into the throne room. "Come, father, we must hurry." His urgency was punctuated by another rock banging against the outer doors.

The King preceded him into the throne room, the sunlight casting sharp beams and creating deep, contrasting shadows. Idrill closed the doors behind them, but neglected to lower the bar down to secure them. He knew that the mob would not make it inside, not in time anyway, and he needed the door unlocked.

His father absently ambled towards the stairs leading up to the throne, shaking his head and muttering. "In all of my reign, the people have never acted this way. I do not understand their hatred. How did it come to this?"

Glancing into the shadows between the stone statues bordering the carpet, the Prince sought any sign of Zairel, hoping that the god would not leave him high and dry. He knew that his actions today were part of a test, but that didn't change his anxiousness, nor dull his excitement.

Walking only half as quickly as his father, he followed towards the throne, until the King stopped at the foot of the steps leading up to the royal chair, and Idrill stopped halfway, between the statues of

King Malgar and Queen Ameila. He eyed Ameila's figure, thinking back to her mother, Amaru. That was considered a dark chapter in Tal's history, but Idrill had always secretly admired Amaru, whose iron rule had given Tal decades of peace.

Except that she had failed to bring the kingdom in line. She had been ruthless, but hadn't foreseen her own daughter betraying her.

Turning back to his father, Idrill saw that he still idly muttered to himself, having half-turned towards his son.

"We stand upon a precipice, my son," he continued. "I fear for our future. If even one more catastrophe befalls us, one more war, it may end Tal."

"Perhaps you are right, Father," Idrill offered. "Perhaps we stand upon a precipice. But it is one that you have brought us to."

His father's mutterings ceased, and he gaped at Idrill. "What did you say?"

Raising his eyebrows, the Prince sauntered towards his father, his hands casually clasped behind his back. "How can you truly be surprised, Father?" He spoke the word 'father' with exaggerated disdain. "We have acted against the will of the Covenant, against the will of the gods, numerous times this past year."

The King scoffed. "Do not presume to know what the gods would think, Idrill. You were here for every moment of the past year, and you know why every decision was made."

"Yes, and who made those decisions, father?"

Turning fully towards Idrill, the King placed his hands on his hips and glared. "I did."

"And look where that has brought us to," he spat back. "A godless man carries the most powerful weapon in the Universe, a great cataclysm befell us, the dead rose, and a great darkness threatens us all."

"Cardin Kataar is one of the most honorable persons I have ever known," the King declared, his voice raised in a commanding tone. "And what do you suppose would have happened had we not allowed him to take up the Sword? Do you believe those other disasters would not have found their way here?"

"We are being punished, Father!" He flailed his hands out, his anger threatening to overcome his senses. "Our entire world is coming to ruin because of your godlessness!"

"That is enough!" The King's voice echoed, and it stirred just a moment's fear within Idrill. The same fear his father had always induced in him.

With a clenched jaw, Idrill thought, *not this time.*

Stopping a dozen feet from his father, he planted his hands on his hips, realizing only a moment too late that he mirrored the King's stance. "Do you admit to your sins or not?"

Staring at Idrill incredulously, the King scoffed. "Do you presume to judge me, S*on*?"

"I am judging you, Father," he spat out. Idrill noticed then that an orange glow had drawn up behind the throne, and he knew that the moment was at hand. "However, I am not the only one who judges you to be unfit."

The glow grew bright enough to attract the King's attention, and he turned just in time to see Zairel come into view, escorted by the new Warrior General, Idann.

Making Idrill's initial mistake, the King immediately recognized whom Zairel's body belonged to. "Pevrin?"

"No, Father," Idrill spat. "This is our god, Zairel."

At first, his father scoffed, but there was no denying the sight of Zairel's glowing eyes and glowing body, the orange light obscuring the Covenant robes that the god wore.

"Your son is correct," Zairel spoke, the inhuman quality unnerving. Even now, after weeks of working with the god, it made Idrill shiver. "I am Zairel. And you have failed your people."

"Impossible..." The King tried to back away, but the Prince placed firm hands upon his father's shoulders. It was the first time in years that he had physically touched his father of his own accord.

"Your son gave you a chance," Zairel continued, "but you squandered that chance. Now you will suffer the consequences."

Idrill didn't know what to expect. So far he had only seen superfluous shows of power from the god in the form of portals and the power to lift himself from the ground. Now, he saw the first taste of the god's raw power.

The orange glow extended from Zairel's body, and engulfed the King. Idrill backed away, having caught just a momentary taste of the power, of the cold emptiness where he thought light would be. This was not a light of life, he realized.

The King screamed a long, terrible cry of immeasurable pain. His body rose from the floor, his arms splayed out and his legs drawn up.

Even through closed doors, Idrill knew that others would have heard that scream. That meant that soon enough, everyone would know the truth.

The shriek died, the light receded, and the King dropped to the ground like a weighted sack, his limbs flailing about as he settled onto the stone and the red carpet. Immediately the Prince could smell a wretched stench, like that of a body long-dead and left to rot, and he knew it was over.

King Beredis was dead.

The front doors flew open, permitting Draegus and several guards to rush in. The sight of their king's corpse stopped them cold, as it did the crowd following behind them. They must have abandoned their efforts to hold back the mob, Idrill realized, and came as fast as they could to save their King.

Admirable, but ultimately useless.

The guards had all drawn their swords, and slowly, Draegus approached, his Warrior's sword lowering impotently. "My...my King. My Lord!" He raised his voice and rushed forward, but at that moment, Zairel's glow flared again, and Draegus noticed him for the first time, stopping several feet from the King's body. "What have you done?!" He raised his sword.

With the flick of his hand, Zairel sent the Guardian's weapon away, to shatter against one of the stone statues. "Do not threaten your god," Zairel spoke, his voice inhumanly loud.

"This is Zairel," the Prince explained, stepping squarely in the center of the carpet between everyone else and his father's body. "The last of the Six. He has come to save us all from evil."

Idrill watched with delight as the realization and accompanying rage drew up within the Guardian. "You," Draegus spat venomously. "You arranged this."

"It was my will," Zairel stated simply, allowing the inhuman quality to remain in his voice. "Your King led you astray. Now it is time for another, more worthy man to take his place." Idrill felt his chest swell with pride. Raising his head, he looked down upon everyone else.

"I suggest you reconsider your words and actions," Idrill stated. "For the King is dead."

None in the crowd said or did anything, but he saw Draegus's clenched fists. He wanted to suggest that Zairel destroy Draegus, but he knew that would be a mistake. For now, anyway.

When no one said anything, Idrill said it louder. "The King is dead!"

There was a flare of light from behind him, and a sudden wind blew through the throne room. Idrill knew what that meant, and pictured Zairel rising up off of the ground.

From behind Draegus, one of the guards finally replied, "Long live the King!" And they all knelt, even the former angry mob. All except Draegus.

Raising his eyebrows, Idrill glowered at the Guardian. Draegus looked at his shattered sword, and then at Zairel. Finally, with his jaw taut, he knelt and bowed his head. "Long live the King…"

Turning to Idann, who still stood beside Zairel, his hand on the hilt of his sword in case anyone tried to assault the god, Idrill nodded. Idann glanced at the mob for a moment, and then approached the King's body and retrieved the silver crown that had fallen off of the withered head. The General gagged at the smell and quickly stood back up before he walked over the King's body.

Idrill drew the smaller silver crown from his own head and tossed it aside in disgust. Then, with deliberate and ceremonious slowness, Idann raised the crown up above Idrill's head, and slowly lowered it down.

The moment it touched Idrill's head, he felt a thrill vibrate through his body. It was finally his. Tal was finally his.

Turning back to the crowd, he saw them staring at him. He wished it was in awe or with respect, but he knew that would come later. For now, they stared in fear. Fear of their god, and fear of the consequences if they rebelled.

Except for Draegus. He looked at Idrill with murderous determination.

In that moment, Idrill smiled. Draegus would be his challenge. He would force the man to capitulate and honor Idrill as King, rather than kill him uselessly. So that when Cardin Kataar returned, he would face his father as protector of Idrill and Zairel, and would be forced to either go through him, or surrender the Sword of Dragons willingly.

It was perfect.

Chapter 22

THE MORNING AFTER

The night of Mayor Warreck Evern's arrest was a night to remember for Kailar. Unfortunately, she didn't remember much. With the deepest level of corruption finally rooted out of Devor, it was a turning point for them all.

No more slaves from Edilas. No more illegal tolls or protection fees. And the Warriors no longer had to fear losing funding.

So naturally, loads of silver and gold were spent at the Inn at Water's Edge, on food and, more importantly, on ale. And from what she could remember as she edged out of her deep sleep, innkeeper Alric was grateful for the business, despite whatever damage may have been incurred.

The moment Kailar drew in a deep breath, she became very aware of two uncomfortable situations. The first was the alarming headache that pounded at her and the buzz she felt in her mind. The second was the weight and warmth of another human against her body.

Her eyes shot open to a mess of red hair. She relaxed then, thanking the gods, whether they existed or not, that it was at least Letan. He faced away from her, scrunched up against the wall that her bed, usually meant for just one person, was nestled against, while she lay on her back, her left arm hanging down from under the covers.

It was Letan. After all of the times they were intimate, they had finally slept together. She expected to feel uncomfortable or panicked at his presence, but she felt neither.

Maybe yesterday had been more of a turning point than she realized. It wasn't so much that Councilwoman Reyla had told her she was a part of Devor now, and that it was her home, but rather it was that Kailar truly felt it.

It should have terrified her. Six months ago or earlier and it would have. Why not now? What had changed?

Idly, she caressed Letan's arm, tracing one of his many scars. For a man who hadn't seen much combat, his torso bore an unusual number of them, but he never spoke about it. As she traced the scar, she wished she could remember last night. Maybe if she hadn't been so drunk, she might have kicked him out again, but still, she wished she could remember it.

He stirred at her touch, and carefully turned his body towards her, his smile mixed with surprise. "Well, then," he whispered, his blazing blue eyes wide open, easily visible in the glow that shone through the drapes. Then he looked around the room, and an ironic grin crossed his face. "Of all the places we would finally stay together, we had to choose the room with the smaller bed."

She laughed at his remark, realizing the irony herself for a change. As an officer, his quarters, though just next door, were larger and had a bigger bed.

"Somehow I don't think either of us cared where we ended up," she replied softly, caressing his other arm now that it was near her. He pushed his left arm under her head and drew her closer into a kiss.

But morning breath was a thing, especially after a night of drinking, and neither of them held the kiss very long. He coughed a little, and she swallowed hard. "I think we both need water."

Closing his eyes for a moment, he nodded. "But that means getting out of bed."

"Maybe we could con a new recruit into being our servant next time," she suggested, already pushing the blanket off completely to stand up.

Only to stop cold when there was a knock at her door.

They frowned and glanced at one another, and then she glanced towards the draped window again, wondering just how late in the day it was.

She pulled the blanket off of Letan, eliciting a surprised protest. Wrapping it around herself, she walked towards the door, while Letan, in a panic, sat up and quickly grabbed a pillow to cover himself. She glanced at him once to make sure he was covered, and then cracked the door open.

Half-expecting Commander Querlin, she was surprised to instead find Councilwoman Reyla standing at her door, a young Warrior standing to the side as escort.

"Councilwoman," Kailar said with a start. "What can I do for you?"

Then she realized that Reyla wasn't in her usual, simple clothing, but rather she wore travel trousers and a warm overcoat. "I apologize for disturbing you," Reyla glanced through the crack at Kailar's blanket. "I thought you would be awake by now."

Feeling herself blush, Kailar replied, "It's okay. We, uh, had a long night of celebration."

A warm smile crossed Reyla's face. "That is understandable. However, if you would be kind enough, I thought I would take you up on your offer to help communicate with all of the towns and cities on Devor."

With the hammer still pounding on the anvil in her head, Kailar frowned and asked, "Today? So soon? I mean, I meant what I said, but I thought you would want to...I don't know. Discuss it further with the other councilors or something."

Reyla grinned and shook her head. "The Warriors were not the only ones to stay up late last night. However, the Councilors and I spent most of our time discussing our future. Until we realized that if that future were to include all of Devor, the other mayors should be involved from the beginning." She shrugged easily and added, "Do not worry, though. There's only two other large towns that necessitated a mayor, so our trip today will be short and productive."

Grimacing and glancing behind her, Kailar sighed and nodded. "I suppose it's better to move quickly. It'll take me a few minutes to get dressed, if you'll permit me."

"Of course," she smiled and nodded. "If you wish, I could wake up the Lieutenant and ask him to accompany us as well. I understand his room is just next door."

With her face again turning pink, she motioned her head towards the bed, still out of Reyla's line of sight, she hoped. "Um, there's no need for that."

At some point, Letan had found his trousers and had put them on, and suddenly was beside Kailar. "I'll be ready to go when Kailar is," he looked over her head at Reyla.

"Oh, I see," Reyla's eyes opened wide, and her cheeks turned a shade of pink. "I'm so sorry to have disturbed you."

Kailar and Letan exchanged amused looks, and Kailar smiled at Reyla. "It's alright, Councilwoman. We're still Warriors, after all."

She felt startled by her own words. In all her time working with Letan, Kailar had never actually identified herself as a Warrior. What in the name of the Six was happening to her?

"I see," Reyla hesitated. "If you're sure..."

"We're sure," Letan insisted. "We just need a few minutes to get cleaned up. We'll meet you soon. If you'll excuse us." He pushed on the door, and Kailar let him close it. They turned to each other, and then snickered quietly, before they both rubbed their heads, her hangover suddenly a bigger nuisance than before.

It was going to be a long day.

Chapter 23

PARTING PATHS

When Dalin awoke the next morning, it was to a catch in his neck and a sore back. The beds that their hosts had graciously allowed them to use were rock hard and lumpy, and his experience last night was just barely better than sleeping on the ground.

One of the three larger buildings in the center acted as an inn for the village, though the accommodations were definitely only meant to be temporary. When Ulpex had shown them to the community structure, essentially a large, shared bedroom with over a dozen beds, he told them that newcomers were always welcomed to the village, but were encouraged to make a home of their own as quickly as possible, if they decided to stay.

Much to Sira and Cardin's chagrin, all of the beds were singles, and they hadn't felt quite right asking Ulpex if they could move two of the beds together. As such, when they awoke, the first thing they did was embrace one another, while Dalin sat on the edge of his bed and worked the kinks out of his back and neck.

It's better than sleeping outside, he reminded himself.

When he finally stood up, his back popped in five places and he felt instant relief. Sira and Cardin cringed at him sympathetically.

"I wish my back would do that," Cardin grimaced.

As if on cue, Ulpex entered from the open entrance carrying a wooden tray with three goblets. Raising an eyebrow, Dalin wondered if their water was fresh enough to safely drink or not. The party had brought their own water skins along, but they were already in need of refilling.

Following behind Ulpex came Naerala, her hands clasped together in front of her, concealed by her long sleeves. She had a thoughtful look on her face, and power radiated from her core, though somehow it felt guarded today.

"Good morning," Ulpex spoke quietly, his voice giving away no hint of early morning sleepiness. "This is for all of you." When Dalin eyed the goblets curiously, Ulpex assured them, "It is clean and drinkable water, from a nearby stream."

Dalin gingerly picked up the closest goblet, but Cardin and Sira showed no hesitance and gulped theirs down. Inwardly sighing, Dalin wished he had learned how to summon his own water, and took a drink. Surprisingly, it tasted as fresh and clean as Ulpex had promised.

Additionally, he felt a tingle that could only have come from a magical enchantment. His first instinct was to inspect the enchantment to determine what it was, but he quickly realized that was unnecessary, since it sent a cool swell of energy into his body, reviving him and making him feel instantly awake. When he looked at Ulpex, the wolf-like man gave Dalin his equivalent of a friendly smile.

Once they were finished and had placed the goblets back on the tray, Ulpex stepped back beside Naerala, who scrunched her face into a concerned frown. "I have thought much about what happened last night," she addressed Cardin. "I believe it would be better if Sira and Dalin remained behind."

Dalin started to protest, but Sira beat him to it, "You can't be serious!"

"I am afraid that I am, Sira," she replied evenly. "The task for which I require Cardin's help is great, and will certainly test his abilities and fortitude."

"I do not believe you understand," Dalin interjected. "We have all sworn an oath to help Cardin, an oath we cannot renege upon. If this task is too great for him…"

"That is why Endri shall accompany us," Naerala interrupted him.

Dalin clenched his jaw in annoyance. "He and I spoke at length this morning, and he agrees. I understand that you both care for him and wish to help and protect him, but ultimately this is a journey that he must make alone." She turned her attention to Cardin and nodded. "You know this just as well as I do."

Cardin opened his mouth to say something, but then released his breath and nodded. "Maybe you're right."

Sira shook her head adamantly, her eyes fixed on Cardin. "I didn't come all this way just to stay behind when it mattered most," she insisted. "I'm not going to just sit around here feeling useless!"

"I understand your feelings in this matter," Naerala began.

"No, I don't think you do," Sira retorted with a scowl. "You can't understand. We made a promise, to him and to each other."

Naerala raised her hands up defensively. "I know, Endri has told me as much."

Dalin raised his chin up and stated, "Then you know that we must accompany you."

"Please," Naerala insisted. "I spent a great deal in meditation on this last night, and if you will but listen to me, I have other reasons to ask you both to stay behind."

Sira and Dalin glanced to one another, and then they looked to Cardin. Rather than flustered or annoyed, he looked at Naerala curiously. "What reasons might those be," he asked.

"Your destinies are tied to this village," the elder woman replied evenly, surprisingly patient. "I have never been so skilled in seeing the future as to know exactly how or why, but I know that there is some vital reason for you to stay behind." Her tone took on a steel edge, and her eyes set hard on Sira in particular. "I know that your fate in particular, Sira, is tied to the crystal's."

That stopped Sira short of a response. She looked down then, her eyes suddenly distant. Turning towards the center of the village, even though they could not see the crystal from within the building, she drew in a deep breath.

Dalin watched Naerala carefully, then, and noticed a peculiar look of fear and annoyance upon her face. The look she gave Sira was one of fear and even anger. He wondered if Naerala was somehow jealous of Sira's connection to the crystal, but then he rejected that notion. What little he had learned of Naerala, that didn't seem to fit her personality.

Then he realized what it was. Naerala was protective of the crystal. It meant more to her than Dalin had previously realized. And that, he deduced, was why Naerala was somewhat short and cryptic towards Sira.

The elder woman then turned to Dalin and nodded. "I also believe that you are meant to stay with Sira for the same reason she is meant to remain in the village. However, Endri has told me that you wish to find an appropriate wood to become a new focusing staff, which I understand all Wizards carry."

Dalin raised a curious eyebrow, wondering if Endri had told her that last part as well. "That is true," he nodded. "I have a focusing stone, but I have not yet fused it with a staff."

Ulpex spoke up next, "There is a wooded forest nearby. I can take you there today to find something appropriate."

Dalin's interest was piqued, and he couldn't help but smile. "I would like that very much

Sira looked at Cardin then, her eyes searching his. Dalin felt his heart go out to both of them, recalling how excited they were to go on another adventure together. Now that adventure would force them to part ways.

"It'll be alright," Cardin reached out and gently caressed her cheek. "Endri will look after me, and I know that you are more than capable of taking care of yourself." Smirking, he nodded towards Dalin, "Besides, someone has to stay here and keep him out of trouble."

Dalin raised an eyebrow and chuckled. "Indeed. You know how we Wizards enjoy making a ruckus."

A laugh escaped Sira and she looked down, her cheeks flushing. "Alright," she assented, looking again towards the crystal before she looked into Cardin's eyes again. "But you be careful, you hear?" Pulling him into a warm embrace, she squeezed tightly. "You come back to me."

"I will," he promised. "And whatever happens with that crystal, watch your backs." When they pulled away from each other, he cusped her cheeks in his hands and looked intently at her. "I don't know what it is, but I don't feel like it's dangerous. That doesn't mean there isn't some other danger surrounding it."

A fair point, Dalin realized. Maybe that's what Naerala saw in her meditations last night. The Wizard looked at their host, who stood by patiently, allowing them to give their goodbyes. Suddenly he worried for his friend, and sought a reason for Cardin to stay longer. "Perhaps a morning meal before you go," he suggested.

Cardin looked at Dalin with a frown, and the Wizard knew immediately that his suggestion would be rejected. They had bread and dried meat to eat along the way, and he sensed an urgent desire from Cardin.

"I think it would be best if we leave immediately," Naerala voiced her opinion. "The journey is long, and it will be dark by the time we arrive at the copse if we depart now."

"So we can expect you to be back by tomorrow evening," Sira inferred.

Smiling patiently at her, Naerala nodded. "If all goes well, yes." She again turned to Cardin, and asked, "Are you prepared to depart, young one?"

Cardin returned to his bed to grab his travel pack, and once that was secure on his back, he nodded. "I am now."

Together, the trio followed Naerala and Ulpex outside. Endri barely fit on one side of the square, having returned sometime during the night, Dalin reasoned, after they had all turned in. The dragon greeted them and asked, *"I assume Naerala has explained our agreement?"*

Everyone nodded. Cardin asked, "Are you ready?"

"Of course. I will meet you on the eastern end of the village." Endri drew down into a crouch, and then leapt into the air to fly over the village.

When the dragon was out of sight, Cardin and Sira exchanged another goodbye hug and kiss. Then, Cardin turned to Dalin and extended a hand. Dalin accepted it and shook it firmly. "Good journey to you, my friend. We will be here when you return."

Cardin smiled warmly. "I know you will. Take care of each other."

With that, he joined Naerala, and together they headed out of town.

Dalin and Sira watched them go, and oddly enough, Dalin felt a knot in his stomach untwist for just a moment, one which he hadn't realized was there before. There was a slight pulse of energy from Naerala, a moment where she let down her guard just long enough for Dalin to get a better sense of her powers. Somehow, the core within her magic soothed his nerves.

Once they were out of sight, Dalin sighed and turned back

towards Sira and Ulpex, only to find that Ulpex had disappeared. The Wizard frowned and searched for the wolfman, only to find him hurrying back out from one of the other large buildings in the square, the tray having been discarded.

"Forgive me," he bowed. "Unlike our evening meal, in the morning, we each generally keep to ourselves to allow self-reflection. As such, I have already eaten. However, you are welcome in my home. I do not usually cook my breakfast, but perhaps a nice steak for your meal?"

Dalin and Sira exchanged glances. It was certainly not a normal breakfast, but it might allow them a chance to get to know their host a little better. Dalin was anxious to head into the forest to make himself a staff, but another hour or two wouldn't hurt. His stomach grumbled its vote, and he nodded. "If you wish," he said to Sira.

"Alright," she smiled. "Just a light breakfast, though."

"As you wish," Ulpex bowed. "Please follow me."

Their host's home was towards the south edge of the village, and turned out to be a very simple hut, even compared to some of the others.

It was made of the same kind of wood that Dalin noticed they had burned in the fires last night, as were many of the houses, and he realized that the forest must be very close for such casual usage.

Inside, the hut was a single room with a small table and two chairs, and a small bed that lacked any sort of covers or pillows. Dalin regarded the bed for a moment, curious about the lack of coverings, but then realized that the wolf's fur probably kept him warm, not to mention that the region's climate seemed relatively mild.

At the back of the hut was a fireplace that was cold, and looked as if it hadn't been used at all that morning. Never-the-less, with a pulse of magic, Ulpex started a fire instantly. Motioning to the two chairs, he nodded. "Please make yourselves comfortable. I shall return momentarily."

A predatory grin flashed across Ulpex's face, and he was out the door in an instant. At first, Dalin felt alert, fearing the wolf's intentions. However, then he realized what was likely about to happen. Ulpex was of a predatory species, like the wolves on Halarite.

"I think he's going to catch our breakfast," Sira echoed the

Wizard's thoughts.

Sure enough, after only about ten minutes, Ulpex returned with a freshly-skinned creature about the size of a giant rat.

Sira and Dalin sat at the small table while Ulpex skewered the fresh kill and began to cook it over the fire. Frowning at the roasting meat, Dalin wondered about Ulpex's common prey, and felt compelled to voice his curiosity. "Last night you were quite friendly towards another creature, much like the foxes of our world, yet you hunt and consume this creature."

Ulpex looked at him briefly before turning his attention back to the roasting kill. "To be honest, if I were ever in dire need of sustenance and nothing else was available, I would consider the...you compared them to foxes, so I shall call them that to avoid confusion. I would consider the foxes prey at that time. However, they are exceedingly friendly creatures, and they are not as disruptive as the rodents to our lives. These things," he nodded at the roast, "like to eat our houses, if left unchecked. So those of us who are carnivorous eat them instead."

Dalin still wasn't used to the idea of consuming freshly killed animals. Everything they ate at the Wizards' Guild had been summoned by Master Wizards who specialized in such magic, and so there was no true meat, not from any actual animals anyway. Over the past year, with all of the time he had spent on Halarite, much of it on the battlefront against the orcs, he had been forced to eat the same meals that everyone else had, but still preferred summoned food when possible.

The wolf seemed intent on his task, slowly rotating the fresh kill and cringing. As they had seen last night, Ulpex prepared his meals raw.

"So, um," Sira stuttered awkwardly. "I, is that what you had for breakfast? Umm, another one of those?"

"Indeed," Ulpex nodded emphatically. "Though mine was considerably larger. I will not need to eat an evening meal tonight."

Sira and Dalin looked at one another, and then Sira asked, "Do you cook for others often?"

"About once every other week," Ulpex nodded again. "The village rotates who helps prepare evening meals." Sira seemed to visibly relax, and Dalin realized she was worried about whether their host actually knew how to prepare meat for others or not.

However, the fact of communal duties brought another question to Dalin's mind. "How many live here?"

Ulpex pulled the bounty out of the fire to inspect it, and then stuck it back over the flames. "It varies, as some leave and new people arrive. I would say probably about fifty at the moment. Some share homes, some are like me and are solitary."

"Why do some leave," Sira asked. "Have they deciphered the secrets of the crystal?"

Although Dalin wasn't surprised by her continued obsession over the crystal, he too was curious. Ulpex shook his head. "No one has deciphered the secret, as far as I know. The reason some leave varies from person to person, but it is generally either a result of lost patience, or because some believe that their purpose for being here has been fulfilled."

Frowning, Sira asked, "But I thought people came for the crystal."

"Present company excepted?" Ulpex grinned back at them. "Yes, that is what draws them here, in most cases. However, every individual's actual purpose for being brought here is different. Those who leave out of impatience may or may not have failed to discern their purpose, but for the rest, they find enlightenment."

Dalin raised an eyebrow. "Oh? Enlightenment about what?"

Ulpex considered his question carefully, his furry brow creasing in thought. "Themselves. The Universe. Their home. Whatever question they came with, if they stay long enough, they eventually learn the answer. Sometimes…" Ulpex hesitated, the turning meat pausing for a moment. "Sometimes, they do not know what it is they seek until after they have found it."

Dalin nodded thoughtfully, realizing that Ulpex spoke of himself. Perhaps that is why he was apparently Naerala's trusted second in the village. He likely had been here the longest, and still sought an answer to his most basic questions.

Then something else struck Dalin. Ulpex had said that everyone comes for their own reason, to find their own answers. While he, Sira, Cardin and Endri had come here for a common purpose, they each also now had their own purpose on Stella.

Dalin had come seeking the wood necessary to build a new staff. Cardin wished to understand how to cope with his connection to dark magic. Sira was somehow connected to the mysterious crystal. And Endri, he realized, most likely wanted to find the elder dragon, so that his people might have a more experienced leader in their fight against Nuuldan.

Then again, Dalin could be completely off about Endri's purpose. He realized that only Cardin knew the dragon, where as everyone else only heard about Endri through Cardin.

Inwardly Dalin recognized his jealousy about Cardin's new friendship and trainer, and he'd felt useless before now. Their separation today didn't help matters. However, he thought back to his final conversation with Master Valkere, and tried to reassure himself that he wasn't useless.

Was this why Valkere insisted he accompany Cardin? Was whatever purpose he and Sira would serve in the village the start of some longer, ultimately vital journey?

Never-the-less, he wouldn't feel complete until he had a staff again. He wanted to head out for the forest as soon as possible.

Thankfully, Ulpex finished cooking their meal and brought it over. He laughed nervously. "I am afraid that I do not have any utensils. However, once the meat has cooled enough, you may use your hands, if that is acceptable. Otherwise, I can find…"

Sira didn't let him finish, and instead, pulled a leg off of their breakfast and proceeded to bite in. After a few moments of careful chewing, she smiled and nodded. "Normally I'd say it could use some spices, but it's cooked perfectly. Thank you!" Swallowing, she then nodded emphatically at Dalin. "You should seriously try it!"

Dalin cringed.

Chapter 24

THE GRAND SANCTUARY

King Idrill Beredis.

Smiling to himself, the new king sat upon his throne, feeling his heartbeat quicken while he looked down upon several of his subjects.

His subjects. The day had finally come.

All because he had earned the respect of a god.

Draegus stood by at the foot of the stairs, his gaze distant, his eyes fixed on the feet of one of the statues, unarmed and unarmored. The Prince grinned at his triumph, at having finally beaten the Guardian. He knew very well that Draegus would rather be anywhere else, likely trying to plot Idrill's eventual downfall, but that wouldn't happen. The only time Idrill let the other out of his site was when he ordered Draegus escorted to his quarters by the other guards, guards Idrill knew to be loyal.

Meanwhile, General Idann Kale droned on about their successful lockdown of the city, and the dispelling of another riotous bunch of peasants from the Green District. That riot had been part of the plan, too, in order to ensure that no additional city guards would come to the aid of the Castle District.

"Several travelers have gathered outside of both gates," Idann continued, the King reluctantly pulling himself out of his reverie.

"But none have attempted to force the matter. From within, several merchants have demanded to see you, though they do not yet know of your father's demise."

Waving a dismissive hand, Idrill remarked, "Tell them I shall address them, and the city, shortly."

"Yes, Your Majesty," Idann bowed. Idrill's eyes turned again to Draegus and reveled in the man's pain. He debated whether to reduce the guard's rank or to force him to continue to serve as guard Captain and leader of the Guardians. It would thrill Idrill immensely to see the man broken further by a demotion, but the King also recognized how much respect Draegus commanded.

General Kale might command the Warriors, and the city soldiers were weak, making Idrill very secure in his position as far as those parties were concerned. The Guardians were another matter altogether. They were the elite. Sworn to serve the throne directly, often on undocumented missions, their voice was considered the same as the King or Queen's. There was a danger to that, one which Idrill had tried to point out to his father long ago. Draegus could claim orders from Idrill when none had been given.

Maybe he shouldn't allow Draegus to live after all.

Idrill's eyes fell again upon Idann, realizing that the General hadn't left yet. Eyeing Idann, he asked, "Was there something else?"

"Yes, Sire," Idann bowed. "I have reports that just before we sealed the gates, Alaia arrived from Erien."

Alaia, the Erien Covenant member, was not due back in the city until the Wizards had chosen a new Grand Master. Until then, the Alliance was in recess. That meant that she had made the arduous journey by horseback or wagon, possibly riding through the night for her to have arrived already. "I see," Idrill frowned. "Why would she have returned?"

"Because I wished it to be so," Zairel's inhuman voice spoke from behind the throne. Idrill craned his neck around and watched the god step forward, his Covenant robes flowing in an unnatural wind around his body. While Zairel's eyes did not glow at the moment, Idrill could still see the underlying power, as if the man's body buzzed with the energy of the Universe. "I arranged to summon her here to coincide with your transition to power."

"I see," Idrill frowned cautiously. "May I ask why?"

Stopping at the foot of the stairs, a wicked smile stretched across

Zairel's face, an unnerving effect since it was still Pevrin's face . "To punish them. Come, witness more of your god's power."

Elation coursed through the King, and he gracefully stood and descended the steps from the throne. Giving Idann a dismissive nod, he said, "That will be all, General."

The General stepped aside and bowed. "Your Majesty."

Together, Idrill and Zairel walked out through the throne room's main doors. He intentionally neglected to provide Draegus with a dismissal order, knowing that his loyal guards would ensure the Captain would not be allowed to leave of his own accord.

The guards bracketing the castle's front entrance pulled open the heavy, groaning doors, allowing Idrill and Zairel to continue undaunted. The road below the terrace was still a mess, with discarded rocks and rags of torn clothing still littering the street. Idrill noticed a dark spot that looked like drying blood in one area, but was unsurprised. The mob had been driven to absolute madness, and the castle guards had to use force to keep them at bay.

As he and the god walked side by side, Idrill stared at his new companion, wondering what his ally's long-term plan was. If he wanted, Zairel could have leveled the entire city, or worse. If that dark dragon could do it, Zairel most certainly could.

So why was there suddenly a moment of doubt in Idrill's heart?

The feeling startled him, and he faltered in his footsteps. He glanced at Zairel fearfully, but the other seemed not to have noticed. His eyes gazed ahead intensely, as if lost in thought.

For weeks, Idrill had worked with or communicated with Zairel to manipulate the citizens of Tal into over-reacting to the disasters that had befallen them. In fact Zairel had been behind the growing unrest from the beginning. While it was true that multiple disasters and wars had raged across the lands in less than a year, and that would have been enough to unsettle any society, the citizens of Tal might have taken it better, had it not been for Zairel's influence.

Idrill's father was good at placating the common folks and the rich alike, even if he sometimes made promises he couldn't keep. Now that Idrill looked back on the past year, and in particular the last few months, events made far more sense.

Zairel and Idrill descended the steps from the Upper City down into the Market district, while Idrill's stomach suddenly felt empty, and the sickly fingers of fear clutched at his chest. Surely Zairel would know of his sudden, inexplicable doubts. What would the god do to him as punishment?

They immediately turned right and headed for the Grand Sanctuary, Zairel still showing no hint of noticing Idrill's sudden change in mannerism.

Like so many other structures within the city, the Grand Sanctuary was massive and ancient, and came within sight the moment they rounded the inner wall. Similar to all other sanctuaries, it was a cylindrical, domed structure, but it was easily a dozen times larger than the one that the Prince had met Zairel in, both in diameter and in height. It sat on the edge of the open space reserved for the Order of the Ages and the entrance to the Catacombs.

The domed roof was made of steel, unlike the stone or wooden roofs of the smaller sanctuaries, its aged iron roof replaced over and over again throughout the millennia, until the latest renovation when its ceiling was replaced with modern steel. It was multiple stories tall, dwarfing all other buildings around it, second only to the castle, though the castle only stood taller because it was built upon the hill. More importantly, the Grand Sanctuary was the largest library and collection of knowledge on all of Halarite, with most of its levels covered in stacks of bookshelves.

Ten thousand years of history, with books either protected by enchantments, or transcribed to new editions by the Order every few decades to preserve their text. It was the heart of the Order of the Ages.

As they approached the massive ironwood doors at the main entrance, Zairel looked to Idrill thoughtfully. "Tell me," Zairel's voice broke his inner thoughts. "Have you ever laid eyes upon one of the Cronal?" Before the King could respond, Zairel interrupted, "Of course you have not. Only the Covenant and their most trusted guardians have ever seen them."

Through his fears and doubts, Idrill felt the familiar sensation of annoyance at being interrupted and talked down upon. However, when he realized exactly what Zairel had said, Idrill took a greater interest, since it probably meant that Anila Kovin had likely seen one of the Cronal.

They were the sacred texts central to the beliefs of the Order, said to have been written in an ancient language that none but the Covenant could decipher. It was one of the Covenant's highest laws that no one may look upon them without every member of the Covenant agreeing to it. If an untrained person were to attempt to read a Cronal, legend said that it would drive the reader mad, or worse.

Which meant that it was left to the Covenant to interpret the words of the gods, and to disseminate that knowledge to the people.

That was when Zairel's earlier words struck him. He wished to punish Alaia, and no doubt the other two remaining Covenant members, both of whom were already in the city to study at the Grand Sanctuary. Had the Covenant lied to the people about what the Cronal said? Is that why Zairel was really here? His mission was to set Halarite back on the correct course. If they had been led astray by those they were meant to trust...

As they passed through the massive, open doors and into the circular rows and rows of stacks, the familiar smell of old books and dust filling his nose, he stopped a moment to stare at Zairel. "Are you saying I will be allowed to look upon the Cronal?"

Zairel stopped, but at first did not return Idrill's gaze. Then the other's shoulders began to shake as he bellowed out a laugh that echoed throughout the Sanctuary, drawing the attention of several clerics and other members of the Order, along with a handful of visiting peasants.

Turning to Idrill, Zairel let out another bellow of a laugh, and the King felt his face turn pink. "Why do you laugh, My Lord?"

Between laughs, Zairel managed to say, "You...you have no idea...what the Cronal actually is, do you?"

Stepping closer while trying to suppress his embarrassment, Idrill hissed, "I fail to see how this is an amusing matter."

Zairel's laughter ceased and his eyes flashed orange, his robes bellowing out more. "Watch your tone, impudent child. You are still my subject, regardless of your kingship."

It hadn't been a whisper, but a full-volume statement that anyone nearby could hear. With so many eyes staring curiously at them, Idrill felt his face burn hot, and his jaw was set tight. He wanted to lash out at the impudence, at being lectured in front of so many.

After countless years of being treated so callously by his father, he thought those days were behind him. Yet despite his ascendancy to the throne, now he had to deal with another, higher authority who openly mocked him.

However, Idrill was powerless, and Zairel was not. Through gritted teeth, the King bowed his head and managed to say, "Forgive me."

Zairel's glare lingered a moment longer, but then his eyes turned to something else. A sudden hunger overtook his eyes, and he turned back and walked onwards, towards the center. Much like other sanctuaries, the Grand Sanctuary did not segregate sections with walls. With six walkways radiating out from the vast, open center, which was surrounded by twelve great marble pillars bracketing those walkways, they had a clear view of the largest crystal ever found in the Ilari Mountains hoisted up in the center of the dome. Situated on a raised circular platform beneath that crystal was an opulent stone altar.

Zairel practically floated up the central platform, and stood in the center so that when he spoke, his voice amplified by magic, everyone could see and hear him on all levels. "You know so little of the Universe, yet it has always been open to you. You have relied upon the Covenant for knowledge that was there for you to see from the moment you were born. You rely upon us, your gods, for guidance! Well here I am, your god, Zairel!"

The King, stunned by Zairel's sudden openness about his identity, stopped at the edge of the open area, where he folded his arms and leaned against the pillar to his left. Idrill realized that Zairel meant to draw the Covenant members out into the open. Whatever his plan was, he meant to be public about it.

It worked. Alaia and the other two members appeared on the second floor one section to the left of where Idrill stood. "Who are you to claim yourself a god," Alaia demanded, her voice dwarfed by the enhanced volume of Zairel's.

An unnatural wind billowed up, and a familiar orange glow surrounded Zairel. With a slow, deliberate gracefulness, Zairel rose above the platform, turning slowly in mid-air to face Alaia.

"I am Zairel," his voice thundered. "You have failed the humans of Halarite, Alaia! You have failed yourselves. Now the time has come to pay for your sins."

The King stepped into the opening just enough to look up at Alaia, and he felt most satisfied by the look of shock upon her face.

No...not shock. A frown fell across his face when he realized that it was fear and recognition on her face, not shock. Idrill then realized Zairel's exact words. 'Failed the humans of Halarite.' Something about those exact words struck Idrill as odd.

"You are not a god," she mouthed. Maybe she said it aloud, but he couldn't hear her above the roaring wind, like that of a great twister, one which reached all the way up to the crystal. Books were suddenly blown from their shelves and whipped around Zairel as he rose to a level just above the Covenant's. Alaia, backing away, screeched just loud enough for Idrill to hear, "You're a wraith!"

There was a flash of movement. Alaia and the others had drawn something from inside their robes. Idrill tensed, anticipating an attack, but they never had a chance. Zairel's hand reached out, and suddenly the three of them were yanked off of their feet and into the center, their thighs slamming against the stone railing with sickening thuds, hard enough that the stone railing cracked and crumbled, spilling chunks down onto the marble floor near Idrill. Whatever weapons they had were tossed back into the stacks.

Clerics fled the Sanctuary, and the King very nearly joined them. It was one thing to see his Father, a man he had loathed his entire life, to be drained of life. It was another to see people he had once respected and revered as the conveyors of the will of the gods thrown about so violently.

His victory suddenly felt hollow. His entire body felt hollow. It was as if all joy were sapped from his body as he watched their ragged, broken forms whipped around the center.

He'd wanted his father punished, and he was willing to punish the rest of Tal if necessary, to help set them all on the right course, leading the kingdom based upon the teachings of the Covenant. All of his dreams were realized and shattered all at once.

"You have kept the truth from everyone," Zairel roared. "To keep yourselves in power. But you should have known, only a god has true power. You are nothing!" One of the other members, the one who had survived the destruction of Sharenth, having been away from the city during Nuuldan's attack, suddenly screamed, and his body crumpled into an ashen mess before he was casually discarded out of the circle. "Only I can command the Cronal!" The Covenant member from Falind met the same fate.

Zairel violently grasped Alaia with magic, instantly halting her from flailing about in the wind. She was upside-down, her robes fluttering in the wind, and she faced Zairel. "You have squandered this gift," he snarled at her. Then he reached for her, and a bright blue glow emanated from her belt pouch. A small coin-like item tore out of the pouch, and the moment that Zairel caught it, his orange glow flashed bright-white, coalescing with the blue and throwing out a great wave that knocked Idrill onto his backside.

The flash subsided. Alaia tried to speak, but only a whimper came from her forcibly-clenched jaw. With a terrifyingly satisfied smile, Zairel scorched her like the others, her scream of pain muffled. When nothing but a husk remained, he flung her into the stacks in a cascade of books.

The object in Zairel's hand continued to glow bright blue, but it did not seem to hurt the god or counter his power. The wind eased down, and the god-like being lowered himself onto the platform, while the King gawked from the floor.

Zairel's glowing eyes were fixed upon the glowing blue stone coin, and a broad smile crept across his face. Idrill tried to get a better look, but then Zairel's eyes fell upon him, and he felt his soul freeze. Should he not have looked? Was Idrill now a liability because he knew too much? Would the new King Beredis be struck down like his father, less than a day after assuming the throne, before his official coronation had even taken place?

No, it wouldn't make sense to kill him now. Not after the god had spent so much time and effort making Idrill the King.

And that was the thought that suddenly made everything coalesce in Idrill's mind. This man was supposed to be a god. Why did he need Idrill?

For that matter, why had he insisted on manipulating the Keeper of the Sword so that he would not be present when they made their move? Surely a god had nothing to fear from the Sword of Dragons, right?

Alaia had called Zairel a wraith. Not a god, nor a demon, but a wraith. Something that the Covenant had never mentioned in their teachings, a word that Idrill was not familiar with. What was a wraith? Why did Alaia fear it?

None of this made sense. Idrill knew he should have trusted Zairel, and believed him when he said that the Covenant had led them all astray, but he didn't. The fact that Zairel seemed oblivious to Idrill's inner doubts, and the fact that Zairel had said 'humans of Halarite,' turned the King's stomach with doubt and anxiety.

Now, more than ever, the King worried for his future.

As the object, twice the size of a gold coin, continued to glow and pulse in Zairel's hands, Idrill's doubts grew further. Was that what this was all about? Did Zairel need those objects to attain more power? Was that why he needed Cardin gone for a while, so that he could obtain the power needed to contend with the Keeper of the Sword?

Zairel, or whoever this being was, was afraid, and gods should fear no one.

The entity descended the platform, the orange glow of his body subsiding along with the stone's blue. The King felt the urge to back away, but he knew that now was not the time to outwardly show his fears or doubts.

So, with great effort, Idrill forced himself to stand his ground.

Zairel stopped a few feet away, and presented the object. "You wished a closer look, and so you shall have it. But do not touch, or I will rend you from this life and the next."

Gulping back his terror, Idrill looked at the object and studied every facet of it. It was indeed a circular object, but he couldn't see the details before. Flat, tiny teeth encircled it, and there were six spokes that expanded out from a center circle, which bore a small, square hole in the middle. In fact, there were six spokes, tapered on either end.

Six, like the symbol for the Order of the Ages.

"This is the Cronal," he blurted out, his eyes darting to Zairel's. "It...it isn't a book?"

With a great smile stretching across his face, Zairel replied, "What is a book, but a gateway to knowledge and experience? This is only a piece of it, and through it, the Covenant has visited a vast library of knowledge beyond this realm." Closing his hand around it, Zairel placed it in a pocket somewhere inside his robes. Idrill recognized the clink of stone or metal on metal, and suspected that there were other pieces already inside of Zairel's robes.

Was that why Zairel had not come to Archanon sooner? So that he could find and take the other pieces?

Confirming his suspicions, Zairel commented, "Only one piece remains unaccounted for. The Falind representative did not have his Cronal piece with him."

Idrill nodded absently. "Wizard King Sal'fe is no fool. He must possess it now."

Zairel scoffed. "That is unlikely. The Covenant has never trusted a king with their secrets." The god's shoulders slouched. "However, I must still confront him with his own sins, and I am weary. I shall rest for now."

A god should not feel weary, Idrill thought, working hard to keep his expression even and emotionless.

Leaving Idrill alone amidst tattered books and a ruined sanctuary, Zairel drifted out. The clerics and other visitors had long ago fled, and the King knew that the story of what happened would spread fast throughout the city, possibly faster than the news of his father's death. A public announcement would be necessary in the morning, he decided. As much as Idrill hated them, his father had been right, and the people needed public reassurance.

For once, he wouldn't be content to delegate that task to someone else.

Chapter 25

GUARDIAN OF SECRETS

Without an open sky above their heads, Reis quickly learned that keeping track of the days was difficult at best. Thankfully, Elaria was able to 'feel what time it was,' as she put it, and told them when night had fallen. Everyone had gathered at that time, even Baenil and his escorts, who practically had to drag the elven archeologist back to the encampment.

Baenil was so intent on exploring the dwarven castle that he refused to sleep. After some discussion with Kellis and Indira, along with the revelation from Elaria that elves could go days without sleep if they chose to, two more marines accompanied Baenil on his continued explorations, with orders to return within a few hours to be relieved by two freshly-rested marines.

Baenil wasn't happy with having to break off his explorations each time, but when both the Sergeant and Lieutenant insisted, he reluctantly agreed. Once he and his two escorts were out of sight, the troupe settled in for the night.

Reis was instantly sleepy, and he realized that the glow panels had started to dim of their own accord, so he laid down on his chosen makeshift bed and prepared for a night's sleep. But when Anila chose the bed next to him, he felt his heart leap into his throat. Then

Elaria chose the one on the other side of him, with Gilrin next to her.

His sleepiness vanished, and it didn't take him long to realize why. He kept glancing at Anila, her eyes already closed and her hands tucked under her head as a makeshift pillow. When he was sure she wouldn't open her eyes again, he allowed himself a moment to stare, his stomach tingling.

"I can feel you staring," she suddenly spoke, her eyes still closed.

Feeling a surge of energy leap up into his chest, he gulped and turned away. "Sorry."

Awkwardly he stared at the dying glow panels, and the patterns on the ceiling from the flickering everlasting torches posted around them. Then he looked the other way, only to find Elaria staring at him with a smile.

He narrowed his eyes at her, and she shook her head before turning to face Gilrin. They whispered something to each other for a bit, but he couldn't make out what they said.

When he turned back to Anila, her eyes were open, and she smiled. His chest fluttered, but then his body grew warm. She reached her hand and rested it on his shoulder before she closed her eyes. After a moment of staring, he looked up and closed his eyes with his hand on hers.

The next day, after an ever-so-tasty breakfast of dry bread and not a drop of alcohol in sight, Reis, Anila, Elaria and Gilrin ventured out into the city to look around. The glow panels in the columns had also dimmed considerably, so the first thing they did was follow Elaria while she relit the panels, starting with the surrounding inner city wall's glow panels.

"Do they dim at night by design," he asked, staring in silent jealousy as Elaria effortlessly lit up another column.

"In a manner of speaking," Gilrin nodded. "Back when this city was alive with dwarves, I believe there were several people in charge of ensuring they remained constantly lit."

"From what I've learned," Elaria nodded as they headed for the next column, "the dwarves had a very organized, very effective government, quite possibly a republic or something similar."

Reis frowned awkwardly at them, and exchanged an unknowing glance with Anila. "I'm afraid I don't know that word. Did your pendant not translate something right? Republic?"

Now it was Elaria's turn to exchange glances with Gilrin. "No,

I'm sure it translated it correctly. You've never heard of a republic?" Reis and Anila shook their heads. "You've really only ever had a monarchy on Halarite?!" They nodded.

Blinking away her surprise, Elaria drew in a breath and narrowed her eyes. "Well, to put it succinctly, it's a form of government where representatives of groups of people within a civilization take part in governing. In a way, your Alliance is similar to one, or the start of one. Each member of the Alliance represents one part of the people of Halarite, and have a single vote each in all matters concerning the Alliance."

Reis took a moment to absorb what she'd said, mulling it over in his mind, wondering how such a government could rule. "By that example," he started, trying to understand, "you mean to say that if Tal were a Republic, there'd be several representatives who vote on matters of politics?"

"Exactly," she nodded. "Perhaps each city has a representative, or each geographical area. Or any other number of possibilities."

"I see," he said cautiously, working the idea over in his head. On the one hand, it sounded strange that individual parts of the kingdom would require a vote in matters. That was the point of the government, to make the appropriate decisions for the people, wasn't it?

Then again, Reis wasn't exactly a specialist in politics, even inter-Guild politics. Feeling embarrassed at not knowing anything about the strange political system, he tried to think of an intelligent question. Finally, all he could think to ask was, "Does it work?"

"Sometimes," she nodded, somewhat hesitantly. "However…well, I guess like any type of government, when it fails, it fails rather spectacularly."

They reached the last column surrounding the inner city and activated it, and with at least the center of the vast cavern lit, they ventured back towards the capitol and began to explore the various out buildings surrounding the capitol.

Half of their efforts were spent clearing out the spider webs that the kiklar had left behind. They tried to clear them out using swords and daggers, but every now and then they risked burning the webs inside of a building. Once this backfired when the webs were so old and so dry, and covered every square inch inside, that it started several pieces of ancient cloth on fire as well, and smoked them out.

They stumbled out of the building, coughing and rubbing at stinging eyes, and then watched as the smoke billowed up out of the door and was caught by a draft above, no doubt heading out towards wherever the kiklar had escaped to.

The fire didn't spread beyond that room, thankfully, and they all agreed not to burn the webbing again. Naturally, the next place they tried to get into was so densely webbed, they simply decided not to explore it yet.

After several hours of searching, and with grumbling stomachs, they returned to the antechamber in the capitol to regroup. Much to their surprise, Baenil had returned and remained, idly munching on a piece of cheese while circling around the statue.

Most of the rest of the troupe had also returned for a midday meal, and as Reis ate an overly salted, dried piece of deer meat, he walked up to Indira and Kellis and asked, "What's Baenil up to?"

Kellis replied, "I'm not sure. He came back an hour ago and said something about missing a clue with the statue."

"He's been circling it like a hungry wolf ever since," Indira added, her voice edged with annoyance. "Won't say anything else to any of us. Makes me think his time in captivity left him a bit...damaged."

Reis nodded slowly and watched Baenil curiously. "I imagine none of us would come out of ten years in captivity with our heads still clear." Memories of what he had almost done to Elaria flashed through his mind's eye again, but he pushed them away. For whatever reason, Elaria had chosen to forgive him, or at least not hold a grudge against him. In time, he hoped he would learn to forgive himself.

Baenil's eyes wandered down, his brow furrowed in deep thought, but then he came to a jarring stop as his eyes opened wide. "It's here!"

His excited shout startled everyone, and those who had sat down sprang up, many drawing weapons, while Baenil dropped down on his knees and began wiping at the floor and blowing on it. Reis, Indira and Kellis hurried towards him, only to stop when the ground suddenly rumbled. Baenil had done something, Reis wasn't sure what, and two semicircle lines of blue light suddenly glowed around the statue base. Several more lines appeared between the inner and outer half-circle at regular intervals, and those sections descended.

By the time everyone reached Baenil, who stood up to watch in excited glee, a semicircle of stairs had formed around the statue, leading down to a door directly in front of the monolith.

The blue glow outlining the stairs dimmed, and the glow panels within the antechamber suddenly flickered brighter. He glanced up at them with a frown, wondering what source of power would suddenly rejuvenate them, but then he gaped back down at the stairs.

Baenil, practically bouncing in excitement, tried to descend ahead of everyone else, but Elaria shot out a restraining hand. "Hold on there, my friend," she chided. "What's going on here, what have you found?"

While the Marines closed in around them, most having drawn swords, Baenil wrung his hands anxiously, glancing down at the stone door at the end of the stairs. The door still had a blue glow of multiple runes carved into it. "Well, when I came back in here, I noticed lines on the floor for the first time," the elf quickly explained. "They were so covered in dirt and dust that I hadn't noticed them before, but all of our walking about revealed them. I had a feeling it was more than just a random pattern."

Reis pointed out, "But you said 'it's here' just before those stairs appeared. What's here?"

"What I've been missing," Baenil spoke pointedly, as if Reis had asked a dumb question. He was pretty sure it wasn't a dumb one, not this time. "Everything in this fortress has been dwarven, no other hint of elves besides the statue. I knew that meant there had to be something hidden, and I knew it had to be in here. This is that secret, whatever it is. Now, can we check it out?"

He tried to descend again, but Elaria held him back. "Alright, we'll go down there. But you and I first, and only the two of us," she glanced at Kellis. "We'll make sure there are no surprises, then we'll call the rest of you down."

Kellis didn't look happy, but he nodded, and then looked at Indira. "Sergeant, deploy your marines in a defensive posture, just in case any other surprises present themselves."

Nodding, Indira doled out orders quickly, while Baenil scoffed. "Lieutenant, I seriously doubt that there are hidden elves around here ready to strike, or any other living threat."

"Perhaps not," Kellis agreed. "But there's no harm in caution, and we're in uncharted territory."

Reis smiled at the naval parlance, probably one the Lieutenant had picked up from Indira over the past couple of days. Still, he agreed whole-heartedly with Kellis – when it came to magic, there was no telling what to expect.

Looking to Elaria, Kellis nodded. "We'll watch from up here."

Drawing her daggers, Elaria smiled briefly at Gilrin, who stood just beside and behind Reis, and then she and Baenil started down the stairs. Baenil was again too excited and quick, and Elaria had to rush to keep up with him.

Since the stairs ran a half-circle around the statue, Reis, Kellis, Indira and Gilrin followed along from above, watching with considerable interest. Baenil's nose practically smashed up against the door as he carefully examined the inscribed runes. There were enough of them that the glow lit up his face in an eerie, soft blue-white glow.

Elaria's curved daggers weren't lit up like when they first arrived, but Reis thought he heard a distinct hum from them, the sign that she had channeled magic into them.

Several minutes passed as Elaria and Baenil examined the door, and with each passing moment, Reis grew more and more anxious. He kept glancing around, waiting for a kiklar to show up or some other deadly creature, some guardian of the elven secrets.

Nothing happened.

Come on, Reis, you're getting jumpy, he thought to himself. *Relax!*

"That's it!" Baenil's excited shout made Reis jump, and he rolled his eyes, both at the excitable elf and his own reaction. "This should open the…"

Baenil never finished his statement. He'd pushed on two separate sections of the door, and the runes flashed brightly before winking out of existence.

Expecting the door to open, Reis frowned when nothing happened. At first.

Several concentric circles lit up around the statue, growing brighter and brighter, as the ground shook again and a low-pitched hum buzzed at his ears. Reis backed away from the stairs, staring around as the glow panels flickered again. The circles grew brighter, and the hum's pitch edged higher and higher.

"Something's happening up here," Kellis called down to the elves. "There's magic building up everywhere!"

Elaria didn't bother to ascend the stairs, she scampered up the wall onto their level. "I feel it," she stated through gritted teeth.

Then a visible field of energy coalesced above the circles and spiraled inward towards the statue, like water towards a drain. As more energy converged on the statue, the tiny inscribed runes on it likewise lit up.

"Back off from it," Elaria shouted, shoving Gilrin back. "Baenil, get out of there! Baenil!"

The other elf didn't reply, but before anyone could get back to the stairs to check on him, the eye slit for the statue illuminated with two distinct points of blue-white lights. And the statue moved.

"By the gods," Reis uttered, his heart racing and his stomach dropping. "What is that?"

No one answered, maybe no one knew. But as everyone edged away from the suddenly-animated giant, it stuck out its hand, and the last of the visible energy in the room coalesced into the shape of a scintillating battleaxe.

"Don't let that axe touch you," Elaria called out, just as the statue raised its weapon up, and then with both hands, brought it down fast and hard. Two marines had to leap out of the way, just as the axe smashed into the ground, driving a large crack into the foundation. That seemed to cut out the glowing circles, and the room was swallowed in darkness when the glow panels winked out.

That left Elaria's lit daggers, three everlasting torches, and the glow from the creature and its bright axe to illuminate room.

The statue pulled its ethereal axe out of the ground with ease, and it stepped off of the platform, its lumbering shaking the building. The marines didn't wait for commands, they immediately pointed their cutlasses at it and released a barrage of arcane attacks.

At first, the attacks didn't even seem to faze the statue, but then it raised up one hand protectively. Somehow it looked angry, and it violently swung its axe horizontally. Reis cursed and dove out of the way. Not all of the marines did, and he heard several screams as the energy weapon sliced through them and their magic shields.

Elaria and Kellis joined in the assault against the creature, but all this did was draw it towards the most powerful of the two, Elaria. It swung again, but both she and Kellis barely ducked out of the way in time, while Reis remained flat on his stomach as the axe slashed over him with only inches to spare.

His mind racing, Reis looked up but didn't dare try to stand. He watched as Anila leapt in at their adversary from behind and tried to cut into it with her impossibly-sharp sword, but he cringed when all it did was clang noisily against the statue's armor. She backed off, and was visibly shaken.

Which meant that Reis would be useless. If her sword couldn't make a dent in its armor, his longsword certainly wouldn't. That didn't stop Elaria from trying. Her daggers glowed bright with energy, but instead of releasing it at the creature, she dodged another swing from its axe, and then leapt in at it, driving her daggers into its chest.

There was a bright flash of light, and all of the energy in her daggers deflected outward, sending her flying across the room and slamming her into the wall with a loud thump.

"Elaria!" Reis called out. He stood up, watching the statue carefully as it turned its attention to some of the marines, and then he sprinted to her. "Are you okay," he asked as he slid down onto his knees beside her. He dropped his sword and he gently pressed his hand against her chest to feel for a heartbeat. She was slumped over, her lower back against the wall. "Elaria, answer me!"

That snapped her back to reality, and she looked up at him, her face contorted in pain as she wrapped her arms around her chest. It looked like she could barely breathe, and he worried she had broken ribs, or worse.

He pressed a reassuring hand on her shoulder, but then heard more screams of anguish from marines after another thump reverberated in the chamber.

Finally she was able to draw in a breath, and she coughed, wincing. "Thank the gods, you're alright," he heaved a sigh of relief.

"None of us will be for long," she said weakly, gulping and then shaking her head. "I think Baenil triggered a trap, and that thing's not going stop 'til we're all dead."

He glanced at it, and noticed Anila suddenly unleash a blast of lightning at it. His heart sank when he saw that. *There's no hiding who she is now,* he thought.

"What if we leave the building," he turned back to Elaria.

"I don't know," she shook her head. "But I get the feeling it'd follow us out." She glanced towards the main entrance, and frowned. "And that would mean destroying a wall. It could bring the entire building down and damage or destroy the beacon."

The ground shook as the statue plunged its axe deep into the ground again, thankfully missing Anila. Reis shook his head, "I don't think it cares about that."

"And I doubt we'd make it to the tunnels before it killed us all," she grumbled, wincing again when she tried to draw in a deeper breath. "And who knows how fast the kiklar would return."

"Well then, what do we do," he asked. "It has to have *some* weakness."

He thought back to the kiklar, recalling that their exoskeletons were extremely strong, but they were weakest at their joints. Maybe this would be, too.

When Elaria couldn't come up with an answer, Reis grabbed his sword and stood up. "No, don't," Elaria's hand snatched his ankle. "It'll kill you!"

Looking down at her, he gave her his typical overconfident grin and shrugged. "Well if I'm gonna die anyway."

Breaking free of her grasp, he regarded the statue, thankful that its back was turned to him, and then he charged at it.

Even turned away from him, it kept moving, attempting in vain to strike at Anila while she dodged and used elemental magic against it. The surviving marines stayed back, watching her work, and Kellis was nowhere to be found. Was the Lieutenant a casualty already?

Reis stopped just long enough to dodge an errant, lumbering arm, and then, trying desperately in the low light to see, he jabbed his sword straight at what he thought was the back of the statue's knee joint.

His sword tip bounced off harmlessly, and his arms jostled painfully. He'd done nothing but get the statue's attention, and he had to jump down the stairwell to dodge its swat.

At the bottom of the steps, he found Baenil and Kellis, the former cowering against the door while the latter stood with a broken sword, watching the commotion above.

"Lieutenant," Reis smiled, feeling his chest lighten for just a moment. "I thought you were dead!"

"Nearly," Kellis grimaced. "Looks like your sword fared better. What the hell are we going to do?"

The sound of another blast of lightning caught his attention, and he looked up just in time to see the creature back-pedal. Whatever extra power Anila had thrown into her attacks, it at least stunned the statue for a moment. However, Reis had the feeling that was the best she could do, and it was doubtful that she could keep it up.

"And where did her powers come from," Kellis added.

"It's a long story," Reis shook his head. "That thing doesn't have a single open joint or weakness in its armor!"

Suddenly Anila leapt over the stairwell, and he watched as the creature turned to follow her, its axe swinging above them, the sizzling energy raising the hairs on the back of Reis's neck.

That's when he saw it. He'd noticed it earlier, the only opening in the statue's armor. The eyes!

The eyes that were suddenly fixed on them.

His mouth fell open as the creature drew the axe back, grasping it with both hands. But there was its only weakness, and with barely a few seconds to spare, Reis knew what to do.

He leapt up the wall to get back to level ground, and then just as the statue swung down, putting its whole body into it, its face came just in range, and Reis jabbed his sword right into one of its glowing eyes.

The axe was just inches from obliterating Kellis and Baenil when it suddenly vanished, drowning them in darkness. Reis's sword smashed into the back of the helmet, and was wrenched from his hand as the statue suddenly convulsed, as if he'd hit a living creature inside, and it crashed to the side, possibly on top of the stairs if Reis heard correctly.

And quicker than it had begun, the battle was over. Reis's eyes adjusted to the dim light provided by the torches, left over by their beds. Before him was the smoldering, smoking corpse of the elven guardian, a hulking shadow that had crashed not over the entire stairwell, as he'd feared, but just the first half of it. His sword stuck out from its head, but lay at such an angle that he knew there was nothing inside of that helmet.

His heart thumped deafeningly in his ears, and his hands shook. He tried to process what had just happened. Had he really done it? Was it really that simple?

Reis nearly jumped out of his skin when a hand rested on his shoulder, but he was relieved when it turned out to be Anila.

"Hey, relax," she soothed. "You did it!"

He looked at her, his chest heaving as he tried to catch his breath, and his nerves. "I...guess I did. I mean..." Shaking his head, he looked again at the fifteen foot tall statue and felt his eyes grow wide. "I can't believe that just happened."

Then reality set in again, and he looked to Anila wide-eyed. "But, your powers, you exposed yourself!"

"It was that or watch everyone else die," she shrugged, raising her sword up. A white glow emanated from the blade now, much like Anila's daggers. "I couldn't let that happen."

"And I am grateful for that," Indira's voice came from the dark. From the darkness emerged the Sergeant, with one of her marines following behind. "I don't know what you are," she said cautiously, brandishing her cutlass. A moment later, she smiled weakly and slid it into her sheath. "But thank you. A lot more of my people would have died if you hadn't..."

Her voice broke, and she looked away from them, towards the lifeless statue. Reis felt his heart sink at that, knowing that at least three had perished, probably more.

Turning towards where he knew the door was below the surface, he saw Kellis climb up the side, the easy way now cut off by the statue. Once he was at their level, he brushed himself off and looked forlornly at Indira. "Sergeant, I...I'm sorry for your marines."

At first she didn't reply, but then another one of her marines approached, this one carrying one of the everlasting torches. Indira smiled at the survivor, then asked for the torch. With it, she climbed up onto the statue and called into the dark, "Alright, marines, sound off and rally to me!"

Reis listened as voices called out from the darkness, but then he remembered Elaria. He looked over and saw that she still sat against the wall, her daggers, having been knocked from her grip, slowly grew dim.

"Anila, follow me," he grabbed her free hand and pulled her along, needing the glow from her sword to light their way. He felt a panic grow inside when he thought that she looked slouched over again, but when they were close enough with Anila's sword, Elaria looked up at the light and smiled.

"Anila," she sighed. "I'm glad you're alright."

Together, Anila and Reis helped Elaria stand, though she winced with every inch of movement. Once she stood, Anila remarked, "As are you, for the most part."

"I wouldn't say 'most,'" Elaria laughed, and then groaned.

Looking up towards the statue and the gathering marines, she asked, "Is Baenil alright? Where's Gilrin?"

"I'm here, lass," Gilrin called out, emerging from the dark just as Indira had.

"Baenil's alright, too," Reis nodded. "Though a bit shaken up."

Elaria shook her head and grumbled. "I'm surprised that thing didn't try to kill him first."

She tried to stand on her own, but when that proved too painful, Reis and Anila helped her over to the others, while Gilrin collected her daggers for her and followed them.

Once everyone was together, between Anila's sword and the three torches, they were able to get a quick headcount.

Of the twelve marines, seven remained. A solemn silence overtook the company for a minute, until it was broken by Elaria. "I am so sorry, Sergeant. I understand if you wish to return to the surface now."

Baenil looked ready to object, but he was instantly silenced by a glare from Elaria.

To everyone's surprise, Indira shook her head. "No. If we stop now, their deaths meant nothing. They were marines, and we take on the dangerous missions knowing that we might not make it back."

The sergeant glared at Baenil and approached him, but he avoided her eyes. "However, I hope nothing like this happens again. Because if it does, I'm holding you personally responsible for it."

Baenil looked up to try to reply, but his voice caught, and he looked down again. Indira glowered at him a moment longer, and then scowled and turned away.

After another solemn silence passed over the group, Reis sighed and asked the obvious question. "So, what do we do now?"

"Well," Elaria released her iron grip around his and Anila's back, finally standing on her own. "We check for any more traps on the door. Then, hopefully, we open it and find out what this is all about."

Reis heard Indira mutter under her breath, "It better be worth it."

Chapter 26

DESTINY'S CHOICE

Cardin's trek into the mountains with Naerala and Endri progressed quickly from the gorgeous, non-woody trees into more familiar surroundings. Within a half hour, they had reached wooded forests that reminded him of the aspen and birch trees on Halarite, and Cardin smiled for Dalin. It wouldn't be difficult for his friend and mentor to find the wood he needed for his staff.

Shortly after they reached the wooded forest, the terrain changed drastically, with extreme hills, rocky surfaces and boulders that they had to navigate around, along with dense underbrush. If not for the well-worn path, their journey probably would have taken three times as long.

Much of their early trip was spent in silence, with Cardin munching on dried bread and a little bit of leftover salted meat from home. As they travelled, however, they came across multiple bushes of berries, their fruit colored bright orange. Before he could ask if they were safe to eat, Naerala picked several from a bush and popped them into her mouth, closing her eyes as she savored them.

Figuring it was better than travel rations, Cardin decided to try one himself, and found it to be very sweet, with barely a hint of tartness that complimented the sweetness perfectly.

Naerala commented, "You are fortunate to have arrived when you did. They are perfectly ripened at this time of year."

As he gathered several more berries and stowed them in his travel pack, he asked Naerala, "How often do you or your villagers make this journey?"

"It varies for everyone," she replied casually, smiling towards the mountains ahead. "For myself, it is perhaps once or twice per year, and that is generally to tend to the copse itself. For others, it is whenever their journey to enlightenment is at its peak."

Cardin looked up at Endri just as he landed on a large boulder next to the path. The wooded forest didn't respond to the massive dragon like the other trees did, and he had to constantly take flight to keep up with them.

"You use the word enlightenment, but…" Cardin hesitated, unsure how to continue. "What exactly does that mean?"

Naerala laughed and looked at him as if pitying a fool. "I am afraid that is not an easy question to answer. It is different for each person, just as each person's reason for coming to the crystal, to this world, is different, and their reasons for leaving are different." Shaking her head, she added, "What I can tell you is that, for many, it involves finding an inner peace," she clenched a fist against her chest. "Learning to tame your inner demons, and learning to be that which you were born to be. For many, the journey begins by discerning what your purpose in life is."

"You're talking about destiny," Cardin suggested.

"No," Naerala shook her head. "The concepts of destiny and fate are intertwined, but they both suggest aspects outside of one's control."

As they rounded the boulder, Cardin saw that they approached the edge of the forest, and the path sloped upwards just beyond the last trees.

He considered Naerala's words for a moment, but then he shook his head and asked, "Are you suggesting our destiny, or our future is completely within our control?" She nodded thoughtfully. "What of prophecy, then?"

From that, a scowl soured her face. "I despise prophecy for one simple reason." Endri leapt into the air again and flew past the edge of the forest, landing only a few seconds later next to the path. Naerala watched him carefully as he did so before she continued, "A prophecy is said to be knowledge of events to come. Yet to know those events gives one the power to change them." She looked at him pointedly, at the Sword handle over his shoulder. "For instance, many prophecies exist regarding the Sword of Dragons, some of which predate its creation, though none knew what they spoke of until after its creation.

"Yet the one that came about after it was forged sent the Star Dragons into a terrified frenzy, and they abandoned it." She shook her head and looked again to Endri, who stared back at them with his starry emerald eyes. "Was the Sword forged because the older prophecies said it would be? Was there no choice to construct such a weapon? Or could the Star Dragons have chosen not to build it?"

Endri tilted his head to one side, watching them curiously as they emerged into the open mountain fields. *"Prophecy or not, we had no choice but to forge the Sword of Dragons,"* he insisted. *"We had to end the Civil War."*

As they passed Endri, Naerala scoffed at him. "It was hardly needed to end the Civil War. Star Dragons have always been arrogant." Endri recoiled at her harsh statement, drawing his head back and curling the back of his lips. "They believed themselves invincible until the first fell to darkness. So naturally, panic ensued, and poor decisions were made."

Endri fell into step beside them, while Cardin watched him carefully, shocked by Naerala's bold statements and curious how his friend would respond to her accusations.

"And what mistakes were those," Endri inquired. *"For that matter, how do you know about our actions during the war?"*

"Do you mean other than the propensity to experiment and explore without regard to the consequences," she asked. "Tessir should never have dabbled in dark magic in the first place."

Endri recoiled again, halting in his tracks and gawking at Naerala. *"How do you know that name?"*

Cardin's eyes grew wide at Endri's reaction, and he looked back and forth between his companions while a chill raced down his back. When Naerala didn't reply, he asked, "Wait, who was Tessir?"

Seeing that Naerala and Cardin weren't stopping, Endri fell into step again and caught up in one great stride. *"Tessir was Nuuldan's name before his corruption,"* the dragon explained.

Now he understood Endri's reaction, but then he thought back to the Celestial Spires and Firdal claiming that Nuuldan's original name was lost long ago. He peered at the emerald dragon and asked, "How do *you* know that?"

Endri caught himself and hung his head. *"Firdal told me, before we left."*

That still didn't explain it, and Cardin wanted to ask why Firdal lied to them, but it was Naerala who answered. "That name is not widely spoken of, and many have tried to forget it. Another example of Star Dragon vanity," she added sourly. "So ashamed that one of theirs fell, that they strike his name from memory. Yet try as they might, not all Star Dragons have forgotten, have they, Endri?"

The path turned to the right as they began their ascent, uneven in this part from weathering, and Cardin noticed that the path wound back and forth across the steep mountain side.

He'd suspected that there was more to Naerala than was obvious, but now more than ever he wondered who exactly she was and how she could know as much as she did. "Don't take this the wrong way," he started cautiously. "But you seem to know an awful lot for a hermit living in a monastery."

She looked at him wide eyed, and he cringed, wondering if he had insulted her. However, much to his relief, she cracked a smile at him. "Oh, a hermit, am I?" She shook her head and looked down. "I have spent only a fraction of my life on Stella. I have always had a thirst for knowledge that perhaps rivaled Tessir's at one time." Drawing in a deep breath, she looked up the mountain and sighed. "Unlike him, I have learned to temper that curiosity with wisdom."

Naerala turned her head back to Endri and nodded. "I apologize, I should not have insulted you. However, my point still stands. The Star Dragons continue to make mistakes. The consequences began with Tessir, and that was compounded by the forging of the Sword of Dragons. I fear the disaster that may come as a result."

Endri favored her with another dark look. *"We were desperate,"* he said, his mental voice quiet. *"Thousands of our kind had perished or turned to darkness. Millions of innocent people perished as collateral casualties. Entire worlds were laid to waste or, worse still, were entirely destroyed. If we had not built the Sword of Dragons and used it on the Dark Dragons, how many more worlds would have perished? Worse still, would the Star Dragons have survived at all?"*

"And tell me," she countered, "who suffered the most for your actions?" She glanced at Cardin before focusing again on Endri. "The Vrol were pulled into a war that had nothing to do with them. The Star Dragons used their influence to convince the Vrol to help build the weapon, and as a result, the Dark Dragons fell upon their world and slaughtered millions, destroying countless cities in their search for the forge." She sighed and looked ahead, her eyes growing distant. "Perhaps their world would have fallen prey to the Dark Dragons eventually, but we shall never know. Every action has a consequence, Endri. For Star Dragons, every action taken may have consequences that echo throughout all of time."

Cardin idly reached back and touched the hilt of the Sword. Consequences like the Sword, he realized. Could the Star Dragons have ever predicted how much its reappearance would affect his world? Not all of the consequences were bad, but he wondered how long it would be before Nuuldan returned. Would Halarite become another world like Vrol?

He considered Klaralin's second war on their world. The evil Wizard had intentionally used the Sword and Kailar to incite war, weaken the four kingdoms, and draw out the other Wizards so that he could directly confront them. Thankfully, whether from arrogance or in his blind pursuit of revenge against the Wizards, Klaralin hadn't counted on the Star Dragons coming back to Halarite and stopping him. It was likely that if the dragons hadn't come back for the Sword of Dragons, Halarite would have fallen.

Cardin realized that if the Sword had never been forged, Klaralin might well have succeeded.

"You focus on the possible negative consequences," Cardin stated. "Yet, what of the good that has come from it? Sure, my society struggles to cope with the new disasters and new reality that has befallen it. But the Sword, and everything that has happened around it, has brought our kingdoms together in a way never before thought possible, and allowed us to survive several catastrophes that would have happened to us either way. In fact," he raised his eyebrow as the idea occurred to him, "Regardless of the Sword of Dragon's existence, Nuuldan would still have crashed on our world. Without the Sword to protect us, he could have destroyed our entire population."

Naerala looked at him with raised eyebrows. "I see. You seek to lecture me on wisdom, now?" He felt his face blush, but he stood his ground, knowing he was right. "Perhaps that may be," she sighed. "Yet it is just as possible that Nuuldan would have ignored your world, and left to immediately consolidate his power and resume his conquest of the Universe." Cardin stopped short of a reply, realizing that she was right. Before the Sword of Dragons, he couldn't imagine there being any reason for a Dark Dragon to stay there.

"Now that you have the Sword, your world has become a target," she added. "Not just for Nuuldan, but for countless other aggressors."

Considering her words, he nodded. "I suppose that's true. Yet it still stands to reason that without the Sword, and the involvement of the Star Dragons, we would have been conquered by one of our own enemies."

"And there is yet another example of the Star Dragons interfering where they should not," she looked at him with a raised eyebrow, as if daring him to defend his position.

Forcing himself to unclench his jaw, he asked, "You'd rather we were conquered and enslaved by our enemy?"

She smiled and nodded her head, not in response to his question, he realized, but in affirmation of her own suspicions. "That is precisely the response I knew you would give."

He waited for another lecture, but when she remained silent, he faltered in his certainty. Exchanging curious looks with Endri, he asked, "Is that a problem?"

With a long, drawn-out sigh, she explained, "There is more going on in this Universe than your own world's needs. The Star Dragons are meant to understand that, and act with the larger Universe, and the consequences that their actions have on the larger Universe, in mind."

Somehow that irked him in a way he hadn't felt in a long time. He caught himself clenching his fists and forced himself to open them back up. "We're not just some inconsequential world..."

"No you are not." Her agreement with his prideful claim surprised him. "That is also precisely the problem."

He was about to rebuke her again, but then stopped and considered that concession. They were not an inconsequential world. Was she implying that by stopping Klaralin, the Star Dragons had set into motion a larger series of events that would reach beyond Halarite?

Considering their interactions with the Dareann Elves, maybe she was right. Halarite was now starting to reach out to other worlds. His presence here was proof of that.

If that was so, what would be the long-term consequences for Halarite? Or for the rest of the Universe?

So he asked the only question he could think of. "Are you saying things will go bad for other worlds?"

Naerala looked at him and appeared quite pleased with his question. "Now that, young one, is the right question to ask." Looking back to Endri for a moment, she then turned her gaze ahead and conceded, "I do not know. I doubt the Star Dragons know. However, what I can say is that your world has the capacity to choose. Your people can choose. And you, Keeper of the Sword, have the ability to influence their decision to a great degree."

Balking at the idea, he shook his head vehemently. "No, no I will not use the Sword to control others."

She smiled warmly at him. "That is good to hear, however that is not what I meant. By possessing the Sword and using it, you've grown in influence on your world, yes?" He nodded. "That is what I mean. Your influence on your people can be good, or it can be bad. No prophecy, no touch of destiny can change the fact that it is ultimately up to you what you do with your power, both literal and metaphorical."

Turning to Endri, she nodded. "As it is with you. What I ask is that both of you remember, your choices have consequences. Please consider the long-term as well as the short-term, because you both have the power to influence the courses of millions."

Endri stared ahead, and Cardin stared at him. He knew it even before he had picked up the Sword that becoming the Keeper would mean he had the power to change everything. He even feared the damage he could do, if he wasn't careful.

Yet despite all of Naerala's lectures, there was one decision she hadn't criticized – Cardin's role as Keeper.

Maybe that was her way of endorsing him as Keeper, without actually admitting it.

"Let me ask you one question in return," Endri spoke at length, turning his head to her. *"The Star Dragons have gone their separate ways, and only now, with Nuuldan's return, are we coming together again. This will once again give us a combined power beyond any others. Do you feel this is the wrong*

decision?"

Naerala's response was not what Cardin expected. A dark cloud hung over her, and she stared at the dirt path passing beneath her feet. "I do not know. I fear there is no good decision the Star Dragons can make in this regard." Looking again to the emerald dragon, she gave a weak smile and nodded. "But as I just told our friend here, it is a matter of choice. Make the right choices, Endri." Her features relaxed into a blank stare. "For everyone's sake."

Chapter 27

DESPERATE PLEA

Draegus grumbled, resisting the urge to draw his black cloak tighter around him. For a spring day, it was unusually cold in Archanon, a bitter wind coming down off of the mountains. From his vantage on top of the inner-city wall, he had a clear view around them of the snow still settled on the mountains.

He, Idrill Beredis, Governor Maral, and the being claiming to be Zairel stood atop the wall above the gates to address the people of Archanon. Hundreds had turned out after town criers had spent the morning summoning them, and as many as could fit in the intersection before the gates were present, with many more crowding the streets and cross streets nearby.

Draegus was still reeling from the events of the past two days. The image of his King, drained of life, of vibrance, of all that made him human, and left a lifeless husk, was seared in his mind. He hadn't slept all night.

Shock turned to anger, rage turned to determination, and he knew what he must do after the assembly. Even though he was being closely guarded and his movements restricted, it was time to stop sulking in his room. He knew of ways to get out without anyone knowing it.

Even though the city was locked down, he knew that there were those capable of sneaking out. He would seek out the assembly of the thieves, and find someone to take a message out of the city. He needed the Guardians. Perhaps together, they could find a way to stop Zairel, or Pevrin, or whoever he was.

A small pedestal was set at the lip of the walkway on the wall, and at that moment, Idrill stepped up and looked upon the crowd. There was no need to wait for them to grow silent, for the mood was already somber, and Draegus knew that rumors had already spread.

"People of Archanon," Idrill began, shouting as loud as he dared without losing his composure. "I come before you with news of great change. Many of you have voiced your frustration and anger over the disasters that have befallen us, some more vocally than others, some more physically than others. Rest assured that your voices have been heard, and that the changes you have demanded, and more, are at hand."

Draegus clenched his jaw, and wished to reach for his sword for comfort, but he no longer had it. Zairel had shattered it in the throne room, and the Prince had ordered him to remain unarmed until he decided otherwise.

"First I must tell you that the rumors are true," Idrill continued. "My father, Eirdin Beredis, is dead." A hushed wave of whispers raced across the crowd, and Draegus waited for an inevitable outcry of regret, or anger, or some sign that the people of Archanon would mourn the loss of their favored King.

It didn't happen. Instead, he felt a pulse of magic from Zairel. Not an obvious one that anyone with an inkling of magic could feel, but something he felt only because of his proximity to Zairel. While he didn't react outwardly, he was immediately suspicious. He knew from experience that magic could be used to influence or even control people, and suddenly he wondered if the pretend-god had those same powers.

When there was no other response from the gathered citizens, Idrill went on at length. "My father, along with the other leaders of the four kingdoms, acted sinfully and disgracefully, turning away from the teachings of the Order of the Ages, away from our gods. In doing so, they have left us open to the prophesied end of days, and the return of Degrin, the first demon. Even the Covenant failed the gods, and that is why one of the gods, the founder of the Order of the Ages, has returned to this plane of existence." Idrill motioned towards Zairel as he spoke. "Through a willing vessel of the only loyal member of the Covenant, Zairel has come to correct the wickedness and sin that has fallen upon our land, and prevent the return of Degrin."

There was another pulse of energy, a very subtle one that Draegus very nearly missed. It was largely directed at the crowd, he realized, which he was thankful for. Whatever influence Zairel tried to inflict, at least Draegus would not be affected. Not yet. Whether that was an oversight on the supposed god's part, or a request from Idrill so that the new king could 'break him,' he didn't know.

Continuing unabated, Idrill said, "From this moment on, the kingdom of Tal shall become a kingdom devoted to the teachings of the Six. We shall follow Zairel's directions, whatever they may be, and do whatever we must, whatever it takes, to prevent the return of the First Demon. I expect all of you to cooperate with both the clerics and the city guard in these matters."

The clerics. Draegus had almost forgotten about them. From what he heard, when Zairel and Idrill stormed the Grand Sanctuary last night, all of the clerics had fled, which meant that there were no witnesses to what really happened. Would they blindly follow Zairel as Idrill did now?

Then, showing just how much he had ignored his father's training, Idrill stepped down from the pedestal. No words of encouragement, no dismissal, he simply stopped talking. Leaving the crowd in stunned silence for a long time, wondering if there was more to come.

Draegus resisted the urge to shake his head, and stared as stoically as he could over the city, keeping his eyes off of Idrill and Zairel. He hoped that he would be dismissed, or better still, ignored again as the Prince returned to the castle.

Unfortunately luck was not with him. Idrill looked directly at him and ordered, "Captain Kataar, you will return with me to the castle. I have assignments for the city guard that I must brief you on."

Draegus looked at him, and then at Zairel, but the god had not turned from the crowd. Draegus felt the pulse again, and as a din of conversation fell over the assembled, he wondered if the false god continued to push his influence.

Looking to Idrill, Draegus bowed lightly. "As you wish, Your

Majesty."

Idrill then looked to Maral and hesitated. "Governor, once Zairel is finished here, please accompany him and see to his needs."

She did not look Idrill directly in the eyes, but she nodded and likewise said, "As you wish, Majesty." Draegus felt for her, knowing that she and Eirdin Beredis were long-time, close friends. She lived in the upper city and had grown up along with Eirdin, and was only too happy to serve as his advisor and, later, as governor.

Leaving her and Zairel, Draegus preceded Idrill down the stairs by the guardhouse, and then walked just beside and behind the King up the main road towards the castle. Draegus tried to remain patient, knowing that once Idrill briefed him on the orders, whatever they may be, he would have the time to leave the Upper City. More than likely he'd be escorted by Idrill's lackeys, but Draegus could deal with that easily enough.

When they arrived at the castle, to his surprise they did not enter the throne room as he expected, and instead headed for the South Wing, where the Allied Council chambers were. But again, they did not go where Draegus expected, and the King led him into one of the waiting rooms in that wing.

The room was empty, with most of the lanterns and candles unlit, only a single everlasting torch burning silently next to the door.

Draegus stood in the doorway stunned for a moment, suddenly suspicious of what was to come, but Idrill quickly closed the door and grabbed the torch off of the wall mount, inspecting the room quietly.

Once he had checked around every piece of furniture, the King came back to Draegus and stared at him silently.

"Uh, Your Majesty?" Draegus was unable to come up with a more coherent sentence. He'd never seen Idrill act so strangely before.

The new King continued to stare silently, his face unwavering at first, but then it broke into a look of terror, and he looked around the dark room again.

"Captain, I…" Idrill's voice shook, his eyes now affixed upon Draegus's shoulder, unable to look in his eyes. "I need your help."

Draegus should have felt satisfaction. Instead, he merely felt suspicious. "With what, Your Majesty?"

After drawing in a deep breath, Idrill finally looked into Draegus's eyes, and suddenly he could see just how frightened the young man was. "I believe I have made a terrible mistake."

Something welled up within Draegus's chest, satisfaction that he knew he shouldn't feel, but he couldn't help it. "Regarding Pevrin," Draegus stated.

The look in Idrill's eyes told him that the former Prince hadn't missed the use of the name Pevrin, not Zairel. "Yes," he whispered. "I no longer believe he is who he says he is."

After the speech he had just given the crowd, Draegus again looked upon Idrill suspiciously. However, considering that Zairel had been there, in the open, side by side with the King, he knew that Idrill would not have had a choice. If he had grown suspicious of Zairel, he could not openly show it.

Perhaps no one could.

"Do you have any way of contacting your son?"

That would be the next obvious question, wouldn't it? Draegus shook his head, "I'm afraid not. I don't think anyone can contact him. And since we have not yet heard from the Wizards' Guild, I doubt that we can rely upon them to help us contact either Cardin or the Star Dragons."

A long grimace spread across Idrill's face. "I was afraid of that. Then there is something else you must do for me."

Draegus raised an eyebrow, irritation boiling up inside, building up to flat out anger. "You must be pretty desperate."

Idrill flashed him a sour face. "Watch your tone, Captain."

Narrowing his eyes, Draegus shook his head. "You just lied to every single citizen of Archanon, and then turned to me for help. With no due respect, *Majesty,* I'm going to savor this moment."

The whites of Idrill's eyes flashed from how wide they opened. "I am still your King, whelp, and I can still have you imprisoned!"

"You can," he conceded, gritting his teeth. "So tell me what you need, and I can go do it before I say anything else you'll regret." He'd chosen his words intentionally, and waited for the King to correct or rebuke him.

At length, Idrill instead said, "I happen to know that Falind, despite all of its proclamations of peace towards us, has spies in our city."

With a barely contained snort of a laugh, Draegus nodded. "I am fully aware of this. The other kingdoms have spies in Archanon as well, just as we have spies within their cities."

Shock overcame Idrill's face, and that combined with his admitting that he was wrong almost made all of this worth it. Almost.

"It is only prudent, *Sire*, and it was always with your father's blessing."

"Which part was with his blessing?"

"Both," Draegus nodded. "Allowing foreign spies to remain while under watch, and deploying our own."

"I see," Idrill grumbled, looking down and allowing annoyance towards his late father to flash across his eyes. "Here I thought I knew about all of our operations."

When Idrill did not continue, Draegus sighed and folded his arms. "I'm guessing you'd like me to ask the Falind spies to tell King Sal'fe what has happened, and to find a way to get those spies out of the city so that they can do just that."

"More than that," Idrill nodded, his dark eyes staring into Draegus's. "Tell them that this being, whoever he is, is far more powerful than anything we have ever seen before. This being that inhabits Pevrin is dangerous, and…he intends to come for Sal'fe next, and the Cronal piece…" Idrill hesitated, and finished, "Pevrin is coming for their Cronal. Sal'fe and Falind are in danger. All of Edilas is."

Draegus huffed a laugh. "You mean, you are."

Idrill's eyes flashed rage again, but he did not refute the claim. "Yes, I fear for my life, so what?"

"Since we're discussing an informal assignment," Draegus narrowed his eyes, "And while we're on the subject of admitting that you're wrong, let me say that this was the only course that could ever have come about with your selfishness, Majesty." He said 'majesty' with sardonic disdain.

"Well fine," Idrill snarled. "Feel high and mighty all you like." He jabbed a finger into Draegus's chest. "However, understand this. I am the King, and I still will be after this is all over."

"Assuming we live through all of this," Draegus pointed out.

"You are pushing your luck, Captain," Idrill spat at him. "I shall let your impertinence slide this one time, because…"

"Because you need me," Draegus interrupted. "And you always will."

Idrill stopped short and slowly withdrew his finger. He narrowed his eyes, and shook his head. "No, Captain. Not always. Do not make the mistake of ever assuming that you, or anyone else, is indispensible. I will do what I must to keep *my* Kingdom safe."

He almost corrected Idrill by saying, 'you mean keep yourself safe,' but he resisted. Instead, he drew in a breath, forcing his hands to stop shaking. "My only question, then, is how I shall smuggle Falind's spies out of the city?"

"That is easy," Idrill smirked. "The city is locked down on my orders. Exceptions can be made, but again, on my orders only. I shall tell the southeast gate guards to allow you to determine when someone may leave the city."

Draegus smiled and nodded. "That is acceptable."

Scowling, Idrill said, "Well I am glad that I have your approval." He reached over to the door and opened it, light from the corridor spilling in. "Carry out my orders immediately!"

Smirking, Draegus bowed. "By your command, Highness."

Chapter 28

THE WHISPERING TREE

After managing to eat some of Ulpex's fresh-cooked breakfast, Dalin slipped out of the humanoid wolf's hut to drink water and wash the taste away, after which he took two massive bites of dried bread and crunched on it as quietly as he could, fearful that Ulpex's wolf-like ears could hear him.

Dalin was grateful for their host's generosity, but he just couldn't get used to the idea of eating freshly killed, unseasoned meat.

When he heard footsteps coming from inside, he stowed his bread back in its cloth and into his backpack, just as Sira and Ulpex came outside. Rays of sunshine broke through the tree canopy and illuminated them both, and Sira closed her eyes and smiled, taking in the warmth.

Looking at Dalin with an expression he couldn't place, Ulpex nodded and said, "I see you are anxious to begin your journey." Was that a hint of sarcasm in his voice? Did he know why Dalin had come outside ahead of them?

Choosing to ignore the tone, Dalin nodded. "Indeed." Uncertainty and embarrassment was quickly replaced with excitement, and he reached into his pocket to grasp the sylaric stone. Finally, today might be the day that he could find the wood for a new staff.

Hefting her pack onto both shoulders, Sira nodded. "Then let's get going."

Nodding in satisfaction, Dalin motioned to Ulpex, who led them north. As they passed through the edge of the village, Dalin noted how quiet it was in the mornings, as there were only a handful of residents outside. With the rays of the sun peeking through the forest canopy, and the serpent-like kaetz swimming around the branches lazily, it made for a serene image.

They came across a well-worn path heading north, along the foothills of the mountains, and set a brisk pace upon it.

After the village was long out of sight, Dalin eagerly asked, "How long will it take us to travel to the wooded forest?"

"Not long at all," Ulpex assured. "Another few minutes, and you'll begin to see signs of the change. It is rather sudden, and we suspect that this whole area was long, long ago covered by the wooded forest."

One of the kaetz swooped down and twirled around Sira excitedly, and she giggled while reaching out to caress one of its fins. That seemed to please it intensely, and it swirled around and around her hand. "Do the kaetz live in the wooded forest as well," she asked.

Ulpex shook his head. "No, they only prefer the altaflos." Dalin raised an eyebrow at that last word, and assumed it was the name of the soft-trunked trees.

As two more kaetz joined the first one in swirling around Sira, Ulpex chuckled and added, "Not to say that they don't venture out of the forest now and again. As you can see, they sometimes have an insatiable curiosity."

After a while of watching the three slither and glide around Sira, they seemed to settle into following just behind her, gliding up and down as if on invisible currents.

Until they came upon the wooded forest. The first trees came into view, looking mostly like aspen trees from Halarite, though with leaves tinted slightly blue from an otherwise normal green. As soon as they came out from under the last of the altaflos, the kaetz scattered back south.

To Dalin's great surprise, however, the currents of magic around them did not grow noticeably weaker. He expected them to, thinking the intense and constant flow of magic was a direct result of the altaflos, but he could feel the power flowing through these trees just as well. The only difference was that the magic had a different quality to it. He tried to pinpoint how it felt different, but could only liken it to the difference between freshwater and saltwater, imperceptible from a distance, but very noticeable once you interacted with it.

He immediately set about looking for fallen branches that might satisfy his needs, but wasn't sure exactly what he was looking for. There were fallen branches all over, far more than he was used to seeing in the arboretum in the former Wizards' Guild. It grew overwhelming, and he felt self conscious about his indecisiveness.

Ulpex and Sira watched patiently, following behind and chatting idly. After a few minutes of Dalin staring at one larger branch with a frown, the two approached and Sira asked, "So how exactly does this work, anyway?"

"What?" Dalin looked up distractedly, and then sighed and ran his fingers through his hair. "We usually take what we can get, often a collection of smaller fallen branches. Well, most of us, anyway," he amended. "Some of the Wizards will cut fresh branches off of trees, however I prefer not to harm life when possible. After we have sufficient material, over the course of several weeks, we will use magic to form the branches together and fuse them into a single piece, always with an open spot at the top to place a focusing stone."

Ulpex's head darted up in surprise. "Fascinating. There have been at least eight or nine villagers who used a similar technique to build their homes. I never thought to build a weapon in such a way."

Dalin was intrigued by their host's statement, but didn't like Ulpex's description of a Wizard's staff. "It is not a weapon, actually. We think of a staff as a tool, or an extension. It can be used for attack and defense, yes, but it is used for so much more than that.

"As strange as it may seem, despite the sheer number of available fallen branches, something is pulling me away from them," he spoke slowly, scratching at his head. It was as he spoke the words that he realized it. There was some force, somewhere in the forest, that called to him.

Closing his eyes, Dalin opened himself up more to the flow of magic, and tried to carefully follow those currents back along their line. He was startled to realize that the currents weren't pulling him exactly, but rather the sylaric stone in his pocket.

Wrapping his fingers around the stone, Dalin felt it pulse several times, tugging at his essence. When he withdrew the gem and held it in his hand, it pulsed brighter, and very quickly he noticed that it oscillated faster and faster with each passing second.

Easing away from him, Sira asked, "What's going on, Dalin?"

"I do not know," he conceded, closing his eyes again to focus. Using the same technique he taught Cardin, he let his powers extend into the world around them, so much so that through closed eyes, he could see all around him as beacons and flowing rivers of power.

It was overwhelming! All around them, magic was a great flood, torrents washing over each other, bashing up against him and his essence. Just as it was when they first arrived, but this time he didn't shut it down.

Arrow-like darts of magic zoomed past, this way and that, startling him. Never on Halarite had he felt or seen such concentrations of magic, and the closer they passed by him, the more they pushed against his soul.

With interest, and against his growing fatigue, he watched them carefully to see if he could ascertain a pattern. Yet the longer he watched, the more he suspected they had nothing to do with whatever tugged on the stone, since they seemed to move in every direction.

Until it occurred to him that the frequency of the magic darts steadily increased. *If they affect my soul, then surely...*

When he opened his eyes and looked upon the stone, he realized that it pulsed with each passing dart of magic.

As he spoke, he intuitively made the connection, "Something seeks the stone." He spoke slowly, working the words over in his mind as they came out, disbelieving his own mental eyes. "Sending out concentrated bursts of magic to try to locate it." He looked to Sira wide-eyed. "To locate me."

The pulse of the stone quickened, and his eyes locked onto it. Sira asked, "How can you possibly know that?"

His mind wandered back to adolescence, to half-remembered lessons from one of the golden-robed masters. "All living beings affect the magic around them," he explained, slipping into the teacher role easily. "Think of it like a stone thrown into a river – all of the water flows around it. The bigger the stone, the more water must alter course. Rapids can form, or should a boulder large enough fall in, the river may be forced to change course altogether."

He closed his eyes again, and carefully watched as the darts of magic grew closer to him. The closer they came, the more they pushed against his soul, and against the stone, which he suddenly realized were one and the same now, since he and the stone were linked on the deepest of levels. As he expected, not only did the darts affect his being by pushing against them, his essence, by nature of existing, pushed back, and they changed their course.

Despite the darts coming from every direction, he knew they had to have a central source. However, without a staff, his ability to concentrate his magic enough to trace the source back was limited at best.

Then his mental eyes fell again upon the stone. He saw it in his hand, saw his powers flowing into it through his finger tips, and back out into his palm, a constant, reassuring connection. The stone had helped him form a portal before, surely it could help him again.

So he channeled more power through the stone, and extended his being outward. Suddenly he could see everything, everywhere on Stella! A dizzying spectacle of power and magic, animals, plants, sentient beings. For the briefest of seconds he even felt Cardin's presence, high up in the mountains now.

His body seized, his soul wrenched about like a flimsy leaf pummeled in a waterfall of magic, gallons upon gallons pouring into him through the sylaric stone.

He collapsed to his hands and knees, the stone falling from his hand.

"Dalin!" Sira's voice cried out to him, and through open eyes, he saw her grasp his shoulders, but he could not feel it. His body had gone numb, as had his soul.

"Too much," he hissed through gritted teeth. "The stone. It is too much for me..."

While he was still connected to it, once it fell from his hands, the connection to all of the life on Stella was likewise broken. Yet the stone's pulse coalesced into a constant stream. Whatever happened, it had been exactly what the entity seeking him needed, and now knew exactly where he was.

Whether that was good or bad, he didn't yet know.

He stared at the stone, regret filling him, and the cold burn of defeat. Valkere thought he was ready for such power, but now he knew that he wasn't. He didn't have the focus or discipline needed to control that power.

Slowly, feeling returned to his extremities. More than that, however, he could feel the pulse of the world around him. In that instant, Dalin felt a connection to something further into the forest. In his mind's eye, he saw a blue-white beam of power link between the stone and whatever sought him.

Sira must have felt it too, even if her powers were minimal compared to a Wizard's, as her eyes, now affixed upon the stone, suddenly grew wide and her mouth fell open in awe.

Whatever it was that called to him, it pulled hard enough that the stone shifted towards it. Then it did so again. Fearful of losing the last gift Valkere had given him, Dalin lurched forward and snagged the stone just as it was yanked on again.

Once again in physical contact, his soul opened up to the world, but he shut down that flow of power, and isolated himself to just the stone, and whatever source connected to it.

"What is out there," he asked Ulpex. "What power could possibly be so strong?"

His eyes likewise wide with wonder, Ulpex shook his head. "I do not know. I know that Stella holds many secrets, but none know of them all, except perhaps Naerala."

Dalin exchanged glances with Sira. Did Naerala know that something would seek out the stone like this?

With feeling fully returned to his limbs, Dalin tried to stand, but instantly felt weak and began to fall again. Sira caught him, and he grit his teeth in anger. Not at her, but at himself. He was better than this, stronger than this! How could he have let magic overwhelm him?

With some great mystery still ahead of them, he knew he needed to regain his strength, and he knew there was only one way to do that quickly. With his jaw still clenched, he pried open his soul, and let magic flow into him. He directed that magic to a specific task, molded it and formed it to give him energy, to physically rejuvenate his shocked body.

It almost overwhelmed him again. Too much energy tried to gush into his soul through the stone, but he focused it, and let the excess bleed off into the world around him. This time it didn't overwhelm him. This time he controlled it. It took all of his concentration, every bit of his willpower, but he did it.

And he stood on his own.

Opening his eyes again, he smiled at Sira and released his iron grip on her shoulder. "Thank you. I am alright now."

She gave him a skeptical look, but she released him. Drawing in a deep breath, savoring the strange pecan-scented flowers that must have been upwind nearby, he looked ahead with determination. "Whatever it is, I intend to find out."

The stone, still connected to whatever called to him, was brighter than a star now, brighter than a Star Dragon's eyes. He wrapped his hand around it, and focused on the connective power through the stone. Again he felt an overwhelming gush of power, but he exerted his will over it yet again. This time it was a little easier, now that he knew what to do. This time, he could follow the connective current between him and whatever power lay ahead.

"If you're sure," Sira said hesitantly, "then we'll follow you."

With Dalin leading, the trio ventured further into the forest. Climbing over logs and boulders, ducking under low branches, they approached the source of the power at a steady, determined pace. After over an hour, they finally came to a clearing, the source being at the exact center of it.

A great tree, larger than any of the other wooded trees of the forest, stood alone in the center. Despite its size, and despite the life force he felt from it, it didn't have a single leaf on it, only an infinitely complex series of branches interwoven with each other.

"I have never before seen this tree," Ulpex exclaimed. "Nor has anyone described it before. It is far off the path that we usually use when seeking wood to burn."

Dalin closed his eyes and could now see that the connective power pierced right into the heart of the tree, and as the trio circled around the tree, the beam remained fixed upon the trunk. "Whatever it is," Dalin nodded, "it seems that it is my destination."

Whatever control he had just learned, he felt like he would need every ounce of it. "It is best if you two remain here."

Sira looked ready to protest, but with a frustrated sigh, she nodded. "Alright. Just be careful, okay?"

He tried to give Sira his warmest, most confident smile, but wasn't sure if it came out right. Turning back to the tree, he shook his head at himself, and started towards it.

As he approached, he opened himself up just a little more to the power flowing through the stone. He wanted to know more about what he was facing, but whatever it was, the tree was just the surface of it, literally. The power pulsing from the tree to the stone came from a source far below the surface of Stella, deep inside of the planet. The tree was merely how it interacted with the surface, he suspected, and he faltered in his steps when he realized that. Was it something to fear?

Steeling himself with another deep breath, he took another step towards the tree. And it reacted by slowly bending branches towards him, creaking and groaning as if blowing in the wind. He stopped cold, and the tree stopped in-turn. Dalin regarded it wide-eyed and terrified, but when he glanced behind him, Ulpex looked absolutely elated and fascinated.

"Should I be worried," he asked their host.

Ulpex blinked twice, as if surprised by Dalin's question, and then quite enthusiastically he replied, "No! This is incredible and wonderful, you must go on!"

Turning back to the tree, Dalin frowned, but was determined to get to the bottom of this.

Dalin took another step forward. Again, the tree branches all bent down towards him. *This is like something out of a frightening campfire story,* he thought, recalling such tales from Warriors during the countless nights in the field last fall and winter.

After another moment of drawing up his courage, he walked forward again, and the tree branches continued to bend towards him, until all but one stopped. The one that came closer came from about mid-way up the trunk. He stopped, surprised by the change in behavior, but the one branch continued to reach out towards him.

Except that it wasn't reaching for him. He realized all at once that whatever he felt was intent on the sylaric stone, and the magic pathway it created. So he held the stone up, open-palmed and as high as he could, just as the branch reached it and slithered around it several times.

There was a sudden flash of light as the branch lifted the stone from his hand, tendrils of blue-white lightning suddenly lancing between him and the branch. His hand seized in pain, his soul screeched in agony.

It wasn't from the tree, he realized. The pain wasn't because the tree or its source of power assaulted his hand, rather all of his life force was being drawn into the branch through the stone!

Panic set in, and he was terrified that he'd fallen for a trap. Maybe some strange magical creature that lured the most powerful to it, with feelings of warmth and assurance, only to drain them dry!

Until he realized how familiar the sensation was, even if it was a thousand times more powerful than the last time. It was just like when his soul had merged with the sylaric stone!

Whatever the source of magic was, it felt excited to have touched the stone, and the branch suddenly transformed, straightening out and raising the stone up. His life force continued to extend into it, and he realized that whatever power lay beneath Stella, it only wanted to help, but it didn't realize how finite Dalin's powers were.

If he didn't slow it down, it would drain him of life.

That wouldn't help Cardin. That wouldn't help anyone. The Staff of Dalin without Dalin was not the legacy he intended to leave behind.

If he could cinch off the flow of magic through him, then surely he could do the same to the energy leaving his soul. Furrowing his brow in concentration, he did exactly that, and instantly felt relief. At the same time, from all around him he called forth magic into him and, just as before, he focused it into a rejuvenating light.

Eager for more, the branch tried to drain him faster, but he kept the flow low, ensuring that he wouldn't lose himself to it. After countless minutes passed, suddenly the flow into the branch ceased, and he collapsed to his knees, grateful for the reprieve.

Seemingly oblivious to how close it came to killing him, the entity within Stella lowered the branch and held it before him, as if offering itself to him.

Drawing in a deep breath, Dalin forced himself to his feet. He gingerly reached for the branch, afraid that if he touched it, it would once again try to drain his life force.

Then he realized that the branch had molded and formed itself, and was as thick as a staff. He finally wrapped his fingers around it. Suddenly the energy in the branch pulsed, and it neatly broke off at the bottom. The remainder of the branch retracted back up to the rest of the branches, all of which now straightened into their natural resting positions.

Slowly, Dalin brought his new staff down and carefully planted it on the ground. He studied the dark-brown bark with interest, noticing that the pattern was almost scaly rather than what he was accustomed to seeing in wood.

It was the perfect height for him, and the sylaric stone was level with his forehead. Furthermore, it felt just thick enough for his hand to grasp comfortably. As if whatever had given it to him knew exactly what he needed.

He turned slowly and looked at his companions in wonder, but then realized how terrifying that must have been to witness. Sira's sword was drawn, but Ulpex held a firm, restraining hand on her. Her face pale, she gaped at him in a mix of wonder and fear.

Dalin looked one more time at the tree, and then at his staff, before he returned to his companions, testing the staff as a walking stick and finding that the seemingly lithe branch was now rock-solid and could easily support his weight.

With a breathless voice, he asked Ulpex, "Is that a normal occurrence on this world?"

Raising his eyebrows, Ulpex shook his head. "This in particular, I cannot say, but I can tell you that this world is unlike any other I have known. Magic here is so very different, so much stronger, and strange occurrences are not unusual."

Closing his eyes, Dalin experimentally called forth power through the staff, and found that doing so was easier than ever before. As if the control he had exercised during the staff's formation was now ingrained into it. Better still, he found it exceedingly easier to rejuvenate himself through it.

"I...never heard a voice," he started cautiously, opening his eyes again to look at the others. "Yet I felt as if some living entity wanted to give me something. To help me in the days to come. I cannot explain it, nor do I understand it."

"Ah," Ulpex smiled. "That is the greatest mystery of all. Here more than any other world, it feels as if there is a presence guiding magic. As if magic itself has intelligence or sentience."

"Preposterous!" Dalin's response was automatic, the idea explicitly discounted by the teachings of the Wizards. However, he then realized that it was Wizard dogma that magic had no guiding spirit. Just like with the Order of the Ages, he realized, dogma could be wrong. Just because it was heretical to think something didn't mean it was inherently wrong.

"Stay here long enough," Ulpex glanced between Sira and Dalin, "and you'll feel it more and more. That much I can promise you."

Dalin looked at his staff, and then back at the tree. It seemed that whatever he thought he knew about magic and how the Universe worked, he was wrong. Or at the very least, not entirely correct.

Tightening his grip on the staff, he smiled at his companions. "Well, then. Shall we make our way back to await Cardin's return?"

Sira drew in a deep breath, and then placed her sword back in its sheath on her hip. "How can you be so casual after something like that," she asked, incredulous. "I thought that thing was going to kill you."

He smiled lightly, but decided against telling her just how right she was. "I am fine, and your concern is appreciated."

She narrowed her eyes suspiciously at him, but then sighed in exasperation. "Are you up for travelling, or do you need time to recuperate?"

Dalin was tempted to use more power to rejuvenate himself, but he decided it would be in excess. He was strong enough now, and his body could recover the rest of the way on its own. Nodding towards the south, he said, "I am well enough, I promise."

Though there was still a look of doubt on Sira's face, she nodded in resignation, and then looked to Ulpex, who appeared amused by the exchange. The wolf-man caught himself, and then laughed nervously. "Yes, well, please. Follow me."

Together, the trio left the clearing, and headed back towards the village.

Along the way, all three were silent. Dalin contemplated Ulpex's claim about magic, thinking back to his training, to his experiences. As far as he could tell, magic was without any form of intent or self-imposed purpose. It responded to commands without variation, and even during his greatest moments of clarity and understanding, he had never felt any presence.

Magic was power, and all it took was the right kind of knowledge to use it, and a connection to that underlying power. It was as simple as that, right?

Then again, he was young, and had barely learned the deepest, most complex secrets of magic. Often in the past, he wondered if there was any real difference between himself, a 'lowly Wizard,' and the master Wizards. Their control and focus was refined, as one might expect from centuries of meditation and training their thoughts and feelings, but that was it. Or so he had thought.

Now he began to wonder if there were underlying truths to magic too outrageous and too difficult to comprehend for younger Wizards. Maybe that was the true separation amongst the ranks of the Wizards' Guild.

If so, then his inability to appreciate the Guild structure may have been wrong all along. He frowned at himself and shook his head. No, that couldn't be true, could it? Certainly that couldn't be the case, not after he had acted in such a headstrong manner.

It couldn't be true.

"Dalin?" Sira's voice penetrated the fog of his introspection, and he was jarred back to reality. He looked at her blankly, and she asked, "Are you okay?"

He tried to think of something to say to her, but nothing came to mind right away. Looking around, he realized how far they had traveled, and based on how magic felt around them, he realized they were close to the edge of the wooded forest.

Dalin opened his mouth to speak. But stopped the moment he felt it.

A pulse of magic not far off to their right, somewhere along the border between the two forests. His head snapped in that direction as he instantly recognized the magic of a portal. Ulpex had felt it too, and he leaned towards it, his nose twitching and sniffing.

"What," Sira asked, stunned by their sudden changes. "What is it?"

"Someone just arrived on this world," Ulpex stated. "Someone new and…very very different." He sniffed. "I cannot smell the newcomer yet, but someone from the village is nearby as well."

Dalin closed his eyes and used his new staff to reach out his awareness, following the currents of magic. He felt the portal close, knowing instantly that its origin was from a world very far away. There were two distinct points of energy near the portal's former location, but before he could focus in on them, he felt a firm hand suddenly grasp his arm.

"Wait," Ulpex hissed quietly. "Something is wrong, and if you focus in on them, they may realize we are nearby."

He gave their host a puzzled look, thinking that their village would

SECRETS OF THE CRONAL

accept almost any newcomers. "What is wrong," he asked.

Ulpex shook his head and looked intently at Dalin. "Whenever a newcomer arrives, we do not know they are coming. So why is one of our villagers already here to meet them?"

"Could it have been an accident," Sira asked. "I mean, if we're this close, maybe they just happened to be in the right place at the right time."

He shook his head. "Even for a world such as this, that would be a very new coincidence. However," he looked at Sira hesitantly. "Perhaps it is better that we find out for sure either way. If you will indulge me, let us look while remaining unseen."

Sira looked at Dalin with surprise, but shrugged and replied, "Sure, why not."

Dalin nodded, "I agree."

With an almost predatory smile on his face, Ulpex crouched down and prowled off of the trail. Dalin hadn't even realized they had found the trail, and chastised himself for having become so self-absorbed earlier.

He and Sira likewise crouched lower, and followed as quietly as they could. Not too long ago, this sort of movement would have been extremely uncomfortable for him, but now, after so many months in the field during the Orc War Campaigns and their venture into the jungles of Trinil, his body was getting used to it.

They didn't have far to go before they heard voices speaking, though they were indistinct and it was impossible to make out actual words. They came upon a cluster of smaller trees. Interspersed among the living trees were several large fallen ones, large enough for them to hide behind.

Ulpex led them up to one such log, keeping low and motioning for them to do the same. They came up on either side of him, Dalin reaching his hand out to gently touch the dead log. Yet even within its core, he still felt some life, some connection to magic.

As carefully as they could, the trio peeked over the log, through moss and the leaves of tiny new trees, into a clearing several hundred feet ahead.

Dalin recognized the villager as Pelick, the elf that they had met shortly after they arrived on Stella. The newcomer, however, was something else entirely. The figure stood much taller than the elf, perhaps at a height of seven feet or more, and was clad completely in

303

blackened, plate armor. He had seen plate armor complementing chainmail on Halarite, but never before had he seen an entire suit of just plate, segmented into many pieces so as to ensure mobility, but otherwise covering every inch of the person's body.

Even the newcomer's face was covered, except that Dalin swore he could see a glow within the eye slits. And their gauntlets were wicked-looking, the fingertips shaped like claws that could rend flesh at the lightest caress.

Whoever the person was, they didn't look friendly. More than that, the color and shine of their armor was very familiar. The exact same appearance as that of the darkened steel armor Klaralin had provided the orcs. Dalin very nearly exclaimed out loud when he realized that, but he managed to keep silent. He looked over at Sira, and saw the same look of recognition on her face as she gawked back at him, her brow very slowly drawing into a frown.

The armored figure reached out with a weapon, and Pelick carefully took it from their grasp, revealing it to be a long, darkened-steel dagger. The figure nodded at him, and then turned on the spot and summoned a blue-white portal. They stepped through and disappeared, leaving Pelick to stare at the dagger.

Long after the armored person had left, Pelick opened his robes just enough to stash the dagger inside, hidden from obvious viewing. The elf then turned towards the trail, towards them, and they all ducked.

"I don't understand," Ulpex whispered, frowning at Dalin and then Sira. "I...what I just saw, it makes me think that..."

"That Pelick is up to something," Sira volunteered. "Yeah. I don't know who that taller person was, but did the material of that armor look as familiar to you as it did to me?" That last question was directed at Dalin.

He nodded thoughtfully. "Indeed."

Ulpex looked even more shocked, and demanded in a raised whisper, "What?! Familiar how?"

Dalin sighed and thought about how best to explain Klaralin's invasion. "A powerful Wizard employed the help of an army of orcs to invade our world nearly a year ago." *Has it really already been a year?!* Shaking that thought out of his mind, he continued, "That Wizard supplied the orcs with weapons and armor that was that exact color and with that same dulled shine."

Ulpex frowned. "The similarity could very easily be a coincidence."

Dalin started to refute that, but stopped himself and nodded uneasily. "It is possible, however I tend not to believe in coincidences until I know for certain."

Ulpex's ears twitched, and he raised a hand to indicate they should be quiet. Dalin gripped his staff tighter, and thought about gathering magic for a possible strike, but that might alert Pelick to their presence.

Then he realized that it was too late. He felt a flash of magic, and the elf came around the far end of the log, immediately launching a magical attack from the darkened-steel dagger.

Dalin raised a shield at the exact same moment that Sira had, and they reinforced each other so that Pelick's attack didn't stand a chance of getting through.

The Wizard rapidly drew in magic and released a bolt of lightning right at Pelick's dagger. He was perfectly on target, and the elf yelped when the dagger was flung from his hand. The elf gaped at them, and then ran. But he didn't get far, as Ulpex took off after him on all fours, catching up in a matter of seconds and tackling him to the ground.

By the time Sira and Dalin reached them, the struggle was over, and Pelick was pinned beneath the wolf-man. Ulpex had his teeth bared, and even under his robes, Dalin could see his hackles were raised. He drew closer to Pelick's face, an inhuman growl reverberating throughout his body.

"Who was that person," Ulpex snarled into Pelick's ear. "Why were you meeting with them? Why did they give you a dagger?"

"I, I, I, please, don't hurt me, please!" Pelick was hysterical, and Dalin started to reach for Ulpex to try to calm him, but then thought better of it.

"Speak!" Ulpex barked.

Pelick nearly jumped out of his skin, and he sputtered out his confession. "I, they, I mean, Darksteel Army." Dalin exchanged another knowing look with Sira. "They sent me. I mean, to watch Naerala and the crystal, to tell them whenever an opportunity came."

"Opportunity for what!?"

Jumping again, he sputtered out, "To get the crystal! They want the crystal. They know, they, I mean, they know that you," he risked opening an eye to look at Ulpex, "are the only other threat. They wanted me to, to, to…"

Pelick clenched his eyes shut and couldn't finish, but Dalin already knew and finished for him. "You were meant to murder Ulpex."

All the elf could do was nod minutely, too afraid to move anymore. Dalin sighed, wondering who would send this man, clearly incapable of bravery, to kill someone like Ulpex. Surely they knew he would never succeed!

Dalin planted his staff in the ground and sighed. "Clearly you have failed."

Sira raised a cautioning hand. "Maybe, but if they were waiting for Naerala to leave the village, and they wanted Ulpex out of the way…"

Very slowly, Ulpex eased away from Pelick's face, his lips closing around his teeth. He stood up and brushed his robes off, the vicious animal persona vanished, leaving the quiet, reserved villager in his place. He looked at Sira, and then at Dalin, before he nodded to Pelick, who still had his eyes clenched. "They will come in force, won't they?"

Pelick stopped shaking after hearing the question, and he cautiously opened his eyes. After looking at each of the trio, he nodded. "They know that most of the villagers have magic," he added.

Ulpex nodded knowingly. "Which means they are coming in force."

Sira sighed in exasperation. "Well, then." She looked at Dalin and shrugged. "So much for our relaxing stay."

Chapter 29

UNLIKELY ALLIES

With a growling stomach, Kailar was grateful to have returned to Tieran after she took the mayors of Edingard, Neolas, and another city near the Plains of Glass home that morning. While Reyla had been keen to use Kailar's powers to gather the mayors, beyond that Kailar had been left in the dark, until called upon once again to take the mayors home.

She knew she shouldn't have let their callous use of her powers bother her, not when she had volunteered to do just that. After all, a good Warrior follows orders and doesn't involve themselves in affairs that are none of their business, right?

Inwardly grumbling, she drew in a deep breath and let it out slowly.

Her frustration was not lost upon Letan, who sat next to her in the Water's Edge tavern, waiting patiently for their food and listening to the crowded, boisterous sailor crowd that occupied most of the tables.

"What's wrong," he asked.

Raising an eyebrow, she tried to hide the annoyance from her voice and asked, "What do you mean?"

They sat at her usual spot at the far corner of the bar, and he turned on the stool to face her. "I can see it in your face. And," he motioned towards the noisy sailors, one of whom slammed his fist down as he relayed an exciting story, "I can hear your frustrated sighs even over them."

Glancing towards the sailors herself, she looked down then, avoiding Letan's eyes, knowing she'd feel compelled to tell him everything she was thinking, even if she knew he wouldn't like it. Maybe someday, she'd feel fine confiding every secret to him. Maybe today should have been that day, after they had finally slept together.

Mulling it over in her head, she clenched her jaw and forced herself to look into his eyes. Leaning closer to him, so that she didn't have to speak so loud over the din of the tavern, she confessed, "I'm starting to remember why I left the Tal Warriors all those years ago."

He blinked once, twice, and then allowed a grimace to fall over his features. "That's...not something I expected you to say."

Narrowing her eyes, she asked, "Why not? You saw how frustrated I've been through all of this, having to follow protocol just to oust a clearly corrupt mayor." She shook her head. "Guild procedure is rarely useful to doing our jobs."

"Guild procedure is what keeps us honest," he replied curtly, his informal tone turning to that of a commanding officer's. It was uncanny how easily he slipped into that mode, and annoying. "Those who fail to adhere to it end up like the Guild in Edingard."

"That's a bold statement," she scowled, her outburst made purely on impulse. She regretted it the moment she said it, but her pride wouldn't let her back-track or apologize for it.

The cool, level eyes Letan gave her let her know she was pushing him more than she should have. Pushing him away, she realized.

"So now you're saying we're corrupted by our policies?" The aggravation in his voice told her he was ready to launch into another one of his speeches about the greater good, the honor serving the Guild, all of those things that both endeared him to her and drove her crazy all at the same time.

"No," she shook her head. "I'm saying they hid behind Guild policy to cover their tracks. I'm saying they hid behind orders. I'm saying the way this entire damned continent is setup is a recipe for criminals, and as long as it stays the way it is, all we've done is give the good people of Devor a temporary reprieve, nothing more."

With a confused frown, he motioned towards the city council.

"Isn't that what we're doing? What was the whole point of you traipsing around with Councilwoman Reyla picking up and dropping off mayors?" She started to reply, but he interrupted, his face turning red as he spoke, "They're trying to form a united government on *your* recommendation, what more do you want?"

"I want to be part of it!" Her voice had raised enough to get the attention of some of the nearby sailors, and Alric gave her a curious look as he delivered pints of ale to patrons further down the bar. "I didn't do all this to be shut out and used like some damned tool!"

Realization dawned across Letan's face, and he drew in a deep breath. His pallor returned to its normal pale-pink as he slowly exhaled and closed his eyes. He was forcing himself to calm down, and somehow that only aggravated her more. She wanted to yell, scream, shout, anything to let out her pent up rage.

He must have realized just that. "That's what this is all about," he nodded. "You're hurt because they aren't involving you." She looked down, feeling her face flush with embarrassment at being called out. Damn him and his logic. "You want to lead the charge. You want to be on the front." He nodded. "You want to be able to control the situation."

She didn't have a reply. Not because he was wrong, but because he was right.

"You can't stand not having control of your life," he continued, "and that's why you left the Tal Guild." There was a shudder of fear in his voice, barely there but strong enough that she could hear it. "That's why you've resisted taking orders from me, why you've pushed for action, even when those actions were dangerous or even harmful to others."

The more he spoke, the more she felt a stinging in her eyes. Panic followed, and she turned back towards the bar. "Alric," she shouted, looking for the now-absent barkeep. "Where's our food?"

"Kailar…"

"Stop," she glared at him. "Just stop. I'm…I don't know…" She shook her head, trying to find the right words.

Only to stop cold when she looked over Letan's shoulder and saw a dark-clothed figure enter the tavern. The person, whom she could barely tell was a woman in her confining black clothes, covered her head completely in matching black cloth, only allowing a slit of her eyes to show through. On her belt was the familiar shape of the handle of a darkened-steel dagger.

Letan must have seen the look on her eyes and followed her gaze, and he acted instantly by shoving the bar stool away, sending it crashing into another group of sailors, while he stepped clear of the bar. As one, he and Kailar drew their swords, Kailar setting hers humming with dark magic.

Alric nearly fell over himself as he stumbled out of the back at the commotion. More surprising, however, was the interloper's reaction – she shot her hands into the air disarmingly. "Wait!"

Kailar and Letan had leveled their swords, ready to release magical attacks, but both stopped short of actually releasing their power. This was a new ploy by the assassins, and Kailar furtively looked around the tavern, searching for any other darkly-clad strangers amongst the sailors.

"Please, I'm not here to attack," the woman insisted. Something about her voice rung familiar in Kailar's memory. "I'm alone," she added quickly.

"Is that so," Kailar asked, noticing now that all of the sailors had stood up in sudden surprise, and any who bore arms had drawn them, though they were unsure who to point them at. "And why else would you be here?"

The assassin hesitated for a moment, and then very carefully pulled the cloth apart at her eyes, revealing that it was, in fact, two pieces that could be separated easily. The tan face beneath shocked Kailar when she instantly recognized it. A face from another life.

"I know you," Kailar spoke slowly, trying to recall the former Mage's name. "Arna, Aren, Aredin…"

Annoyed, the woman corrected curtly, "Ardelle. Former Captain of the Falind city guard."

Kailar grimaced and felt a pit of guilt form in her stomach, though she didn't dare show it on her face. Ardelle was the first person that Kailar had controlled through the power of the Sword. A year ago, she made Ardelle help her assassinate the King of Falind and assume control as the first step in Kailar's conquest of the four kingdoms.

She observed the assassin carefully, and noticed that her brown hair had been cut shorter since her days serving Kailar, but her brown eyes still had the intense stare that sometimes made Kailar uneasy, even when Kailar had controlled the Mage's thoughts.

"If you're not here to kill me," Kailar eyed Ardelle carefully, glancing at Letan to find that he had not dropped his guard one bit. "Then why are you here?"

Ardelle glanced at the sailors and Alric reluctantly, but then sighed and said, "I am here at my master's command, to ask you for your help."

Kailar felt her eyes grow wide, and she exchanged stunned looks with Letan. "Um…excuse me?"

Visibly clenching her jaw, Ardelle continued, "Edilas is under a grave threat from a being more powerful than any Wizard, even Klaralin, and perhaps growing more powerful than Cardin Kataar." Kailar tensed at hearing that name, but did not interrupt. "He is posing as one of the Six and inhabits the body of a former member of the Covenant. Furthermore, he has murdered King Beredis and the rest of the Covenant, and now controls all of Tal through the King's son."

As the events were spelled out, Kailar's sword drooped lower and lower, as did Letan's. This was not the news she would have expected from Edilas, not now, not after they had weathered so many catastrophes. How could things have possibly gone so wrong now?

She should have known better. Things can always get worse.

Ardelle worked her jaw around, grinding her teeth in aggravation. After hesitating longer, the woman took one step closer and said, "I am to formally ask you to come speak with Wizard King Sal'fe about this grave threat to all of Halarite."

Kailar laughed, but then clamped her mouth shut, not sure where the laugh had come from. "And why exactly would I do that? For all I know, everything you've just told us is a lie, and this is a trap, meant to finally capture me for Sal'fe's own purpose."

Ardelle grimaced. "My King predicted such suspicions from you. That is why he has ordered me…" She closed her eyes for a moment, obviously steeling herself for her next words. "I am to surrender myself to you," she opened her eyes and looked directly at Kailar. "To do with as you please."

With the same slow, deliberate motions from when she unmasked herself, Ardelle reached for the sheath of her dagger and unlashed it from her belt. Once it was free, she set it on the bar and slid it past the other stunned patrons to Kailar, who grasped it tightly the moment it reached her.

There was no concurrent surge of power that she felt, but she didn't expect there to be. Despite the darkened color of its blade, it was still a weapon of star magic, not dark.

Ardelle then raised both of her hands disarmingly, and eased down onto one of the barstools. "My Lord wishes you to believe his sincerity, and knew that our history together would help in this instance."

Kailar's jaw tightened. "You mean because of what I did to you, and how you no doubt despise me for it."

Ardelle nodded. "I believe the situation is serious enough to warrant these actions."

With a frown on his face, Letan glanced at Kailar and asked, "Wait, what did you do to her?"

She closed her eyes for a moment, and slowly lifted the dagger off of the bar to bring her hand down by her side. Kailar had intentionally neglected to tell Letan the details of her campaign with Klaralin, and never confirmed anything he learned through word of mouth. Would he understand? Would he continue to be as forgiving of her if he knew the depths she had gone to on Edilas?

Finally, after drawing up as much courage as she could, she looked at him, looked into his striking blue eyes, and through a shaky voice, said, "I took control of her will through magic. Forced her to help me. Forced her to do..." The memory of her ordering the murder of the Falind King played out in her mind. "To do terrible things for me."

His face slackened, but only a little, and he nodded and looked at Ardelle. "I see." He paused, and Kailar wanted to ask him what he was thinking. "So Sal'fe believes that by having you, someone who would clearly despise Kailar, surrender to her, we'll be more likely to believe the sincerity of his request."

Ardelle nodded curtly, her eyes flashing with rage at Kailar.

A long silence ensued, and suddenly Kailar was aware of their audience again. This was a rather awkward conversation to hold with so many people watching, especially when one of those persons was a friend, and another was her lover. Maybe that was why Letan wasn't pressing her for more information, but she knew that as soon as he could, he would ask her.

When Kailar didn't say anything one way or another, Ardelle huffed impatiently. "Look, if you still need proof, I'll stay here, in the dungeon or wherever you want to put me, while you check out Tal and ask around. Apparently they've locked up Archanon and aren't letting anyone in or out, but one of our assassins spying in Archanon was allowed out to come warn us." Kailar frowned at Ardelle's statement – allowed out? Who allowed them out, and why? "So time is short, and I ask you to make your decision quickly."

Kailar raised an eyebrow. "I see." It could still be a trap. Falind would sing Sal'fe's praises if he finally managed to capture or kill her, the butcher who had sent their Warriors on a hopeless mission against Tal. Plus it was not beyond the realm of possibilities, since Sal'fe was known for being manipulative.

Ardelle, on the other hand, was another matter altogether. Even as an assassin, Kailar couldn't believe Ardelle had a deceptive bone in her body. Even while under Kailar's direct control, her personality had shone through in that week together in Falind. Better still, she knew from experience that Ardelle was a terrible liar.

Kailar shoved the dagger hilt under her belt and sheathed her sword, and then looked at Letan. "I guess I'll go see what old Sal'fe has to say, then."

Letan's eyebrows shot up. "Not without me, you're not."

She shook her head, her expression dark. "I can't let you come along. Whether it's a trap or not, I can't protect you and unleash my full power if I need to."

Sliding his sword into its sheath, Letan shook his head resolutely. "You're still under my command. Consider this an order."

Shaking her head, Kailar started to object, "But I said…"

"It's that or I walk her to the dungeon and we sit on this information," Letan folded his arms.

Her previous anger flared up. Conscious of their audience, she managed to hold back her sharp retort, but this was exactly why she hated being part of the Warriors' Guild.

On the one hand, she wanted to leave the Devor Guild, to get out from under the control of anyone else. On the other hand, if she did, she would become a hunted fugitive again, and she'd have lost any hope of making a real difference.

"Fine," she nodded curtly, trying to hide her emotions.

Stalking past Letan, she felt her stomach growl, and she grimaced as she glanced at a full bowl of soup in front of one of the other patrons. Looks like she'd be missing lunch today, too.

"Standup and turn around," she ordered Ardelle. "We're going on a short trip."

Apparently suspicious, Ardelle looked at Kailar curiously, but did as she was told. The moment she faced away, Kailar opened a portal at the entrance to the tavern, straight into the Falind throne room. She looked at Letan and nodded. "After you."

Nodding once, Letan came forward and grasped Ardelle by the arm, and then preceded Kailar through the portal, with her hot on his heels, unwilling to let him go into danger alone.

They came face-to-face with a throne room full of people, and guards surrounding them with swords drawn. Sal'fe stood in front of the throne at the far back, a concerned look on his face initially, but then it turned to one of annoyance upon seeing Kailar.

"Stand down," the Wizard King's voice, enhanced by magic, boomed over the chatty crowd. "You must forgive these new guests, I did not expect them at this hour." The guards cautiously lowered their swords, but their gazes remained fixed upon Kailar. Sal'fe's voice took on a threatening tone as he glared at Ardelle, "In fact, I expected them early this morning."

Ardelle's head hung low, and that incensed Kailar. "She is not to blame. I was gallivanting around all of Devor this morning, and she could not possibly have caught up to me." Maybe it was because of what she had done to Ardelle, but Kailar felt compelled to defend her former guard captain.

"I see," Sal'fe's eyes fell upon Kailar.

Looking around at the assembled court, she realized that they had interrupted an audience. It looked as if some peasants had come before Sal'fe for some reason, and looked upset by the interruption. Worse still was when one of the guards recognized Kailar, and raised his sword again.

"Kailar," he growled. The moment he said that, her name echoed in whispers throughout the assembled crowd, and except for a few of the guards, who probably knew to expect her, the wave of shock that passed amongst the assembled was palpable.

The guard that said her name advanced, and Ardelle had to snap, "Eamon!" That halted the guard instantly. "She is here to answer to the King, not your personal vengeance."

The one named Eamon looked at Ardelle with no small amount of surprise, and then he looked back at his King and bowed.

"Forgive me, Your Majesty."

Sal'fe ignored the guard, and instead ordered, "Everyone out now." Looking at the peasants, he added, "We shall conclude our business at a later hour."

Whatever look of annoyance they had was instantly gone the moment they looked at Sal'fe, and they bowed deeply. "Yes, Your Majesty," one spoke.

A moment later, the guards escorted the court out, and closed the doors behind them. Kailar took a moment to look around the throne room, and noticed that a wooden frame with curtains was setup near where the marble floor had been damaged during her last visit. When she turned to look at the large curtains to the balcony, she grinned when she saw the familiar dark-blue curtains now hanging in place of the ones destroyed during her confrontation with Sal'fe. "I love what you've done with the place."

"Yes, well," Sal'fe drew closer, glancing at the curtains. "Your assistance was most unwelcome in that regard."

She looked at him curiously. "And yet you need me for something else."

The Wizard King stopped a few feet away, his staff clenched in his hands. "It is unfortunate, but yes. What has Ardelle told you?"

Looking to the former guard, Kailar relayed her words about the murder of King Beredis and the supposedly powerful entity that now controlled Tal. "Other than that, she hasn't said much. Not that we let her go on for long."

Sal'fe nodded, but then looked at Letan's grasp upon Ardelle. "Now that you have arrived, must you hold her so? She is one of my subjects, after all, Mister…"

"Oh," Kailar grinned. "Where *are* my manners before royalty? This is Lieutenant Letan Velethar of the Devor Warriors."

Sal'fe again eyed Letan, his distaste for the Warrior's grip on Ardelle apparent in his glower.

Letan looked around the throne room again, no doubt searching for any hidden assassins, before he nodded and released Ardelle. "Very well," he said as he stepped away from her. "Assuming your request for our help is genuine, I'll show a little good faith. But I'm not dropping my sword."

Ardelle looked at Kailar with a blank expression, and then crossed the distance to stand with her master. Kailar looked pointedly at

Sal'fe and added, "But you already knew who he was, didn't you? I'm sure former Mayor Evern told you all about him."

There was barely a flicker of surprise on the old man's face. "Former mayor, you say. Interesting."

She gave him the slightest hint of a smile. "Yes, well, running a criminal empire that spans a continent does tend to get a politician into trouble, doesn't it?"

"I know nothing of that," Sal'fe replied. "However, we have strayed from the central topic." Kailar didn't reply, and instead patiently waited for Sal'fe to actually say the words. After a moment of waiting for some quip from her, he gripped his staff tighter and sighed. "I am afraid that my information about this entity is minimal. He inhabits the body of a man named Pevrin, a former Covenant member, and claims that he is Zairel, come to punish humanity for straying from the teachings of the gods."

Kailar frowned and glanced at Letan, but he looked as confounded as she was. He shook his head and said, "I don't recall the clerics ever teaching that a god would return to Halarite like that."

"They never have," Ardelle grumbled. "Whoever he is, he's lying."

"Obviously," Kailar remarked. "The question is, why?"

"An astute question," Sal'fe replied. "It is exactly what I wish for you to find out."

When his words registered on her, she let out a cackle before she knew what she was doing. Her face warmed when everyone gawked at her. Clearing her throat, she said, "Sorry, but I'm not one of your subjects, oh great King. Sorry, *Wizard* King. You can wish all you want, but this is Edilas's problem."

She turned and made a big show of summoning a portal, but Sal'fe called after her, "I know that you still care about the four kingdoms."

Stopping short, her earlier rage was added to by an older, harsher anger, and her hands tightened into fists. "Oh yeah?" She turned back to him and wished she could strike that smug look from his face. "The same kingdoms that exiled me? And placed a bounty on my head? The same ones that sent assassins after me?" Her voice grew louder with each question, and her hands shook. "Tell me, which of those actions are supposed to endear this wretched place to me?"

Sal'fe was unfazed by her outbursts, and he simply grasped his staff with both hands so that he could lean on it. "You failed to conquer Edilas, but I was there when Cardin Kataar was interviewed by the Alliance afterwards. I know why you did what you did."

"You don't know anything about me," she spat back.

Sal'fe nodded. "Perhaps not. However, if you would not do this for Edilas, then do it for your new home." The Wizard glanced at Letan. "Do it for him, and any future you wish to have with him."

Letan frowned at Sal'fe. "What do you mean?"

Sal'fe scowled. "Oh, do not pretend that a being as powerful as this would be content to conquer only one land. I thought you would be smarter than that."

Kailar's fists tightened further, her fingernails digging into her palms. "Alright, let's say you're right," she folded her arms. "What does that have to do with me? Why me and not you, or someone else? Why not Cardin Kataar? Or another Wizard?"

An exasperated sigh escaped Sal'fe and he walked away from her in frustration. "Do you really believe I would invite you here under peaceful conditions if there was someone else who could face Pevrin?" After walking halfway to the throne he turned and waved his arms. "You are Falind's most wanted criminal! Working with you undermines my authority, especially after your grand entrance today!" He gripped his staff tightly and a menacing quality gave his voice an edge. "My people want your head for what you did to Falind, and I would give it to them if I believed that there was another way."

She slowly reached for her sword, suddenly very afraid that he might decide she wasn't worth keeping around after all. However, his temper subsided and he lowered his staff. "Unfortunately, I truly believe that you may be the only one capable of helping us. You see, Cardin Kataar has left Halarite on another matter of great importance, and…"

She scoffed. "What idiot thought that was a good idea?"

Sal'fe's jaw clenched, but he otherwise continued undaunted. "I believe you are the only other person on Halarite who has the kind of power that is a threat to this false god."

That made her pause. The only *other* person? Did that mean that Cardin had the ability to use dark magic as well? If he did, then it solved one of her outstanding mysterious. It wasn't the Dark Dragon that had unlocked the dark powers within her. The Sword of Dragons had, they had just remained dormant for half of a year.

"If this 'false god' as you call him is so powerful," Letan interrupted her thoughts, "why would Kailar stand a chance over anyone else? Is his weakness dark magic?"

Sal'fe leaned on his staff and considered Letan's question carefully. "I honestly cannot say for certain. However, I infer from his actions that he is afraid of dark magic. With the Prince of Tal's help, he ensured that Cardin would leave. Originally he probably intended for Cardin to simply be unreachable, but when a need for travel off-world arose, I believe they encouraged the Keeper to go."

Thinking about her next words carefully, she asked, "He was manipulated to leave so that his dark magic wouldn't be a threat?"

"I believe so, yes," Sal'fe nodded, the crack of a smile appearing on his face. She grimaced, realizing that it hadn't been a slip of the tongue, and he had meant for her to glean that information on her own.

At first, she chastised herself for letting Sal'fe manipulate her that way. Then she realized it didn't matter, not right now. This god, or false god, or whatever he was, sounded like a master manipulator in his own right.

And even if she denied it to others, Sal'fe was right that she still cared about Edilas. Especially Tal. She had tried so hard to make things better for her home kingdom, but she had failed spectacularly and had opened the door for one of their most dangerous enemies to rise to power again.

Maybe this was the Universe giving her a chance to make up for her past failures, more than she ever could on Devor.

Kailar looked to Letan, searching his eyes for his thoughts. He stared back, determination on his face. She suspected she knew his thoughts, but after the lecture he had just given her, she knew she had to let him make the decision. "This sounds like a legitimate threat to all of Halarite," he nodded. "So if you're looking for an official sanction of this as a Guild mission, you've got it."

"Do we need to get the Commander's blessing first," she asked, hoping she kept most of her sarcasm out of her voice.

If she'd failed, Letan didn't appear to notice. He simply shook his head and replied, "No. I consider our current situation as 'being in the field' and as a Lieutenant, I have authority to make command decisions in the field."

A grin tugged at the edges of her mouth. "Let's say I do this," she started, looking towards Sal'fe. "Let's say I agree to help. Where do you suggest I start?"

The Wizard tried to hide the relieved look from his face, but he failed spectacularly. "My spies tell me that Pevrin's intent is to take the Cronal from Falind. It was not with our Covenant representative when Pevrin murdered them. In fact, it is in my possession. If his focus is on the Cronal, then the answer may lie somewhere in the Grand Sanctuary."

Her eyes grew wide. "In Archanon. The most heavily fortified city on Halarite, and from what Ardelle tells me, is currently locked down."

Sal'fe gripped his staff tightly and gave her a sardonic look. "I would assume that someone of your talents could easily find a way in. Is my confidence in your abilities unfounded?"

Kailar allowed a murderous glare to cross her face. "I hate you."

Chapter 30

MISSING PIECES

Following the defeat of the statue, Baenil and Gilrin set to work examining the door, trying to make sense of the runes and other symbols on it. While they no longer glowed, the runes were still readable. While Kellis and the remaining marines attempted to gather the bodies of the fallen, Reis accompanied Elaria and Anila to the roof to ensure that the beacon hadn't lost power with the rest of the capitol.

Thankfully Elaria's concern that it was drained of power when the statue awoke were unwarranted, and it still glowed brightly at the top of the tower. Never-the-less, she recharged it to ensure it wouldn't fail on them anytime soon.

The trio took a moment to look out upon the city, into the shadows beyond the columns that they had re-lit earlier that morning. Elaria lowered her head and drew in a deep breath, before she looked in earnest at Reis and Anila.

"I should warn you two that…" She stopped short, and Reis and Anila exchanged curious glances. After another moment of warring with herself, Elaria looked Reis squarely in the eye. "I'm concerned that what we're going to find down here might shake the very foundations of Dareann society." She laughed and looked down at the courtyard in front of the capitol. "More than it already has, anyway."

"What do you mean," Reis asked. "Shake it how?"

Her face slackened into a deadpan look, her eyes growing distant. "I don't know. But, to be honest...I think it needs to happen." When she looked at him again, it was as if she saw through Reis, like she was looking into the distant future, or perhaps the distant past. "This whole situation, the elven language on the statue, the attack, it's like someone tried really hard to hide something big."

Anila voiced the question forming in Reis's mind when she asked, "Aren't you the least bit afraid of what we might find under the statue?"

Elaria nodded solemnly. "Very much so. But change is always frightening, and I think that it is now inevitable." Clearing her eyes, she smiled weakly. "Anyway, I just thought I should warn you. Gilrin and I both are very vocal about our distaste for how dwarves are treated, and I'm really worried about how Gilrin will react to whatever we find down there."

Motioning towards the stairwell, Elaria led the way as they headed back for the antechamber. Reis asked, "Do you think he'll be a danger to the rest of us?"

"Towards any of us, no," Elaria glanced back at him and shook her head just as she began to descend the stairs. "I doubt he'll do anything against myself. Nor is he likely to harm Baenil, since he's never seemed to care one way or another how dwarves are treated. Then again, Baenil's apathy might incite Gilrin. In any case, I'll do my best to keep him calm."

Once they returned to antechamber and the statue, Elaria hopped down to help Baenil and Gilrin, while Indira and Kellis came over to talk to them. Reis noticed that several of the makeshift beddings now had irregular forms beneath them. He grimaced at that, wondering if even one of the casualties were relatively intact. Would their loved ones get to see them one last time?

After Reis reported that the beacon was functioning fine, Kellis planted his hands on his hip and nodded in relief. Then a great smile overcame his face and he looked at Reis. "That was a hell of a smart move you made there."

Letting his characteristic grin spread across his face, Reis nodded. "Yeah, it was, wasn't it?" In his peripheral, he saw Anila roll her eyes.

Kellis laughed quietly. "What made you think to go for the eye socket like that?"

Thinking back to their fight against the kiklar again, Reis replied, "I figured it was the only visible weak point, especially after hitting his knee joint didn't do a damn thing. But I'm honestly surprised no one else thought to try for its eyes."

"Elaria and I both did," Anila volunteered, "but with magic attacks. Not even lightning or ice shards broke through, as if blocked by a barrier."

Reis felt his pulse quicken when she mentioned her magic attacks, and looked at Kellis and Indira with apprehension. Indira mentioned it first. "About that." Anila met her gaze unflinchingly. "I didn't sense any power from you before the attack, and I still don't. What..." She caught herself and rephrased, "How did you do that?"

For the briefest of moments, Reis saw Anila's eyes flicker in uncertainty, before she folded her arms in front of her and sighed. Looking to Reis, she asked, "I suppose I can't hide it anymore?"

Before he could reply, Kellis asked, "You knew about her powers?"

Reis grimaced, wondering if he would be in trouble for covering for her. "Yeah. It's a long story."

When he didn't volunteer any more information, Kellis raised his eyebrows, and then looked to Anila for further explanation.

After heaving another defeated sigh, Anila explained, "My parents were what you might call a mixed relationship. My father was an exiled Wizard, and my mother was a Mage."

Reis watched Kellis and Indira's expressions closely, wondering how they would react. He knew that his response a few months ago had been less than friendly, but he'd also had a personal stake in the matter, and had felt betrayed. Would anyone here actually be offended?

Both were obviously surprised, and they looked from Anila, to Reis, to each other, and back. Kellis finally spoke, "I thought Wizards didn't intermingle with us lower beings."

Reis grinned inwardly, recalling he had said something similar during Anila's confession to him.

Anila cringed at the Lieutenant's tone. "Not all Wizards are bad. Then again, I never actually knew my father. I can't even picture his face in my head. My mother said he preferred isolation, and that was a lifestyle that she couldn't get used to. She told me that one day, before she even knew she was with child, he disappeared." A dark look overcame her face then, but she didn't elaborate further.

A thought suddenly occurred to Reis when he thought about Dalin, and he frowned at her. "Wait, you said your mother *was* a Mage. Where is she now?"

Even in the dim light from the flickering torches, he could see Anila blush. "She was killed during one of the Lesser Wars," she cautiously admitted.

Now it was his turn to exchange surprised looks with the others. "The last Lesser War ended when I was a child," Reis pointed out.

Indira pointed out, "She didn't say the last one, she just said 'one of them.'"

So his suspicions were correct - Anila was older than she looked. He wanted to ask, but didn't wish to be rude. Thankfully, or rather not thankfully, she admitted, "I'm just shy of one hundred and fifty years old."

At first he felt too shocked to think of or say anything. Most Mages didn't live past one hundred years old, though the oldest in recent times turned one hundred twenty before she died, and that Mage had very much looked her age. For a Mage, anyway.

Anila looked like she was thirty at most. Not even a hint of grey in her hair.

Indira eyed her carefully, and asked, "So where do your loyalties lie?"

Giving the Sergeant a dead-pan stare, she replied, "To the Covenant, and the Order of the Ages. Why would that change?"

"The Wizards do not believe in the Order," Kellis folded his arms.

Anger flared across her face. "I'm no Wizard," she spoke through clenched teeth.

"Not to mention I think she's proven herself today," Reis defended, pointing towards the fallen statue. "She could have let us all die to cover up her secret. She chose to fight."

Indira and Kellis both looked at him, and then looked at each other, their suspicious features softening.

"I think we have it," Elaria suddenly called up to them.

While Indira immediately turned her attention towards the door, Kellis stared at Anila for a few moments longer. Finally, he turned away as well, and the four of them gathered around above the door, while the marines started gathering nearby.

Looking up at them, Elaria deferred to Baenil, who explained, "I misinterpreted the runes as having no impact on the actual elven words written in between them. They actually are meant to modify each statement, and I pressed the wrong series of glyphs."

Reis's head spun at the use of words like glyphs and runes, and wondered what the difference was. He kept his ignorance to himself, and just nodded at the statements.

"I am confident that I know the correct combination now," Baenil stated resolutely.

The archeologist reached for the door to begin pushing them, but Kellis stopped him, "Hold on!" Baenil pulled his hand away quickly, as if stung, and looked up at Kellis with a confused look. "Are you absolutely certain?"

"Uh, I, well." He stuttered and stammered over his response, and then nodded emphatically. "Yes. I made a mistake before, I was too quick, and I am so very sorry for that mistake." He looked pointedly at Indira. "I am sorry."

"I've gone over it with him thoroughly," Elaria defended. "I believe he's right, and we can safely open it."

Reis glanced nervously at the statue, recognizing all too well that they hadn't actually destroyed the armor itself, and that it could potentially be revived if the trap was sprung again. Kellis and Indira looked to one another, and then Kellis asked, "Gilrin, what do you think?"

The dwarf, standing between Baenil and Elaria, shrugged. "I don't know one way or the other, lad. Everything about this door is elven, so I have to rely on my friends here to make the right call."

Kellis drew in a breath, looking around at the gathered marines, before he nodded. "Alright, give it a try. Everyone give the statue a wide berth and be ready. Remember, if it comes back, try to get in close enough to stab it in the eye."

"No magic," Reis added, drawing his sword and backing away into the darkness of the chamber. Elaria hopped up to ground level, drew her daggers, and lit them up to provide extra light. Anila did the same with her sword a second later, and Reis wondered if using those powers would make their weapons ineffective.

Once everyone was ready and far enough away from the statue,

Kellis nodded, and Elaria called out, "Alright, Baenil."

There was a long pause, and Reis tightened his grip, his leather gloves grinding into the sword handle. He watched for any hint of a blue light or glow, any sign that the statue would come to life.

Instead, he felt the ground tremble just a little bit, and he heard stone grinding on stone. His heart leapt into his throat, but the statue remained lifeless.

Baenil's excited voice called up, "It's open!"

Letting out a breath he hadn't realized he was holding, Reis lowered his sword in relief. The rest of the team approached, but most of the marines kept their weapons ready. Reis was tempted to do the same, but decided to sheath his, and he and Kellis looked down as Baenil and Gilrin beamed up at them. "We're in the clear," Gilrin declared triumphantly. Then he looked into the open door and added, "It's time to find out what the devil this is all about."

Elaria dropped back down into the stairwell and shone her daggers inside. Then she stepped halfway in and pushed her hand against what looked like a glow panel, and much to everyone's relief, several lit up, illuminating a spiraling stone staircase downward. Reis grimaced, hoping it didn't go down too much further. He already felt like they were further below ground than any person should have ever gone.

"My marines are used to that kind of close quarters," Indira suggested to Kellis. "We can scout down there."

However, Elaria had stepped a little further in, and then ducked back out to shake her head. "There's no need. It's just a room directly beneath the statue's pedestal, and it looks like it's pretty small."

Without waiting for further orders, she went back inside. Baenil and Gilrin looked to one another, and then followed.

Too curious for his own good, Reis hopped down, while Indira and Kellis sheathed their weapons. As he stepped inside of the doorway, he heard Indira order her marines, "Set a perimeter around us, just in case we set off another trap. Stay alert, and watch that thing closely."

As Reis followed the others, and Kellis hopped down and followed behind him, he discovered how right Elaria was. Just a couple of feet down, the wall of the staircase opened up inside, revealing what looked like a small circular library, with bookshelves lining the entire wall except where the stairs came down, and the glow panels lit up the wall just above the shelves.

In the center of the room, however, was something new, a pedestal with some sort of contraption atop it, shaped like a dais.

As he descended, Reis looked closely at the books lining the wall, and noted that they looked extremely old, but were well preserved and somehow showed no hint of dust. He wondered if the room had been sealed well enough that no air got in. The markings on the bindings looked strange to him, but he thought they might be written in the same language as the markings on the statue. Until he came to other books that had completely different markings, ones he recognized as having seen throughout the dwarven city.

Baenil came to the same conclusion, exclaiming, "There are both dwarven and elven books in here!"

"More evidence that our two people once cooperated," Elaria asked Gilrin. The dwarf didn't reply, as he was more concerned with the apparatus in the center.

Baenil, Elaria, Gilrin, Reis, Kellis, and Indira gathered around that pedestal, and stared at the strange stone and metal contraption. It was unlike anything he had ever seen before, almost like an open book, but flat instead of bent at the binding, and they could see inside of it, the inner workings of which were a mess of strange, circular objects with outlying teeth.

It was Elaria who recognized them. "Those are gears. This is a device!"

Reis looked at her curiously, his eyes scrunched up at the unfamiliar description, and the word 'gears.' "A whatsit, now?"

"I have seen similar devices before," she replied confidently. "In fact, one of our allies uses them prolifically."

Indira raised an open hand above the 'device' and closed her eyes. "I can feel magic imbued within it."

Elaria nodded, "I can feel it too. If I'm right, every component inside of this thing is enchanted." Closing her eyes, she also raised an open hand above the dais. Reis watched her expression go from wonder to confusion. "In fact, there's more to it than just this pedestal. I can feel the enchantments going deep underneath. I believe we're on top of a much, much larger device."

Reis looked to the others, wondering if anyone else had the same question he did. When they didn't, he asked, "What does this 'device' do?"

Retracting her hand, Elaria opened her eyes to inspect it closer. "I have no way of knowing." She drew closer and peered at the inner workings. "And it seems we will not find out anytime soon. There are four gears missing."

Reis tried to look closer as well, along with everyone else. Sure enough, he saw four tiny poles sticking up where it looked like more of the circular pieces were meant to fit in.

Looking at the others, Baenil suggested, "Maybe there are answers in these books."

Everyone gawked around at the library, and Gilrin nodded. "Aye, and between you, me and Elaria, we should be able to decipher some of them."

Then the trio looked at Reis and the others, and Elaria smiled sheepishly. "This is going to take a while…"

Chapter 31

STRENGTH IN SHADOW

When Cardin had set out on the journey into Stella's mountains, he thought that it would be a leisurely hike up one pass and then down into the valley where the copse would be. He should have listened closer when Naerala had said that it would take all day to reach their destination.

Granted, days on Stella were definitely shorter than days on Halarite, but by the time they had crested the second pass and begun their descent into a valley, the sun had already dropped low enough to cast them in the shadows of the mountains.

Unfortunately for Cardin, the temperature dropped a lot more in the mountains when night set in, far more than in the village. Despite the cold, they trudged on, with Cardin wrapping his travelling cloak closely around him.

Similar to the trees around the village, there was no need to light torches or other light sources, since much of the flora around them, specifically a type of red and purple mountain flower, glowed bright and lit up their surroundings. In fact, those very flowers were closed during their daytime journey, and it was only at night that they opened up, as if to catch the rays of the moon. When they unwrapped, the entire valley swam with the scent of almonds, and he wondered if all the flowers on Stella smelled like various nuts.

The trail was easy to follow at night, the path well-worn from multiple pilgrimages, and Cardin was thankful for that. After Naerala's lecture about the Star Dragons, the trio had mostly hiked quietly, with Naerala picking up the pace. She was surprisingly fit, and Cardin had to work hard to keep up.

By the time they made it to the bottom of the pass, all pretense of twilight was gone, and the stars shone bright, with hardly a twinkle to them. Staring up at those stars, Cardin couldn't help but feel a closer connection to them now than he ever had as a child. He was in awe of Stella, and promised himself that he would return someday, whenever there was a pause between crises that would allow him a break.

They hiked along the valley for another couple of hours, but the further they travelled, the greater the density of flora that surrounded them. They entered another forest, this one half-filled with wooden trees and half-filled with the unusual trees from the village.

When they came upon their destination, Cardin knew it instantly, not by the sight, but by the sensation. As it was everywhere on Stella, when he would close his eyes and reach his senses out, he could feel all of the life around him radiating with magic. But here, at the copse, he could see a well of energy radiating everywhere, and the flora and fauna thrived off of it.

More than that, he could see the dome of energy, a protective shield that prevented anyone from entering the copse through any place other than a naturally-formed rocky arch that blocked the shield from reaching the ground. The arch was at least ten feet tall, and several vines and flowering plants adorned it, all of them shining in the night.

Sitting beneath the arch was a collection of rocks and stones roughly shaped like a humanoid meditating, though its 'knees,' if that's what they could be called, were drawn up close to its chest, and it appeared to be completely still. If Cardin didn't sense the life force within it, he might have dismissed it as nothing more than a strangely arranged pile of rocks.

Naerala stopped them a few hundred feet away from the entrance, while Endri came up from behind and hovered over them, staring at the creature. Cardin looked at Naerala, and then up at Endri. Some past legend he remembered reading during Guild training came to mind, and he asked, "Is it a golem?"

Endri looked down, his starry eyes shining bright even in the ambient glow around them. *"An educated guess, however I do not believe so."* Motioning his snout towards the dormant rock creature, he concluded, *"It is an elemental."*

A frown crossed Cardin's face, and he stared at the rocky creature. Another name he had heard in passing reference, but only in regards to Wizards. Legends spoke of some of the most powerful Wizards being able to summon creatures from the essence of the elements, but none were known to have done that since Klaralin's reign.

If this was an elemental, then it was obvious that it was an earth-based elemental. "And you say it will not allow anyone to pass?"

Naerala nodded thoughtfully. "That is correct. Many have tried, even some of our most skilled warriors have tried to defeat it or make it past. It is slow and lumbering, but it may extend its arms quickly, and can catch you easily."

Endri raised his head up, and declared, *"I could easily defeat it."* But then he stopped himself, and looked back down at Naerala. *"However, the power I would need to destroy it would likely damage the surrounding area."*

"Yes, I knew as much," Naerala glanced up at him. "Thank you for restraining yourself." Turning to Cardin, she added, "I would ask the same restraint of you. Please try not to harm the surroundings. This is a sacred place."

Nodding solemnly, Cardin cursed inwardly. How in the name of the Six was he going to do this, then? He recalled his battle against Kailar in Archanon, where even simple, but powerful arcane attacks caused collateral damage, in some cases destroying entire homes around them.

This would be his greatest challenge in focus and control yet.

"Stay here, Endri," he spoke, faking confidence as he worked the problem over. "I'll see what I can do."

Drawing in a deep breath, he stepped forward and reached back to grasp the Sword. He willed the enchanted scabbard away to free his weapon and brought it forward, the feather-light claymore-sized weapon visibly blood-red even in the low ambient light. Cardin looked at it carefully, realizing that it had been months since he last physically used it against an opponent. He knew that the weapon was unlike any others, and he suspected that if anything could cut through the enchanted rock, the Sword could.

After only taking a few steps forward, he felt himself cross a magic threshold that he hadn't noticed before, setting his hairs on end, and a pulse of invisible energy drew across the open path to the elemental. It suddenly stirred, the rocks rumbling against one another.

If there was a ward that set it off, he realized, then this was not some accident or happenstance. Someone or something had set that ward, and tied the elemental to it.

Moving with the kind of slow deliberate motion he expected for something its size, his opponent emerged from the archway to stand tall.

Very tall.

Cardin gulped as he gawked up at it, realizing that this would be even more difficult than he thought. He frowned when he noticed that the elemental's height seemed to fluctuate, and he noticed that as it grew taller, its frame grew thinner, and that the opposite would happen when it shrank.

Some kind of moss grew on several of its rocks and stones, the flora naturally lighting its frame, and Cardin smiled. At least that would make it easier to see it in the dark.

Drawing in power from all around him, Cardin infused it into every muscle in his body, while he simultaneously charged the Sword with what he thought was just enough energy.

An approximation of a face appeared on the creature's head, noticeable only by the recesses that vaguely imitated eyes and a mouth, and on that face came a scowl. It groaned, or rather the rocks ground against one another, and it raised a fist up and lumbered at Cardin.

With all the strength of magically-enhanced muscles, Cardin charged at it. The elemental brought its fist down upon him, but he was ready with his most powerful shield. The fist exploded against it, scattering rocks all around. Cardin didn't break pace and released a blast of magic straight into the elemental's chest. Rocks scattered everywhere from the blast, opening a hole into its core.

With as much strength as he could muster, Cardin leapt and buried the Sword into that gap, slamming his shielded body into his opponent's. The Sword pierced through to the creature's back, and he released the last of the pent-up energy within the Sword into the creature's body. As it fell backwards from Cardin's impact, it exploded in a shattering shower of rocks.

When Cardin landed on his feet, he felt elation inside, realizing that he had done it in one try! The elemental was defeated.

He turned to smile at the others, only to realize that the creature's energy had not dispelled. And almost as quickly as he had 'defeated' it, it reassembled itself, and towered over him again.

"Dammit," he cursed, and leapt up over a surprisingly fast-swinging arm. He landed on top of the elemental's left shoulder, and buried the Sword into the top of its head, releasing another blast of energy that dissipated just shy of the ground, strong enough to blast the creature apart while sending Cardin flying away from it, and away from the copse entrance.

He tucked into a roll and allowed his momentum to naturally die, and then he was on his feet, facing the creature as it reassembled itself and faced him. Somehow it looked a lot meaner now.

"What the hell are you," he reflexively asked. It replied by swinging its arm and detaching one of its larger constituent rocks, hurling it straight at Cardin. He leapt aside in a roll, and then as the rock sailed past him, he turned and blasted at it with magic, hoping to at least disintegrate it, but his attack went wide, and suddenly the rock came sailing back, barely missing him.

When it's ranged attack had failed, it leapt at Cardin, its errant rock colliding with its chest unharmed, and it brought both of its arms down on Cardin. He stood his ground, letting the creature's fists explode against his shield, and then he swung the Sword at its neck, decapitating it. The scattering of rocks gathered into the creature again, and a new head formed atop its shoulders.

It pounded on his shield again. And again. And again. Over and over, scattering itself each time, but reforming and attacking again. Cardin hoped he could outlast the creature's magic, but he felt no diminishment from its essence.

Then he panicked when he felt the cold void form inside of his chest again. "No, no, no, not now!" His shield waned, his powers sputtered, and he was vulnerable. He dove out of the way of the next attack, barely in time as the elemental's fists pounded the ground inches away from where he landed. He scrambled back onto his feet, grasping the Sword tightly, but feeling no magic in it, only a void.

Another fist came down upon him, and he rolled in a different direction. He got to his feet again and faced his opponent, hoping that the Sword could at least still stand up to the creature, and he cut down on its arm before it could lift it up from the ground.

The Sword rattled and rang out upon impact, jarring his arms and chest. The elemental didn't pull back, but instead swiped at Cardin, slamming into his chest and sending him flying over the trail. He tumbled across the ground, pain wracking his entire body. He knew that several ribs were broken now, and he swore he felt his left shoulder pop out of place.

Struggling to breathe, Cardin looked at his opponent, and it slowly turned to face him. He looked at where he was, and realized that it had sent him flying outside of the ward. Did that mean it wouldn't attack him anymore?

If its job was to guard the copse, then it would not come after him. He held his breath, watching as it stared across at him, as if daring him to get up and try again.

But he couldn't. Not in his current condition, not without magic.

He realized that he'd lost his grip on the Sword at some point, but it was only a few feet away. He tried to reach for it with his left hand, but his strength gave out and fresh bolts of pain shot into his body. *Definitely dislocated.*

Cardin thought he heard a whisper, someone's voice in his head. Star magic was coming back to him, slowly seeping in past the darkness, and it was Endri's voice, growing stronger and louder with each passing second.

"Cardin! Are you okay? Cardin!"

"I hear you," he turned towards where the voice came from, sensing Endri's reassuring presence as the dragon came to tower over him. Naerala was with him, and she knelt down next to Cardin, resting a hand on his dislocated shoulder and sending strands of healing magic into it.

Wincing and groaning, he closed his eyes and clenched his jaw. This hadn't gone his way in the least.

He had failed.

A jarring sliding sensation, and suddenly his shoulder was back in place, the pain instantly fading under Naerala's healing touch. She pulled her hand away and was about to press it against his battered chest, but he waved her off. "No. No, I can do this part myself." He opened his eyes and stared into hers, swearing for a moment that there was a light of magic behind them. "Thank you, though," he nodded. "You took care of the hard part."

She smiled, but replied, "I do not believe that for a moment, but you are most welcome."

"You held your own quite well," Endri encouraged.

"Yeah," he growled, standing despite the pain in his chest and the difficulty he had breathing. "Until dark magic asserted itself again." He sighed in frustration, but then winced.

Closing his eyes, Cardin summoned the power needed to heal, allowing the green light to wash over him and mend his broken bones and bruised muscles.

"No," Naerala's voice came out of the darkness. "It did not assert itself."

Cardin's eyes shot open and he looked at her in confusion. Had *she* made it happen to him somehow? No, she couldn't have. She had no apparent ability with dark magic. "What do you mean?"

His healing efforts had tapered at his distraction, but he refocused his thoughts and continued his efforts while Naerala spoke. "You were failing to defeat the monster," she supplied. "You were growing frustrated and desperate, but at the same time, you maintained control over your powers, for the most part." His errant blast earlier flashed in his mind, and he hoped that the blast would miss anything living and dissipate into the air. "Tell me, in the past, how have some of your greatest breakthroughs in powers occurred with the Sword?"

He frowned at her question, thinking back over the last year. Learning to summon a portal moments before a meteorite incinerated him. Learning to heal when that little girl almost died from her burns. Summoning his avatar against Nuuldan when his powers were ready to fail and Nuuldan was ready to destroy him.

Realizing the point she wanted to make, he grinned. "Always when the moment was dire, and I was desperate." Nodding, he added, "And usually when I wasn't ready for it, and I had to learn to adjust to my new powers afterwards." He shook his head, and added, "I still don't know how to do some of it on command, even though I know I can do it." He thought of his failure to summon his avatar, and of how he only recently learned how to summon a portal on command.

"Exactly true," she smiled thoughtfully.

He narrowed his eyes, and then looked back at the elemental, which lumbered back towards its resting spot under the archway. When the darkness had grown within him during battle, his shield was raised, and the creature smashed at him relentlessly. Though its wear on him was negligible, it was still constant, and he had taken that moment to consider what he could possibly do to defeat a creature that hadn't even wavered against his attacks.

The darkness had come when he needed a solution. The Sword, he recalled, always seemed to intuitively know when he needed a power. It had saved him in times when he had no business being saved. It was the only reason he was still alive.

Dark magic.

He looked again at Naerala, and she nodded, as if reading his thoughts. "Cardin, if you are to be the Keeper of the Sword, there is one thing you must always and forever understand. Nothing is inherently evil. Nor is it inherently good."

With a slow nod, he thought he understood. He feared dark magic, feared that it might corrupt him like it would a Star Dragon. But he was not a dragon. And the Sword had only ever given him what he needed.

He looked down at the blood-red blade, its black hilt a shadow in an otherwise well-lit area. Then he looked again at the elemental. Its essence, he realized, was pure star magic. He thought back to his encounter with Nuuldan, at how the Dark Dragon's first attacks against his star magic-powered shield had eaten away at it, until it felt like it had never existed in the first place, and all of Cardin's strength was drained from him.

Bending over, he picked up the Sword and examined the lines inlaid into the blade.

"I think I know what to do," he looked at Naerala, and then up at Endri. "I don't know if it'll work, but…"

"Believe that it will," Naerala insisted. "Or else it will not."

Raising a curious eyebrow, he nodded and turned back to the elemental. It had just reached its spot and turned, ready to sit down again. Cardin closed his eyes for a moment, and focused within. He thought about how he summoned power, and realized that dark magic was the opposite of star magic. So did that mean he had to perform the opposite actions to summon its power?

The moment he thought of that, the darkness welled inside of him and star magic was pushed outwards, away from his core. It was cold, and felt so empty.

Except, it wasn't.

There was power in that emptiness. Strength that he had not noticed before.

In those moments, he was cut off from star magic, and he could no longer feel the life around him, the power. Even Endri's ever-present and reassuring strength was gone.

But within himself was renewed power. And he used it.

Drawing in a breath, Cardin opened his eyes, and stepped across the threshold. He didn't feel the pulse of magic, but he saw the creature stop halfway as it sat, and it pushed itself back up, its 'face' glaring at him. Its mouth moved as if to roar, but no sound came from it. It extracted itself from beneath the archway and lumbered at him, gaining speed.

Cardin channeled the absence within himself into the Sword, feeling the cold, dark energy streaming into the blade. He pointed the Sword at the elemental, and when it was only halfway across the field from him, he unleashed his power, and a blast of darkness, surrounded by a purple haze, lanced out and shattered into the creature.

The glowing moss on the elemental's rocks suddenly went out, and every rock and pebble that made up the creature exploded backwards, away from Cardin's attack, and scattered across the field.

He waited patiently, enduring the darkness, letting it remain within him, knowing that he might need to use it again. But the creature did not stir. Nor did its moss light up again.

Hoping it was over, Cardin focused inward, and willed the void to be filled again. It washed over his soul, like hot bath water pouring over every inch of his body, and he felt life again. He sensed Endri's core, and Naerala's. Only this time, everything was in stark contrast. He had a much sharper understanding of the magic that surrounded, passed through and swirled around him.

Including the deep, intense, warm power within Naerala, which felt stronger than anything he had ever felt before. He looked at her, and she smiled. His earlier suspicions were right, she wasn't exactly who she appeared to be. She was far more.

Endri's voice reached his mind, sounding terrified and impressed all at once. *"That was..."*

Cardin glanced up at his friend. "Speechless? Well, that's a first, isn't it?"

The emerald dragon smiled down at him. *"Indeed it is."*

Cardin looked again at the Sword of Dragons, and let out a satisfied sigh. It seemed that there were deeper mysteries to the Sword than he realized, even after everything he had been through with it.

With practiced ease, he reached back and placed the Sword within its enchanted sheath, and then looked to Naerala. "Now what do we do?"

Her eyes darted towards the archway. "You have passed the test." He raised an eyebrow. Had she set the ward? "Now you must enter the copse."

Glancing over his shoulder, he asked, "What will I find?"

"Only you can answer that question."

Chapter 32

REVELATIONS

After the initial discovery of the hidden library and the 'device,' Reis settled onto the steps along with Anila to watch the elves and dwarf work, just in case they set off any other traps. Indira and Kellis went back up into the antechamber to inform the marines and to relieve some of them for watch duty.

The mix of dwarven and elvish books fascinated him, even if he couldn't read any of them. The very oldest books were ready to fall apart, but when Reis mentioned his surprise that millennia-old books survived at all, Elaria pointed out that all of them had enchantments meant to preserve them through the ages, though even enchantments were limited in how long they could protect.

Fearful of destroying the older books, the team moved on to newer ones, finding that the oldest were stored directly beneath the stairs, while the age decreased along the right, and the very newest were near the foot of the stairs. Elaria said this was 'clockwise,' but Reis had no idea what that meant.

Baenil stuck with the older texts for a time, while Elaria and Gilrin looked for newer books that they had some chance of understanding.

For a long time, Reis and Anila sat in silence, his mind wandering to the events that had transpired, and the possible implications of

Anila's secret finally getting out. If Kellis and Indira's reactions were any indication, she would be met with trepidation and uncertainty at the very least, and possibly open hostility from a few.

He tried to remember if she had ever mentioned if the Covenant knew her secret or not, but he suspected they would have to know. Maybe that was even why she worked for them, because they would gladly take advantage of her talents without letting the world know. Reis also realized that the Order was known for protecting and providing for those without homes or families, and that certainly seemed to fit Anila.

Reis then wondered if they would be able to spend more time together. He wasn't exactly sure what her duties were, just that she was considered a guardian of their secrets. *Go figure,* he thought. *They guard her secret, and she guards theirs. It makes perfect sense.*

With his elbows planted on his knees and his head resting in his hands, he looked sideways at her, a question on the tip of his tongue, until he saw the distant look on her face. Frowning, he followed her gaze to the apparatus in the center of the room. Her look was remote, but she was definitely focused on the apparatus.

"You okay," he asked, his voice quiet so as not to disturb the others. When she didn't reply, he waved a hand in front of her eyes. "Hey, you there?"

Blinking in surprise, she focused on him. "What? Oh. Sorry, I was…thinking of something."

After a beat, he said, "Copper for your thoughts."

A wry smirk crossed her face. "Do you actually have a copper piece on you? Or are you going to have to owe me?"

"Actually," he pretended to reach for a non-existent money pouch. He had known he wouldn't need money on this mission, so he hadn't bothered to bring any.

Anila chuckled, but then looked at the dais again. Reis let out an obvious sigh and shook his head. "Something's obviously bothering you. Is it something I can help with?"

Her eyes narrowed and she looked down, apparently considering his question. After another prolonged silence, when he was ready to give up pestering her about it, she asked, "Do you think that…after the last secret I kept from you, that you would begrudge me keeping another?"

Raising a curious eyebrow, he considered her question for a

second, and then shrugged. "It depends, I guess, on why you're keeping that secret, and whether or not it would hurt others." A tingling feeling grew in his stomach, an uneasiness about the topic that made him curious about what she hid now.

Shaking her head slowly, but still avoiding his look, she said, "It's nothing that is harmful to anyone right now. However, it *is* something I was ordered to keep secret by the Covenant. Perhaps the biggest secret of them all." A grimace drew down her face, and she let out an exasperated sigh. "Then again, given everything that's happened in the past year, maybe it is a dangerous secret."

Reis shook his head and commented, "All secrets are dangerous for someone, and that's why they're usually kept secret."

The tiniest hint of a smile brightened her face. "That's a good point."

Leaning back on his elbows on the step behind him, he looked at the researchers just as Baenil, a deep frown on his face, put one book down and crossed over to the very newest books at the foot of the steps, and picked one up after browsing through them.

"To be frank," Reis started, "keeping a secret as part of your job, as part of your *honor*, is important. That's always something I can understand. As a Warrior, we've always been taught that it's important not to tell civilians about our deployment plans, because it might allow bandits to know where to expect us, and where not to expect us. In that case, lives actually depend upon secrecy."

"Another good point," she conceded. After staring at the dais a while longer, she looked at him and asked, "When did you get to be so wise?"

He laughed, louder than he meant to. "No, I'm most definitely not wise. If I was, I wouldn't have treated you the way I did." His face grew warm. "I wouldn't have messed up our friendship like that."

Anila didn't reply, and after a moment of thinking about it, he was glad she didn't. They may have been friendly towards each other again, perhaps even with a hint of more, but he didn't feel like he deserved her forgiveness. He hadn't earned it yet.

Reis's gaze fell again upon the trio reading, his eyes only half-focusing on them, while his thoughts went back to his time on the sea with Elaria and Anila.

Before he could go too far into his reverie, however, he heard

Baenil mumble something, and he noticed that the elf's deep frown had grown even deeper.

Elaria picked up on it, too. "You found something?"

At first, Baenil didn't appear to hear her, but then he looked up, his expression still the same. "I think so. This was a journal from an elf who helped build this entire chamber and the apparatus. The name of this elf is familiar, too, but more importantly, he speaks of what this is supposed to be."

That caught everyone's attention. Elaria and Gilrin set down the books they were working on and gathered around Baenil, while Reis and Anila leaned forward with interest. "Well, tell us, lad," Gilrin insisted. "What does it say?"

Baenil looked back at the book, his expression troubled. "Some of it uses language that I am unfamiliar with, so I cannot be exactly certain of everything. However, from what I understand, this chamber, the books, the device, it was a centuries-long project built cooperatively between the dwarves and elves. There's a passage here that reads, 'once ancient enemies, the elves and dwarves had become such close allies. With both of our peoples strong with magic, we began to unravel the secrets of the Universe together.'"

Turning the page, Baenil scanned over the pages before he continued to summarize, "This was meant to be a gateway." He paused and re-read a passage. "A gateway to knowledge and power."

Elaria exchanged glances with Reis and Anila, and he thought of Elaria's earlier suspicion that they were on the brink of a shattering discovery. "What kind of knowledge and power," Elaria asked.

After another moment of reading, Baenil's eyes grew wide. He scanned the same section several times before he finally replied. "All knowledge." He looked up at Elaria, his mouth ajar in shock. "All power."

Reis felt himself grow skeptical. How was that even possible? That would put them on the same level as the gods! But then he reminded himself that the Six were once human, and had ascended to their godhood. "Maybe the elf was talking about ascension," he suggested. Everyone turned to look at him, so he supplied, "I mean, it makes sense. Ascension is meant to be the ultimate end to our existence. Well," he hesitated. "I mean, according to the Order. Ultimate knowledge, ultimate power, unending existence. Basically, to become godlike."

Elaria considered his suggestion, and nodded. "That's a sound supposition."

Baenil nodded. "Under normal circumstance, I would agree. However, I don't believe that's what this is meant to be," he nodded at the device. Turning the page again, he read some more before adding, "This seems to reference a vast library of knowledge. And…" He looked around at the books surrounding them, and then again at the book. "And not this library. These were just books referenced to understand how they might construct this device. The library they talk about is 'beyond our realm, beyond the next.' I think I'm reading this word correctly, 'a nexus of everything.'"

Reis felt a deep frown crease his face, and he turned to look at Anila, only to find that she didn't look at all surprised or perplexed by any of this.

Before he could ask her about that, Baenil continued. "Once the device was finished, a group of elves and dwarves used it together, but found themselves in separate places in this…in this 'plane of knowledge.' In fact, everyone who used this device always found themselves alone on the other side."

Turning the page again, Baenil's eyes grew wide. "These next passages were written much more recently. The language is a more recent dialect, I think I can directly translate it. 'Fifty centuries have passed since we last visited the Library, and the guilt still weighs heavily upon me. I am fortunate to have found my journal intact, for it will allow me to record the last moments of my life before I sacrifice myself to protect it for all time. If you have defeated the guardian and find this journal, heed my warning, do not use this device! Not all knowledge is safe, and I have learned that knowledge without wisdom is the most dangerous of all.'"

The team looked around at one another, but then kept their eyes focused on Baenil, hungry to hear more. Reis felt something twist in his stomach, recalling that this was a similar lesson taught by the Order of the Ages. That was one of the core missions of the clerics and the Covenant, to teach the people both knowledge and wisdom from the books of the sanctuaries.

Baenil continued, turning the page and reading, "I know that I can never justify our actions, but if you still doubt whether the Library is dangerous or not, understand that when my people acted, it was because we wished to preserve the futures of millions of worlds. In the Library, you can learn absolutely everything. What was, what is, what will be. We learned of the future that we had created with this very device, a future where the dwarves used the power and knowledge from it to conquer world after world. They claimed it all as their own, feeling it their divine right. After all, what is a god but one who is all knowing, all powerful?"

All eyes fell upon Reis. He gulped and tried to smile innocently.

Pushing past the distraction, Baenil read the last lines of the journal. "So we did the only thing that we could think of. We denied them knowledge. We denied them power. We severed all connection between the stars and the dwarves, leaving them in the void, never to use the device again, never to use magic again. It left them vulnerable. It destroyed them. We destroyed them." Baenil glanced nervously at Gilrin, as did Reis, and the look of shock and rage mixed upon his face made Reis's stomach turn. "We were wrong," Baenil continued. "We did not understand that the future is never set in stone, and the consequences of our actions will echo throughout eternity. Do not make our mistake. Leave this place buried and forgotten. Destroy it if you can."

An emptiness welled up deep inside of Reis's chest. Everyone remained deathly silent, while Baenil lowered the journal. A chill ran through the chamber, up Reis's spine and raising the hairs on the back of his neck. He looked upwards, towards the defeated statue. He gulped hard, and wondered if he had just destroyed the spirit of the very elf that had written those final words.

The one who had helped sever all dwarves from magic.

The group watched Gilrin carefully. His eyes were almost impossible to read, but in his own heart, Reis felt a twinge of anger, growing stronger as the elf's final words sunk in. Reis knew what it was like to be powerless and at the mercy of those with magic. His rage grew stronger when he realized that the elves now treated the dwarves, the people they had violated, as slaves.

"It was you," Gilrin glared at Baenil, his voice menacing while his chest began to heave. "Your people did this to us. Your people enslaved us! You did this!"

His voice rose, his fists clenched, and he looked ready to murder Baenil. Elaria rested a cautious hand on his shoulder. "Hey, that's not fair, Gilrin." His head snapped around to glare at her, and he shrugged her hand off. "Baenil didn't do anything to your people, and we can't be blamed for something our ancestors did!"

"Maybe not," he growled. "Yet you're more than willing to take advantage of the situation created by them! Stepping all over our accomplishments, burying them, hiding them, making us feel inferior and reminding us of it every day!"

"Gilrin," she pleaded, but he cut her off.

"You did this to us!" His shout was loud enough that it caught the attention of those above, and as Reis and Anila stood, they heard Kellis and Indira rushing down the stairs.

"What's going on," Kellis asked, his hand on the hilt of his sword.

"We're leaving, lad, right now," Gilrin demanded. "I'm going to tell my people, all of them!"

Kellis looked bewildered, but Reis stepped up by him and quickly whispered the explanation, "Ancient elves used this place to strip the dwarves of their magic."

The wide-eyed look on Kellis and Indira's face mirrored the horror in Reis's stomach.

"No," Baenil suddenly said, surprising everyone. "No, you cannot!"

Gilrin's hand was instantly on his short sword. "No?! How dare you!"

"Things are already tense between the dwarves and elves on Darea," Baenil defended. "Even I noticed it."

Elaria nodded, "This could incite an uprising."

"Yeah, so what?" Gilrin pulled the short sword just enough that it clicked free, though he didn't yet draw it. Reis very carefully reached for his own sword, but wasn't sure what he would do if it came to blows between the elves and the dwarf. He empathized with Gilrin, and found himself growing increasingly angry with Baenil and Elaria, even if they didn't deserve their malice. He glanced at Anila, and suddenly remembered the anger he felt towards her a few months ago. This was a far worse offense, and he considered Gilrin's reaction to actually be tempered.

"It would tear the very fabric of Dareann society apart," Baenil defended. "Everything that we are, everything that we have…"

"Yeah, you wouldn't have dwarves to step all over anymore," Gilrin spat out. "You'd actually have to serve your own damn food, clean your own pots, build your own homes. Such a pity, isn't it!? Isn't it! And your lot, you would deserve every bit of it!" With each shouted statement, he drew his sword a little more, until it was free and he held it menacingly at his side.

Baenil backed away, and Reis noticed that Kellis and Indira had begun to ease their weapons free. He looked over at Anila, saw her doing the same thing, and then looked down at his own hands, grasping his sword tightly, ready to draw. Could they rightly interfere? Was it their place to defend one or the other?

Thankfully, he didn't have to decide. "Maybe he's right." Everyone gawked at Elaria, her hands slowly moving away from her daggers, still secure in their sheaths.

Baenil's eyes grew wide, and he stared at her. "You can't be serious!"

She glared at Baenil, the first time that Reis had ever seen her look at another elf that way. "We've built our society on the backs of slaves, Baenil, you cannot deny it!"

"I know, and I hate it," he tried to defend. "But, the College! Our studies, our research! It would all end in such an uprising."

Elaria raised her chin up. "It's no less than we deserve."

Reis exchanged glances with the others, and then drew his hands away from his weapon. He noticed that Gilrin looked less incensed now, the dwarf's eyes looking appreciatively at Elaria.

Staring at Gilrin with a mournful stare, she shook her head. "I have always hated how my people have treated yours, my friend. I'd rather it not come to an uprising, but this," she motioned at the device, "it's just too much. I can't just bury this." She glared at Baenil again, and added, "If it comes to it, if no one will let you speak or listen to you," she turned again to Gilrin, "then I will also stand up for you. It's time things changed on Darea."

Baenil gulped, and he leaned against the book shelves, defeated. Sighing, he glanced at the journal, and his gaze lingered.

"If you destroy it," Elaria said cautiously, "you'll only delay the inevitable. I won't let the truth die. Neither will Gilrin."

Looking at her astonished, he shook his head quickly. "No, that's not what I was thinking. Actually, I was thinking that this would provide irrefutable evidence, and if we present it to the College, the Board will have to acknowledge it and bring it to the attention of the Emperor."

Elaria looked surprised, but then smiled. As Reis realized the implications of Baenil's words, he too smiled.

Turning to Kellis, Elaria said, "Lieutenant, I believe our mission here has come to its natural conclusion. Would you be kind enough to escort us to the surface, so that we may leave Halarite?"

Kellis hesitated, his face somewhat pale. However, after considering her request, he clicked his sword back into place and nodded. "Of course. This matter is far outside of our purview, and we cannot interfere." Turning to Indira, he ordered, "Please designate some of your marines to remain behind to guard. I don't want something this dangerous left unguarded."

"Yes, sir," she nodded, and then headed upstairs to issue orders.

Reis drew in a great big breath, but then suddenly felt very afraid. He looked at Elaria, and he realized what this meant. If an uprising did happen on Darea, then it could be years or even decades before he saw her again, or never.

"Pack up camp," Kellis snapped him out of his worries. "We leave as soon as possible."

Chapter 33

OVER THE WALL

From the Falind throne room, Kailar and Letan returned to Tieran in order to don their light-leather armor and travel cloaks. Kailar asked if they should alert the Commander to their actions, just to follow protocol, but Letan agreed that time was of the essence, and Kent was not expected to be in the Guild today due to a summons by the city council.

Knowing that, after preparing to head out, they met back in Letan's quarters to make a plan.

"I pretty much grew up on Devor," Letan folded his arms and leaned against the door frame, while Kailar stood in the open center of the room, prepared to make a portal once they were ready. "I don't really know anything about Archanon or its layout, so we'll be relying on your knowledge to get us in." He looked at her cautiously, and asked, "Do you remember any vulnerabilities from the, uh…last time you were there?"

Their conversations in the tavern was not forgotten, and Kailar felt a rumbling of her previous aggravation resurface. She knew that Letan meant her attempted invasion with the orcs last year, but she still kept so much guarded that he looked surprised when she said, "I used to live there, so I know the city pretty well, and let me tell you, it won't be easy."

Recovering from his surprise, he dropped his hands to his sides and stood up straight. "How did you get in last year?"

Kailar's eyes narrowed. "You sure you want to do this now?"

"Yes," he replied, but then hesitated. "No. I mean, I need to know *something,* after what you told me about Ardelle."

"I thought you said we were pressed for time," she deflected.

"Just…tell me why you did it, then," he planted his hands on his hips, a habit she noticed he had when his stubborn streak asserted itself. "I need to at least know that! Surely you had good reason…"

Kailar's stomach turned, and she impatiently rubbed her temple. This wasn't the direction she wanted her day to go. But she also knew that she owed him something. Especially if he was going to essentially go behind enemy lines with her, against a reportedly powerful enemy.

Drawing in a deep breath, she looked him in the eyes. His stare almost made her falter in her resolve to tell him, fear edging into her peripheral.

Thinking carefully about how to explain it, she started, "It's not a simple answer. It goes back to why I left the Guild, why I thought I needed to take control of the Kingdoms. I told you…" Her voice wavered, and she looked down to regain her composure. "I told you I'd done some pretty horrible things."

"I've read the updates from Edilas," he nodded. "You led a coup on Falind and killed the king; you pitted the Falind army and Tal army against each other; and you led an orc invasion on Archanon. I've accepted those as part of your past, Kailar, you know this. But…none of those reports said anything about controlling the will of individuals. That's what I need to know about."

Shaking her head, she thought the reasons behind that were obvious. "It was the easiest way to do it."

Letan's eyebrows rose up expectantly. "That's it?"

Gritting her teeth, she nodded. "Basically. The Sword of Dragons was supposed to give me the power to control the kingdoms. What I didn't know until after I had it was that it would take time, possibly years, to become powerful enough to affect anything on a grand scale, at least directly. Klaralin…mind you I didn't know it was him yet, but he suggested I could control minds based on my exposure to and use of his pendant, as well as my ability to summon drakes. It was a quick and easy way to start the revolution I needed."

Looking down, he nodded absently. "I see. So what you're saying is that you were impatient, and you let your impulsiveness guide you."

A grimace drew across her face, and the disappointment in his eyes was enough to make her turn away from him. She had a feeling about what he would say next.

"Not much has changed, after all, has it," he asked.

Her jaw went taut, and she clenched her fists tight enough to dig her nails into her palms. "I guess not," she said, her words barely coming out as a whisper.

A dreadful silence fell between them, and she didn't dare look at him. Her heartbeat thundered in her ears when she realized this could spell the end between them. If he was with her because of her desire to change, but now she had shown him that she hadn't changed, not really, then would he leave her?

Kailar waited for the dreaded words to come. She feared what it would do to her.

When he spoke, she tensed further, "Look, no one can deny what you've done here." His voice was careful and measured, any emotion in it suppressed. "Your tenacity to see a goal and go for it, no matter the cost, turned out for the best this time around. What about next time?" She felt his hand on her shoulder, and he gently pulled to turn her towards him. His eyes were surprisingly sincere when she looked into them. "If someone gets in your way, will you plow over them like you intended to do with Warreck? If I hadn't held you back, would you have killed him?"

It was a good question. That moment in Warreck's office, when she summoned flames for the first time, played out in her head, and she imagined how far she might have gone without Letan. She didn't think she would kill the Mayor, but then she thought of the miner she had murdered in Edilas. The image of the young man, desperate to get out from under the thumb of a slave master, haunted her every day.

Her silence apparently wasn't what Letan wanted, and his sincerity plummeted into resignation. "I see."

"I am trying," she insisted, reaching her hand out for his. He let her take his, but there was no warmth in his grip. There was no grip at all.

"I know you are," he nodded without looking into her eyes.

It felt like a wall had suddenly been built between them. They were back to how things were before she had revealed her identity to him. Except instead of her being the one to block him, he had just put up a wall to keep her out.

Could they get past this? Could she regain his trust?

Did she really want to?

That's what scared her more than anything. Her impatience with due process, with the Warriors, her desire to leave them again, it was all tumbling back towards her default mode. Do what needed to be done, regardless of the consequences. Because if she didn't, no one would, and nothing would ever change.

Maybe this had all been a folly on her part. Had she really thought she could become anything else?

Suddenly Letan shook his head, and his eyes became hard-set. "Listen, we're about to do something extremely dangerous. I'm going to have to rely heavily on your knowledge and experience in Archanon, but I also need to know that if I give you an order, you'll follow it."

He stared at her expectantly, and she had to swallow down the lump that had formed in her throat. She still wanted to try, she decided, even if she would fail in the end. So she gave him as sincere a nod as she could, and she said, "I will. I promise."

"Good," he drew his hand away from hers. "Now tell me, how do we get into the city without alerting Zairel, or whoever he is?"

Setting her jaw tight, she forced the welling emotions within deep down, as deep as she could bury them. They wouldn't serve her right now. Maybe that was the best place to keep them anyway. That was the only way she could rise above them and do what needed to be done.

And then the idea hit her.

"Well I can't portal us directly into the city," she started slowly, narrowing her eyes as she considered her powers. "However, Archanon was mostly fortified around the idea that only Warriors would attack, not Wizards or anyone else who could create portals."

"But no one can create portals within the walls," Letan pointed out.

"Right," she nodded, "Thanks to Klaralin three thousand years ago. But the northern mountains that partially cover the wall. There's watch towers all throughout that tiny little range, and one blow of a horn and the shield goes up. However, that defense is predicated on one fact – the mountains are almost impossible to climb. But once you're up there, it's another matter altogether."

Letan nodded thoughtfully. "They're counting on seeing anyone who tries to climb up to give them enough lead time to get the city shield going." She nodded. "But you could portal us up past that point."

"I think even past the towers," she smiled, an overall plan forming in her head. "They're situated on the western and norther edge to watch for climbers. The energy field that prevents portals is further back than that. And..." Memories of her time as a Tal Warrior patrolling the Archanon wall gave her yet another idea. "I think I even remember a boulder that we could portal in near, and it would be between us and the towers." She added after a second, "Not that anyone in the towers ever really looks towards the city."

He frowned at her and asked, "Wait, how do the guards get to the towers?"

"The part of the wall that goes into the northern cliffs," she nodded, "there's a tunnel that leads to an underground barracks, and that tunnel continues on to the rest of the wall once it emerges from those mountains. But, there's also several small branch tunnels that lead off into those towers."

Narrowing his eyes, Letan asked, "Are you thinking we'll try to break into a tower and take the tunnels?"

Shaking her head adamantly, she said, "Absolutely not. There's nowhere to hide if we do that. We'll have to find a quiet corner of the mountain to descend into. However, that shouldn't be too hard." Her smile returned. "After all, the part of the city reserved for the Order of the Ages, the grounds of the Sanctuary, they're all nestled up against those mountains."

He must have realized what she intended, and he smiled. "It's perfect."

Nodding once, she moved past him towards the door, and then turned. "Well, then, ready to go?"

The gravity of their earlier discussion wasn't lost on her, but her efforts to bury her feelings worked. They had a task before them, and as long as they could put aside everything else, maybe they could work together once again to make a difference. Letan hesitated a moment, but then joined her by the door, giving her the space to summon her portal.

With her emotions trying to bubble up again, Kailar turned her focus from Letan to the task at hand, and focused on creating the strange void within herself that would allow her to summon dark magic.

A portal sparked to life on command, and Kailar drew in a deep breath, and then motioned for Letan to precede her. She followed close behind, and only a second after he passed through the wall of purple-white light did she follow.

They emerged exactly where she intended, facing the rising sun in the east, and a massive twelve-foot-tall and thirty-foot-wide boulder behind them. The portal closed the instant she was through, and they pressed themselves against the freezing cold, hard and grainy surface of the boulder. Beneath their feet was the slate-gray rock face of the Ilari Mountains, and to the east, their view of the city was blocked by other boulders, hills, and rocky faces of the mountain they stood atop. Any south-facing hills or shadowed places beneath rocks and boulders were still covered in a thin layer of leftover snow.

She should have known how cold it would be this high up, and almost at the same time, she and Letan drew their cloaks tighter around themselves, a sudden shiver rattling her body.

"By the gods," Letan whispered through chattering teeth. "I thought winter was over up here."

"It is," she shuddered. "Welcome to spring on top of a mountain."

"I swear it's colder up here than Edingard Pass in the spring," he shook his head.

Ignoring his complaint this time, she started to edge to her right and tried to peak over the boulder at the nearest tower. Even though anyone on duty probably paid no attention eastward, she didn't want to risk being seen.

However, as she peaked over the stone monolith, expecting to see smoke from a fire on top of the watch tower, she was shocked to find no evidence of guards.

"What the..." She frowned and moved out a little more to get a better look.

"What?" Letan asked.

Her feet crunched on some shadowed snow, and that should have worried her, but she grew more confident that the guard tower was empty.

"There's no one there," she remarked. "But…that shouldn't be."

"Well it is damn cold up here," Letan shivered. "Maybe they're below for a break."

"That's why there's a fire pit on each tower," she shook her head adamantly. "You don't understand, those towers are the only real defense against someone dumb enough to climb the mountains. That and regular patrols along the base of it, but when I was a Tal Warrior, those towers were *never* left unattended, day or night."

Letan looked east, worry set in his face. "Maybe they don't have it manned because they've left the shield up. Sal'fe said the city was locked down, right?"

A grimace drew across her face. "Maybe." She looked around, but found no loose rocks nearby, so opted instead to grab a clump of snow and packed it into a snowball, thankful that she had worn leather gloves. "Only one way to find out."

Kailar drew her arm back, hesitated when she wondered if anyone was around to see it, and then threw with all of her strength.

She had a vague idea of where the magic shield should have started, and held her breath as the snowball sailed towards, over, and then well past that point, and splattered against the rocky surface a good two dozen feet past.

Letan let out a breath, but then looked at her. "You're sure you remember where the wall should be?"

"Not precisely," she shook her head. "But for now, we're safe, and with no one watching from the tower, we should be okay." She glanced again at the tower, and sighed. "If they're leaving the city this unguarded, things are worse than I realized."

Letan nodded his agreement. "Well, let's get to it, then. How well do you know the terrain up here?"

"Only a little," she admitted. "But well enough that I can get us to the northern edge. We should be able to climb down near where the wall comes down, but far enough away that no one on the wall will see us."

Without looking at him, she walked past and trudged north and a little east, keeping her cloak wrapped tightly around her, especially when a biting wind suddenly crept up on them.

They trekked along for a short time, Letan following behind her silently, while her own mind worked over their conversations that day, both at the pub and in his quarters. Her anxiety started to rise up again, threatening to bubble out and overtake her mind again.

Now wasn't the time. She needed to focus. So she turned her mind elsewhere, to the situation at hand. It was frustrating how little they knew about the situation, or what they could expect. Sal'fe suggested they look for clues in the Grand Sanctuary, but what clues were they actually looking for? What would they find in the Sanctuary? Was it abandoned now that the Covenant members were all dead?

She grumbled about it in her head, but then realized that she had merely redirected her anxieties elsewhere. Worrying about it now when she knew there was no more planning they could do was pointless. *Let's just make it off this mountain first, then tackle the next problem, and then the one after that.*

As they approached the edge, and the mountains began to slope steeply downwards, she got her first look at Archanon in nearly a year. They hid as best as they could and looked to the north, at the wall escaping the mountain to the left, and part of the city nestled up against it beyond the foot of the mountain. Many people mistakenly believed the Archanon outer wall was a perfect circle, but from up here, it was easy to see that its path was most definitely not a perfect curve.

It was too quiet. They crouched and observed for at least a quarter of an hour, waiting to see one of the regular patrols that she knew should have walked along the wall, but there was no sign of them. Not one guard.

"This makes no sense," she whispered, even though the howling wind would have concealed her voice from any guards. Moving to get a better vantage of the city, she could see streets, houses, and other buildings, with people moving about as she should have expected, but the wall was empty.

"I agree," Letan nodded. "But it gives us the chance to get down quickly and unseen."

She glanced at him, realizing he was right, but she still didn't understand how the guard captain or the Warrior general would allow it.

Shaking her head, she led the climb down, still cautious regardless of the lack of guards. The descent was difficult at best, but this side was considerably easier than outside the wall.

They passed the level of the top of the wall unhindered, with still no guards in sight, and were thankful that from this point on, the mountain leveled out enough so that their greatest task involved keeping behind cover, so no one in the city noticed them climbing down.

By the time they reached the bottom, it was well past noon, and that put them in the shadow of the wall. It was warmer down at this level, but the shade did nothing to chase away the chill in her bones.

No one was around this part, and they decided to immediately use that to their advantage, following a stone guard path east away from the wall and avoiding the city proper, eventually coming out onto a cobblestone roadway that traveled directly between the open green space for the Order and a row of homes. Strangely, the street was relatively empty, with only a few people traveling in either direction upon it. Ahead of them, they had a clear view of the Upper City wall, and in front of that, the monolithic Grand Sanctuary.

"By the gods," Letan declared, while Kailar drew her hood around her face. They hadn't run into any guards yet, but that could change at any moment, and she couldn't risk being recognized. "I had no idea such things could be built."

She tugged on the hem of his cloak to keep him moving along, and they hurried. It hadn't occurred to her that there were no great castles, walls, or other impressive structures on Devor. Now Letan was laying eyes upon the most impressive city in all of Edilas.

Despite her fears and anxieties, Kailar smiled at Letan's awe. It was a reminder to her that, despite its failings, society on Edilas had performed some pretty impressive feats.

They had closed about half of the distance to the Grand Sanctuary when their luck finally ran out. She hadn't seen any guards, but they had passed by so many cross streets that it shouldn't have surprised her when a commanding voice called out, "You two, stop right there!"

Recognition set in for a split second, and she froze, terrified. Could Cardin Kataar have returned? If so, she couldn't let him see her face.

Letan was quick to cover, and he turned to face the commanding voice fully, while Kailar didn't dare look towards them.

"Hello, there," Letan said lightly, nervousness edging into his voice. "Have we done something wrong, sir?"

Boot steps drew closer on the cobblestone road, crunching on loose dirt and gravel. "What business do you have in this part of the city," the voice asked. It wasn't Cardin after all! But it sounded similar. Color drained from her face when she realized it might be his father, whom she had heard was the Captain of the Tal soldiers and castle guards. Surely he would know her face.

"Why, uh, we're just out for a stroll," Letan defended, holding his arms out defensively. Kailar knew how much of a mistake that was, and Letan did as well, as he drew his arms in quickly. His cloak would have opened, and the interrogator would have seen how armed and armored Letan was.

"In full combat gear?" the voice asked. "Warrior garb, if I'm not mistaken, but I'm pretty sure I've met most of the Archanon Warriors." The voice paused. "And you! Turn and face me."

Kailar turned ever so slightly, but kept the hem of her hood between her and the speaker. Trying to lighten her voice, she said, "These are dangerous times, sir. Is it a crime to defend ourselves?"

She saw boots now, and recognized them as standard issue. Yet despite those boots and the leather armor above them, she didn't see a sheath for a sword. The person moved to try to get a better look at her, and she moved to keep her face hidden. It was probably a useless gesture, but she really didn't want to have to fight off anyone, let alone the guard captain.

"No," the voice agreed. "But it *is* illegal to enter the city over the mountains." She felt her heart rate quicken. How could he have known? "Awful brave of you, but you do realize that the Military District is up near this part, don't you? Three of my soldiers and I saw you climb down."

She cursed, and felt immense embarrassment.

At the same time that she thought of a question, Letan asked it, "If that were the case, why would you not have brought more guards?"

The boots stepped closer, and the man spoke in a quieter voice. "Because I assume King Sal'fe sent you, though you came much faster than I anticipated." Stunned, she unconsciously looked into the face of the man, and felt even more shock when she realized she was right. He looked much like Cardin, but clearly older, his hair longer and graying.

As stunned as she was, he certainly hadn't been prepared to see her.

"You!" The venom in his voice could have poisoned her, and he stepped back. The shock and hatred that simultaneously passed over his face told her she was in trouble, and she grasped the hilt of her sword tightly.

"You're right," Letan quickly spoke, raising his hands disarmingly, which likewise opened his cloak to show that he hadn't drawn a weapon. "King Sal'fe sent us. At your request, I believe."

The guard captain glanced at Letan, but then kept his eyes affixed on Kailar. He reached for his sword, only to find nothing there, which drew a frown across her face. Why would the captain of the guard be unarmed?

He clenched his fists tightly, along with his jaw, and drew in a deep breath. Finally, through gritted teeth, he asked, "And he sent you, of all people?"

Defensively, she snapped, "He didn't *send* me, he asked me to come."

"How did he even know where you were?"

"It's a long story," she grumbled. "I know this may come as a surprise to you..." She hesitated and looked down at her hands, debating if she should show him her powers or merely tell him.

Letan said it instead. "Sal'fe believes she may be able to contend with this man pretending to be a god." She looked up, and Draegus looked at Letan skeptically. "Because she has the ability to use dark magic."

Expecting further shock on his face, instead a morbid look of recognition drew down his face. "Oh," was all he managed to say at first. He let out a great sigh and stroked his goatee. "That makes sense, actually."

After a long time standing silently, with Draegus continuing to stroke his beard thoughtfully, Letan cleared his throat. "Look, we're not exactly sure what to do here. Sal'fe thought we could search the Grand Sanctuary for clues as to what this Zairel impersonator wants, but beyond that..."

Draegus dropped his hands to his side and nodded. "Considering he attacked the Sanctuary last night, it might be a good starting place. He wanted something from there, but I don't know if it was just to murder the Covenant, or something else." Glancing around, he nodded his head. "I've been given some leave by the new King to move around the city, especially if it is to help resolve this situation, so I suppose I should come with you. If any guards ask, I'll tell them I'm escorting you on the King's order. However," he looked pointedly at Kailar, "Maybe keep your face hidden. If anyone else recognizes you, there could be some very difficult questions."

Kailar agreed, and allowed Draegus to take the lead. As they walked along the road, she felt a greater weight on her shoulders, and a lot more paranoid. She drew her hood further forward to better conceal her face, but also begrudged that act, knowing that she could not easily watch her surroundings that way. She would have to rely almost entirely on Letan and Draegus.

What insanity has this world come to, she thought. To rely on the father of the man that was her greatest nemesis seemed ludicrous, and she could hardly believe that he was actually willing to work with her!

It was well into the afternoon by the time they made it to the broad, circular Sanctuary. Given the attack on it last night, she was not surprised that there wasn't a single citizen or cleric in sight. In fact, the only people present were pairs of guards at every entrance.

Draegus frowned, and commented, "There shouldn't be any city guards here."

Letan peered at the guards, and nodded, "Yeah those definitely aren't Warriors. Is this why there are none on the walls?"

The guard captain gave them a stunned look. "None?!"

"How do you think we managed to make it as far as we did," Kailar remarked.

Lowering his eyes, Draegus slowly shook his head. "His influence is spreading. But, I can't imagine why he would want to leave the city unguarded."

Kailar frowned, and asked, "We should still be able to walk in under your orders, right?"

Draegus looked at her hesitantly. "Perhaps. This entity, he seems to have the ability to influence others, though it seems limited for now. We can try to get past them, and hope they are still loyal to me."

He led them on towards the western-most entrance. The guards didn't seem to notice them until they were almost on top of them, and that struck Kailar as odd. When they did notice, the two raised their hands and immediately ordered, "Halt!"

Draegus looked the guard on the left up and down, and then ordered, "Step aside, Astrin."

"I can't do that," the guard replied, her eyes half-focused and her voice monotone.

Raising his eyebrows, Draegus glanced at Kailar and Letan, and said more forcefully, "That is an order."

"Our god's orders supersede yours," Astrin replied.

Kailar's stomach dropped at that statement, and she glanced around nervously. She noticed then that several other guards seemed to have appeared around them, though none moved. Yet.

"You do not fall under the orders of the Covenant," Draegus spoke sternly. "I am your commanding officer, and you will step aside immediately."

Astrin and the other guard's hands moved to their swords. "Our god's orders supersede yours."

Kailar's eyes grew wide when she realized what was happening. "Captain," she warned. "I don't think they're in control of themselves anymore."

Even through his leather armor, she noticed the guard Captain's shoulders tense up, and he eased backwards. She had made others act this way, but only when she exercised direct and precise control over them with the Sword of Dragons. It required considerable will power to hold that sort of control over one person, let alone several, and she had found it easier to simply influence than to manipulate.

Kailar and Letan likewise backed away with him, but it was too late. Astrin and the other guard drew their swords and stepped towards them. "Our god wishes to see you. Now."

Kailar glanced at the other guards that had appeared, and they, too, drew weapons.

"Dammit," she reached for her weapon. "I think we're in trouble."

Glancing around, Draegus nodded. Letan and Kailar drew their weapons, but Draegus merely clenched his fists. "We can't let them capture us," the Captain said.

"No," Kailar shook her head. "But where do we go? What do we do?"

Draegus looked around in a panic. "I don't know. We need to

get somewhere safe. We need allies."

"Come with us now," Astrin repeated, bringing her sword up and grasping it with both hands. "Or we will take you by force."

Kailar filled her sword with dark magic, setting the blade humming. "If it's a battle they want…"

"Try not to hurt them," Draegus glared at her. "They're not themselves."

"To hell with that," she growled. "It's them or us!"

"At least try," Letan snapped at her. A weight formed in her chest, but then she nodded.

"Alright," she grudgingly assented. "But if we get caught in a prolonged battle, their god is gonna come calling."

"The Catacombs," Draegus suddenly stated. "We have people down there that might be able to help us!"

She didn't bother to ask who or why, she just stated, "Then go. Now!"

At once, the trio sprinted, while the two guards immediately lunged at them. Kailar and Letan batted their swords away and kept moving, heading for the stone fence surrounding the open space just beyond the Sanctuary grounds, and right towards three other guards.

Draegus was no slouch, and he released a surprisingly well-focused blast wave from the palm of his hand, but two of them were Mages and blocked his attack with ease. Realizing that they were vulnerable, she quickly enveloped herself and the others with a dark shield, easily blocking return blasts of magic.

Letan met the remaining guards with a flurry of parries and strikes, and quickly pushed in past their defenses to shove them down. Draegus paused by one to punch him full-force in the face, and then he took the other's sword. Kailar passed by the stunned guards just as Draegus took up his run again, and she glanced down at them as they seemed to barely register that they were on their backs.

The trio was at the stone fence a heartbeat later. The two men clambered over it, but she used her powers to simply leap over and land in the open field, with nothing between her and the catacombs entrance, which she noticed for the first time had apparently been damaged at some point, the ancient archway gone and rubble strewn around the tunnel. The normal Covenant guardians were noticeably absent, and not even city guards stood in their place. This would be easy.

Until something hit her shield like a sledge hammer, instantly draining her.

"That's far enough!" The booming voice had an unnatural tone to it, and when she turned to face her new opponent, she saw a man enveloped in an orange glow floating towards them from the Sanctuary. His Covenant robes fluttered in an unnatural wind. Before she could respond, he released a torrent of magic upon her shield, further fatiguing her. That must have been the imposter, and he was incredibly powerful!

But she was no slouch, either. The power she had built up within her sword was still ready for her to command. Thrusting the blade towards her enemy, she released the pent-up energy in an overpowered blast that sent out a shockwave along its path, obliterating the stone fence and the ground around it. The false god tried to dodge the blast, but he was still caught in the shockwave and was sent tumbling to the ground. She grinned.

Turning again, she saw that Draegus and Letan had run past her, but then stopped to try to help, only to watch stunned at the full strength of her powers. "What are you waiting for?! Go!"

They clamped their mouths shut and took off running, Kailar right behind them. They were about a hundred feet from the tunnel when she suddenly noticed a flickering light from within, and the trio came to a sudden stop when shapes emerged into the shadow of the mountain. One of whom she instantly recognized as the elf that she had manipulated last year.

"Look out!" Draegus called out to them.

The elf, Elaria, reacted quickly and leapt in front of the emerging party, raising a large shield just in time to block another attack from Zairel. But it overwhelmed Elaria, and she was driven onto her back by sheer force.

Kailar guessed that they were the allies that Draegus mentioned, and if Elaria was the best they had to offer, then they weren't much help.

Which meant it was up to her. She stopped in her tracks, turned back towards Pevrin, and prepared to fight.

Chapter 34

THE FINAL PIECE

The world exploded around Reis, and Elaria crumpled to the ground before him, a blast of magic exploding against her shield. "Elaria!"

He was at her side in an instant, while Kellis stepped ahead and drew his sword to defend them. Lifting Elaria's head up, Reis called out again, "Elaria! Are you okay?"

She blinked her eyes rapidly, and then tried to focus on him. "I...I think so."

Another deafening explosion reverberated, and Reis looked up to see a purple-black shield surrounding the area, having just deflected another orange-white blast of magic. Looking towards the edge of the field, he saw a figure in a dark cloak point her sword at the floating attacker and release another ground-shattering blast. She missed her target, but this time instead of her attack disappearing into the clouds, it slammed into the second floor of the Grand Sanctuary, devastating the structure and sending chunks of stone and metal into the city.

Then Reis noticed Draegus Kataar racing towards them along with a man with flaming red hair and a matching beard, both with weapons drawn and their faces hardened for combat.

"Captain Kataar," Kellis called out, keeping his sword ready.

"Kellis," Draegus replied, his relief palpable. "Where are your marines?"

Reis helped Elaria stand, though she wavered in her footing. Anila caught her as she started to fall, and together Reis and Anila held the elf up.

"We left them behind," Kellis told Draegus, watching the battle as the orange-glowing man released another attack against the shield. "It's a long story, but what the hellfire is going on here?"

Once the two men reached the group, they turned and readied their own weapons. "It's...a long story," Draegus huffed out, breathing heavily. "For the moment, just know that the orange one is the enemy."

If that was the case, they were in trouble. After yet another attack against the shield, the woman was driven to her knees by the effort to maintain the shield.

"Then why did she just destroy the Sanctuary," Anila demanded.

No one answered, but when the woman turned towards them, Reis's heart froze, and he and Elaria clenched each other's hands. It took only moments to register who it was, but when it did, a blind rage overcame him. "It's Kailar!"

She started to stumble back towards them, obviously exhausted. Another blast of magic slammed into her shield, further fatiguing her. Reis almost cheered the attacker on, but Draegus explained, "For now, she's our ally."

"Ally or not, she's losing," Baenil observed.

That's when they noticed that the shield began to shrink, and Reis realized they had only moments of safety left. Setting his jaw, he hefted Elaria and grudgingly said, "We better get over to her."

No one had to be told twice, and the troupe rushed to Kailar as quickly as possible. Elaria was able to help run, but she was still too weak to do so on her own. The others got to Kailar faster, just as she was driven to her knees again.

"He's too strong," she huffed. Then she saw Gilrin and frowned. "What the hell is he?"

Gilrin's annoyed response was drowned out by another blast from the enemy, and Kailar looked ready to break.

The red-headed man ordered sharply, "Kailar, burn him!"

At first she frowned, as everyone else did, and that's when it occurred to Reis that she had magic when she wasn't supposed to.

Then, seemingly realizing what her companion wanted, she turned around, and with a war cry that could have rivaled an orc's, she released a stream of blue-white fire from her hand.

The attacker tried to dodge, but the stream was too wide and it engulfed him, lighting up his covenant robes and hair. He screamed out in agonizing pain, the unnatural tone of it sending shivers down Reis's spine.

And then Kailar's shield fell. They were exposed.

"We need a portal," Kailar shouted, spinning around and looking about wildly. "I can't last long enough to get us…"

She stopped talking mid-sentence, and Reis felt an unusual wind stir around them just as a flash of light blinked from behind. Everyone turned at once, and were stunned to find a purple-white portal behind them, with streaks of harmless lightning lancing out irregularly.

"How in the six," Kellis started, his face as stunned as Reis felt.

"Everyone move," Draegus snapped. "Through the portal, go, go, go!"

It wasn't wide enough for more than one person, so Reis let most of the group in ahead of them, Elaria still needing his and Anila's help. Baenil and Gilrin were the first ones through, followed by Kellis, and then Draegus, who glanced at Reis just as he and the others made it to the portal. Once Draegus was through, he looked at Anila and said, "You go first."

Thankfully she didn't argue, and while still holding onto Elaria, she passed through the portal, but as Elaria entered, Reis let go and pushed her through, and then turned to Kailar. He wanted to command her to stay behind, and was about to draw his sword to force her to stay behind, but she collapsed into his arms before he could. The portal flickered, and he saw that the attacker was blindly heading towards them, screaming and flailing about across the now-burning field. Reis cursed and pulled Kailar through the portal moments before it collapsed.

Only to find himself in another dreadfully familiar location, the last place that he had fought against Kailar – the Falind throne room.

"Oh, you've got to be kidding me," he whispered to himself. Everyone had made it okay, but they were surrounded by several Falind guards, including some in strange, all-black outfits.

After a few moments of gathering his wits, he looked at Kailar, still collapsed in his arms. "Hey," he shook her. "Hey, wake up. You alive?"

With her eyes barely open, she looked up at him, and then grimaced. "Oh gods, not you."

Letting out an airy laugh, he shrugged and said, "Would you rather I drop you?"

The red-headed man appeared next to him and extracted Kailar from Reis's arms. "I've got her."

Reis nodded his thanks, and just barely stopped himself from a wry remark. However, he then turned to Draegus and planted his hands on his hips. "What the *hell* is going on, Draegus?"

The guard captain gave him an exasperated look, but then his expression slowly melted to a desperately sad one. Glancing at Kellis, Draegus shook his head. "It's difficult to...I mean." Drawing in a deep breath, he looked Reis in the eye and said, "The world has fallen apart in your absence."

"What do you mean," Kellis asked. "Who was that man?"

"It was Pevrin," Draegus replied, much to Reis's shock. "But not Pevrin, exactly. He's possessed by some *thing* claiming to be one of the Six. Though I don't believe it's a god for one second, especially since it couldn't blast right through Kailar's shield."

"He nearly did," Kailar weakly chimed in.

"Yeah, and how do you have powers," Reis glared at her. "The dragons were supposed to have taken care of that. For that matter, how did you make a portal inside the city borders?"

"Dark magic," she replied tersely, adjusting her posture as she hung off of the red-head. "Just like Cardin, apparently."

He wasn't sure how that explained it, but then realized what she meant. If the Sword had given her the ability to use dark magic, the Star Dragons probably wouldn't have been able to take those powers away.

Thinking back on everything that had just happened, Reis suddenly remembered what Draegus said a few moments ago. "Wait, what do you mean the world has fallen apart?"

The look on Draegus's face drove a pit of darkness right into Reis's stomach.

"King Beredis is dead," Draegus began. Reis suddenly felt weak, and it took all of his will power to keep from collapsing in front of everyone. The world threatened to spin around him, and he held his stomach tightly. "Murdered by that thing."

The throne room doors burst opened, and two guards entered, followed by King Sal'fe. However, when Sal'fe saw the assembled group, he paused at the threshold. Then, with a long face, he approached the troupe and asked, "Dare I ask what transpired?"

Shocked that the Wizard King wasn't surprised they were there, Reis's jaw dropped when Kailar replied, "Pevrin was at the Grand Sanctuary. I don't know why."

"I see," the Wizard nodded solemnly.

Then Draegus stepped before Sal'fe and bowed. "King Sal'fe. I am Captain Draegus Kataar, commander of the Guardians of Tal."

Yet again, Reis felt his stomach drop in surprise. He'd heard of the Guardians of Tal, but he never knew that Cardin's father was their leader! It seemed that today was a day of surprises.

"I want to thank you," Draegus continued, "for asking Kailar to aid us. And I ask you for sanctuary."

The Wizard King clutched his staff tightly, and he glanced around at the assembly of Falind guards. He seemed to consider the request for a long moment, his eyes eventually surveying Reis's party as well, before they settled back on Draegus. "I am afraid that I cannot grant your request."

Feeling completely lost, Reis none-the-less frowned at Sal'fe's refusal. Somehow he had the feeling that they had barely scratched the surface in bringing him and the others up to speed.

"Your Majesty, please," Draegus replied, stunned. "We have nowhere else to go, and I know of the defenses you've added to your city."

Sal'fe lifted a surprised eyebrow. "Do you, now? Then it seems I have not successfully rooted out all of your spies." Draegus didn't reply. "However, I am afraid that even my defenses are inadequate against this entity. Especially because I know how much he desires this." From his robes, Sal'fe produced a small cylindrical piece of stone, and Reis felt his eyes open wide when he recognized the shape.

Before he or anyone else could say anything, Anila demanded, "How did you get that?"

Sal'fe looked at her curiously, but then he seemed to realize who she was. "It was entrusted to me, or rather its secret was, by the Covenant."

Anila shook her head dubiously. Reis noticed that her hand rested on the hilt of her sword, and he groaned inwardly. The last thing he wanted now was to go up against an ancient and powerful Wizard. "I seriously doubt that," she spoke darkly. "Hand it over."

"Oh I intend to," Sal'fe nodded and held the piece out towards Draegus. "This is a piece of the Cronal."

For a moment, no one said anything. Most everyone was too stunned. Reis couldn't comprehend it at first, it was too much of a coincidence. However, when he looked at Anila, she looked back at him, and then lowered her head. Was that the secret she referred to in the hidden library?

Because the item in Sal'fe's hand looked just like one of those 'gears' from the dais.

All eyes fell upon the Covenant's guardian, and Anila simply nodded her confirmation of the object's identity.

"I see," Draegus turned back to stare at the Cronal piece. "I guess this explains why the Prince started to say piece, not book or copy." Reis clenched his jaw, realizing that if the Prince was still alive, he was likely still in line for the throne, unless the King had left behind succession orders excluding the Prince.

With deliberate hesitation, Draegus reached for the piece, but then Sal'fe closed his hand and retracted it just a little. "Before you take this, you must be cautious. If you have ever touched an enchanted item before, like a Wizard's staff, you will know the rush of power you will feel. This is beyond any of those, and could be dangerous if you do not control yourself."

If it's so powerful, why are you letting it go? The moment the thought occurred to Reis, he realized the answer, and was stunned. Sal'fe was terrified of Pevrin, and didn't want to defend the Cronal from him.

Hesitating, Draegus backed away. "I don't want it. I shouldn't be allowed to…"

"I'll take it," Anila stepped forward. "I've never used one, but I've handled Cronal pieces before."

Sal'fe regarded her carefully, but then nodded. "Very well." He willingly handed her the piece, and then backed away from them.

The room remained quiet as all eyes were fixed on Anila. She visibly blushed, and then carefully placed the piece inside one of her belt pouches. Clearing her throat, she asked the Wizard, "So if it isn't safe to stay here, where do you suggest we go?"

"To the Wizards' Guild," Sal'fe said plainly, as if they should have figured that out themselves. *Maybe we should have,* Reis thought. "Whatever Master Wizards there are left will be more powerful than I am alone."

"What about your assassins," Kailar, her voice still weak, motioned to one of the black-clad guards. "We could use their help."

Sal'fe shook his head. "They stay here, to protect my kingdom."

Kailar scoffed and muttered, "Naturally."

The Wizard King narrowed his eyes. "Make no mistake, every king and queen acts in the best interest of their kingdom first, and I must do no less. That is why I have helped Tal as much as I can, but now it is up to all of you."

Grimacing, Reis looked about the group, and realized how weakened they already were. Two of their strongest combatants were already beaten down. Then he realized what else that meant, so he cleared his throat and nodded at Sal'fe. "I, uh, don't suppose you could at least make us a portal to the Wizards' Guild?"

The Wizard scoffed, but then regarded Kailar and the others, and with a heave of a sigh, he nodded. "Very well." Turning on the spot, he planted his staff in the marble floor, and the blood-red gem flashed brightly. A moment later, a blue-white portal formed several feet ahead of the Wizard King. "Please go quickly."

Noticing that Elaria still struggled to stand, Reis moved over to her and helped her walk. Together, they moved out.

Just before Draegus preceded them through the portal, Sal'fe added, "Make no mistake, I place my kingdom above all others. When Pevrin comes for the Cronal, I will willingly tell him where it has gone. Which means he will be coming for you."

Reis wanted to curse him out, but surprisingly, Draegus simply nodded and said, "Thank you for the warning."

With that, he ducked through the portal, followed closely by Kellis. Reis glared at the Wizard King, before he led Elaria through.

Chapter 35

DARK VISION

Passing through the rubble left behind from the elemental, Cardin walked under the archway leading into the copse. The copse was densely packed with trees whose leaves glowed bright purples and blues, and some kind of moss that grew on the bark illuminated everything else in a cold, green hue.

As densely packed as the trees were, there were only a handful of pathways into the copse, but they were all heavily worn trails, which left him the question of which one to take. Then again, it was a small enough copse that he suspected it didn't matter.

Amidst the rustling of leaves from a light breeze, he caught the sound of falling water, and suspected that whatever lay ahead of him, it would be at the source of that sound. So, picking a path at random, he entered.

The feeling of life all around him nearly overwhelmed him, and just as he had done upon arriving on Stella, he focused his attention to tuning out much of it. Doing so meant that he might not sense danger if it existed within, but he suspected that there was none.

Just before he reached the center, he glanced upwards, following the tree trunks up and seeing a vast field of blue and purple in the crowns of the trees, interlinking so much that he swore the trees were, in fact, connected to one another, as if they were a single entity.

Following the path and the sound of water, he emerged on the other side to a tiny clearing that was well-tended, with weeds cleared out and rocks arranged so that they neatly surrounded a pool of crystal-clear water. The pond was fed from a broad waterfall six feet tall, and the water eventually drained down another waterfall into a cave beneath the copse.

More than that, however, the clearing was alive with swarms of the floating, serpent-like kaetz! There were hundreds, he thought, and the way they moved together like a flock of birds or a school of fish enchanted him.

Some of them noticed him, and the swarms lazily moved towards and around him in a twister-like motion. He reached a hand out to caress one, but it darted away from him, perturbing the swarm momentarily. As soon as he retracted his hand inwards, the perturbation disappeared, and he was again surrounded by a wall of circling kaetz.

With deliberate care, he walked over to the pool, the kaetz following along as if they anticipated his every move. Once at the edge, and being careful not to touch any of the smooth stones, he glanced first into the water, and then down into the cave, where the water disappeared into blackness. Was he supposed to go down there?

As if sensing his question, the kaetz reacted by speeding up their circular motion, faster and faster, until they swirled around him at dizzying speeds and he felt nauseous. Then, all at once, they sprung up into the sky like a splash of water, and then they darted towards the waterfall.

Falling into place, one by one in rapid succession, they splashed through the falls and halted just behind the stream, until it looked like a floating, writhing single creature glowed beneath the water.

Their coloration fluctuated, changing from blues and reds to green, then yellows, and each one changing to different colors, the changes happening more and more rapidly, until all of a sudden, an image formed, as if projected against the water.

An image of a terrible, ruined battlefield. He saw himself standing amidst a sea of bodies on an open, scorched field, the Sword of Dragons in-hand, with red, green, and blue blood dripping from it. His image faced away from him, towards a great grey stone pyramid in the distance, the pyramid's top opened up in slits and forming pikes. Those pikes looked metallic, but not like shiny steel, more like tarnished metals. Surrounding the pyramid was a vast wilderness of trees that reminded him vaguely of the jungles of Trinil.

He wore no armor in the image, only simple trousers and a shirt, and a black cloak, torn and soiled by battle and blowing in a breeze. As the breeze caught up his cloak more, his image turned to the right and looked down. Following his eyes, Cardin's heart froze, a deep, dark void forming in his stomach.

Sira's battered and broken body lay crumpled on the ground.

His image stumbled over to her, and he heard his voice cry out, "Sira!"

Slamming his fist into the ground, his image released a blast of magic in a great wave all around him, magic that Cardin knew was both star magic and dark magic, blowing away all of the littered bodies like ragdolls, all except Sira's.

Cardin's hands shook, and he wanted to look away from the horrific image as his projection gently caressed dirt off of her face. He saw now that her chest was caved in and singed, as if from a blast of magic from some powerful opponent.

The image grew blurry, and then re-coalesced to show Cardin standing in the throne room of Archanon. The Sword was sheathed on his back, and he wore clothing that he knew was far more expensive than anything he owned, including a black cape with silver embroidery. No one sat upon the throne, but he stood before the stairs leading up to it like it was his.

Two indistinct soldiers brought a man before Cardin, the man's steel mail and plate armor broken, battered and bloodied, and his brown hair soiled and mussed up, covering his face at first.

Cardin heard his projection ask, "Did you really think you could win?"

The prisoner looked up, a flash of brown eyes appearing behind the hair, but he didn't answer.

"Was it worth it," Cardin's projection asked, his voice shaking with rage and pain.

The prisoner jerked his head to the side, clearing some of the hair from his face. Cardin's stomach dropped again, and he stepped backwards in absolute shock.

It was Reis!

"She's dead because of you," Reis's image growled, his voice hoarse but still recognizable.

Cardin's projection shouted, "You brought this down upon us! You killed her!"

Suddenly Reis broke his right hand free and thrust it at Cardin, and even more shocking, he released a blast of arcane magic. But Cardin's projection anticipated the attack, and it bounced harmlessly off of a shield.

Then, in one fluid motion, Cardin's projection drew the Sword and cut off Reis's arm at the elbow. He howled in agony and was driven to his knees by the guards. Cardin's projection grabbed him by the hair and forced him to look through agonizing tears at Cardin. "I'll make you suffer a lifetime for this, you bastard!"

His projection then placed his hand on Reis's face, and...

Cardin looked away, unable to watch the horrific scene play out any more. He shut out the sounds, clenched out the vision, tears burning his eyes while a horrifying, sick feeling overcame him. Falling to his knees, he dry-heaved, barely holding back what little dinner he'd had.

Was that the future? It couldn't be! Reis didn't have magic! He never could! Not unless...

Not unless he somehow got his hands on the Sword of Dragons.

And what of Sira? He was tempted to turn back to the projection, to try to force it to show him what happened to her, how she died, but he couldn't do it. He couldn't bear to look again. Never again. That couldn't happen.

Moments passed, minutes, maybe even hours, he wasn't sure. Finally, when the sick feeling subsided, he forced himself onto his feet and looked around, at everything except the waterfall. The kaetz had resumed their idle swimming throughout the clearing.

Cardin wanted to scream at them! How could they show him that? What was the point? To drive him into a depressed stupor? To give him a chance to change the future? Was it even really the future?

He had to know, and only Naerala could tell him. Determination overcame him, and he marched out of the clearing and through the copse. The journey seemed to take a lot longer, and he went over in his head what he was going to ask her. What he would demand from her.

When he finally emerged and passed under the archway, he saw Naerala waiting patiently just outside of where the ward had ended, while Endri was absent. He glanced around, realizing that he had blocked out all feelings of magic, but then he saw the emerald dragon sleeping some distance back up the path they had travelled down.

Cardin stopped in front of Naerala and planted his fists on his hips, his mouth half-open. All of the questions he had rehearsed were suddenly gone, replaced by the deep, terrible emptiness that the vision imbued in him. She raised her eyebrows curiously, and folded her arms in front of her. "Yes?"

"What just happened," he demanded. "I just saw...the most horrific images!"

The green light of Endri's eyes appeared, and he raised his head curiously. Naerala looked amused, and Cardin wanted to scream at her. *This is no laughing matter!*

As if reading his thoughts, her smile faded, and she let out a deep sigh. "What you saw, whatever it was you saw, is the course that you are on right now. It is your destination if you do not change your journey."

Glancing impatiently at Endri, he asked her, "That's what that place does? Shows your future?"

"No," she shook her head. "Sometimes it shows nothing. Sometimes it shows the past. Sometimes it shows you your greatest fear or your greatest weakness, and sometimes your greatest strengths and sources of courage or inspiration. It is different every time for every person."

Frowning, he asked, "Then how did you know it showed me the future?"

Unfolding her arms and letting them fall to her side, she looked intently at him. "Because I know the ebb and flow of star magic. I know the will of the stars themselves." Her eyes suddenly flashed bright red, and that flash turned into pinpoints of light. He felt the magic around her suddenly shift, like a river flowing differently around a rock that was just thrown in.

Before he could react, her features changed. Her face grew scaly, and larger, her entire body rapidly shifting until he stared up at a great red dragon.

Endri bolted to his feet and gazed at her slack-jawed, having to look up at the much larger dragon.

Lowering her head to better look at Cardin, her next words came through his thoughts, like Endri's. *"It was vital that I bring you to this copse,"* she explained. *"For the sake of all, I knew that there was something you needed to see, even if I did not know exactly what it was."*

"Astaria," Endri exclaimed. The red dragon looked at him as he approached, and she nodded. *"It was you all along."*

Suddenly Cardin's sense of her earlier, and the flash he swore he'd seen in her eyes, made perfect sense. "But, why? Why the deception? Why hide?"

Looking to him again, Astaria replied, *"I left behind the Star Dragons and all involvement with them, and I have no desire to return to the fold."*

"But we need you," Endri insisted. *"Now more than ever! If we do not stop Nuuldan…"*

"No," she shook her head adamantly. *"Not again. Last time our war destroyed billions of lives, and it shattered our culture. With every innocent killed, with every brother and sister lost to darkness or torn apart, we forgot what it meant to be Star Dragons."*

Looking around at the copse, the mountains, the stars above them, she spoke with passion, *"I came here to rediscover our roots, to find why we were created in the first place! And more,"* she looked at the green dragon. *"More than I am willing to admit at this moment."*

Endri began to argue, but she growled, a deep, vibrating, foreboding sound that forced Endri's silence. Cardin was dazed, both by her growl and Endri's sudden unwillingness to argue his case. He had never known the green dragon to back down when he was adamant about something, not without at least talking it out.

Astaria looked again at Cardin, her red, starry eyes penetrating deep into his soul. *"I still do not agree with the forging of the Sword of Dragons, but it is in the past. Now you, Keeper of the Sword, must deal with the present, and shape the future. You have the power,"* she emphasized the word, *"but I fear that you do not yet possess the will. You were horrified by the future you saw. So change it. Make it better."*

Opening his mouth to respond, Cardin's voice caught, and he thought carefully about her words. He thought about Reis, about the strain on their friendship, and about what his friend had said in Archanon before they parted ways.

"I understand," he finally said. With a glance at Endri, he then remembered why they had come to Stella in the first place. "Can you at least tell us about the Shadow Quartz? What it is and where we can find it?"

Through his mind, he heard Astaria sigh, accompanied by a strong huff of breath from her nostrils.

"The Shadow Quartz was Nuuldan's final solution," she finally said, even her mental voice cracking with barely-contained emotion. *"As it was ours. I did not agree with the other remaining First Ones, the last ones to fall in the Civil War, when they gave their lives to forge the Sword…"* Cardin exchanged a surprised look with Endri. *"I remained on the surface to help defend the Vrol from the descending Dark Dragons. However, they knew that even the most powerful star magic by itself could never contend with the swarms and swarms of Dark Dragons."*

She hesitated, but had already said enough, and Cardin made the connection instantly. "They used the Shadow Quartz to forge the Sword of Dragons!"

Astaria hung her head shamefully. *"Yes. I begged them not to, for it would mean that the Vrol who would take up the Sword would feel the conflict between light and dark, and it could destroy him. I thought that no being in the Universe could ever live with both powers. When the Vrol leader fell after destroying the Dark Dragons, I thought I was right."*

Astaria then looked at him with an expression he couldn't read, as if she was both surprised and afraid. *"You have proven me wrong, Keeper. That was why I had to test you, to see if you could control the void without succumbing to it."*

Cardin's face grew warm, and he looked away from her piercing gaze. She had seemed so confident when she helped him realize what he had to do, so much so that he had assumed she knew exactly what would happen when he used his dark powers. Except that he had surprised her. Was that why she didn't want Sira and Dalin to come along? If he turned to pure darkness like a dragon, she probably expected to have to fight him.

Another thought then occurred to him. "So Nuuldan was right to look for the Shadow Quartz with the Wizards." He looked at Endri with his face slackened. "When the Star Dragons entrusted the Sword to the Wizards, they essentially gave the Shadow Quartz to them." He frowned and turned to Astaria. "But the Star Dragons should have known that."

"Only the First Ones knew," she replied. *"As I was the only one left, I did not wish it known by anyone else, in case any other Star Dragon fell to darkness in the future. It was my last act before coming here."*

Cardin nodded solemnly, and he saw Endri hang his head low. He could only imagine how his friend felt. It was a monumental piece of Star Dragon history, and it had been kept from him.

Sighing, Cardin asked, "I don't suppose you might know who else would have known that, and told Nuuldan to attack the Wizards?"

"I am afraid that I do not. No one else should have known. So it seems," she turned to Endri, *"That while I kept secrets from you, the other First Ones must have kept secrets from me. Or there is another survivor out there that neither of us is aware of."*

Endri looked at her curiously. *"It is unlikely. However, at least we know that as long as the Keeper is safe, so too is the Shadow Quartz."*

"It may be best to keep it a secret from everyone else," Astaria nodded towards Cardin. *"Or you will make yourself an even greater target, along with your world."*

Grimacing, Cardin nodded. "Unfortunately, I think you're right." He considered whether he would tell Sira or not, but that would be a decision he'd make at another time. He knew she wouldn't tell anyone, but it was a heavy burden to bear.

Looking up at the moon, he realized that he had spent at least an hour in the copse, probably longer, and he longed for Sira. He had to make sure she was okay after the images he saw.

As if reading his thoughts again, Astaria turned towards the path. *"Your journey here is nearly complete. Let us go home."*

Chapter 36

CONSUMED

When the first boom thudded throughout the castle, Idrill Beredis was stirred from a terribly boring meeting with the city Governor. Maral was visibly shaken before from an earlier private meeting with Pevrin, but the echoing boom that shook the castle rattled her almost beyond reasoning. The Governor dropped a cup of tea that she had been nursing, letting it shatter over the marble floor in the Allied Council Chambers.

"By the Six…" Maral stopped herself and seemed to bite her lip in fear.

She and Idrill were by themselves, and he noticed and was annoyed by the fact that no castle guards came rushing in to make sure he was okay. A deep frown crossed his face, and he and the Governor quickly left the room to investigate.

Except, the halls were strangely empty. Not a single guard was in sight. Then an even louder boom shook the castle, reverberating up through the floor and into Idrill's soul. A moment later, what sounded like hail pelted the roof, but only for a moment.

Glancing at one another in a panic, they raced towards the castle doors, trying to find a guard along the way but coming across none.

"Someone's head will roll for this," he growled as they

approached the doors.

Confused, Maral asked, "Sire?"

"Where are the guards?!"

Glancing about, she only just noticed the distinct lack of any soldiers. "That is odd…"

With his mood increasingly sour, they raced outside, only to stop cold when a piece of flaming debris the size of his head slammed into the castle behind them, carving out a chunk from the centuries-old structure. Maral screamed, and Idrill fell back trying to scramble away.

Once he knew he was safe, he glanced up at Maral, but then noticed the rising column of dust and smoke beyond the Upper City wall. From the direction of the Grand Sanctuary.

Looking around again, he realized that there were still no guards in sight. Cursing, he sprang back onto his feet and raced towards the wall, Maral bustling along after him, mumbling about seeking cover and saying this was a bad idea.

They quickly made their way out of the northern-most courtyard of the castle, but then it took the Prince several minutes to find the nearest stairs up onto the wall. Once he did, he took them two at a time, ignoring Maral's plea to wait for her.

When he reached the top, a great void welled up inside of his stomach. The Grand Sanctuary was missing a sizeable chunk, and it burned, along with much of the grass and trees around it, a thick plum of white and gray smoke growing larger and rapidly rising into the sky.

Once Maral made it to his side, she took in the terrifying visage and muttered, "By the gods…"

Idrill suspected a god, or false god, did indeed have something to do with it, and his eyes darted around, looking for a glowing figure but finding none. He did, however, notice several burning figures stumbling out of the flames before collapsing. From his vantage, it was difficult to tell, but he was almost certain they were armored guards.

His thoughts flashed to Draegus, and wondered if the fool had tried to gather a force to attack Zairel. Cursing, he wondered if he was next, and he knew that he had to figure out some way to hide or protect himself. Without a word to Maral, he turned and raced back down the stairs.

"Sire? Your Majesty!" Maral noticed his absence, and tried to follow after him. "Where are you going?"

Bounding across the grass as fast as his wiry legs would take him, he didn't bother to answer. There wasn't time. His heart raced, not from running, but from terror.

Dashing into and through the courtyard again, he didn't even try for the front entrance, he found and burst through one of the side entrances into the north wing, and immediately turned and ran through the doors into his old bedroom. He had already begun to move into the King's room, but he still had his weapons stored in his old bedroom.

Tearing open the chest, he grabbed his dagger and unsheathed it, but the moment he looked upon the silver blade, he knew it would be useless against Pevrin. He cursed, but then spun around when he heard Maral let out a squeak of a scream.

She had just ran into the room behind him, but her eyes were fixed on the far window. Following her gaze, his heart froze when he saw Pevrin, or what was left of him, glowering inside of his bedroom. The false-god was totally naked, his flesh scorched and his hair gone, but more terrifying were the numerous cracks all about his frame, all of them glowing bright white, as if the power within him were ready to burst forth.

Almost saying 'Pevrin,' Idrill corrected himself, "Zairel! What happened?"

The god stumbled forward, and another crack suddenly opened in his face, accompanied by a flash of light that destroyed the bed frame as he continued past it. Maral jumped back, and then raced from the room in terror. Idrill intended to follow her, but he knew he probably wouldn't get far.

"I need you," Zairel spoke, except his human voice was now completely gone, and all that was left was a terrifying, deep, resonating voice.

"My Lord?" He gulped, and edged towards the exit.

"This vessel can no longer sustain me. I need another."

Idrill froze, terror filling him with panic. Then he realized that he still had the dagger in his hand. If he couldn't run, then maybe he could kill the weakened entity!

Lunging forward, he tried to plunge the long, steel blade into the other's chest. But he made it only a few feet before he was suspended in midair, with Zairel pointing his finger at him.

"It is time...to serve your god," Zairel stumbled over his words. He suddenly opened his other hand, and the three Cronal pieces fell out, landing on the carpet with a soft thud. "One last vessel. One last time."

There was a flash of light that seared into Idrill's eyes, and the glow within Pevrin launched out of the being and at him, engulfing the King.

Searing pain! His insides wrenched as if something pulled them inward, and then again, and again. He felt boiling heat and burning cold all at once. Idrill's senses dulled, he didn't even feel his body crumple to the floor.

A voice boomed inside of his head. *"If you do not resist, there will be less pain."*

There was a scream, but he didn't know if he really screamed or if it was in his head. He couldn't feel his body, couldn't do anything with it, and yet the pain grew worse and worse.

What's happening to me?!

"I am taking your body."

But it's mine! I can't die like this! Please, I beg you, leave me! I have served you well!

"And you shall continue to, but not in the same way."

More searing pain, more heat and cold. His vision darkened at the edges. His mind grew dull. Forming thoughts became difficult.

Until, for the briefest moment, his mind and the other's enmeshed. He knew then what was happening, he knew then that he had moments left before he would be consumed.

Worse still, he finally knew who the imposter was. Not a god. Not Zairel.

Degrin.

I am Degrin.

Idrill Beredis was gone, leaving only Degrin. Like with Pevrin, it felt clumsy to inhabit and maneuver in another human body.

Degrin stood up, but he had to focus carefully on moving, and concentrate on keeping his overwhelming essence contained in the shell. He wasn't done yet, he couldn't let this body fail him.

Turning to the old body, he observed through cold, raging eyes. He had seen into Idrill's mind in those last moments, saw what he had done.

It mattered not, his betrayal was now dealt with. Degrin had gained the last bit of knowledge he needed from the Grand Sanctuary before it was destroyed. He had leverage on the Wizard King now.

Idly, he wandered over to his former body, learning to walk all over again. The clothing felt smooth, and when it rubbed against his skin, it didn't itch like the Covenant robes had.

Pevrin's body had turned to ash, and as Degrin bent over to pick up the Cronal pieces again, he brushed his fingers against Pevrin's face, starting a chain reaction that sent the ashes into a pile of dust.

Holding the Cronal pieces before him, he smiled.

It was time to retrieve the last piece.

Chapter 37

REFUGE

When Kailar passed through Sal'fe's portal to the Wizards' Guild, she emerged with the others several dozen feet south of the complex, and she had to raise her hand to block the afternoon sun from her eyes. While she waited for those behind her to file through, she took in the monumental complex before her, surprised not only by how colossal the buildings were, but also by how spread-out they were.

Artists' renditions had depicted the ancient complex as grand, but not nearly of this scope, and all of the structures in the old renderings were interconnected, unlike the new one. The Grand Hall itself stood center before her, with a stone courtyard between her and it. The Hall was easily tall enough to accommodate any dragon, the massive copper and iron doors open to the cool spring breeze that blew locks of hair into her face. Several incomplete spires surrounded the entire complex, and in the courtyard before her, the foundations of several small structures were being laid.

Brushing hair behind her ear, she looked at the other stone, marble, and steel structures, and felt violated. These ruins had once served as her refuge, a place that no one else came to except occasional treasure hunters, and it was where she used to come to think when the world turned against her.

It was also the place where she had first learned to summon drakes after obtaining the Sword of Dragons, and where Klaralin, whose identity she hadn't yet discovered, helped her unlock more of her powers. Glancing at Elaria, she remembered when she first met the Dareann Elf right here, where the brand new structures now stood.

Their arrival hadn't gone unnoticed, as several Wizards, all working on the various structures with a combination of magic and manual labor, swarmed towards them. They had their staves raised suspiciously, but as they drew close enough, someone recognized members of Kailar's troupe and called for everyone to be at ease.

One middle-aged looking Wizard, which Kailar guessed meant he was at least a thousand years old, stepped ahead of the rest, his burgundy robes fluttering about in a sudden breeze. "I am Alabran," he announced, planting his dark oak staff into the ground beside him. "Acolyte of the Wizards' Guild."

Kailar was about to announce who she was, but then stopped herself and glanced at Letan beside her. His eyes were wide open in wonder, though his attention was more on their surroundings and the Guild complex than the actual Wizards.

It was Draegus who stepped forward and took charge at that moment. "I am Captain Draegus Kataar of the Tal Guardians. We…" The guard captain glanced about him at their eclectic group, his eyes settling on Kailar for half of a beat longer, before he looked at Alabran again. "We request asylum."

The shock upon Alabran's face was almost comical, and he looked at his companions, flustered and uncertain. Hesitantly, he spoke, "I am afraid that I do not understand. Why would you require asylum with us?"

Kailar raised an eyebrow and watched Draegus carefully as pain and sorrow etched across his face. "Much has happened since the Wizards retreated to your Guild complex. Tal…Tal has fallen." His voice increasingly shook as he spoke, and even Kailar felt a pit form in her stomach. Tal was no longer home to her, but it had been for a long time. "And we are now hunted by a terrible enemy. We need your help."

Alabran rearranged his robes nervously. "Well. I see. In that case, you may wish to speak to the Masters. I believe all votes have been tallied this morning and a new Grand Master elected, so they should be ready to receive you." Kailar's eyebrows perked at that. A new Grand Master? Apparently more had happened than she knew. "Please, follow me."

Alabran led the way, with the other Wizards parting for them. Kailar glanced again at Letan, and smiled at the wonder and awe still present in his eyes. He noticed her staring, and his cheeks suddenly flushed, almost matching his hair. "What?"

Kailar shook her head and nudged him forward. "Nothing. Come on."

The troupe followed Alabran onto the stone courtyard, allowing Kailar a moment to look closer at the half-finished foundations. They were set together in pairs, she realized, but were much too small to serve as any logical buildings, even watch houses, and they were raised too high off of the ground. What could they possibly be?

A wave of fatigue suddenly overtook her, as the aftermath of her battle with Pevrin caught up to her while her combat high faded away. Letan's firm hand grasped her arm and helped steady her, but he knew not to ask if she was okay. Even if she wasn't, she would never admit it in front of anyone else. Instead, she took comfort in his grip, and channeled energy from her dark magic into her body to help her recover.

She glanced around to see if anyone had noticed, and grimaced when she saw Draegus staring at her. After a moment of returning his stare, she gave him a wide-eyed look, silently asking 'what are you staring at?'

He answered her question with a question. "How did you make that portal in Archanon?"

Alabran's head jerked when he overheard the question, and the Wizard suddenly took great interest in their conversation. Shaking her head, Kailar replied, "Like I said in Falind – dark magic. I'm guessing whatever blocks portals in Falind only does so for regular magic, not dark."

The guard captain nodded thoughtfully, but Alabran glanced backwards with a frown on his face. Kailar narrowed her eyes at him, a spiteful comment on the tip of her tongue, but he quickly looked away.

The troupe passed through the massive open doors, revealing the interior of the Grand Hall. She had never visited the Wizards' otherworldly version, but she imagined it looked somewhat like this, with giant marble pillars reaching high up to the ceiling, skylights at regular intervals, and matching windows along the tops of the wall. The floor was covered by ornate rugs directly beneath each skylight, and the symbols inlaid into them vaguely reminded her of some the symbols she noticed in the trim embroidery on the older Wizards.

At the far end of the Grand Hall was another set of very large doors, only slightly smaller than the entrance doors. Those doors, made of some white metal with gold details, stood wide open. A mass of ancient-looking Wizards milled about inside the room, which Kailar surmised was the famed Council of Masters.

All motion within stopped when the masters noticed the approaching group. Alabran brought their troupe to a halt several feet away and waited patiently to be acknowledged. One particularly old Wizard, her robes the color of a plum, emerged and stepped ahead of the rest. Her voice was cracked and gruff with age. "Alabran. What have we here?"

"Grand Master Syrn," Alabran bowed deeply. "Congratulations on your election. This is Captain Draegus Kataar of the Tal Guardians. He has come to seek asylum."

The Grand Master's ancient eyes widened in shock. "Asylum?"

Draegus stepped forward, his dirty and worn armor in stark contrast to the clean and tidy Wizard robes. "Yes, Grand Master. May we address the Council of Masters?"

Kailar wasn't sure if it was the dark tone in the Captain's voice or his title that demanded attention, but Syrn acknowledged his request, dismissed Alabran, and ordered the other Masters to find their seats. The troupe was admitted into the Council of Masters chamber, which contained a three-quarter circle marble table surrounding the center where they stood. She looked up and closed her eyes as a sliver of a sunbeam from a large skylight warmed her face, and she waited for the elders to sit.

Syrn remained standing until all other Wizards were seated and then, just like the others, she rested her staff on her chair's back, and sat. The white and gold doors behind Kailar closed of their own accord, giving them privacy amongst the Masters.

Nodding her head, Syrn implored, "Please explain."

After gathering his thoughts for an additional moment, Draegus Kataar launched into the tale by first telling the Wizards about King Beredis's assassination at the hands of a former member of the

Covenant, one who now appeared to be possessed by a powerful entity. Draegus described how he was outside trying to settle a crazed mob when he heard the King's screams, and he rushed into the throne room to find the King already dead. He spared them the full gruesome details of how he died, but Kailar's imagination ran wild with the basic description. Draegus added that he tried to attack the one named Pevrin, only to have his sword shattered and his magic defenses nullified by whatever possessed the former Covenant member.

The Guardian further explained the possessing entity's claimed identity of Zairel, and then explained his interactions with the Prince and his subsequent conversation with a known spy of Falind. Then he turned his attention to Kailar.

She in turn launched into her story of being approached by one of Sal'fe's assassins, which garnered more than a few stares. Kailar wagered that none of them knew about Sal'fe's secret training of Mages before now, and she reveled in spilling his secret. After that, she finished her tale by describing how she and Letan had snuck into the city, and then fought Pevrin.

The assembled Master Wizards remained silent after that, all of them looking to their newly elected leader for guidance. Syrn simply stared upon the troupe silently, bringing her hands up to her lips and thinking carefully. Finally, she looked at Draegus. "Captain, you mentioned asylum."

Hesitantly, Draegus nodded and motioned for Anila to join him at the head of the group. "We have in our possession one of the pieces of the Cronal, which apparently this entity seeks. He has the other three, and needs only this piece."

A deep frown formed crevices upon Syrn's face. "Pieces? Not volumes?"

Anila looked hesitantly to Draegus, who nodded encouragingly to her. "I realize that keeping the Order's secrets is core to your duties," he said. "In this case, however, I think it is time for the truth to come out."

Drawing in a deep breath, Anila nodded and withdrew the Cronal piece from a pouch. She cleared her throat, and began, "I am Anila Kovin, trusted guardian of the Covenant. And this," she held the small piece out for all to see, "is one of four pieces of the Cronal."

The Master Wizards all leaned forward to get a better look at the tiny cylindrical piece, but they remained silent and allowed Anila to continue explaining. "This is so much more than a text could ever be. You see, Zairel found these ten millennia ago. I didn't know where until recently, all that was told was that it was in a place no one could find unless they knew where it was. If I'm right, however, Zairel found these pieces in the dwarven city beneath Archanon, in a magical..." Anila glanced at Elaria, and asked, "Device?"

Elaria nodded. "Yes. A magic-powered machine, though apparently even more than just that."

Addressing the Grand Master again, Anila continued, "The legend says that Zairel and his closest companions, all of whom were magic-sensitive, were able to touch these and focus their souls through them to access a place of knowledge."

At this, Syrn's jaw grew slack, her eyes opening wide. "The Library."

Kailar frowned at that, surprised both at the revelation of the truth of the Cronal, and at the fact that the Wizards knew about this 'library.' She glanced at Letan, but he still seemed to just be in awe of it all.

The other elf that accompanied Elaria asked, "You know of it?"

Syrn nodded. "It is known to all Wizards, and achieving a level of consciousness that takes one there has always been one of our greatest goals. None ever have, at least none who lived. Some assume that when a Master Wizard's powers destroy them, it is because they discovered the Library, and the knowledge was too great for their mortal bodies."

"That sounds similar to the legends," Anila nodded. "As well as how it is treated now. Members of the Covenant train for many years before being selected, with emphasis on mental and emotional control.

"In any case, Zairel founded the Order of the Ages and the Covenant shortly after finding the Cronal, and having learned of a fourth kingdom far to the east, he took the fourth piece with him, along with several others of the Order, to find that kingdom and leave the final piece in their care. You see, he believed that having all four together was too dangerous, and it was vital to keep them hidden from the common population."

Anila looked at Reis and grimaced before she asked, "I wonder if he knew that this day would come."

"Based on everything I have heard today," Syrn began, "I assume that no one believes that this Pevrin is possessed by Zairel?"

Kailar withheld another snarky remark, thinking it obvious by now. Draegus replied, "He is too cruel, too inhuman, to be one of the Six."

Anila nodded her support. "Zairel was compassionate, a man of learning. Destroying and threatening were never his style. If anything, I would sooner believe it was Degrin."

Even Kailar felt a sudden chill run down her back after those words. She didn't believe in the Order of the Ages, but if she was wrong, and the first demon was real and had come back, then the end of days were coming.

That was probably how the entity had attained so much control over a short amount of time. Whether it was Degrin or not, the threat of the end of days could easily force the populace to fall into line and follow the orders of one claiming to be their god and savior. That on top of his ability to influence people made him beyond dangerous.

Syrn sat back again and placed her fingertips together, her brow furrowed in deep concentration, her eyes lost in thought.

"With respect, Master Wizard," Draegus spoke impatiently, "This is a grave threat to us all, and the Wizards represent the greatest power still on Halarite. Perhaps by working together, we can protect the final Cronal piece, and stop this Pevrin or Zairel or whomever it is."

Syrn raised a skeptical eyebrow, and Kailar felt her temper flare. Were the pompous asses going to refuse to help?

Another Master Wizard to Kailar's left asked, "What about the Keeper of the Sword? Can we get word to him, or the Star Dragons?"

Kailar almost lost it, and sputtered out a scoff. All eyes fell upon her, so she asked, "You're kidding, right? Is that always going to be your answer? Run to the Star Dragons for help?"

"It worked against you," Reis grumbled.

With a scornful sneer, she reeled on him, "Can it, moron. That was the Sword of Dragons, something they were involved with forging, something that was *their* problem to deal with. This isn't, it has nothing to do with them, *especially* because the fabled Keeper of the Sword isn't involved." Reis didn't take too kindly to being told off, but she didn't let him say anything. "This is our problem, isn't it? A man claiming to be one of *our* gods has come to apparently punish us, and we're just going to sit by and let him?" She glanced at Elaria and her companions. "No offense, but this is our world." She looked again at the others. "This is our world, our problem, and I think that it's one we can deal with."

The look that most everyone gave her reminded her just how hated she was. In particular, those who lived in Tal glowered at her with absolute disdain. "Maybe you haven't noticed," Reis scolded, "but we've been through our fair share of disasters lately. We've endured countless losses, including some of our most powerful allies," he waved towards the new Grand Master, piquing Kailar's curiosity again about what happened to the previous Grand Master. "And now you want us to face this new threat on our own out of some selfish sense of pride?"

Kailar began her retort with a curse word, but Elaria interrupted her, "First of all, you're not alone. I'm here now, and as before, I'm honored to fight alongside the humans of Halarite. Second, I think that Kailar's point is Valid." Kailar almost snorted out a laugh at the incredulous look on Reis's face. "Hey, don't look at me that way," Elaria defended. "I'm not picking her side over yours." She looked pointedly at Kailar and added, "As far as I'm concerned, she deserves to burn for her crimes." A part of Kailar took that as a threat. Another part recognized that she deserved those words. The same guilt she felt over Ardelle gripped her chest now.

"However," Elaria continued, addressing everyone else, "as an experienced explorer and occasional diplomat, I'm saying that if your people don't learn to stand strong on your own against threats from your own homeland, you'll be perceived as weak by other worlds, and a ripe fruit for picking by those less interested in peace." She smacked her fist into the palm of her hand, "*This* is your chance to prove otherwise."

"To which other worlds do you speak of," Syrn frowned questioningly at Elaria. "You and your companions are the only other ones here at present."

Elaria shook her head in exasperation. "You don't have anything to prove to us, believe me. But word will get out sooner or later. This could be your moment to shine, and to make any hostile worlds second guess ever crossing you. Believe me, there are plenty of hostile worlds out there looking for easy prey, at least as many as there are neutral or friendly, and the stronger image you can project, the more likely they'll go off looking for easier prey."

"Think about the story you could tell them," the other elf encouraged. "A world battered and beaten by apocalypses and invasions, yet when incredibly powerful beings attack, you stand strong and defeat them on your own. If I were someone looking to pick a target, and I heard that, I'd find somewhere easier to pick at."

Kailar grinned at the elves' enthusiasm, and looked to Reis, daring him to counter their impassioned speeches. He didn't say a thing.

Syrn nodded thoughtfully. "You all make a compelling argument. Furthermore, as Halarite is once again our home, and it is the will of the Council to remain here, we have as much of a stake in securing Halarite's future as anyone else." She looked around the room with a raised eyebrow, and hesitantly added, "Unfortunately, our defenses are not yet ready. We will need to act quickly to prepare."

Another violet-robed Wizard nodded to Syrn. "I believe we can at least raise a shield around the complex with relative ease. If six or eight Masters worked together, I doubt even this Pevrin could penetrate it."

Nodding, Syrn replied, "That would likely be enough. Without our spires working, however, if he should break through, it will be up to individual Wizards to mount a defense." She looked at Draegus and asked, "Can we expect Pevrin to come alone?"

Even Kailar knew the answer to that, and Draegus solemnly shook his head. "I doubt it. My guards...it seemed as if Pevrin had enthralled some of them. They followed his will, disobeying all of my orders and attacking me."

A thought occurred to Kailar, and she looked very carefully at the Captain. "Yet he didn't think to enthrall you?"

Without a connection to star magic, Kailar had no way of detecting if there was such control being exerted upon Draegus, so she watched his facial expressions very carefully for any sign that his thoughts weren't his own.

When he looked directly into her eyes, all she saw was contempt. "As I understand it, Idrill Beredis wanted to break me down on his own, without Pevrin's help." A wry grin crossed the Captain's face. "As it turned out, that was a good thing, otherwise the King might not have had anyone to turn to for help, once he realized his mistake."

Syrn listened quietly until that moment, when she said, "His abilities greatly complicates matters."

"No kidding," Draegus gulped.

Kailar considered the situation for a moment, and began, "I know you're all going to hate me for saying this…"

"So don't say it," Reis glowered.

She almost said it anyway, knowing that someone should. Surprisingly, it was Syrn who spoke the needed words. "We will of course try to subdue any such enthralled people without killing them. However, unless Kailar can give us insight into how to interrupt such control, it is likely that we will have to hurt many of them, and possibly kill some."

Kailar shook her head solemnly. "I don't even know how to exert control over others anymore." An unfortunate truth, she grimaced. Maybe someday she would learn that ability with dark magic. Then again, what would she do with it this time?

"One more thing," Anila quipped. "If the Wizards' shield should fall, Pevrin will be after this," she held up the Cronal piece again. "Even though we do not know exactly why, the knowledge and potential power it could give him could make him unstoppable. Our priority should be keeping him from getting it."

"We could send it away," Kailar suggested, glancing at Letan. "Hide it on Devor somewhere, or even on Asirin or Trinil."

Syrn shook her head. "Unfortunately, I do not believe there is any true way to hide the Cronal from this entity, if what everyone has said is true. He will discover that it is not here very quickly, and will leave to continue his search. The Wizards' Guild represents our best defense."

"We should hide it somewhere in the complex," another Master suggested.

"I agree," Syrn nodded.

"In which case, I will hide with it," Anila stated, wrapping her fingers around the piece tightly. "As the only representative of the Covenant here, it is my responsibility."

"I'll help," Reis quickly volunteered. Anila smiled, but continued to face the Wizards, while Kailar rolled her eyes. Clearly those two were a thing.

"Agreed," Syrn nodded and stood up, followed quickly by the

other Masters. "Then let us call this meeting to an end, and prepare the Wizards' Guild for a siege."

Chapter 38

CHRYSALIS

When Sira, Dalin and Ulpex had caught Pelick and convinced him to spill his guts about the impending attack, Sira had expected the invasion immediately. They had rushed back to the village and sounded the alarm, and the villagers leapt to action, surprisingly organized in their efforts to prepare for invasion.

But then it didn't happen.

Sira in particular had stayed close to the crystal, along with about a quarter of the villagers, while the rest had gone further out to defend the perimeter and, should the assailants portal directly into the village, the villagers would then surround them.

The day passed by silently, tensely, the sun travelling fast across the sky, and night coming quickly. When it was clear that they were in no immediate danger, some of the villagers decided to at least feed the defenders, and fires were struck up to cook evening meals. As the night wore on, some took turns sleeping, but Sira refused to, not while the crystal was in danger.

Instead, she used techniques she had learned in Warrior training to infuse her body with magic, revitalizing herself without having to sleep. It wasn't a long-term solution, and their teachers had always warned that their senses would still dull as time passed, but in a pinch, it kept them going long after non-Mages could not continue to fight.

Sira took little comfort in the kaetz becoming active, or any of the other fauna throughout the village, though the kaetz in particular continued to show interest in her and sometimes swarmed her. More than once she had to shoo them away, but they always came back, individually at first, and then in groups.

She was grateful when the sun rose, and the kaetz returned to their trees to float lazily around the branches. Did they ever sleep? Or were they constantly revitalized by magic, like she was now?

Shortly after dawn, Ulpex left to tour the front line, and she realized then that he was once a military commander, or at the very least, he had once been a part of a military. He very effectively organized what were almost all civilians into a capable defense, and he knew that the 'troops' were no doubt demoralized already by having to maintain watch throughout the night. She respected him for that, and smiled upon his return to the square to check on the core defense.

"I stopped by to chat with Pelick before I came back," he casually said as he stopped beside Dalin and resumed surveying the square. "He is as surprised as we are that no one has come to attack. I am wondering if they thought he would need extra time to complete his mission."

"Was he supposed to report success to them," Sira asked.

With a shrug, Ulpex replied, "If so, he did not admit to it."

Dalin smirked. "Pelick does not seem like the type of person able to resist questioning from you, my friend."

The back of Ulpex's mouth curled up in a smile. "Indeed. However if we do not see any activity by the end of today, I-"

Ulpex was cutoff at a surge of magic not far away. Then Sira felt another. And another.

Suddenly a dozen portals opened up throughout the square. Someone near the front sounded a horn, indicating more portals had opened further out. Sira drew her sword and charged it with magic, stepping into a defensive stance and facing the nearest portal.

The enemy had come.

The first darksteel-clad soldiers came through in a wave from each portal, and Sira, not caring so much about what they looked like, unleashed her first attack upon them. The attackers, however, came through prepared, and her blast of magic slammed into magic shields.

Remembering the enchanted weapons that the orcs had wielded, she knew she couldn't fight them from afar, so she shouted a battle cry and charged the nearest invader, feeling more than seeing other defenders following her lead. The portals closed, each having deposited only four attackers, but that meant there were more than two dozen in the square alone, and she was on top of the first one.

Or rather, she lunged in underneath, since it was a much taller person than she expected. She dove in and jabbed her recharged sword at him, but it deflected off of his magic shield just enough that her weapon only scraped his armor.

And he was fast. The assailant swung his battleaxe down on her at lightning speed, but she too was fast. With the help of her shield, she was able to avoid death, and she swung again, managing to scrape against his gauntlets, but missing his skin, which she noticed for the first time was a deep purple color.

Looking up into the slit of his helmet, she saw deep, yellow eyes glaring at her, and white teeth flashed as he smiled, and swung his arm wildly to try to backhand her.

She ducked and lunged in again, this time making it through and impaling into the attacker's armpit, where his armor was weak, and she felt her sword stop short against bone.

The attacker roared in pain and tried again to swat her away, but she pulled her sword out and spun around, charging her weapon up again and swinging with all of her might to release a powerful blast. Wounded and distracted, the attacker had dropped his shield, and her blast crushed into him, cracking and crinkling armor while sending him sprawling.

Around her, the battle raged on, with most of the villagers having at least some connection to magic and able to hold their own at first. Dalin blasted at one attacker with lightning, which she recalled was effective against the orc commander during the war, and it was just as effective here.

But then another attacker was upon her, and she had to roll out of the way of his advance. It was another of the purple-skinned, larger brutes, but thankfully there were only a handful of them.

Sira was on her feet instantly to face her new attacker, when suddenly Ulpex leapt onto the attacker's back and dug claws and teeth into their neck and shoulders, anywhere there was a weak spot in the armor. The attacker roared in pain and tried to grab Ulpex, but Sira saw her opportunity and rushed in, driving her sword up beneath the breastplate and into what she hoped was their opponent's heart.

Not knowing for sure, she yanked her sword free then, and darted backwards. But the opponent was defeated, and he fell to his knees before dropping his broadsword and falling over dead.

Sira felt a pulse of intense magic, and she turned to the west towards the source. There stood the tall being they had seen Pelick meeting with, their body still completely hidden by armor, but the claws on their hand had extended several inches, and looked absolutely terrifying.

Worse still, the clawed attacker's magic was potent, and they released a blast of arcane power from the palm of their hand against a villager, penetrating the villager's magic shield and sending her sprawling away.

The attacker then looked to the crystal and ran towards it.

"Oh no you don't," Sira called out, and unleashed a blast of magic from the tip of her sword. The blast caught the attacker off guard and made it past their shields, sending them stumbling to the side, but it looked like the armor had mostly protected them.

The attacker looked at Sira, and she saw the glow in their eyes again, orange like that of a fire. At first she thought it might be the same species as the other two that she had just helped take down, but if so, it was shorter than they were by at least a foot, even if taller than Sira by a margin.

The opponent bent down then, as if coiling up, and sprung at Sira. When they were on top of her, they brought both clawed hands down, and she barely dodged, and then tried to counter. The attacker was fast, however, and the armor didn't seem to slow them down much. They grabbed the blade of her sword with one hand, and swiped at her with the other.

She dodged, but didn't let go of the sword, nor did the attacker, and they swiped again.

Grinding her teeth at the sudden stalemate, Sira charged her sword with magic, and tried to release it from the edge of the blade without swinging. It worked, and blasted away her opponent's grip, freeing her weapon and allowing her to dodge back as the other clawed hand swiped at her again.

Sira was immediately on the defensive again, the attacker swiping left and right, and Sira having to dodge or parry and back away, drawing them closer and closer to the crystal. She suddenly felt completely out of her element, having trained against mostly sword-wielding opponents, along with some other familiar weapons like daggers or axes, but never an enemy like this!

Ulpex came to help her again, trying to match the attacker claw for claw, but he had no armor. Suddenly the opponent slashed deep gashes into Ulpex's arm, and then sent him sprawling away with a blast of magic. Sira glanced around, saw Dalin, and called for his help.

And then the attacker was upon her again, only this time, they grabbed her sword and tried to yank it from her grip. Sira held on strong, but was suddenly dangling from the hilt, her feet a good six inches off the ground.

The attacker pulled back with their free hand and prepared to impale Sira, but in that instant, Dalin unleashed a blast of lightning at the attacker, blinding Sira temporarily from the flash, but forcing the attacker to let go of the sword.

There was another flash, and another, and Sira had to keep her eyes shielded as the bright spot in her vision faded. When she could see again, the attacker was not falling back like she had expected, but instead advanced upon Dalin, taking each blast of magic with a grunt.

Something sounded strange about the grunt, but Sira couldn't tell what it was. She stood up, pushed as much magic into her sword as she could, and released it in a pinpoint attack against the opponent.

They must not have expected the attack to come from behind, and stumbled forward with a surprised yelp. Dalin unleashed another attack against their foe, sending them back towards Sira. She in turn forced them the other way.

They had them! Surely the attacker's armor couldn't take much more of this.

Suddenly the attacker dove for the ground, anticipating Sira's next attack. She missed, and instead hit an unsuspecting Dalin, whose shield was only partially formed, and he spun around and crashed to the ground, having taken some of her attack by accident.

Enraged, Sira leapt at her opponent, but they were ready and backhanded her, sending her flying towards the crystal again and knocking the wind from her.

It took her several heartbeats to try to recover, gulping in breaths. She looked up just in time to see her opponent release a blast of magic towards her. Sira hastily raised a shield and tried to dodge, but part of the blast slammed into her, flinging her sideways while the rest of the blast shattered into the crystal.

There was a colossal pulse of magic, and a bright beam of purple light lanced upwards out of the crystal. She gawked at it wide-eyed, her stomach sinking when she realized she had failed to protect it.

"No!" The attacker's shout was distinctly female, only mildly surprising Sira. It was impossible to tell through her armor, but there was no mistaking that voice.

However, the attacker then looked at Sira, and stalked towards her. "I needed it in one piece!"

Sira stood up again, even though her right shoulder screamed in pain, and she realized it was dislocated. Weakly, she tried to swing her sword with her left hand, but the attacker used Sira's momentum and swinging sword to spin her around, and then claws raked across her back. Her world exploded in pain, and she sprawled down onto the ground, crying out.

Sira tried to move, to stay in the battle, but the wounds tore with every movement, and her dislocated shoulder refused to work. She cried out in agony, but had to keep moving, had to protect what was left of the crystal.

A shadow fell over her, and she looked back to see the clawed attacker standing over her, heaving angered breaths and ready to end Sira's life. Until another blast of lightning from Dalin slammed into the attacker. Followed by a shard of ice. And then another blast of lightning.

"Sira."

Freezing, Sira's eyes shot open wide, the voice coming from everywhere and nowhere, just like Endri's voice, but not Endri's voice. In fact, it had sounded like her own voice.

She tried to turn over, to reach her sword, which she had dropped a few feet away, but her wounds tore again, and she cried out.

"Sira, I can help."

Confused, Sira looked around to try to find any sign of a dragon. Except, why would a dragon speak to her in her own voice? Endri's voice was unique, as was every dragon's at the Celestial Spires.

Who are you?

"We can help each other," the voice spoke again. *"We are both wounded and cannot survive alone. But together, we have a chance."*

Her eyes grew wide, and she looked towards the crystal. More cracks jutted into it, and some chunks had fallen out. There was still a beam of light straight into the sky, but it looked like it had grown weaker.

Are you...in the crystal?

"The crystal is my...how do you say? Womb? That may not be right. But I am not ready to come forth. I am still too undeveloped."

The raging battle around her forgotten, Sira stared at the crystal dumbfounded. That was the secret! It wasn't just some random magical artifact, it was like an egg!

Wait, what do you mean, together we have a chance?

"I can heal you. And you can provide my essence with a vessel."

Her eyes grew wide in shock and she felt an impulse to reject the offer. *You mean like a child?*

"No. Much different from that. I do not know if I can explain it. I will imprint upon you, become a part of you. And you will be a part of me."

I don't understand. She hesitated, but pain fogged her mind, and her vision blurred with darkness surrounding the edges of her sight. Her body was giving up, and she felt cold. Whether or not she was dying, she was now out of the fight, and since she couldn't feel her legs, she probably wouldn't ever recover again.

You can heal me?

"Yes, but only if we act quickly. I am growing weaker by the moment. You must let me join with you, now, or neither of us will survive."

Blinking away blurriness, Sira looked around, trying to find Dalin to see if he could help instead. That was when she saw the Wizard fly backwards from another blast of magic, his body tumbling across the square.

Several of the Darksteel were vanquished, but more rushed into the square, and most of the villagers had fallen. They were losing the battle.

Sira thought she heard a roar in the distance, but she could barely process it, and only scarcely noticed the clawed lady look to the east. And then Sira's vision darkened.

It was over. She had failed.

"Together, we might yet pose a challenge to her. We can defend the village."

As her mind faded, Sira latched onto that fact. She couldn't fail.

She wouldn't.

Do it.

She felt a pulse of magic envelope her. Consciousness was slipping away, but was suddenly revived by an invigoration of power. The cold numbness in her body was replaced by warmth, and by pain that had earlier faded.

But the pain subsided. Her vision cleared, and she realized that a purple light surrounded her, emanating from the crystal. That light pulsed, as the entity within it flowed into her.

She tensed up, as a terrible thought occurred to her. *Did I just make a mistake? Will you consume me, take over my body?*

"*No,*" her own inner voice replied, sounding stronger and more confident. "*Do not worry. I will never harm you, I promise. I will protect you. We will co-exist, and defend those we love.*"

A broad smile crossed Sira's face, and she pushed herself off of the ground, realizing then that she no longer felt any pain, her back healed, her shoulder affixed and fully functional.

She looked at the clawed attacker, and her smile grew larger. Even without seeing her face, Sira knew her opponent was suddenly scared.

And then a portal opened near the square's eastern edge, allowing Cardin to step through, Sword ready.

Chapter 39

STARCHILD

It happened when Cardin, Astaria, and Endri had just crested over the first mountain pass, a bright, purple beam of light pierced the sky in the west. They had walked through the night, mostly at Cardin's insistence, because he knew that if they stopped, he wouldn't sleep anyway. Not after the visions from the copse.

The trio came to a jarring halt, with the two dragons looming on either side of Cardin, and they stared at the beam.

Then they noticed rising smoke.

"The village is under attack!" Astaria shouted in panic, and she instantly took to the skies, pumping her wings hard to move as fast as possible while she let out a deafening roar.

"Astaria, wait!" Endri leapt up after her, leaving Cardin alone, while the image of Sira broken on a battle field flashed through his memory. With his heart pounding and all fatigue vanished, he opened a portal to the village square, drew the Sword of Dragons, and rushed through.

The square was a mess, littered with bodies and debris, and several buildings outside of the square were set ablaze.

The first thing he saw was a frighteningly armored person, covered from head to toe with segmented, serrated, darkened steel plate armor, and claws where fingers should have been. Cardin's eyes locked with hers, eyes glowing bright orange in the darkness of her helmet.

Then he saw Sira standing a few feet away from the crystal, which at that very moment exploded as the last of the energy contained within coursed through the flowing magic of the world and into Sira. Her armor was torn and bloodied, her face a mix of blood and dirt, but she stood tall, despite not being armed. Cardin saw her sword on the ground only a few feet beside her.

The clawed enemy appeared to recognize him, stating, "The Keeper of the Sword. You should not be here!"

She coiled back and then lunged at him, her clawed hands opened at her side, and Cardin braced himself, drawing power into his body to enhance his muscles and reflexes.

Tall and brutal, the attacker assaulted him ferociously, swinging her hands in quick, trained swipes. Cardin twisted and swung the Sword to bat away one attack while using a magic shield to block the other, and then performed the same actions a second time. He spun around, swung at her, but was likewise blocked by magic.

He spun again, thrust the Sword towards his opponent, but missed, and she grabbed the blade, her larger hands easily wrapping around it, and she held firmly.

But when he pulled back, the Sword ripped free, cutting her armor and hand. She cried out and backed away, gawking at her wounded hand, and that was when Cardin noticed that her blood was a green color.

And then a blast of violet magic slammed into her and sent her sprawling. The blast had felt incredibly strong, and he expected to find that Dalin had cast it. Except it hadn't come from the Wizard, whom Cardin had yet to see on the battlefield. It had come from Sira, who was armed again and brandished her sword at the attacker. She prepared another blast, setting her sword glowing purple and humming.

Then Astaria's roar echoed across the skies, and the clawed woman looked up in a panic, just as the dragon's shadow fell across them.

An alien word escaped the clawed woman, and she raised her uninjured hand into the air and released a red flare skyward. Suddenly the rest of the attacking force stopped what they were doing, and several of them summoned portals for the rest to retreat through.

Cardin grinned, realizing then that at least the attacking army was afraid of dragons.

The woman stood up and looked at Cardin menacingly, so he prepared to defend himself again. But then she opened a portal horizontally above her and leapt up into it, the portal closing a second later.

And then it was over. The last of the attackers were gone before Astaria or Endri had even arrived.

Lowering the Sword, Cardin looked about the square in awe, and a great weight settled over him when he realized how many bodies belonged to the peaceful villagers.

When his eyes settled on Sira, she smiled at him, but there was something new in her eyes. They flashed a purple-white, and then she collapsed to her hands and knees, dropping her sword again, and her head drooped. He rushed towards her, seeing that her armor on her back was ripped to shreds. Through those slashes, her flesh looked torn, but a purple glow engulfed the wounds before he could tell how bad they were.

Magic swirled all around the square in that moment, and it flowed directly into Sira. Dozens upon dozens of kaetz emerged from the trees and swarmed around them. The power coalescing into Sira felt familiar, and he realized that it was just like with the crystal – the energy went in, but never flowed back out.

Securing the Sword on his back, Cardin knelt down and tried to grab her shoulders, but was physically repelled, as if by an invisible force. Not a shield, but like two magnets pushing against one another.

Though silent, she looked up to him, the glow in her eyes slowly receding. "Cardin," she said weakly, pain evident in her voice. "I'm still not…ready. Not done healing, I think."

His jaw hung open as he watched the glow recede, but her eyes remained a bright, vibrant shade of purple. He knew those eyes, knew every detail of her irises, and every detail was still there, only the color had changed.

Her head drooped down again, but she did not collapse further, and that was when he noticed the glow on her back diminishing. Through the torn armor, he saw that her flesh had healed, but something else was there. Not scars, but a purple image crisscrossing across her back.

Astaria landed hard at that moment, her feet finding the few gaps between bodies, and she looked down upon the remnants of the crystal, which Cardin only now noticed had lost its mystifying sheen. Astaria's voice echoed through his thoughts, crying out, *"No!"* followed by an agonized, enraged roar that pierced his ears and made him wince, her roar crying up to the stars.

Then the power within Sira pulsed, momentarily reversing the direction of magic flowing into her, and that caught Astaria's attention. Her roar ceased abruptly, and she looked down at Sira in shock.

"My child," she cried out, and started towards Sira, transforming in the blink of an eye back to her human form, as she rushed to their side. "What happened?"

"I'm not sure," Cardin shook his head. He tried to look into Sira's eyes, but her head was still too low.

"She was badly wounded," came Dalin's voice from across the square. He was in the middle of extracting himself from debris. Blood trickled down from the corner of his mouth as he hobbled over, having to rely on his staff for support. Cardin smiled briefly at his friend's new staff, but otherwise was more concerned about his friend's health, and Sira's. "And the crystal was cracked by the clawed attacker."

As Dalin came closer, Cardin asked, "Are you okay?" Cardin motioned towards the corner of his mouth, and Dalin dabbed at it, seeing his own blood.

"Yes," he grimaced. "Mostly. I feel some broken ribs, and I bit my tongue." He wavered in his posture and almost fell, but caught himself. "I shall be feeling the aftermath of this battle for days to come."

Endri finally landed in the square, right where Astaria had originally, and looked on in deep concern. Astaria, however, had her eyes fixed on Dalin. "Tell me exactly what happened after that."

When Dalin finally made it to their side, he leaned heavily upon his staff and looked at Sira, deep crevices forming around his eyes from concern. "I blacked out momentarily. However, from what I could see, whatever power was in the crystal seemed to…to transfer to her."

Astaria's taut face slackened a bit, and she lowered her head, nodding once. "I see," she spoke mournfully.

"You said 'my child' when the energy pulsed," Cardin said.

Astaria nodded again and looked upon Sira, the sadness in her eyes making Cardin's heart hurt. "Yes, I did."

Endri's green eyes lit up brightly for a second, his face showing shock. *That was a dragon chrysalis!*

"Yes," Astaria replied. "It was. However, it needed decades more before it was ready to hatch. It...is lost to me now."

"No, it isn't," Sira suddenly spoke. She looked up and pushed herself onto her knees. "It is here," she placed her hand on her chest. "It asked to join with me, to heal me and to provide it with a vessel."

Cardin shook his head, trying to process her words. "What do you mean, joined with you?"

"I don't know, exactly," Sira replied, her brow creasing in confusion. "The effort of healing me drained it considerably." Looking at Astaria, she nodded encouragingly. "It, or she, or however you define gender, is still there. I just don't think she'll be conscious again for a while." Sira frowned and shook her head slowly. "Does that even make sense?"

The first hint of a smile crossed Astaria's face, and she nodded. "Yes it does. This has never happened, in all the history of the Star Dragons, but it does not surprise me." She drew in a shuddering breath, and clenched her eyes shut. "My child may not ever be born now, not while residing with another entity. But..." Astaria's voice caught, and the first tear streamed forth. A forced smile spread across her face, and she looked upon Sira, her eyes flashing starlight for a brief second. "At least they can live on in you."

She clenched her jaw tightly then, and hung her head. Cardin wanted to say something, anything, but felt that any words he could possibly give would fall so short of encouraging as to be insulting. He watched Astaria's expressions as she shook her head, and then turned away. After another moment, she walked towards Endri, while she surveyed the wreckage and the casualties.

Endri looked upon her mournfully, lowering his head to eye level with her, and she rested her head against his snout. The green dragon's eyes turned towards Cardin, and he explained, *There has not been a newborn Star Dragon since the Civil War.*

Cardin's eyes grew wide, but then he noticed Sira trying to stand, and he helped her up. He was grateful when he wasn't repulsed again, and he drew her into a tight embrace.

The explanation from Endri could wait. He was just glad to be with Sira again.

Chapter 40

IMPASSE

In his private study, Sal'fe walked along a row of bookshelves that doubled as the back wall and contained not only his personal collection of books, but many of the books he had found in Falind's sanctuary that he deemed vital to his research.

Today, his original research was secondary, and he tried to grasp for some vital truth he might have missed. Something that would ensure the survival of his kingdom, no matter the outcome of the inevitable conflict between Pevrin and the Wizards.

Part of him knew that Pevrin, or rather the entity within him, would win. It was likely inevitable, unless Sal'fe found some secret, some method of dispelling the entity or destroying it. What little he had learned did not bode well.

He was growing frustrated, having looked through the titles twice over in the past hour, hoping something would spark his intellect or lead him to an answer. So when there came a knock at the light wooden door, he barked, "What is it?"

The door creaked open just enough to permit one of his assassins to edge inside quietly, and her unique pulse of magic allowed him to identify her as Ardelle.

"Forgive the intrusion, Sire," she spoke cautiously. "The King of

Tal is here to see you."

He was so engrossed in his search of the bookshelves that he initially was shocked, thinking she meant Eirdin Beredis. But then he brought himself back to the present, and realized it would be Idrill.

In and of itself, that was a surprise. Sal'fe had the impression that the former Prince was a prisoner in his own kingdom. Had he slipped away? Or had something happened and he was forced to flee?

Sal'fe considered seeing the young King in the throne room, but he knew that time was short, and it was essential to continue looking for an answer. "Show him in," he ordered without looking at her. Then he realized that it would still be wise to show strength, especially if Idrill had come seeking help, so he walked along to the side of the stacks and picked up the Staff of Aliz. With a satisfied smile on his face, he turned to the door, and felt pleased when he realized that Ardelle had slipped out without him noticing. She was easily his best student.

Closing his eyes momentarily, Sal'fe centered himself, drawing in deep breaths and letting them out slowly, trying to flush the frustration from himself so that he did not make any mistakes. Somewhere in the back of his head, he heard an inner voice insist, *you've already made a terrible mistake.*

Sal'fe didn't make mistakes. He scoffed at the idea. But then he decided to extend his senses outward to find any hint of danger. That was when he realized what was wrong.

Sensing the overwhelming presence moments before the door opened again, he steeled himself and opened his eyes just in time to see Idrill step inside, with Ardelle bowing and closing the door to give them privacy.

Still wearing his royal black and silver robes, Idrill's eyes flashed orange briefly, and he smiled. "Halarite's first and only Wizard King," the young man bowed to him. "How I have wished to meet you."

With an ever-tightening grip on his staff, Sal'fe eased towards the center of the room, giving himself space in case he would be forced to fight. "I cannot say that the feeling is mutual," he spoke curtly. "I hear that you have worked over Tal quite handily."

Leering at Sal'fe, Idrill replied, "It was an interesting experience, though hardly a challenge. When one has the knowledge that I have, manipulating people becomes easy."

Already growing impatient with the exchange, Sal'fe decided to challenge him directly. "I know what you are."

Idrill raised an eyebrow and folded his arms. "*What* I am, not who I am?"

Though he did not show it on his face, Sal'fe cued in on that word choice. Deciding to fish for information, he planted the staff beside him, drawing Idrill's eyes to the red gem, before he continued. "You are a wraith. A half-ascended being who cannot fully take physical form in this world, nor can you take full advantage of the Great Library."

The wraith was visibly surprised and impressed, and nodded his head slowly. "Interesting. And quite correct. Bravo, Your Majesty." He considered Sal'fe's words another moment before adding, "There's nothing on this world that speaks of such things, so I can only assume you yourself have been to the Library."

Sal'fe swallowed hard, but otherwise controlled his outward expression tightly. "Indeed I have, thanks to my kingdom's Cronal piece. And once I learned what you were, and that my presence could create another channel for you to come to our side, I immediately left."

"A pity," the wraith sighed dejectedly. "I can only imagine how delectable your soul might have been. It still could be." Sal'fe tensed, the voice in his head urging him to attack pre-emptively. Drawing in magic surreptitiously, he continued to project his outwardly calm demeanor.

The wraith continued, "I am impressed. You navigated the library quickly and efficiently to have discovered such vital information without alerting me. I have my attention fixed upon Halarite, after all."

A grin tugged at Sal'fe's lips. "You underestimate me."

"Perhaps," the wraith nodded. "Perhaps not. Your attempts to draw magic to yourself have not gone unnoticed." Sal'fe tensed again, but did not cease his efforts. "Be careful, Wizard. You cannot possibly win against me."

"Oh? Even for a wraith, that is quite a claim." Sal'fe shook his head in admonishment. "You are not invincible."

"My body isn't," the wraith corrected, the orange glow returning to his eyes. "But if you destroy my body, I shall require the use of another. How convenient that such a powerful one stands before me." He nodded to Sal'fe's staff and added, "Not to mention the things I could do with that staff. Tell me, have you told anyone the secret of the Staff of Aliz?"

Sal'fe's composure faltered for a moment, and he ceased drawing power into himself. What did the wraith know? Or was it a bluff? *No*, Sal'fe thought, *it is no bluff, not if he exists within the Library.*

"Ah, so you have not," the wraith smiled. "Excellent. Shall I tell your guard outside? Shall I announce it to your people? No?"

Clenching his jaw, Sal'fe drew in a deep breath and nodded. "I know what you have come for, but it is no longer here. However, if you promise to leave my kingdom alone, I will tell you where you can find it."

The wraith narrowed his eyes and regarded Sal'fe carefully. Then he closed his eyes, and Sal'fe felt him flex his powers, a sensation he recognized as extending his senses out to search the currents of magic in the area. "You speak the truth," he opened his eyes a moment later. "A rather brave thing for you to do, sending it away from me."

"I want no part of this struggle," Sal'fe defended.

"Then you should have kept it to give it to me," the wraith sneered.

Sal'fe almost reacted, almost leveled his staff at his adversary, especially when he felt another flourish of power from the wraith. But then he recognized the antics, and knew that the wraith was impatient. More than that, he saw cracks form in Idrill's skin when the wraith flexed his power, and he suspected that the wraith was losing the ability to maintain his essence within a human body.

Somewhere in the back of his mind, an answer clicked. If the wraith had occupied Pevrin for weeks or months without issue, yet now he could scarcely retain his form within Idrill Beredis, was there a correlation to magic? After all, Pevrin, like all Covenant members, had a highly trained mind and a deep connection to magic. The Beredis family was devoid of magic.

That also meant that Sal'fe could not afford to get into a battle with the wraith. If it did take control of Sal'fe's body, it might be too powerful for anyone else to handle.

After several tense moments, the wraith relaxed. Scowling, he waved his hand towards Sal'fe. "Very well! I have no need for your kingdom now. But be warned, there will come a time when you cannot defend against me, even with all of your enhancements to your city's defenses." Sal'fe started at that statement, but should have realized the wraith knew about everything he was doing to Falind, if not because of the library, than through Tal's obviously effective spy network.

"I have your word, then," Sal'fe asked, even though he had no choice but to give the wraith what he wanted.

"Yes, yes," the wraith waved his hand dismissively. "Now tell me where it is!"

Nodding in satisfaction, Sal'fe rested his free hand in the nook of his elbow and stated, "It is at the Wizards' Guild to the north."

That made the wraith lose face for a second, but he quickly recovered. "I see. No matter. It will soon be mine," he leered, "and then I will have what has always belonged to me."

Half-bowing in mock respect, the wraith smirked, and opened a portal then. He stepped through quickly, and his portal closed.

Sal'fe's shoulders slouched, and he let out a relieved sigh. Just then, Ardelle made her presence known. He had sensed her entrance, just after the wraith flourished its powers, but Sal'fe did not dare cue the wraith to her presence.

The grim look on Ardelle's face matched the pit in his stomach, and he nodded to her. "Go," he ordered. "Tell the Wizards that the entity now inhabits Idrill Beredis, and that he is coming." He hesitated, a realization dawning on him when he thought back to the conversation, and he nodded. "Tell them that the entity may be Degrin."

Looking even more shocked, she asked, "My Lord? How do you know this?"

"The things he knows," Sal'fe started, but then looked at her. "And his final words. More than that, I have spent enough time on Halarite, overheard enough sermons from clerics to know the myths and legends."

She clamped her mouth shut and nodded. "I shall leave immediately." Grasping the pommel of her dagger, she summoned a portal.

Before she left, Sal'fe cautioned, "Do not tarry, Ardelle. Give them the information they need, then return immediately. Let them fight this battle."

Bowing deeply, she replied, "As you command, Your Majesty."

Once she was through the portal and it closed behind her, he turned back to the bookshelves and stared at them absently. The answers weren't in there, he knew that now. It would be up to the Wizards and Cardin's friends now to figure out how best to defeat Degrin.

They will turn on you afterwards, the voice in the back of his head insisted.

He had to see to the defense of Falind.

Chapter 41

KAILAR'S CHOICE

Even though only a couple of hours had passed since their arrival, Kailar was impressed with how quickly the Wizards prepared their defenses. Especially considering how long they had lived in luxury and isolation, they defaulted to ranks quickly, and efficiently doled out assignments.

There was considerable debate about where Anila should hide, in case Pevrin managed to get through their defenses, but it was finally decided she should go into the restricted section of the library, since it already had additional magical defenses to prevent unauthorized access. Although Reis had volunteered to protect her, Draegus decided to accompany them as well.

After that, Kailar and Letan split off from the rest of the group, unsure what to do except watch the Wizards prepare. Kailar's presence amongst everyone else was decidedly unwelcome, and through mere association, so was Letan's.

As the flurry of activity continued around them, Kailar watched absently, unable to sense any of the power being used by the Wizards. It was somewhat disconcerting, seeing magic being used non-stop and not feeling a thing, and she thought back to her days as a simple Mage.

An awkward silence had fallen between her and Letan. They had ventured out into the field where they had first arrived, and idly paced around the short grass. When Kailar looked at Letan, she saw that his eyes were distant, looking towards Daruun Forest to the west.

Taking a guess at where his thoughts were, she nodded towards the forest and commented, "I used to travel extensively through that forest. It was the easiest way to stay hidden."

His expression darkened, and he looked down, avoiding her eyes.

When he didn't say anything, she sighed and demanded, "Ask your questions."

"What?" He frowned at her. "What questions?"

"You want to know more about what I did on Edilas," she narrowed her eyes at him. "Don't pretend that's not what you're thinking about."

Letan's jaw tensed. "Are you saying you're a mind reader as well as a controller?"

So that was it. He was still stuck on that bit. Kailar planted her fists on her hips and squared off with him. "I can't control people's minds! Not anymore."

"But if you still could?" The question was direct and simple, his tone even. There was an underlying anger she sensed, but maybe also fear.

He folded his arms and looked her right in the eye, searching no doubt for a hint of dishonesty in whatever her response was. The problem was that she wasn't sure she had an answer for him.

Kailar began to close up inside, sealing off her feelings like she used to do. There was no way she could come out of this on top, she decided.

"It doesn't matter," she looked down.

"Oh yes it does," he stepped closer to her, unfolding his arms and reaching to grab hers. She retracted from him, apparently catching him off guard.

The silence created a gulf between them, and her heart ached, so she pushed those emotions aside, too.

Finally, he flailed his arms out, and raised his voice in exasperation, "Would you stop pushing me away like that? Stop hiding! We've avoided this conversation long enough, and…"

"And now, before a great battle, is *really* the perfect time to talk about it, yeah?" Her accusatory question dripped sarcasm, and it made him back off. She pressed on, "You don't want to hear about it, okay? I had to do a lot of distasteful things while I was here, and yeah, I'm not proud of it, but I tried! Alright? I tried! And I tried again on Devor, only this time I did it your way." She shouted, "But now all I feel is guilt! I'm tired of guilt, I'm tired of fear, I hate it, I hate it all!" She pointed a finger at him and said, "I never felt any of this before you, and it's made me weak."

She said it before she realized that her lid on her emotions had failed, and everything spilled out all at once. The stunned look on his face stopped her short of going on any further, and an immense guilt overcame her.

The very guilt she despised. That, the conflict inside of her, is what she hated more than anything.

Letan didn't reply. She couldn't blame him. What could he ever possibly say to that?

It wasn't his fault, she realized, and she was being unfair. So, with fists clenched to stem her frustration, she said, "You're a good man. And you're absolutely right about me. I can't change."

The gulf between them widened. She could see it in his eyes, and she felt it in her chest.

There was no going back now.

After a moment of thinking about it, Letan asked, "Then what do we do? Where do we go from here?"

Before she could answer, a flash of light caught her attention, and the eyes of every Wizard nearby looked towards it. Kailar saw that a portal had opened up about twenty feet to the south of where she and Letan stood, and she felt her pulse quicken.

Thankfully, Ardelle's familiar form stepped through.

She let out a sigh and relaxed her hand off of her sword. Ardelle spotted them and headed towards them immediately. With only moments to spare, she looked at Letan and said, "For now we have a job to do. After that…I don't know. We'll talk then."

He didn't look satisfied with her answer, but they didn't have time to debate further, since the Falind assassin was upon them.

"Kailar," Ardelle began, the urgency in her eyes and voice sending a surge of renewed energy through Kailar. "I come bearing news. The entity has changed hosts to the former Prince of Tal, Idrill Beredis." That came as a surprise, but not as much as Ardelle's next words. "King Sal'fe believes the entity to be Degrin."

Some of the approaching Wizards stopped cold upon hearing that, and even Kailar felt a chill run through her entire body. She still didn't believe in the teachings of the Order of the Ages, not after everything she had seen and experienced, but to hear a Wizard claim that a mythical being existed?

Ardelle finished, "And King Sal'fe wished me to inform you that Degrin is coming. Now."

A rushing sensation took hold of Kailar, and she nodded. Their time was up.

"Thank you," Kailar bowed appreciatively. "I take it you won't be staying?" Ardelle shook her head. "You'd better go now, then, because we're about to seal off this whole area."

Kailar didn't bother to watch Ardelle portal out, she and Letan turned and ran for the center of the complex, a square just north of the Council of Masters. That was where they would find Syrn, and the six Master Wizards chosen to summon the shield.

They ran into Elaria and the Daruun Lieutenant, Kellis she thought his name was, along the way, but when they asked what was going on, Kailar didn't bother to explain, so the elf and Warrior ran to stay with them.

They careened around the corner of the Guild Hall, and as soon as they saw Syrn, Kailar shouted, "He's coming! We need to get the shield up now!"

Syrn, standing next to and talking with Master Phaern, didn't question Kailar. She gave the group of six Wizards nearby a knowing look and nodded. They in turn formed a circle, and placed the tips of their staves in the center.

Kailar and Letan skidded to a stop next to Syrn and watched as a bright flash engulfed the six shield bearers, and suddenly a white beam of light pierced into the sky. A blue-white translucent dome began to form, extending outward from the beam of light and down around the entire complex. While it formed, the Wizards all around took that as the cue to get into final positions, taking up defensive lines all around the complex until they knew for sure which direction Degrin would attack from.

As the dome finished forming, she explained to Syrn, Phaern, Elaria and Kellis what Ardelle had told her, their expressions of surprise mirroring her previous one.

"That may be why he needs the Cronal pieces," Syrn stated. "He may need them to connect to this world."

"Or worse," Kellis added. "If he knows about the device down in the dwarven city, he may be able to use the Cronal to effect things on a cosmic scale."

"Bad news all around," Kailar agreed. Motioning to the shield bearers, still engulfed in a bright white light, she asked, "How long can they keep that up?"

"For days, if necessary," Phaern replied.

A low rumbling suddenly echoed across the sky, and Kailar looked to the south, though her view was occluded by the Grand Hall. "Somehow I don't think they'll have to wait that long."

The group rushed to the western side of the Grand Hall to see what the noise was, but what they saw was unexpected – a deep, thick fog rolling in from the south, engulfing the grasslands in a wall of shadow.

Kailar gulped. "I guess he's coming from the south."

Syrn frowned at her. "Obviously."

She bit back a retort, and instead led the group into a run for the southern line. Moments later, the edge of the fog came up against the shield, though it didn't cause a flare up of any kind, and instead it rapidly rolled up and around. It reached the top of the dome in a matter of seconds, and dimmed the sun, casting everything into a gray haze.

An oppressive silence fell upon the area, the kind that only comes from a thick fog. They reached the southern line of Wizards, and then waited.

Kailar's heart raced, and suddenly she wished things were back to normal with Letan. She wished to reach her hand out to his. But that's something she probably would never get to do again.

When nothing else happened at first, it only put her further on edge. Why announce his arrival like this? What did the fog accomplish?

Peering into the murky haze, she tried to find any sign that the shield would fall under assault, but nothing happened. The Wizards all around them shifted uncomfortably. Even Syrn appeared uncomfortable, flexing her skinny, bony fingers around her staff. Kailar rested her left hand on the hilt of her sword, a reassuring sensation, though she didn't draw it yet. As long as the shield was up, they were safe.

Weren't they?

Quick movement above caught her attention, and she glanced up, but there was nothing there. She looked around at the others, but no one else seemed to have noticed. Had she imagined it?

She looked up again, and watched, waiting for it to happen again.

There it was! A brief swirl through the fog, like a bird swooping through a cloud. There was another to the right of it. Then another.

Others noticed it now, and more eyes looked up, staring in confusion at the swirling patterns, growing more and more pronounced and frequent. Then the shield flared near one of those swirls. And again near another.

"What in the Six is that," Kellis asked.

Sighing in frustration, Syrn raised her staff up, and her plum-white crystal flared. Suddenly a wind blew outside of the shield, and Kailar stared at her in awe, wondering how she could affect magic outside of the barrier like that.

When she looked up again, however, she was even more surprised. Though the fog had blown away from the shield above them, tufts remained, shaped like giant eagles, and they swooped about, some diving towards the shield and exploding against it in a puff, releasing enough energy to visibly affect the shield.

"By the gods," someone said.

"Elementals," Syrn stated, a hint of awe and fear in her voice. "My goodness, I never thought to see elementals in person."

Letan looked at Syrn with a frown. "What are elementals?"

"Creatures literally summoned from the elements," she explained, her eyes fixed on the elementals as they continued to assault the shield. "A powerful magic that even Wizards have scarcely ever mastered, and none in my lifetime. Those would be a type of air elemental."

Kailar looked curiously at the bird-shaped clouds, wondering just how much damage a cloud could possibly do. The flaring caused by their attacks was minimal, and there was barely a sound from them. Were they merely testing the shield? Or were they more powerful than she realized?

She looked down, and noticed for the first time that the fog continued to recede beyond the shield, and at that instant, human forms took shape. "Is that another form," she asked.

But as everyone looked south, she realized that it wasn't more elementals she saw. The mist pushed away further, and the forms cleared up.

It was an army of people.

Her heart froze for a moment when she realized that it wasn't just soldiers, either, nor Warriors. It was blacksmiths, tailors, farmers, all brandishing instruments of their trade as weapons. A hundred. Two hundred. Her stomach sank further as the mist cleared further.

Hundreds of them.

At the very center stood Idrill Beredis, his eyes glowing bright orange.

"Just like the soldiers in Archanon," Letan murmured. "They're enthralled by him."

"How do we fight without hurting or killing them," Kellis asked.

Shaking her head, Kailar replied, "We don't." All eyes fell on her, but she kept her eyes fixed on the enemy. "If we try to defeat him without hurting the others, he'll overwhelm us in seconds."

Kellis's response was immediate, "Don't you dare hurt them. They're innocent people!"

"I don't care," she glared at him. "I won't give up my life to save a few peasants, and I certainly won't sacrifice the world for them!"

"Kailar," Letan cautioned her, as useless as that might be. "We're not here to slaughter innocents."

"No kidding. We're here to keep a dangerous, malevolent being from doing who knows what to our world." She waved her hands about and added, "The whole damn Universe, actually! That's what you said," she jabbed a finger towards Kellis, "Right? If he gets his hands on that piece, he could affect changes on a cosmic scale."

Kellis looked ready to object, but then stopped himself, and a grimace drew down his face. He didn't say anything else.

But Letan did. "Fine, we have to save the Universe. But that doesn't mean we have to needlessly slaughter them. We're Warriors, not monsters!"

She looked towards the advancing army just as Degrin stepped ahead of the rest by a few paces before they stopped their advance. Even from this distance, she saw a sickening leer on his face. Suddenly he raised his hands up, and tiny fires ignited all across the field between the two forces, lighting the grass on fire. Those tiny fires flared, swirled, and coalesced into humanoid forms with flames for hair. There were hundreds of them.

"And now fire elementals," Syrn stated. "This is not going to go well."

As if to prove her statement, the elementals all lined up, the surrounding grass blackened like a scar upon the world. They raised their hands, and without warning, released streams of fire upon the shield. The barrier flared brightly, and the effect upon it was immediately noticeable, as it changed colors against the onslaught, weakening and losing its brightness.

Syrn tensed. "The shield will not hold long against this." She raised her staff up, and sent a bright red flare towards the center of the dome, alerting all Wizards to converge on their location.

Kailar drew her sword, as did Letan and Kellis, while Elaria drew her daggers.

The impact points on the shield began to turn a strange pinkish color, and then more orange, turning to the color of the flames, Kailar realized. She charged her sword with dark magic, setting it humming, and at first prepared to raise a shield, but then she realized that everyone else around her would do the same, and a dark magic shield might be counterproductive.

She had an idea and stepped back a few paces, eliciting a confused look from Letan. "Kailar?"

"I know what I'm doing," she replied, her jaw set tightly.

He was about to inquire further, but then the shield broke, and a torrent of fire engulfed them. Every Wizard and Mage raised shields to block it, but as long as they were on the defensive, the elementals could continue undaunted. Kailar knew they had to do more.

Pushing magic into her legs, she leapt up as high as she could, much higher than anyone should have been able to, and then she swung her sword, releasing the full extent of power within her sword outwards as a deadly wave aimed at the line of fire elementals.

The blast was devastating, and when it discharged into the enemy lines, it carved a divot out of the ground, destroying every last fire elemental.

When she landed, the air elementals had broken through from above and dove upon the Wizards en masse. Blasts of magic, elemental and arcane, lanced up into the sky, piercing and destroying the ghostly forms in waves.

Then the ground rumbled violently, and all around them, columns of rock, dirt and grass rose up into behemoths, in and among the defenders. The Wizards reacted instantly, but the rock elementals only added to the chaos and casualties.

The three rock elementals closest to Kailar took a particular interest in her, and she had to leap and dodge around to avoid smashing dirt and rock fists. She cut the arm off of one in a single neat slice, her sword recharged already and helping it cut through the rocks, but it didn't stop the elemental, and it pounded against her hastily erected shield.

Kailar jabbed her sword upwards into the chest of the elemental and released a burst of magic, blowing it apart and ending its fight. But the other two smashed her shield.

She rolled away, and recharged her sword while turning around to face them. They barreled towards her, the ground shuddering with every step, but she was fast, and she released a wave of energy just powerful enough to destroy them both.

When the rain of dirt and pulverized rock settled, she heard the sound of a roaring, charging army, and saw the citizens of Archanon advancing upon them in a crazed rage. The Wizards were handily dealing with the elementals, but they would soon be overrun by the enthralled, and things could get really sticky then.

It would be so easy, she thought. All she had to do was get out ahead of the Wizard front line, and release another deadly wave of magic. She could knock out a quarter of the army in one blow, and then do it again. Then the only threat would be Degrin's elementals, and Degrin himself, much more manageable.

It would be so easy.

She caught sight of Letan then, his shield failing and his head nearly being smashed in by an earth elemental, but he ducked out of the way in time. Kailar released a pinpoint blast of dark magic at the monstrosity, disintegrating it.

He looked at her to thank her, but the look she gave him in response conveyed everything she thought. They both glanced at the enthralled army, and then at each other. "Kailar," he shouted amongst the rumbling of the elementals.

Looking again to the rushing army, she bit her lip, thinking hard about what options they might have. How could they possibly stop that army without hurting or killing them? How could they do that and survive themselves? Or keep Degrin from finding the Cronal while they were occupied?

Letan dodged around another elemental, and rushed over to her. "Kailar, don't!"

"I have to!"

"They're innocent people," he shouted.

"Right now they're our enemies," she bit back. "We don't have time to debate this!"

"Kailar!"

Ignoring Letan, she pulsed magic into her legs, and ran for the front of the defensive line, while simultaneously charging her sword. One of the elementals tried to get in her way, but she leapt over it, and landed in front of the line.

She hesitated for only a fraction of a second, but by then the enthralled were on top of her, so she swung her sword, and released the wave of magic into them. The blast wave instantly slammed into the front line, throwing bodies into one another, tearing up the grass beneath, tearing apart bodies.

Tearing apart lives.

The miner from Edingard flashed through her memory again, and she felt a void rip apart her insides.

But the army wasn't defeated yet, and those that weren't killed or stopped by her blast kept coming. She channeled more power into her sword, stepped forward, and swung, releasing another blast as powerful as the last. Her attack had to travel further this time, and lost a bit of its edge, but it did the job, killing or disabling more people.

Her eyes felt wet, but she ignored it. Her heart felt heavy, but she ignored it. She charged her sword and released another wave.

When her throat caught, she cried out in rage to clear it, and released another wave.

But when she prepared to attack again, the grass all around her erupted in flame, and fire elementals swarmed her. She raised her shield before any could harm her, but then she was engulfed by fire, and even through her shield, she felt the heat.

The torrent spilled upon her incessantly, like a rushing river that never gave up. Kailar could feel the star magic negating her dark magic, and she had to thrust more power into the shield, but it was almost impossible to keep up the needed flow. The shield flickered, flames licked at her armor, her hair singed, the scent bit at her nostrils.

She was trapped.

"NO!"

With a massive surge, she poured every ounce of strength into her shield, pulsed it outward, expanding, shoving and pushing the elementals away.

But she wasn't done. The ache in her heart grew worse, the images of all of the bodies she'd destroyed, all of the lives she'd destroyed passing through her thoughts. "NOOOOO!"

The shield fell, replaced by a field of purple-white lightning, deafening as it crackled and danced about her, disintegrating every elemental it came into contact with. They weren't alive, she could destroy them, unleash her rage, unleash it all on them!

When there were no more left to destroy, she looked for more targets. More elementals to devastate. Her fists crackled with energy, her sword hummed and glowed, the blade turning red-hot.

Until her eyes fell upon Letan. The deep shock within them, the horror on his face as he watched her unleash her rage.

He was afraid of her.

The power within faltered, the crackling energy disappeared. A cold, deep ache grasped her heart, suffocating her.

Kailar fell to her knees, and she gazed around her. Indeed, the fire elementals were gone, with naught but charred grass to mark their passage. But atop that charred grass lay broken, torn, and burned bodies, mutilated by her magic, by the fires, by the lightning.

Looking again to Letan, she wanted to cry out, but in that moment, she knew what she had done. For the first time, he had seen what she was truly capable of.

The battle against the earth elementals raged on behind Letan, the Wizards destroying one, only to have two more take its place. More air elementals coalesced above, falling upon the Wizard forces even as they were reinforced by more Wizards from the other fronts.

Suddenly Elaria was at her side, her daggers out and charged, and Kailar wondered if the elf had come to put her out of her misery.

Instead, she asked, "Where is Degrin?!"

Kailar's heart leapt into her throat. There were still enthralled humans alive, far to the south and steadily charging towards them, but their numbers were significantly dwindled.

Degrin was not among them.

Chapter 42

BURNING STACKS

The sounds of battle outside of the Wizard library boomed and thumped, reverberating the marble and stone walls and floor, and setting Draegus on edge.

"So much for the shield holding up," Reis muttered. Draegus, Reis, Anila, and two Master Wizards were holed up inside of the restricted section of the Great Library, which itself was protected by an anti-portal ward, according to the Wizards, and the restricted section was protected by defensive barriers on top of that.

Draegus wanted to command Reis to watch his words around their hosts, but the Master Wizards were themselves too nervous to react. Before the battle had begun, they had boasted about how rapidly they had rebuilt and expanded upon the ancient Wizards' Guild complex, and how unlike the now-destroyed complex in their pocket universe, they were keen to put windows everywhere. Except, of course, in the restricted section. While this meant that they could not see what was going on outside, it also meant that the attackers would not be able to find them easily.

Draegus looked to Anila, who had knelt on one of the colorful rugs set out in the precious little open space in the library and closed her eyes, her hands resting on her thighs as she meditated calmly.

Even he, a seasoned Warrior and Guardian of Tal, was in awe of her composure.

The walls shook hard, the ground rumbled, and Draegus felt a storm of magic as the Wizards fought whatever the entity threw at them. "What do you suppose is going on out there," he asked one of their hosts.

"Whatever it is," the blue-robed one replied, "It is power beyond anything I have ever felt."

"Oh," asked the green-robed Wizard, while Draegus tried to remember their names. "I suppose you claim you can sense exactly what is going on through the wards when I cannot?"

"Maybe I can," Blue frowned. "I am older and wiser than you."

Green scoffed. "Older, yes. But..."

Draegus rolled his eyes, but before the argument could continue, they heard a great crash and shattering of glass through the sealed steel gate of the restricted area. Blue and Green ceased their banter and stared through the gates, though from their position in the center of the room, no one could see out into the library itself.

Draegus reached for his borrowed sword anxiously, wishing for the familiarity that his old Guild sword once gave him. Reis stepped up next to him, likewise prepared to draw his weapon, but Anila remained in her meditation.

A sense of dread crept into Draegus's heart, though he didn't know why, and he felt his heart race. The feeling didn't get any better, regardless of how much time passed, and for no reason that he could account for, he drew his sword. Reis followed suit, and this finally brought Anila out of her meditation. She stood up, and drew her unusual sword.

"He's here," she stated with dead certainty.

The other Wizards frowned at one another and looked back at her. Draegus likewise looked at her curiously, but when he and the Wizards looked forward, their hearts froze.

Idrill Beredis stood inside, somehow having made it through the shield and wards without alerting the Wizards, but instantly Draegus knew that it was no longer the former Prince before them. His eyes and entire body glowed bright orange, and his face was cracked with power bleeding through the fissures. Draegus sensed the well of magic all at once and couldn't understand why he hadn't felt it before that moment.

The Wizards reacted, but so did Idrill. He raised his hands, and the Wizards raised a shield. A field of magic surrounded them and assaulted their shields from every direction, crushing their barriers and forcing them to contract.

The Wizards looked at one another, a look of respect and resignation in both of their eyes, and then they dropped their shields while blasting Idrill full-force with magic. Idrill flew back and slammed into the stacks, grunting as he did so, but when their shields fell, the Wizards succumbed to Idrill's attacks, and they screamed in agony as their flesh burned.

Knowing that they were outclassed, Draegus shouted, "Run!"

Before Idrill could recover, they rushed past him, through the opened gate, and into the larger library. The stacks and stacks of books were only half-full, thanks to Nuuldan's attack, and their steps echoed off of the dark redwood shelves. The skylight above provided ample light for them to see as they fled.

The trio ran through the ten-foot-tall stacks, hoping to lose Idrill amongst the maze, but they didn't make it far. Draegus felt a surge of magic behind him, and raised a shield just in time to intercept an assault from his former Prince and King. The blast was powerful, and his mind instantly turned bleary and his vision blurry. He stumbled onto his knees, his sword clattering out of his hands, and pain wracked his body.

But then Anila turned around and unleashed a focused arcane blast of magic from the tip of her sword. The pain wracking his body ceased, and he fell forward onto his hands, breathing heavily like he'd been suffocated.

It took several moments to register what had just happened, and he looked at Anila in shock, but she only looked determined, and stepped past Draegus to defend him and Reis. When Draegus looked to Reis for answers, the Warrior whispered, "I'll explain later."

"Well, well, well," Idrill's mocking, inhuman voice spoke. "This is most unexpected. This host had no idea you were so powerful!"

Draegus took up his sword with one hand while Reis took the other and helped him to his feet, but his legs nearly gave out. Whatever Idrill had hit him with, it had taken everything he had out of him.

When Draegus finally turned around, he saw the former Prince with his hands clasped together and a delighted smile on his face.

"He assumed that you had no powers whatsoever. If only he could see you today."

Draegus gulped, and though weakened, he managed to ask, "Is…is he still in there?"

The entity's face slackened and he shook his head. "Oh no, most certainly not." Sneering, he stepped closer to them. Anila tensed, her blade hummed with magic. With a menacing tone, the entity announced, "I consumed him. Shall I do the same to you?"

Idrill's advance stopped when a wicked leer drew across his face. Then, he raised up his right hand, and snapped his fingers.

A pulse of magic, a flare of light and heat, and suddenly several books behind them were alight with fire, startling them. The flames swirled around in the middle of the aisle, and coalesced into a humanoid form, face of molten rock and red glowing eyes glaring at them.

"What in the Six," Reis cursed.

"All these books," Idrill waved his hands about. "All this wood. So many fuel sources to make an army. Shall I set the entire library on fire? I can burn every single one of you, right here, right now."

"No!" Anila's protest surprised Draegus, and he looked at her shocked. "Wait, please."

Idrill stared at her for a long time before a dark, frightening smile slowly drew across his face. "I thought as much. You are a guardian for the Covenant. They who value knowledge over all else. Knowledge, history, philosophy. You know that I can do exactly as I say. There is no escape, no possible way you can contend with me." As if to prove his point, the fire entities drew closer, their hands open with balls of fire ready to be unleashed.

Idrill raised his hand up and prepared to snap again, but Anila lowered her sword. "Please, don't!"

"Anila," Reis cautioned, his back now facing Idrill so that he could watch the fire creature. "What are you doing?"

Slowly letting out a sigh, she looked back towards Reis and rested a hand on his shoulder reassuringly. "We're trapped. There's no way out, and he could kill us in an instant if he chose." Draegus frowned and looked at Idrill, wondering why he hadn't actually done so yet.

Anila pulled out the Cronal piece from a pouch on her belt, presenting it to the former King. Idrill looked upon it greedily, his eyes wide with anticipation. Anila held it up, and stated, "We'll fight you again. But not here."

Ignoring her threat, Idrill walked towards them. That was when Anila made her move, pointing her sword at the possessed King and unleashing bolts of lightning upon him.

Her blasts found only a shield that deflected them right back at her, slamming into her chest and sending her careening into one of the stacks. As Reis caught her before she could fall, Draegus watched in awe as the Cronal piece hadn't moved, floating in the air where Anila had held it only moments ago, a blue glow surrounding it.

Idrill reached out and grasped the piece, his orange-hued essence clashing against the blue, and a magic-fueled wind kicked up all around them, raising the hairs on Draegus's arms and the back of his neck.

"Finally," Idrill shouted into the air.

Draegus tried to raise his sword and prepare an attack, but it still felt so heavy in his arms, and he couldn't focus his thoughts enough to call forth magic. But someone had to stop their enemy!

The entity looked upon them, and Draegus felt his heart stop. Idrill smiled, and raised his free hand, preparing to snap again and summon more fire.

A violet-white portal opened behind Idrill. Draegus blinked, seeing it with his own eyes, yet not feeling a stir in magic of any kind. A moment later, he knew why when Kailar stepped through, rage and murder in her eyes. She pierced her sword through Idrill's back, as a gasp escaped him, all air forced from his lungs.

The swirling magic that had come from Idrill moments ago ceased, and his face slackened. He looked down at the blade sticking through his gut, shocked.

"We're not finished, you and I," Kailar growled.

Before she could do anything else, Idrill's power flexed, and a wave of energy flung Kailar back away from him, her grip on her sword pulling it out of their enemy's back. Just then, another skylight shattered above them, and Draegus, Reis and Anila ducked and covered their heads from the falling shards.

A piercing shriek resonated through the stacks, and a giant, grey, cloudy eagle swooped down. The glow around Idrill's body returned, and he rose up into the air, where the eagle caught him and flew back up through the skylight. All of this happened so quickly that Draegus and the others barely registered it until it was over.

Once Idrill was gone, a sudden, deafening silence fell upon them all. The sounds of battle outside ceased, and Draegus felt only one more pulse of magic from above. He knew without having to see what it was – Idrill had used a portal to flee.

Kailar, having slammed into one of the bookshelves, groaned and tried to pull herself up. She stared after their enemy, but then collapsed backwards again, blood trickling from her mouth. Draegus tried to make his way over to her, but his legs gave out and he fell to his knees.

An empty void opened up in his chest, and he stared at the marble floor as despair overcame him.

They had lost.

Chapter 43

ASHES

As the morning wore on, Sira felt her strength return minute by minute. As if something within her regenerated her, and she knew that was exactly what was happening. The unborn dragon's spirit, or essence, or whatever it was, still slumbered within, but it recovered its strength alongside hers.

The day wore on, and as they looked for and helped survivors, with Endri, Cardin and Astaria healing those who needed it, they found even more villagers' bodies, some mangled or burned beyond recognition.

The only relief was in the beginning, when they found Ulpex alive, if severely wounded. Even Cardin couldn't heal him, and it took the combined strength of the dragons to bring him back from the brink, but he survived.

None of the invaders left behind lived, there was no one left to question. Even Pelick was gone, either burned in one of the buildings or escaped. As they found the bodies, they dragged them into a single area and left them to be dealt with later.

Cardin recognized the armor the same as they did, and the weapons. "The design, the craftsmanship, how the enchanted weapons feel," he remarked, shaking his head. "There's no denying the fact that this is the same as what Klaralin gave his orcs."

Sira and Dalin agreed. This was no mere coincidence. "What do you think it means," she asked.

It was Ulpex who answered, coming up behind them, freshly healed from Astaria's efforts. "I have heard of an unstoppable army," he spoke solemnly. "They invade entire worlds, one by one, and have done so for centuries or longer."

Staring down upon the bodies, his eyes were distant, fearful. Sira tried to read into those eyes, to glean any bit of extra insight from them. Ulpex drew in a deep breath, and he nodded. "I do not know what they call themselves, but those who survive and escape their invasions call them the Darksteel Army. We are lucky," he looked at Cardin, and then over towards the dragons in the square. "We are but a single village on a largely uncivilized world. They could have overrun us with hundreds of thousands of troops."

Sira nodded, none of what Ulpex said surprising her. The orc shaman that Cardin encountered had warned them about such an army. This attack and Ulpex's information only proved the army was real.

Once the fires were out and the survivors accounted for, they set to work trying to take care of the bodies as best as they could. Astaria knew most of the villagers' cultures and death rites; those who were normally buried were entombed beneath the ground on the northern edge of the village, and a graveyard previously sparsely populated now carried the weight of dozens. Others came from cultures whose funeral rituals involved burning the bodies, and this they did, using wood from half-destroyed homes, and setting more bodies than she cared to count atop them.

Silently, the village gathered around the square, where the pyres were built, and watched as each was lit, and a morbid silence fell upon them. While Astaria remained in her humanoid form, Endri stood at the edge of the square, looking over everyone and mournfully paying his respects.

Sira and Cardin stood by one another, her travel cloak covering her tattered and ruined leather armor, and she clenched his hand in hers. In front of so many, she tried desperately to keep the tears from coming, but she could still feel that her eyes were wet.

Until her own voice spoke within her head. *"What is death?"*

She blinked, the voice surprising. *Uh, hello?*

"Hello. What is death? I do not understand."

Sira glanced at Cardin to see if he heard the voice as well, but he gave no sign of having heard anything. Whatever was within her spoke only to her, it seemed.

Turning her attention back to the question, she frowned. *How do you not understand it? You just prevented both of us from dying.*

"So death is what happens when your light fails?"

It was an interesting question, but given the nature of the creature within, she decided it was an accurate description. *Yes. Our light fails within. We cease to exist, and only our bodies remain behind, although they then decay.*

She felt a shudder within, but it was not her shuddering. *"That is a terrifying prospect."*

Sira nodded once out of habit. *Yes, it is. How did you not know, though? You knew how to communicate with me before we joined.*

"Indeed. But what is magic, if not knowledge and power? As I grew within the chrysalis, magic flowed into me, and with it came knowledge. Surely you feel that now." Again she nodded. *"As much as I learned about life and the Universe, still there is much that I do not know or understand."*

Cardin suddenly squeezed her hand, drawing her eyes to him. Whispering, he asked, "Is something wrong?"

Feeling her face grow warm, she smiled and shook her head. "No," she whispered back. "It's just…the thing…being within me, whatever you want to call it. It's talking to me again." She frowned at her own word usage, and thought, *What do I call you?*

"I have no name," it replied. *"I would not have been given one until I came forth. I know your name is Sira. How did you come by your name?"*

She considered the question for a moment, realizing that what she took for granted, the unborn dragon might not have any concept of.

My parents gave me my name when I was born. I could ask Astaria what she would have named you.

"You could," the being conceded. *"But I think I would like it better if you gave me a name."*

Sira's eyes grew wide, and the request caught her off guard. She had never thought to name anyone or anything, and it was still technically Astaria's offspring. In fact, Sira had already decided to never have children, since she was unwilling to incur the months of being placed on inactive duty a pregnancy would necessitate.

This was something far different. Not even adoption could cover what this was, and her head swam as she tried to grasp what had really happened. Somehow, she felt responsible for the unborn.

Sira felt a sour taste in her mouth when she thought of it as 'the unborn' and decided never to think of it like that again.

"Thank you," it said. *"I do not like being thought of as unborn."*

Another smile lit up her face, and she felt warmth inside from it, as if the being within also smiled. She realized, then, that despite all of the horrible messes around her, the creature kept making her smile. So she thought of the ancient language, of a word she remembered from school that meant smile, but it didn't work as a name by itself.

But it was a good base, and she immediately knew how to alter it to something appropriate. *How about I call you Raida?*

After thinking about it, she felt the warmth again, and associated that sensation with it smiling. *"Raida. I like that. Thank you, Sira. I am Raida."*

She smiled, but then noticed Cardin staring at her, concern etching lines into his face. "I'm fine," she whispered, wondering how long he had been watching her. "Really. We can talk when we're home."

While he probably didn't fully accept her claim to being fine, she was glad that he knew enough to drop it for now.

Once the pyres had burned long enough, the villagers dispersed to assess the damage and decide how to rebuild. Sira walked west with Cardin, Dalin, Ulpex, Endri and Astaria, the western edge of the village their destination, and she realized then that the time to go home was upon them.

Her travel pack! She just remembered it, but then realized that it had been in one of the buildings surrounding the square. The only one of the three that had burned down.

When she pointed this out to Dalin, he grimaced. "So much for my only other possessions in the world," he sighed. Looking at his new staff, he nodded solemnly. "At least I have this. I may not be a Wizard by Guild anymore, but with this, I feel whole again."

"I am pleased that you found what you were looking for," Astaria said, her tone like that of one forcing joviality.

Sira glanced back at the village, most of the buildings having either been damaged or destroyed. "What will become of the village?"

Surveying the relatively deserted village, Astaria sighed and shook her head. "I shall remain here."

Endri looked down at her in shock. *"But we need you, Astaria. Your leadership, your wisdom."*

"I will not go back." Her voice had such finality in it that Sira knew there was no arguing, and apparently so did Endri, as he did not speak on it anymore. "My place is still here. These people came to Stella looking to find answers, to find their place in the Universe. The least I can do is continue to help them find their way." Setting her jaw, she added, "And defend them."

Thinking of Raida, Sira asked, "Will you try to have another child?"

Astaria's face slackened, but she simply stared in front of herself, watching her feet take one step after another. "I do not know."

Feeling an intense urge to comfort Astaria, Sira sought the right words, even as she wondered if the feelings in her were her own or Raida's. "I am so sorry for all that has happened," she spoke, sincere remorse in her voice. "I wish I could have protected the crystal better. I wish..."

Astaria's eyes flashed, her inner starlight coming to the surface for a brief moment. Was it in anger? Pain? Sorrow? Sira couldn't tell, but she was afraid for a brief moment. "You did the best that you could," Astaria stated plainly. "For now, I wish you to leave."

Sira hesitated, wanting to say more, wanting to find a way to reassure Astaria. When she realized that there was nothing she could say, she kept quiet, and merely nodded.

Astaria stared up into the sky for a moment, and seemed to draw some strength into herself. Enough to say to them, "Farewell to you all. May the stars guide you." She barely glanced at Sira, but she looked directly into the eyes of Dalin, Cardin, and finally Endri.

We could stay behind, she thought, thinking then that at least Astaria could communicate with Raida through her, but the twisting in her stomach told her immediately that she couldn't do so.

"I fear to do so would only bring her more pain," Raida said. *"For now, it is best that we continue upon your journey through life."*

Ulpex likewise gave a fond farewell, but when he came to Sira, and she saw the pained look in his yellow eyes from the losses he had suffered, she couldn't help it and she wrapped her arms around him. He seemed surprise by her act, but then relaxed and returned the hug. His fur tickled her neck, and she giggled warmly. "Thank you for being such a wonderful host," she told him, pulling back and looking him in the eyes. "Now it's time to take care of yourself, okay?"

"Thank you," he replied warmly, covering his wounded arm self-consciously. "However, if this village is to survive, what few of us remain must all do what we can for each other. I will help the others, and in turn, they shall help me."

"Good," she nodded, trying to broaden her smile but having a hard time mustering herself. "I'll hold you to that."

And then one last surprise came to them all. Swarms of kaetz suddenly floated down from the trees, and began to swirl all around them. Sira stared in wonder as she counted a dozen, two dozen, three, four, until she could no longer keep up. A smile blossomed across her face as she watched the spectacle, as if they knew that their newest curiosities were about to leave, probably forever.

She looked to Cardin, wishing to share the moment with him, but her joy faltered upon seeing the look of fear and pain on his face. His eyes bore into hers, and she suddenly worried for the future. What had he seen up in that copse? Why would the kaetz scare him?

"I have never seen such a thing," Ulpex broke her from her thoughts. "The kaetz are curious, yes, but never have they shown such attachment to newcomers!"

Sira's eyes fell upon Astaria, who stared at the ground mournfully. Even before Raida spoke, Sira knew why, *"They sensed the future. They could feel the flow of time. They knew that you and I would one day become linked."*

That only further fueled her suspicions of why Cardin was made anxious by the swarm. She looked at him again, but in that moment, the kaetz dispersed, their movements slow again as they lazily found tree branches to whirl around.

With their farewells given, Astaria and Ulpex headed back into the village, which left the original four to themselves. Dalin asked the obvious question, "What do we do now?"

Endri stared after Astaria for a long time, but he replied, *"I shall return to the Celestial Spires to tell the others what has happened and seek further guidance."*

Sira took Cardin's hand and interlaced her fingers with his, but the tension in him radiated. He stared up at Endri, and said, "I don't think we should tell them everything."

Endri looked down at Cardin in shock. *"But we must. They must know about the Shadow Quartz."*

Cardin had quietly told her and Dalin about it while they helped with the village. Endri had objected to his decision to tell them, but she was glad that Cardin was open with her about everything.

Cardin insisted, stating, "If even one Star Dragon who learns about it falls to darkness…"

Endri's head shot back like he found the idea of that happening offensive, but then the scales around his eyes seemed to slacken a moment, and he lowered his head. *"That is a fair point. But then what shall I tell them?"*

"I'm not sure," Cardin shook his head. "Definitely tell them about the attack that happened here, though. And…" He looked at Sira, silently asking her what should be said about her condition.

Smiling, she looked up at Endri. "Tell them about what happened to me. And tell them they need to stop hiding from the Universe. After all, the Universe would be a lesser place without Star Dragons."

Endri's lips curled back in an approximation of a smile. *"Very well. I shall do just that. Be safe, my friends. I will return to Halarite as soon as I can."*

With that, he lowered himself down, and then sprung up into the air, extending his jade wings to catch the wind. Moments later, as he pumped his wings to gain speed, he disappeared through a portal, leaving just the humans.

"Well then," Cardin looked to Dalin and Sira. "Where shall we go? Daruun? Archanon?"

Sira's heart stirred, and she longed to return home, to see her parents and assure them that she was alright. But then her stomach turned, an uneasiness filling her at that thought. How would she explain to them what had happened to her? For that matter, how would she explain it to anyone?

Would her work with the Warriors continue, or would she be considered compromised? *Oh gods,* she thought. *How is this going to affect my life?*

She felt a pang of guilt from Raida, but other than that, Raida didn't respond to Sira's thoughts, probably as uncertain as Sira was.

"We should return to the Wizards' Guild," Dalin suddenly said.

"The Guild," Cardin asked, startled. "I thought you turned your back on them."

"In a manner," Dalin nodded. "However…" He looked down at

his feet, his eyes betraying how worried he was. "We should…well, we should not tell them about the Shadow Quartz. Then perhaps we should go there to see who the new Grand Master is. Or…"

Cardin and Sira exchanged looks, and then together, they rested a hand each on his shoulders. "It's okay, my friend," Cardin said. "You want to check to make sure Nuuldan hasn't attacked them again."

Chuckling at himself, Dalin nodded. "Am I so transparent? But yes, that is my desire. I may have turned my back on the Guild, but that does not mean that I do not care about them."

Nodding, Cardin turned, and Sira felt him gather magic into him. Somehow, she was able to sense it easier than ever before, and she wondered if that was thanks to Raida. A moment later, however, he stopped and looked at Dalin. With a grin, he motioned to Dalin's staff. "Would you care to do the honors?"

A smile blossomed across Dalin's face, delight in his eyes, and he stepped forward and planted his new staff in the ground, almost instantly summoning a portal. Looking to them, the Wizard said, "After you, my friends."

Taking one another's hands, Sira and Cardin stepped up to the portal. It may not be Daruun, but it would still be Halarite. It would still be home.

They stepped through the wall of light together. Only to face a line of a dozen Wizards, their staves pointing at them.

"Um," was all Sira could get out.

"Hold on," Cardin raised his hands defensively. "We're not here to…cause…"

In that moment, they noticed their surroundings, and realized that something terrible had happened. Dalin came through and bumped into them, his portal closing a second later.

They had appeared in the square south of the Grand Hall, and all around them, anywhere there had been plant life, was scorched and burned earth. Massive divots and craters pockmarked the landscape, and there was obvious signs of damage to every building in sight. Behind them, Sira's gaze fell upon a field of bodies, torn asunder, battered, burned, or worse. Her stomach twisted at the horrible stench of death.

The dozen Wizards surrounding them relaxed once they realized who had come through, and they lowered their staves. One of them,

Cardin noticed, was Master Syrn, her robes singed and her face covered in ash.

"Keeper," she sighed, her chest heaving a sigh of relief. "Oh your timing could not have been better."

Sira looked at Cardin wide eyed. Never would she have expected a Master Wizard other than Valkere to be happy to see Cardin.

"What has happened here," Dalin asked, an edge in his voice that she had never heard before.

Syrn opened her mouth to speak, but then stopped short. "A great deal," she finally said. "This goes far beyond the Wizards. It is best if we gather the others to tell you, but we must be quick. I am afraid a new threat came to Halarite in your absence."

The Grand Master then dispatched the other Wizards to find 'the others' and bring them to the Council of Masters. 'The others,' it turned out, were Reis, Anila, Draegus, Kellis, Elaria, Baenil, and Gilrin. When Draegus saw Cardin and the others, he ran to his son and nearly crushed him in an embrace, but she also noticed that he had a distinct limp, and his armor was torn and bloodied. As was everyone else's, except for Baenil and Gilrin, who looked untouched.

And then the one person Sira hoped never to see again showed up – Kailar.

"What the hell is she doing here," Cardin recoiled, his hand grasping the Sword of Dragons. Kailar saw that and scowled.

Master Syrn raised a halting hand before Cardin or Sira could draw their weapons. "Please," the Master shook her head, stepping between the two of them. "There is no time for old grudges."

"What about new ones," Reis seethed.

Sira looked at Reis, her mind suddenly racing. What had Kailar done now?

"There is too much going on, and too much at stake for us to fight now," Syrn insisted, suddenly summoning a shield around her to separate Kailar and Cardin. "Halarite stands on the brink of disaster, so I am telling you to stand down!"

The tone of her voice and the fact that she commanded rather than asked stopped Cardin short, and it shocked Sira. The situation was dire indeed if the Master Wizard felt like she could command him, even if she had been elected Grand Master.

Cardin's hand clenched the black handle of the Sword of Dragons, but he did not draw, and after glaring through the shield at Kailar, he finally nodded and let go, his hand coming down. Sira took his hand, and he grasped hers firmly, trying to reassure him while at the same time trying to control her own emotions.

"Who is she?" Raida asked. *"Why do you revile her so much?"*

I'll explain it later, Sira thought shortly. She felt Raida recoil at her shortness, and felt guilty for treating the entity so, but she couldn't allow herself to be distracted right now. *I'm sorry. Just please let us handle this situation first.*

Syrn let her shield drop, but for the moment remained between Cardin and Kailar. "That is better."

"What's going on," Cardin demanded, looking around. Everyone looked disheveled and broken, and Sira felt a cold pit forming in her stomach. He waved his hand behind them, at the bloodied battlefield. "Who did this, Nuuldan?"

Sira knew it wasn't, recalling what had happened to Sharenth. Nuuldan wouldn't have left bodies behind.

It turned out it was far worse than even she imagined. Syrn turned to Draegus, who began with, "It was not Nuuldan, it was something else. But first, I must tell you…King Beredis is dead."

Sira's heart stopped for a moment, and she felt as if a great sledgehammer smashed into her chest. She wanted to collapse to her knees, the weight in her heart growing a thousand times stronger. The tears that she had barely held back earlier on Stella came back, stinging her eyes and turning everything blurry.

She wished that had been the worst of it, but after he let the King's death sink in, Draegus continued on. He told them about the entity claiming to be Zairel, who was really Degrin; how that entity inhabited first Pevrin, and now Prince Beredis; how Degrin sought the Cronal pieces, which were in fact enchanted objects rather than sacred texts.

Kellis then explained what they had found in the Dwarven city, and Anila added how the Cronal and the device in the Dwarven city were meant to work together. Gilrin then angrily conveyed how the elves of ancient times had used the Cronal to strip all dwarves of magic power.

And finally, Draegus told them how Degrin was able to enthrall the people of Archanon, and brought hundreds to fight the Wizards, to claim the final piece of the Cronal.

Sira grimaced, and felt a vice grip on her chest. No one said it, but she knew what that meant. Hundreds of dead people. Those were the bodies that now littered the fields around the Wizards' Guild.

"Degrin has the final piece," Kailar finally growled. "And if what you say is true," she looked at Gilrin and the others from the underground expedition, "I'm betting he's on his way to the dwarven city now."

"Which means we need to stop him," Cardin stated.

"Obviously," Kailar glowered.

"But he has a considerable lead on us," a red-haired man standing next to Kailar pointed out, cutting off Cardin's incensed reply.

Kailar smiled. "I can fix that easily."

Cardin and Sira looked at her curiously. "How so," Sira asked.

With a self-satisfying smile, she said, "I can create portals inside of Archanon."

Sira was shocked, but the look on Cardin's face told her he wasn't as surprised. "I knew I sensed something strange about you. You have power again, but it isn't star magic."

"Right," Kailar nodded. "And dark magic can circumvent the star magic barrier around Archanon."

Cardin shook his head slowly and looked around at the crowd. "We...we were gone less than a week."

"Indeed," Syrn nodded. "I would guess that Degrin waited specifically until you were no longer on Halarite, so that you would no longer pose a threat to him."

Cardin looked at her skeptically. "Why me? The combined might of the Wizards is far more powerful than I am."

It was Kailar who replied. "Because he's afraid of you. He's afraid of dark magic."

Sira raised her eyebrows, and looked at Cardin. "If that's true, and both you and Kailar have dark magic now..."

"Then we have a chance," Cardin agreed.

Chapter 44

BATTLE OF THE CRONAL

Kailar was sorely tempted to go alone, once Kellis, Reis, and Elaria described exactly where the dwarven cavern was. She wanted to go there and face Degrin alone, to once and for all wipe him from existence.

Unfortunately, she knew that he was too powerful for her, and she would need help from the others, if only to distract him.

There was little preparation to be made, everyone was already set for combat. The disgust and hatred she saw in most everyone's eyes didn't faze her one bit. The disappointment and disgust she saw in Letan's eyes, however, fueled her growing rage.

She needed to rend Degrin to pieces.

Once everyone was ready, Kailar opened a dark magic portal to the dwarven city, hopefully right inside the capitol, and waited for the others to go through. Cardin stepped up, ready to lead the charge in case Degrin was already there, but then he stopped and looked at Kailar suspiciously.

"How do I know you aren't sending us all into a pit of lava or something?"

Kailar scowled. "If I wanted to kill you, I'd do so with a blade or crush you with magic." With narrowed eyes, Cardin studied her carefully. Impatience fueled her already short temper, and she grit her teeth. Finally, she shook her head and started for the portal. "Fine, I'll kill him myself."

"Wait," Cardin demanded, stepping in front of her. She almost barreled right over him, but stopped, and looked at him impatiently. Cardin drew in a deep breath, drew the Sword of Dragons, and looked at the portal. Finally, after waiting far longer than she cared, he stepped through. Sira, Dalin, Kellis, Draegus, Letan and Reis quickly followed, and then Anila, Elaria and the dwarf, Gilrin. Finally, three Master Wizards, including Syrn, passed through, leaving just Kailar. The other Wizards stayed behind, reasoning that having too many powerful magic users in battle could risk bringing down the entire cavern. Other than that, the only one who stayed behind was the elf Baenil, who had no combat capability. The only reason they brought Gilrin with was because the dwarf insisted, and he had brandished his shortsword with the promise that he could hold his own.

Drawing in a deep breath, Kailar drew her weapon, and stepped through.

As it turned out, she had brought them right to the capitol square, and the columns surrounding the square were lit up, just like Reis and Kellis had described to her. Those who preceded her had spread out to ensure no one blocked the portal, but Kellis had run up the stairs towards the capitol building and was calling out the name of the marine sergeant who had been left behind.

To everyone's relief, Sergeant Tein emerged, her cutlass drawn and ready in case of battle, but relieved to see Kellis again.

Degrin hadn't made it down to the city yet. And that meant they had time to prepare. While Kellis brought Tein and the other surviving marines up to speed, Kailar, Cardin, Sira, Anila, and Dalin headed into the capitol and down the secret stairs to the hidden library, and the device in the center.

Cut off from star magic, Kailar couldn't feel any sort of enchantment or power coming from the device, but Cardin certainly did. Anila pointed to the exposed inner workings, and pointed specifically to four spots where pieces were missing. "Elaria called them gears," she stated. "And given the magical nature of this device, basically replacing all four of them will likely turn it on, and allow Degrin to do whatever he wants to do with it."

"Do we even know what he intends to do with it," Cardin asked, gingerly touching the housing of the device, no doubt exploring its enchantment.

"I'd guess he'll use it to completely return to this realm," Anila grimaced. "With the full extent of whatever power and knowledge he has gained in the Library. Or even just fully connect his two halves and try to control both realms. But as the journal indicated, he'll have the ability to effect changes across the entire Universe if he desires."

Sira let out a soft whistle of surprise. "That's...dangerous. Even Raida has never heard of such a powerful device."

Everyone stared at her blankly, and she blushed. "It's the name I've given the dragon connected to me."

Stunned, Kailar thought, *they neglected to mention anything about that before now.* "Can it help us win this battle," she asked.

Sira looked at her curious, but shook her head. "I...don't know. I mean, I'm still figuring all this out. I don't know if Raida can actively fight, or enhance my powers, or what."

"What matters most is Degrin's fear of dark magic," Cardin interjected. "That's what we have to focus on." Suddenly his head jerked upwards, and his expression grew hardened. "He's here. Let's go."

Kailar's pulse quickened, and she was the first to run up the stairwell, drawing her sword the moment she was in the antechamber, and then she was out the door. Everyone else had sensed the coming enemy, and at Elaria's insistence, the dwarf ran in the opposite direction, seeking refuge within the capitol building.

All weapons were drawn, and everyone gathered on top of the steps to the capitol, looking towards where Kailar guessed the secondary entrance from Archanon was. The furthest column of light was already turned on, barely visible from their vantage, and just as she looked out over the wall surrounding the inner city, she saw a second one come on, much closer.

Kailar raced down to the bottom of the steps, intending to lead the assault, but then Cardin was next to her, and then Letan. She wanted Letan to stay back, but one look in his eyes told her he wouldn't leave her side. She reasoned that it wasn't because he cared for her, not anymore. It was because he wanted to try to keep her from doing anything worse than she already had.

Another column, just outside of the wall, lit up.

It felt as though their enemy was covering ground quickly. And suddenly Degrin appeared through one of the archways, standing inside as if he had always been there, his glowing orange eyes surveying them menacingly. His face was a cacophony of cracks, with light spilling out through them. The wound that Kailar had inflicted in his chest was lit up like a beacon, and his face was incredibly pale.

He was weakened, she realized, and they had a chance.

With an inhuman voice, Degrin demanded, "Let me pass."

Brandishing her sword, she shook her head. "I don't think so. Your journey ends now."

Cardin added an ultimatum, "Leave that body, return to the plane from which you come immediately, or we'll destroy you."

Degrin's eyes darted back and forth between Kailar and Cardin, and then he let out a bellow of a laugh, raising the hairs on the back of Kailar's neck with how otherworldly and menacing it sounded. Looking around at the dwarven city, he shook his head. "You have no idea, do you?" His eyes flashed again, and he smiled. "You will not deny me my prize."

Suddenly, in a great wave starting where Degrin stood, every single kiklar web ignited. Kailar's stomach sank when she realized what that meant, and she knew they had only moments. She leveled her sword at Degrin, and unleashed a blast of dark magic upon him, as powerful as she dared in the ancient city, but his shield managed to absorb it.

That was the last chance she had to attack him, as the flames all around and above them coalesced into humanoid fire elementals that dropped down upon them.

Kailar rolled to the side to prevent one from landing on her, and then she stood and swung her sword at the nearest. This time, they were summoned with ethereal swords, blood red like the Sword of Dragons, and the closest opponent blocked and parried her attack. She raised her shield, but knew that she couldn't attack as effectively if she kept it up, and as she shuffled around her first enemy, she strategically lowered it to strike, successfully getting past its sword and decapitating it.

She raised her shield again just in time to block a sword attack from behind, and she spun around, slicing through the elemental's torso in between shields.

An overwhelming number of elementals fell upon them, all while she could hear Degrin somewhere in the background cackling. Magic burst and crackled everywhere as their forces defended with all of the power that they dared use, destroying one flame elemental after another.

But then something new happened. For every three elementals they slew, their remaining fire coalesced together, and formed blue-white fire elementals, their swords now white-hot and as big as a claymore, and their attacks were stronger.

Her shield almost failed when one struck from behind, her mind and body growing fatigued. Growling but not turning around, she pointed her sword behind her and unleashed a blast of dark lightning, which sizzled across the creature's frame, and a moment later it was gone. With a grimace, she wondered if the defeated blue ones would reform into even deadlier forms.

The only saving grace was that the elementals seemed particularly susceptible to dark magic, and she capitalized upon that weakness. As she cut through two more and shredded a third with magic, she heard Degrin's cackle again, but it had moved. Through the sea of blue and orange fire, she saw him ascending the stairs towards the capitol building, and he reached one of the Wizards.

The Wizard unleashed a flurry of elemental attacks upon Degrin; fire, water, ice, lightning, everything he could, but Degrin's shield took it all. And then with the flick of a finger, he sent the Wizard careening to the side, as if he had been nothing more than a fly to be swatted.

Another elemental attacked Kailar, and she had to dodge and retaliate, first taking one of its hands off, and then stabbing it directly in the chest. Degrin's cackle taunted her further, so she hurried in that direction, reaching the foot of the stairs instantly, but halted again by two more blue elementals.

The first one she cut through quickly, but the second one sliced through her shield, and its sword clashed against hers, exploding in sparks. It didn't pull back or attempt to parry in any way, it kept its sword on hers, and pushed her down. Her sword glowed red where the contact was made, and its sword began to cut into hers, despite her efforts to reinforce it with dark magic.

She tried to step to the side, but missed the step and stumbled, breaking the connection, but leaving her vulnerable.

It never had a chance to act on her vulnerability. Cardin suddenly leapt over her and cut through the elemental's sword and body in one swipe, destroying it.

Kailar caught her balance at the bottom of the steps, and then she rushed up the stairs. She barely caught a glimpse of Degrin facing off against the marines, before another elemental was in her way. As she cut through it, she heard multiple screams, and once she could see again, there were four smoldering bodies on the steps, and Degrin was at the top.

Gritting her teeth, she knew she couldn't let him get away, and there was only one method to get ahead of him. Spinning around, Kailar cut through another elemental behind her, and then summoning what little concentration and strength she had left, she made another portal and leapt through, placing her inside of the doorframe, and in Degrin's way.

"Nice try," she spat, and then hurtled at him.

He waved his hand, and her shield failed, his invisible attack sending her sprawling back through the door and sliding across the smooth marble floor into the antechamber.

As Degrin followed, he cackled again. There were a handful of cobwebs up near the ceiling, and he torched them and brought down three more elementals.

Pushing herself up with a grunt, she felt a wave of nausea, and her head hurt, but she still summoned a shield around herself, just in time to stop Degrin's invisible assault.

Her focus wavered, and the elementals came at her. She couldn't stand up to Degrin and the elementals by herself.

Thankfully she didn't have to. Degrin suddenly scowled and leapt to the side, a blast of arcane magic flying past him and passing over Kailar's head to explode against the wall behind her. Draegus, Sira, and Dalin rushed in through the door, and the elementals turned their attention on them, as did Degrin.

Kailar stumbled then, and thought of summoning another portal behind her enemy, but knew that she didn't have the strength. Yet his attention was completely off of her, and that left him vulnerable.

He could sense the others, she realized. He couldn't sense dark magic, or her presence. Willing strength into her muscles, she circled around him as quickly as she could, her feet feeling like lead weights.

A ball of cascading blue and orange light sparked between Degrin's hands, growing larger by the second. Recalling what she had seen in the library, she surmised he was using both his own innate powers and the four Cronal pieces to create a devastating attack. The others could not possibly survive it, even the Wizard.

She had to act, now.

Pushing every bit of magic she had left into her legs, she leapt up through the air at him, raising her sword. Just when the ball of magic looked ready to release, she sliced down from his left shoulder, through his torso and all the way down to his right hip.

All of the magic from his attack and within his body released at once. The blast flung her backwards and knocked the air from her lungs. Her sword snapped where the elemental had cut into it earlier, and she skittered and slid across the floor, slamming into the back wall. Something broke in her right arm, raking pain across her entire being, and setting her head spinning, her vision blacking out for just a moment.

When it returned to her, Degrin was gone, his body destroyed, and his royal robes a pile of smoking ashes.

It was over.

Except, Cardin, who had rushed into the door just in time to see her cut him down, didn't look convinced of that, and his face twisted in pain.

Chapter 45

THE GREAT LIBRARY

When Cardin rushed into the antechamber, he expected the worst, having watched Sira and his friends follow Degrin in less than a minute before. What he found was his friends holding their own, but with Degrin preparing to unleash a destructive blast upon them.

At the same time that Cardin summoned a shield to surround all of them, even the elementals that his friends battled, he saw Kailar leap through the shadows and cut down Degrin. All of the magic pent up inside of their enemy unleashed, but it splashed harmlessly against Cardin's shield. Harmless, except that it was strong enough to fatigue him and shake the entire capitol, stirring up dust and dropping chunks of debris from the ceiling.

But their enemy was defeated, and the elementals winked out, like a flame doused by a candle snuffer.

Degrin was beaten. And Cardin let out a great big sigh. Kailar had done it!

Walking towards his friends and his father, all of whom looked around for any other sign of an attack, Cardin spotted Kailar then, having been flung to the other side of the room. He wondered if she had survived the blast, but then she stirred and locked eyes with him.

But it wasn't over. From Degrin's ashes, a wisp of light appeared and raced at Cardin. He didn't have a chance to raise a shield before it engulfed him, and racked his body with pain. There was a presence, powerful and menacing, and it tugged and pulled at his soul, dragging it towards oblivion.

It was Degrin! And he had chosen Cardin as his next vessel.

His eyes shot open, and everything had an orange haze to it, while his chest felt like it was on fire. He fell to his knees, but he held onto the Sword of Dragons tightly, not willing to let it go, not willing to fail his mission.

He tried to push the entity out, tried to protect himself. Somewhere in the back of his mind, he heard a voice calling out to him, Sira's voice. But he was lost to her, the dark, oily black crawling over and into his soul, infesting it inch by inch, sapping all of the warmth and strength within him.

Then, when he thought he had lost the battle, the entity touched the dark core in his soul. It recoiled from the dark magic, and practically exploded out of him. He gulped in air, not having realized that he'd stopped breathing, and he tumbled backwards from the force of expelling Degrin from his body.

The Sword had protected him. No, not the Sword itself, but dark magic. He realized it instantly, his mind going back to the copse and the earth elemental. Star magic and dark magic were never meant to coexist with one another, and Degrin's spirit couldn't handle it.

Which meant Degrin was weakened, but not yet dead.

He opened his eyes, and Sira was at his side, her face pale, and the worry on her face sent a pang through his heart.

Degrin was still in the room, he could feel it now, more than ever. There was even a hint of Degrin's thoughts just at the edge of his peripheral, and Cardin felt the other's annoyance at having failed to take the Keeper of the Sword. Then there was a delighted sensation, as a new target was chosen.

Draegus cried out and fell to his knees.

"Father!"

Cardin strained to stand, but his legs felt numb. His father howled again, grasping at his head. Cardin's chest compressed in fear, his heart raced, and he crawled over to his dad, aided by Sira.

From behind him, Cardin heard all of the surviving combatants rushing in to see what was going on, and as Cardin reached his father, they all gathered around.

"Fight it, Dad," he said, wrapping his arm around his father's torso. "Fight him off, you can do it!"

Draegus writhed and jerked in pain, his body trembling. Cardin closed his eyes, using his powers to see into his father's soul, to see Degrin's surrounding his entire being, and pressing in, consuming. "No!"

He tried to intercede, tried to figure out how he could send his darkness into his father, knowing that doing so might kill Draegus or drive him insane, but he had to try. Cardin looked at the Sword of Dragons, still clenched in his right hand, and willed it to give him the knowledge he needed, the power he required.

Another cry of pain, and Draegus collapsed onto to his side. Cardin looked within his father again and saw that Degrin had almost won.

"Somebody help him, please," he cried out, his eyes stinging. "No, Dad, don't go! Don't go, please." Desperation rushed through him, but he was helpless!

His father's eyes opened, not by Degrin's will, but by his father's, opening against pain and anguish, through blurring tears. He looked at Cardin, as the orange glow surrounded his irises. He looked into his son's eyes.

"No," Cardin whispered. "No…"

The glow flowed into the irises, and he felt the last bit of Draegus fade away.

Degrin was all that was left. And he laughed.

Pressure boiled up inside of Cardin. He pulled his hand off of the shell of his father, clenching it into a fist. He felt his powers flex and contract, pulsing like never before, control starting to slip away. The star magic and dark magic within roiled around each other dangerously.

He backed away, with Sira and Reis helping him stand up. Degrin laughed again, an inhuman sound with only a bit of his father's tone in it. Degrin stood up and brushed himself off, and looked at himself before he smiled at Cardin.

"I think I'm going to like this new body," he spoke, the orange in his eyes pulsing.

Cardin leveled the Sword at him, but Degrin raised up a cautioning hand. "Ah, ah! Now now, all you'll do is kill your father. And then I'll have to find yet another body to take." He looked around at everyone present, but then settled his gaze upon Sira and smiled. "Perhaps hers, next. And then his," he pointed to Reis.

"No," Cardin growled. "You will not harm another."

The smile on Degrin's face darkened, and he shook his head. "I will destroy every life here. There is nothing that you can do to stop me."

He almost did it. For a brief moment, Cardin saw past his father's shell and almost obliterated Degrin. It would have been easy, and the fury he felt inside compelled him to do so.

But then the image from the copse flashed through his memory again. Sira's body, the field of blood, and his rage unleashed upon Reis.

He could change the future. Astaria said he could. His path was his to choose.

The balance within him returned, the two powers no longer combating one another. His temper cooled, easing off just enough so that he asserted control over all of his powers. The dual powers he had funneled into the Sword dissipated back into the ether.

Dark magic. It was the key.

He knew what he had to do, then.

As his strength returned, he shrugged Reis and Sira's hands off and stepped closer to Degrin. "What do you want?"

Degrin's eyes pierced into him, his mood decidedly sour. "Let me complete my task," he spoke quietly. "I will leave your father, then. You may have him back once I finish."

It wasn't true, Cardin knew that. Degrin would never let his father go, if his father was even still alive in there somewhere. However, he had already decided to let Degrin do what he wanted.

Motioning towards the ashen remains of the Prince's body, Cardin nodded. "Fine."

"Cardin, no," Dalin cautioned.

"That is most unwise," Syrn added. "He will destroy everything if we let him."

Cardin glanced at the others and tried to convey what he knew he had to do through his eyes. "Trust me," he said slowly. "We have to let this happen. There's no other choice."

Degrin smiled. "I am that glad you see it my way, son."

That almost sent Cardin over the edge into rage, but he forced himself to resist the urge. He had to, if anyone was to survive. "Do it," he demanded.

Degrin sauntered over to the ashes, Cardin watching the strange spectacle of his father moving in a manner that was completely unlike him. With deliberate slowness, Degrin brushed the remains aside and picked up the four pieces. Suddenly his entire body flared orange, just as the Cronal flared blue, and the magics swirled around one another.

Looking back to Cardin and the group, he smiled. "A wise choice, indeed."

Degrin walked past the defeated, armored statue from Reis's earlier adventure, and dropped down to the stairs confidently, smugly. As his head dropped beneath sight, Cardin looked to his friends, and then to Sira. "Trust me. And stay here."

"Cardin," she shook her head. "I think I know what you're going to do, but...what if you don't survive?"

Looking back at the stairs, he drew in a deep breath, and then let it out slowly. "I have to. It's the only chance we have."

He wanted to embrace her, to kiss her one last time, but the timing of his plan had to be just right. Cardin reached out and squeezed her hand, and then he walked away from her, passing through the solemn group. They parted for him, and some reached out hands to pat his shoulders encouragingly. Reis was the last one he passed, and he and his friend exchanged knowing looks.

Much to Cardin's pleasant surprise, Reis gave him one last, characteristic grin, and a mock salute.

When Cardin reached the stairs, he bent down and used his hands to lower himself as quietly as possible, and then he descended the steps on tip-toes. The Sword felt heavy in his hand for the first time ever, so he reached back and placed it in its sheath. He wouldn't need it for this.

Passing through the doorway, he saw Gilrin down in the library, his back against the bookshelves as he watched Degrin with terror. Their enemy had taken up position at the device, but as Cardin quietly descended, Degrin appeared not to notice, his focus entirely on his task. First he looked at one cronal piece, and carefully placed it in its spot. Then another, and another.

All that was left was one final piece, and then it would be complete.

It had to happen. As long as Degrin's spirit lived in the Great

Library, he would remain a threat.

As Cardin passed Gilrin at the bottom of the stairs, Degrin placed the last piece, and a bright blue light flashed. A grinding, clicking noise started, and the gears inside of the device all turned at once. Cardin felt a pulse of magic shoot downwards, deep into the world. He closed his eyes to try to watch it, but couldn't believe it when he realized that the entire area beneath him lit up with magic. Through his mind's eye, he saw it extend outward, probably as far as the city's border, and downward, far below, farther than he could comprehend.

Cardin opened his eyes, and watched as Degrin placed his hands on either side of the apparatus. His orange glow grew outward and touched the apparatus, and then something beyond the physical realm happened, something that Cardin barely felt.

Until he stepped up to the podium as well. Degrin's eyes shot open, and he glared at Cardin. Staring back at Degrin, he touched the other side of the dais.

Searing pain.

Blinding light.

His fingers felt like they burned and were frozen all at once, and that sensation raced up his hands and arms, right into his core, until he felt everything inside of him twist and warp.

Dark magic. He called upon that shadowy force, a void between matter, willing it into the realm around him, through his body, through his hands. Like he did when he pushed dark magic into the Sword, he pushed it into the apparatus. Where it intermingled with Degrin's spirit.

The magic went beyond that, beyond everything. Degrin recoiled, but he was committed, because now he was fully linked to his other half.

An earth-shattering, ear-splitting scream reverberated through magic, from the realm beyond realms. Darkness engulfed that soul, and Cardin coerced it further, surrounding Degrin with it just like the malevolent entity had done to Cardin's father.

It ate away at Degrin, bit by bit, piece by piece, dismantling his power, his soul. Like the ashes of a log, he blew apart then, scattered into the nether of the beyond. Nothing was left behind.

Cardin ceased to call forth the dark power, but he didn't know what else he could do. He wasn't anywhere familiar, in fact he didn't seem to be anywhere. There was no physical sensation anymore. No pain, no heat, not cold. No pleasure, no happiness.

Just nothingness.

This is the end, he thought.

"No it isn't."

The voice surprised him. It was the first physical sensation he noticed. And then he felt pressure on his feet and legs, as if he stood atop something. His eyesight returned, but the light was blinding. No, it was more than just light. It was energy, all around him, flowing and coursing like great currents, some of it passing right through him.

The floor he stood upon was made of pure light, as was the sky above him. But everywhere else, all around him, there were books. Stacks and stacks of books in never-ending shelves, reaching miles high and extending miles below.

The Great Library!

The stacks towered higher and higher, disappearing into the light, but he knew that if he climbed up, he could climb forever and never reach the top. He could walk forever in any direction, and never reach the end.

Then he remembered the voice, and he turned to discover that he was not alone. A man stood behind him, with dark skin, hardened from countless years walking in the sun, along with short, messy hair, and a face that hadn't been shaved in at least a week. His clothes were simple tans and light browns, very modest.

But his eyes were a blazing, glowing blue-white, and the power that he possessed was overwhelming and calming all at once.

"Who are you?"

The man smiled. "Who do you believe I am?"

Cardin looked around the library, feeling dizzy for a moment from the scope of it all. "I don't know. But if you're here, you're not mortal." His eyes grew wide, and he gawked. "You're an ascended being."

Nodding, the man clasped his hands behind his back and drew in a breath. Except, what was he breathing? For that matter, what was Cardin breathing? Were they physically here, or was it some sort of illusion?

"You know me as one of the Six," the man announced. "Though despite what the Covenant has told you, we were not the first to ascend. However, I am afraid that is a story you must find on your own."

Cardin blinked a few times, trying to process what he had just been told. He looked around at the library, and asked, "You mean, find it here?"

The man raised an eyebrow and glanced around. "You could, I suppose. But that is not what I meant."

Cardin nodded, trying to grasp his meaning. "What you're saying is that I should experience it for myself. Learn the answers...wait, you said 'no it isn't' before. I'm not dead. I'm here because of the Cronal." He drew in a deep breath as he took in the man's visage again, the desert robes, the hair, the sun-worn face. "You're Zairel! The real Zairel."

He nodded. "Yes."

"Then that really was Degrin?"

Zairel's face darkened. "Yes."

Rubbing at his face, and marveling at the fact that he *could* rub his face here, Cardin shook his head. "Then the Covenant was right. People can ascend, and you are our gods."

Zairel placed a hand firmly on Cardin's shoulder, forcing him to look into glowing eyes. "No, Cardin Kataar. We are not gods. We do not wish to be worshipped. Yes, the Covenant and the Order of the Ages was right about a lot of things, but not that. We have never wanted the people to worship us."

Cardin felt light-headed at the monumental occasion, and his mind swirled with the words that were spoken to him. He felt a great well grow inside of him, but it was not a happy one. Grimacing, he inquired, "Why are we speaking? Why am I here? If I'm not dead, does that mean I will return to Halarite?"

"Of course you will," Zairel nodded once. "Your journey through life has just begun, and there is much that you must teach your people."

Cardin looked at him skeptically. "Did you bring me here to...what, make me your emissary? To bring your will to the people?"

Zairel's serious face suddenly cracked into a smile, and he bellowed out a great laugh. "Oh, goodness, no! No, no, no, that is not up to you." He patted Cardin's shoulder a few times heartily. "No, the search for knowledge is a personal endeavor. Believe me on that, I have had more than enough time to discover that truth."

Cardin smiled awkwardly, but then looked at Zairel curiously. "What's wrong," he asked Cardin.

With a chuckle, Cardin replied, "Nothing, nothing, it's just...I never really imagined something like this happening, but still, I expected you to speak and act...differently."

"What, you mean all high and mighty like some Wizard?" Zairel scoffed and waved a dismissive hand. "No, never. I'm as human as you. Or at least, I was."

Cardin laughed, and folded his arms. "No one's going to believe me when I tell them about this." He raised an eyebrow and asked, "Can I tell others?"

"Certainly," Zairel nodded. "In fact, unless you want to stay here for a while longer, you can go tell them right now."

With eyes growing wide, Cardin glanced around at some of the nearby book titles. The Staff of Aliz. The Pyramid of Trinil. Volumes and volumes of Halarite history, much of it dated far beyond the present.

It was all here for him. He could learn the future, he realized. And by extension, he could change it. Prevent whatever war was to come. Save Sira's life. Stop Reis from ever becoming his enemy. It would be a simple matter.

Even better, there was knowledge here that would allow him to change the future right here, right now, without ever leaving the Library. He could give Reis powers, or keep him from ever getting them. He could restore magic to the dwarves, all he had to do was find the correct book.

All I have to do, he laughed at himself, staring down the endless stacks of shelves. He could spend lifetimes searching and never find the answer. And what would it truly get him?

His existence on Halarite would end. Sira would be left to deal with her new reality alone. All of his friends would go on without him.

He looked at Zairel cautiously, who regarded him patiently. "That would be a bad idea, wouldn't it?"

Zairel grinned. "Yes. That's how all of this started, you know. One of the Covenant, Pevrin, went looking in parts he shouldn't have. Went back to the past to find out the truth about the history of the Order. He found Degrin at the moment of his ascension, and then brought a little bit of Degrin back with him."

Cardin shuddered. "So it isn't actually just knowledge within these books. It's more than just reading, much more. And there's no telling what I could take back with me if I stayed here."

"The Cronal is dangerous in the wrong hands," Zairel nodded. "Or even in the well-meaning hands. So you and your friends must decide what to do with it. It is not my place to tell you what to do."

Laughing a little at that, Cardin shook his head. "Is it really *my* place to decide what to do with it?"

Zairel shrugged casually. "I'm not your master or keeper, Cardin Kataar. Your fate is in your hands."

Before Cardin could ask him anything else, Zairel reached out and pushed Cardin's shoulder. Cardin lost his balance, fell backwards, through the floor of light, through the planes of reality. Right back to Halarite.

Back home.

Chapter 46

AWAKENING

Was it a dream? That was the first thought Cardin had, but as soon as the cool air of the dwarven city whispered across his face, he knew that it was real.

Cardin opened his eyes and expected to find Sira standing over him, just like in Daruun after the meteor showers. Instead, he saw Gilrin's quizzical face peering at him, his nose taking up a large portion of the view.

Cardin's body suddenly spasmed in coughs, his body's way of reminding him to breathe. He jerked upright, almost smacking his head into Gilrin's, trying desperately to suck in air and revitalize his body. His arms and legs tingled, as if waking up from a forever sleep.

Something told him that he *had* died in his efforts to destroy Degrin, but somehow, he lived again. Was it through some secret power of the Sword? Or had Zairel brought him back?

"Easy, there, lad," Gilrin placed a comforting hand on him. "I thought we'd lost you, until you started breathing again."

The sound of rushing feet on stone steps echoed, and his companions rushed down into the chamber, with Sira in the lead. "Cardin!"

Relief and joy washed over him, but when Cardin tried to stand, his legs gave out and sent waves of tingles all throughout his body. She leapt down from the stairs and caught him, and nearly crushed him in an embrace. "You're okay! I thought...I swear I'd felt your spirit vanish."

Trying to gasp in air again, he shook his head as much as he could. "No, not yet," he breathed. She loosened her grasp then, and pulled back, holding him up under his armpits as his legs found their strength again. "Not exactly, anyway," he shook his head, looking towards the Cronal.

Then he saw the legs of his father sticking out from behind the device. "Dad!"

Ignoring the prickling muscle fatigue, he extracted himself from Sira and rushed around the apparatus to his father's side, kneeling down and placing a hand on his father's chest. Draegus's face was pale and clammy, but his chest still rose, even if very, very slowly. There was a heartbeat, and then nothing. Cardin's stomach dropped, and he thought he'd felt his father pass on, but then there was another heartbeat.

Confused, Cardin looked over his shoulder at Sira and the others as they all gathered around. "I don't understand." Another heartbeat. "His breathing and heartbeats are so slow."

Syrn and Elaria both knelt down by Draegus's head and placed their hands on either side of his temples. They looked at each other, shocked by their mirrored actions, but then focused on Draegus. Cardin felt their magic flux and extend into Draegus, but all they managed to do was warm his skin a little.

"He is alive," Elaria nodded. "But...I don't feel him in there. There's no magic within him, no sense of him."

Cardin grasped his father's tunic, the panic in him rising again. "Father..."

"There is nothing we can do for him now," Syrn stated. She stood up and looked at the others present. "We must get him under a healing blanket as soon as possible, and have our best healers look after him."

"Has anyone seen Kailar," Anila asked. "She could teleport him to the Wizards' Guild right away."

Cardin remembered seeing her battered body earlier. "She's in the antechamber," he replied. "She was hit pretty hard. Someone see if she's alive."

Sergeant Tein was at the highest point of the stairs and nodded, rushing up to carry out his request.

Looking to his father again, Cardin felt his eyes sting, but he tried as hard as he could to hold back the tears. "Come on, Dad, stay with us," he choked out. "I already lost Mom, I can't lose you too."

Sira knelt down next to Cardin and wrapped her arms around him, rocking back and forth and rubbing his back. He allowed himself to fall into her embrace, to try to find comfort in it. He extended his senses out to her, to feel something familiar, but when he did, he felt more. She wasn't alone anymore, and it had changed her.

He sighed in frustration, clutching his father's armor and bowing his head against the slowly-rising chest. Nothing was the same anymore, and he longed for something familiar, something reassuring. Even he felt different inside now. Better, yes, more in control of both the star and dark magic, and he should have felt comfort in that, but all he felt now was a terrible emptiness.

"What are you doing," someone asked. He looked up, and saw Syrn reaching for the pedestal. His conversation with Zairel came to mind, and he shot up and snatched her hands before they touched the pedestal.

"Don't," he warned.

Yanking her hand out of his, she glared at him. "How dare you!"

"Do not touch this device," he insisted. Cardin placed himself between her and the Cronal. "No one touch it. You don't know how dangerous this really is."

"I think we do," the other surviving Master Wizard intoned. "We all fought against Degrin, and we know he came from it."

"It goes deeper than that," he insisted. "Degrin was dangerous, but I'm worried there are worse things that can come from the Great Library."

When he looked at Syrn again, her eyes were wide. "You were there."

With a nod, Cardin folded his arms resolutely. "I was, and I met someone there. It's a lot to explain, and I will, but just know that it's more dangerous than we realized."

Elaria stood up, breaking contact with Cardin's father, and she nodded. "He's right in that regard. We heard Baenil read from the journal," she looked at Gilrin and then at Reis.

"Aye," Gilrin nodded. "We did. And that's precisely why we

need to use it. To give my people their power back."

"No," Cardin shook his head, holding up a halting hand. Gilrin looked ready to tear him apart, so he quickly added, "Not yet. If someone goes in there without knowing what they're doing, they could make things worse instead of better. They might accidentally destroy every dwarf in the Universe, or accidentally take away all other civilizations' powers while giving you yours back."

Gilrin's eyes grew wide in excitement. "Really, now? That doesn't sound so bad."

"No!" Cardin tried to leave no room for debate in his voice. "And if anyone tries to use this thing without consideration for how dangerous it is, I'll destroy it." He reached back and touched the Sword, but didn't draw it. "I cannot overstate how dangerous this could be."

Everyone considered his statement for a long while, but then it was Syrn who made the inevitable suggestion. "Maybe it should be destroyed anyway."

"Absolutely not!" Gilrin shouted, his voice echoing. The dwarf rushed towards the apparatus to protect it, his short sword drawn and clenched in his fist. "This is my people's only chance for freedom! Anyone tries to destroy it, and they'll have me to answer to."

Someone somewhere snorted a laugh, but Cardin glowered and looked around. "This isn't a joke," he stated to everyone in general. "And Gilrin is well within his right to defend it. But," he looked at the dwarf resolutely, "I stand by my statement. We need time to understand it, to understand the implications of using it. For now, we must protect it from misuse, and see if we can figure out how to use it safely."

"If that's even possible," Kailar called down from the stairs. She descended from the antechamber, with Letan and Indira holding her up and helping her. "I have my doubts about that."

"As do I," Syrn agreed.

"I don't give a rat's backside," Gilrin growled. "I'll be caught dead before I let anyone destroy it!"

Sira came to the fore front as the voice of reason. "Can we even destroy it? Is it possible to destroy something of this magnitude? I mean, I don't know about anyone else, but I felt how encompassing it was, how big the device actually is beneath the surface. I'm sure every Mage up topside felt it, too."

Cardin agreed with her, but he held back one key thought – they might not be able to easily destroy the entire device, but if they destroyed the apparatus, it would be next to impossible to use it again.

He also held back another thought that terrified him – something that big, and that powerful, if they managed to make the magic inside release all at once, it could end up destroying everything above it – the dwarven city *and* Archanon.

"For now," he took his hand off of the Sword cautiously, "we will guard it. Protect it from anyone using it for ill or good, and then we can discuss it further." He looked at Syrn, and then back at Gilrin. "Agreed?"

Raising an eyebrow, Syrn nodded. "Agreed."

"Aye," Gilrin nodded. "You seem like a good lad. I'll hold you to that agreement."

Cardin looked then to Kailar as she stopped near the bottom of the stairs. Could she use it with dark magic? A second later, he knew it would be impossible. The Cronal's power was based entirely on star magic.

"So," Sira started hesitantly, grasping and squeezing Cardin's hand. "Is Degrin…"

"He's gone," he nodded reassuringly. "From both realms." She smiled, and there was a collective sigh of relief from everyone.

Looking again to Kailar, he noticed that she cradled her right arm, and appeared exhausted. "Kailar, I know that I have no right to ask you, but…if you have the strength…"

She glanced at his feet and saw Draegus lying unconscious. She seemed to consider it for a moment, a war going on behind her eyes that worried him. Finally, she sighed and nodded.

"Very well. But one trip only." She glanced at Letan uncomfortably, and made a show to stand on her own. "And then we need to go home."

Squeezing Sira's hand, Cardin knelt down and gathered his father's motionless form into his arms and stood up, grateful that his full strength had finally returned.

He would need it in the coming days.

Chapter 47

THE GREATER GOOD

After Kailar had taken Cardin and his father's lifeless body back to the Wizards' Guild, she and Letan immediately returned to Tieran. Whatever reason Letan had for his eagerness to return, for Kailar it was out of prudence – there was no telling how long it would be before the others turned on her for what she had done.

She brought them directly to the Tieran Warriors' Guild's courtyard, if you could call a grassy yard without even a fence a courtyard. Once they arrived, she avoided Letan's gaze and tried to head in. It was barely noon in Tieran, and behind her, she heard the usual bustle of the city. One of the other Warriors stepped out of the double wooden doors in front of her and was startled by her appearance.

Without looking to see if Letan followed, she headed straight for her room. She was in no mood for another argument or discussion.

Once there, she locked her door and stood leaning against it, listening for his footsteps. She never heard them.

After a while of anxiously waiting for him, she decided it was time to strip out of her armor and tattered cloak, discarding all of them in an untidy pile at the foot of the bed. Once she was clothed in black trousers and a grey shirt, she sat on the edge of her bed and stared at her hands.

It seemed as if she had a big decision before her – leave the Devor Guild, go back into hiding again, and try to figure out how to make the world better from the shadows, or remain and endure the unbearable bureaucracy and procedure, the self-limiting 'honor' that was only observed when convenient, and the ever-annoying restrictions on her freedom.

Neither choice is all that appealing, she grimaced.

Of course, there was another aspect that she realized she was avoiding in her own thoughts. Letan. If he couldn't look past what he had learned from Ardelle, she doubted he could get past her actions against the enthralled.

Whatever they were only a day ago, it was lost now.

Which came back to her original question of what to do with herself.

Aggravated with her indecision, she pulled on her boots and headed back out to find something to eat, realizing that it had been too long since her last meal.

Her heart thumped in fear as she made her way out of the Guild, wondering if she would run into Letan or not, but thankfully that didn't happen. Once outside, she made a beeline for the Inn at the Water's Edge.

She hoped for a quiet afternoon lunch and idle chatter with Alric, and was ever so grateful when she stepped into a largely empty tavern. The crowd from before she had left were all gone, and other than a single old man sitting at an empty table in the back, everything was empty.

"Kailar, love," Alric beamed when he saw her walk in. "You're back! That's a relief."

Trying to fake a smile despite the emptiness she felt inside, she nodded. "Alric. I could use a hearty meal, if you don't mind."

"I've got just the thing," he said with a great big grin before he disappeared into the back.

Kailar took her usual seat in the far corner, and stared off into nothingness while she waited for Alric to bring back her food.

When he came back, he had a steaming mug of broth to warm her soul, and a while later, he brought out a juicy steak, salted to perfection and cooked the way he knew she liked it. It was a welcome change, and she savored every bite.

After a while, he sauntered over again and set to cleaning some mugs. His usual antics when he wanted to talk.

"So how'd your adventure with that assassin lady go," he asked, failing to cover the curiosity and worry in his voice. "Sounded like Edilas was in a bit of trouble."

She stared down at her plate, her stomach suddenly souring. "I...don't really want to talk about it," was all she managed to say.

Alric stopped mid-wipe on a mug and stared at her, his face growing long. "That bad."

Without moving her head, she looked at him with glowering eyes. He didn't take the hint. "I hope whatever happened doesn't bring trouble to Devor. The last thing we need is another apocalypse."

Ignoring his attempted fishing for information, she finished the last bite of her steak and set her utensils down, clearing her throat and taking a sip of the broth. *Maybe I should have asked for ale,* she thought. *Or something stronger.*

"Still, if you came back," Alric resumed his task, "everything must have worked out, eh? Say, where's Letan? He came back too, didn't he?"

She drew her lips into a fine line, and nodded curtly. "Yeah. We're both fine." *Physically,* she added mentally.

"That's good," he sighed in audible relief. "Just surprised you two aren't in here celebrating, or, you know, whatever needs doing. Either way, I'm glad you're back."

Surprised, she looked at him with wide eyes. "You are?"

"Of course," he nodded encouragingly. "You've done more for this cursed land than anyone ever has. Plus," he hesitated, and glanced at the only other patron before he leaned in closer. "The fact is, I'd miss you if you ever stopped coming in. Business matters aside, you're one of my favorite persons to talk to."

Kailar smiled at that, and she felt the tight grip on her chest and heart suddenly release. It was nice to be acknowledged, and she realized that despite everything that had happened, it wasn't the first compliment she had received in recent days.

Letan may not like how she did things, but others did.

In that moment, she made her decision to stay. If not for anyone else, than for those who had come to rely on her to change things for the better on Devor. Assuming, of course, they would let her stay.

Her lighter mood soured again when she realized that the moment

Commander Querlin learned of her actions, he might not want her around anymore. So she decided she would tell him herself. Besides, she and Letan owed him a report.

After she paid Alric and finished off the broth, she headed back to the Guild. When she tried to find the Commander, he wasn't in his office, so she tried his quarters. When no response came from knocking, another Warrior, Arnbor, happened to walk by and see her.

"He's not there," Arnbor remarked, not bothering to stop. "I saw him and Lieutenant Velethar heading out a while ago."

Just as Arnbor passed her by, she grabbed him by the shoulder to stop him. "Where were they headed?"

Taken aback by her gruffness, he stumbled with his words for a second before saying, "I think I overheard him say they were headed for the City Council."

That surprised her at first, but then she realized that if the Council was trying to organize all of Devor into a singular government, they might want to know about events on Edilas, since it could impact Devor's interactions with the kingdoms.

The more she thought about it, the more it angered her – she was being excluded again. She should be there to help give the report.

When she said nothing else to Arnbor, he shook his head and walked away. She, in turn, headed for the exit, intent on bursting in on the meeting. If they weren't going to voluntarily include her, then she'd have to force her inclusion.

She didn't get far. Just as Kailar marched out the doors of the Guild mansion, she saw Letan briskly walking back from the direction of the Council, his head down and his eyes focused on the ground before him. Stunned, she watched as he approached, his brow furrowed and his eyes lost in thought. When he realized someone stood before him, he looked up and halted, likewise surprised.

"Kailar," he said cautiously. "I was just coming to find you."

A tingling sensation drew up inside of her chest, and she felt a rush of anticipation. "Funny. I was just looking for you, too."

"I see," he replied uneasily. "Well. I've come because Commander Querlin and Councilwoman Reyla would like to speak with you at once."

There was no urgency in his voice, only hesitance, and that made her stomach drop. Something had happened. Or was about to happen.

She didn't know what to say, so she motioned behind him and said, "Well, then, lead the way."

He avoided her eyes and simply nodded, and then turned to head back for the Council. She followed along absently, realizing she had never strapped her sword on. Would they decide to arrest her? If so, would she let them?

Shaking her head, she discounted that possibility. First of all, they knew they couldn't contain her, even if they wanted to. Second, if she was to be arrested, her conditional pardon rescinded due to her actions on Edilas, Letan would have brought along shackles.

He didn't say a word to her the entire walk over to the capitol building, and that only set her on edge further. No lectures, no reproaches, no idle chatter, just silence.

Until they reached the front door. She noted that it was a pair of Warriors now, not city guards, who stood watch on either side of the entrance. Once there, Letan stopped them and turned to her, though he couldn't quite look into her eyes.

"Listen, I just wanted you to know..." He paused and looked at her feet again. This was the first time she had ever seen him need to work up his courage to say something. Finally, he looked her in the eyes. "I've gone over it in my head, over and over. And for the first time in my life, I don't know what exactly is right and what is wrong. Killing all those people was terrible. But how much worse would it have been if we had been stuck fighting them off and trying to subdue them?"

"A lot worse," she said impulsively. "Degrin would have killed Anila and the others, and we wouldn't have known he got his hands on the Cronal piece until too late. Even if the Keeper came in the middle of battle, it still would have taken too much time to..."

"I know, I know," he interrupted. "And for all we know, Degrin could have wiped us from the face of Halarite. We might all be dead by now." He nodded once. "Whatever is happening between us, just know that I think you probably did the only thing that could be done. Right or wrong, it saved us all."

It wasn't exactly an endorsement, but it wasn't a condemnation, either. She supposed it would have to do, for now.

After staring into her eyes, he sighed and motioned into the doors. "Let's head in."

She nodded, uncertain about what to expect. Did he feel compelled to say those things because she would not get as much understanding from the Commander and the Councilwoman? Steeling herself for whatever was ahead, she preceded him in. The steward in the antechamber, retaining his services after being forced to cooperate with them during the Mayor's arrest, directed them to head straight into the council chambers.

Surprisingly, only Kent and Reyla were present, the rest of the city council was nowhere to be seen. They stood at the closest end of the long table, and turned fully to face her as she entered. Letan closed the doors behind them, and then stood off to the side, apparently unwilling to pick a side in whatever was coming.

"Thank you for bringing Kailar," Kent nodded to Letan, before he turned his attention back to her.

Before the Commander could say anything, Reyla smiled warmly at her, catching her off guard. "Thank you for coming on short notice, Kailar."

Uncertain of what to expect now, she nodded. "Of course. What can I do for you two?"

Kent glanced at Reyla, and then stepped forward while clasping his hands behind his back. "I'll get right to it. Lieutenant Velethar filled us in on your actions today in Edilas. I wish you two had found me before you left," he gave an intent look at Letan, "but I understand that time was of the essence."

He let out a long sigh and lowered his head. "In short, while you may have helped save the world, your actions reflect very poorly on the Warriors of Devor." His tone grew dark with those last words, anger and disappointment rife in his voice. "Once again, you have the blood of innocents on your hands."

A lump tried to form in her throat, but Kailar pushed past it and started to say, "I did what had to be…"

"Stop," Kent raised a hand, impatience deepening his troubled look. "I'm not interested in hearing it." Her inner rage boiled up again and threatened to spill out. They damn well should listen to her side of the story! "I cannot allow you to represent the Warriors after a show like that. To have you as a part of our organization knowing that you treat life so casually would undermine everything we stand for."

"And what do you stand for," she demanded. "What exactly-"

"I said stop!" Kent's booming voice left no room for argument, stifling even her rage. She gulped back her words, and folded her arms, impatiently waiting for him to continue. "I get it. You did what had to be done to save the world, maybe more. Letan made that very clear." She looked at Letan appreciatively, while her mind worked to figure out where all of this was going. She already had one suspicion, but why involve Reyla?

"Effective immediately, you are hear-by removed from the Warriors' Guild," Kent continued at length. "As soon as you can find appropriate quarter elsewhere in Tieran, you will be barred from entering without official escorts, and your room and all Guild attire and weapons surrendered."

Then she was right. After only a few months, she had lost her place. The decision of whether or not to stay had been made for her, whether she liked it or not.

She had nowhere to go now.

"Having said that," Kent interrupted her deepening depression. "Councilwoman Reyla and I have a proposition for you."

Again catching her off guard, she fumbled her words, "I, uh...what?"

Reyla stepped forward now, standing side by side with Kent. "This may come as a shock to you, but all of the leaders you helped gather before were quick to jump on board with the idea of uniting. The details are still being worked out, of course, which brings me to why I'm here."

All at once, Kailar understood. "You still need me. You need my portals."

Reyla shook her head. "It goes beyond that. You have made such waves on Devor that you do not even realize, and your name is well known throughout the lands. The only ones who speak ill of you are those whom you oppose, namely the criminal underground and those associated with it.

"As such, I would like to make you an offer." Reyla nodded at the Commander. "As you are no longer bound by oath to the Guild, and the Commander and I consider the terms of your pardon satisfied given your contributions to all of Devor, you are free to choose. And I offer a choice of serving the new government, whatever it will be, in the coming days. Not just as one who can facilitate communications between the regions of Devor, but also as an advisor to us."

Kailar faltered in giving any response, her mind racing to wrap itself around what Reyla had just offered. "You mean…even after everything, you're willing to let me stay?" *Better than that,* she realized, and added, "You want me to take a more active role in shaping Devor's future? Even after I've been condemned by the Warriors' Guild?" She looked pointedly at Kent.

Reyla sighed and planted her hands on her hips. "The fact is, the most difficult times aren't behind us, they are yet ahead of us. Your tenacity, your fervor, your desire to actively change things and make them better, *that* is what we need. And while the Commander believes me to be callous in saying so, you sacrificed the lives of Tal citizens, not Devor." She met Kailar's gaze evenly, determination and willfulness in her eyes. "If you can use that same resolve to protect Devor against all threats, I strongly believe that we need you."

At this point, Kailar had lost count of how many times she was surprised in the past few minutes. She thought she knew what kind of person Reyla was based on how she had acted when they arrested Warreck. It seemed as though Kailar was wrong.

All at once, she admired Reyla, and she worried about her. Could she be dangerous? Or could she be Kailar's greatest ally in the days ahead?

Perhaps that was Kailar's choice. What she did now could shape their future relationship, and by extension, shape the future of Devor.

Another thought occurred to her, and she said cautiously, "You realize that now, more than ever, Edilas will not be happy with us if I am officially a part of the regime."

With a curt nod, Reyla replied, "This I know. However, considering we mean to become an independent nation, they no longer have a say in the matter." She thought for a moment, and amended, "They never really did, or you would never have been allowed to join the Warriors."

Kailar smiled at that, and realized how right the Councilwoman was.

The idea of being in the thick of it, voluntarily placed in a position of authority and power, with the ability to help shape a new government – it was everything Kailar had wanted.

Finally, things were actually starting to go her way.

Stepping forward proudly, Kailar said, "I accept."

EPILOGUE

The Allied Council Chambers in Archanon were eerily empty, creating an air of uneasiness that had Cardin shifting his weight from one foot to another, back and forth like an impatient child. The Chambers weren't just empty because the current session was considered a closed session, but because of how many members were lost.

As it stood, he and Governor Maral were the only representatives of Tal, while Queen Leian and King Sal'fe were the only monarchs present. Grand Master Syrn rounded out the leadership present. The Covenant was wiped out, Saran still had no leadership, and Tal was without an heir to the throne.

It would take Tal considerable time to select a new king or queen. Without a known successor to the throne, the governor would act as a steward of the throne while the most influential of Tal would decide on who would rule next. Cardin didn't look forward to witnessing that sort of political debate, especially not in these uncertain times.

The mood was somber, and instead of sitting at their respective tables, the four had gathered around Tal's table to discuss things more intimately.

Cardin had told the leaders everything that had happened, after having been brought up to speed by his friends at the Wizards' Guild.

Queen Leian was the only one present who had no involvement with the matters over the past week, and she was mortified by all of the news, especially of King Beredis's death.

Cardin finished explaining the events then, but nodded to their Falind counterpart and said, "King Sal'fe was kind enough to come to the Wizards' Guild and resurrect as many Archanon citizens and Wizards as he could without charging Tal a single copper." The unfortunate truth was that not all could be brought back. Some were so completely destroyed that their bodies were beyond saving, even for the healing powers of the Staff of Aliz.

Sal'fe nodded, a distant look in his eyes. "We have all suffered during these trying times," he spoke quietly. "It was the least I could do."

Cardin eyed him suspiciously, but did not voice any of his reservations. Sal'fe wasn't one to give charity, as was evidenced by him nearly bankrupting Tal during the Orc War Campaigns where he charged for every single Warrior healed or resurrected. Why the charity now?

Queen Leian decided at that moment to voice her opposition to being left out of everything over the past week, and Cardin had to resist rolling his eyes. Thankfully, Syrn pointed out that if she had been a part of it, her kingdom might have been left in greater disarray than it already was.

She conceded the point, but then mournfully shook her head. "I cannot believe what the world has come to. How much chaos has been sown, how much death and devastation. Where do we go from here? How do we recover?"

Governor Maral nodded her support of Leian's question. "Without the leadership of the Covenant, I fear our citizens will fall prey to greater fear and panic. Our world stands closer to disaster than ever before."

"Maybe," Cardin shrugged. "But maybe not." All eyes fell upon him, and he felt his cheeks flush. He'd given this a great deal of thought in anticipation of the Council meeting, and he was prepared to cheer everyone up, even if he didn't feel cheerful himself. "I think there's a great deal to be said about our fortitude and strength. We fought against someone who was practically a god! And we came out on top. We worked together, not just as an Alliance, but also with a former enemy, to stop him. I think that is the message we should be sending out to the people of Edilas. The message of hope. We overcame Degrin. We've survived Nuuldan and a meteor shower. We've persevered against Klaralin. We can do anything!"

Looking at the others, he forced himself to smile, big and broad, thinking about his experiences in the Great Library to boost his own morale. "*Together*, we can survive anything."

The others all smiled back at Cardin, and they each nodded and voiced their agreement. "Perhaps you should be the one to spread that message," Leian suggested. She looked him up and down appreciatively. "You have a knack for speeches."

A part of him shied away from that idea. He wanted to say no. As it was, all he wanted was to sit by his father's side and try to find a way to bring him back. It was killing him to be here, in the council chambers, rather than back at the Wizards' Guild with his father.

But who would he really be serving if he did that? The fact was, he had made a choice a year ago to stop serving himself, and to do what he could to make the world a better place. Now was not the time to fall back on his old ways.

With no outward reluctance, he nodded. "If you believe it will help."

"The people need someone to look up to," Maral encouraged. "Someone to rally around. You, as a soldier of the Allied Council, and as someone with a natural charisma, can be that voice."

He didn't know what to say, and hadn't expected *that* kind of statement. But maybe Maral was right. Maybe he could do more than just fight. It'd be a nice change of pace to do something other than take lives or train to take lives.

The rest agreed, even Grand Master Syrn. Then there was the question of what to do about the Cronal in the dwarven city. Sergeant Tein and two Wizards remained below to ensure that the Cronal was guarded and the anti-kiklar beacon remained active, though relief guards had already been dispatched that very morning.

"Where are Elaria and the others," Leian asked. "I expected them to participate in this meeting, given their involvement."

"They've already returned to Darea," Cardin replied. "I think they have their own problems to deal with in the coming days, and as much as I hate to say it, we're going to be part of it. They'll be back, I have no doubt about that. Only this time, we might have to open official negotiations with the Dareann leadership."

"Assuming they don't have a civil war on their hands," Sal'fe pointed out.

Cardin drew in a deep breath and nodded. "About that. About Darea, and this Alliance, and Kailar and Devor." He looked around at all of them, and felt a pang grow in his chest, a pang of fear and uncertainty. He spoke his next words carefully. "There's another matter we really need to give attention to that might affect our entire world. The Darksteel Army."

"The soldiers you fought on Stella," Leian intoned. "You didn't go into much detail about them."

"Oh no, there wasn't much more to say," he shook his head. "They practically wiped out that village."

"The villagers were hardly a military force to reckon with," Syrn stated pragmatically. "I think we would fare much better."

Cardin shook his head slowly. "No. I don't think you understand. That was only a single unit of their soldiers, perhaps not even a battalion. I didn't see much of their attack, but based on Sira and Dalin's description, they were well trained and well armed. And I am convinced that they are the very force we've been warned about."

The others exchanged confused glances with one another, all of them except Sal'fe, who stared intently at Cardin. "You refer to the invaders that the orc shaman spoke of."

He nodded. "Exactly."

"What makes you think that," Leian asked.

"Their armor," he intoned. "Their weapons. The same kind of darkened steel that the orcs under Klaralin's command wore. Enchanted in the same way, resistant to magic attacks the same way, built in the same style. It would be an unbelievable coincidence if that armor didn't come from the same source."

He let those facts sink in, and thought about what he would say next. There was already so much on their plates, and he was about to add more to it. "If the Darksteel Army is, in fact, a force capable of invading entire worlds, then we are probably already one of their targets. I can think of no other explanation for Klaralin having access to the armor. They probably cooperated with him. And that means we need to prepare for that invasion now."

An unnerving silence followed, and Cardin had to consciously keep his fists from clenching. He had expected them to deny it, like he was used to happening in Council sessions. Usually it took multiple meetings, or at least hours of talking in one session, to convince them of difficult facts.

This time, there was no such delay, no such objections. "What do you propose we do to prepare," Leian asked.

When no one refuted his conclusion, he sighed in relief. "We need allies," he stated plainly. "Not just each other, either. Darea would be a start."

"I see," Sal'fe nodded absently, his attention seemingly only half-concerned with the meeting. "Which means it would be in our best interest to ensure they do not fall into a civil war."

"And we have the means to influence them," Syrn added. "The Cronal will become a center piece in their political and social conflict."

"Exactly," Cardin said, suppressing a grimace. He didn't like using such a powerful device in that way, but it was one of the many things he had considered since he defeated Degrin. What he didn't say to them, however, was that he would also try his hardest to find a way to destroy the Cronal without destroying Archanon. He felt that someday it would be absolutely necessary.

The Council meeting went on for much of the rest of the day, discussing possible ways to work with the Dareann Elves and the Dareann Dwarves, and how they might strengthen their own forces. But fatigue quickly fell upon the members, and the session was adjourned swiftly.

Syrn offered to take him back to the Guild to see his father, but he said he would be along on his own shortly. For now, he wanted to see Sira, Dalin and Reis. He had another task ahead of him that he hoped would once and for all end the feud with Reis.

When he went to his guest quarters in the castle, he was surprised to see Reis and Anila already there, deep in conversation with Sira in front of a warm fire, extra chairs brought in from somewhere else in the castle.

Everyone stood up when he entered, and Reis looked at him briefly before his eyes fell downwards. Their last real conversation had been an argument, and it hung over them like a dark cloud. Now, Cardin couldn't help but think of his vision in the copse, and the hatred in Reis's eyes before Cardin had...

Pushing the image away, he closed the door behind him and

walked in, embracing Sira in a hug. "Reis," he nodded. "Anila. It's good to see you both again."

Reis looked at him with slight surprise, and then he smiled, that characteristic roguish grin finally gracing his friend's face again. "Yeah, you too," he nodded. "We...actually, I wanted to talk to you about something."

Sira glanced between them, and offered, "Anila and I can step out if you'd like."

"No," Reis held up his hand. "Please, stay. I just, well..." He looked at Anila, and she nodded encouragingly. It was a pleasant surprise for Cardin to see the two of them getting along again. "I wanted to apologize for the way I treated you," Reis looked at Cardin. "You kept her secret as best as you could. I just wish..." He looked at Anila sheepishly. "I wish we could have kept it longer for you."

She shook her head. "We've already talked about this, Reis. It's okay. I'll just be hated by the Wizards for the rest of my life."

Cardin gave a sour expression. "Well for what it's worth, you don't have to worry about any of us treating you any differently."

She beamed at him. "Thank you."

"Anyway," Reis nodded. "You really surprised me down there in the dwarven city. You didn't flat-out refuse Gilrin's request to use it, you just wanted to be cautious about it. You could have destroyed the apparatus right then and there and deprived him and his people of ever having a chance at power again."

Cardin's stomach fluttered for a moment, but he chose not to tell Reis about the Council's plans to use the Cronal as a bargaining chip.

Instead, Cardin decided that now was the time for their conversation, even if Dalin wasn't with them yet. He looked at Sira, and nudged her away so that he had room to pull the Sword of Dragons from its sheath. "About that," he said nervously. What he was about to do might have been a mistake, but after he, Sira and Dalin had discussed it, they had come to the conclusion that this was the only way to prevent that future, as ironic as it might seem.

Cardin presented the Sword of Dragons to Reis. "I know how much you've always wanted to have magic." The image of Reis attacking Cardin with magic flashed through his mind, but it was Sira and Cardin's hope that giving him the power up front would remove the possibility of continued jealousy. Maybe, he hoped, it would mean he would not come to despise Cardin, and vise verse. "I thought about what you said before all of this craziness happened, and you're right. Having magic opens doors up for people on Halarite. I talked it over with Dalin even, and while I think he'd prefer to be here when we do this, he agreed to it."

Reis gawked at the Sword, but as soon as Cardin mentioned Dalin agreeing to it, he shook his head. "Now *that* I have a hard time believing."

"I mean, we can see if he's in his quarters," Cardin motioned his head next door. "Assuming he's there."

"He's not," Sira pointed out. "I tried to invite him over, too."

With a nonchalant shrug, Cardin said, "Regardless, all you need is a few seconds with the Sword. Then you can be a Mage."

Anila stepped closer to Reis and wrapped her arm around his, the look of shock on her face mirroring Reis's. He looked at her, looked at the Sword, and then looked at Cardin, a range of emotions playing across his face.

But his hands never rose up to accept the gift, and after staring at Cardin for a few moments longer, he shook his head. "No. I can't. I won't."

Cardin raised a questioning eyebrow, but inside, all of the little knots twisting in his stomach suddenly relaxed.

"I don't think you get it yet," he narrowed his eyes at Cardin. "And please don't take this as an insult, because I'm glad that you understand what magic does for people in society. But that's still the problem. If I become a Mage and then work my way up the ladder, all I'm doing is perpetuating an unfair system."

As Cardin pulled the Sword back, he listened to his friend intently. He would never make the mistake of not listening to him again.

"I need to make it as I am, and then work to make changes from the inside out," Reis continued, folding his arms. "It's time for me to stop whining about the world and actually step up and do something about it."

With a broad smile on his face, Cardin nodded his appreciation of Reis's position, and he carefully placed the Sword back into its sheath. "Well, you have my full support, my friend."

A giant smile spread across Reis's face, and he stepped forward with his hand out. Cardin took it, shaking it firmly. "Thank you." And suddenly Reis pulled him into a tight hug. "My friend."

When they separated and shook each other's hands one more time, Sira let out a giddy, happy laugh. "Oh gods, it's about damn time you two made up!"

The tension was broken, and the four of them erupted into laughter. For the first time in ages, things felt like they were back to normal between the three of them.

When there came a knock at the door, Cardin extended his senses out, and felt his spirits soar even more when he felt Dalin's familiar presence, along with two other souls. He went to the door and swung it open. "Dalin! Perfect timing, my friend." Then he noticed that Kellis was with him, along with a nobleman that Cardin had never met before, but he knew he had seen.

Dressed in fine blue and black silks, the nobleman was grey and balding, though his goatee was neatly trimmed, and his blazing blue eyes were confident and serious. Recognition clicked, and Cardin realized he had seen the man in the upper city countless times.

"Cardin," Dalin nodded. "I ran into these two on my way in, and they asked if I knew which room was yours."

"Well, come on in," he nodded warmly, but looked at the nobleman curiously. He had the sudden impression that the mood was about to turn somber.

The three entered and gathered around the chairs near the fireplace. "Cardin," Kellis started, "may I introduce Sir Jeric Ferel."

Jeric bowed deeply, far deeper than Cardin would expect a rich man to bow to him. "It is an honor to meet you, Keeper," Jeric stated curtly.

Cardin glanced at the others, but then returned the bow. "As it is for me, Sir Jeric. What can I do for you?"

Jeric hesitated and looked about the room carefully, peering intently at each of the persons present. It was Kellis, however, who answered. "Jeric is an old friend of mine, and as it turns out, his family was one of the most trusted by King Beredis."

"I didn't know who to trust after His Majesty was murdered," Jeric added. "Even after the crisis was averted, I knew that the new Warrior General could not be trusted." He nodded at Cardin and added, "The only other person I thought I could trust was your father, and when I learned that he had taken ill…"

Cardin gulped, a pit of emptiness opening up inside. Sira's hand immediately grasped his and tightened.

"Cardin," Kellis looked at him intently. "Is your father okay? Is he still alive?"

He nodded, and barely managed to croak out, "Yes. He...he's alive. Though the Wizards don't know how to revive him. They don't know if they *can* revive him. They're..." He felt his body shudder, but somehow, he kept tears from resurfacing. "They're not sure he'll ever wake again."

Kellis and Jeric exchanged disheartened looks, and the Lieutenant sighed. "I was afraid you would say something like that."

Frowning, Cardin asked, "Why? What's wrong?"

"After he was poisoned," Jeric began, "King Beredis feared another such attempt on his life, and he wanted to appoint a successor in the event his son turned against him. He was still hopeful, 'til the very end, that Idrill would learn his lesson and become a worthy successor. But in case he didn't, he left my family with a sealed order dictating who would be King next."

Kellis held up a parchment with a broken royal seal. "Which Sir Jeric showed me. I broke the seal and can attest to its authenticity." He handed it to Cardin, but when he took it and before he could look inside of it, Kellis told him what it said. "It seems your father had earned the King's ultimate respect. He was to be the next King of Tal."

Cardin drew in a sharp breath, echoed by Sira. He quickly opened the parchment, and read the decree, confirming what Kellis had told him. "My gods," he muttered. "My Dad...King?"

Kellis nodded. "Which means that you, Cardin Kataar, are now the Prince of Tal." Cardin gaped at Kellis. "And rightful ruler in His Majesty's absence."

DID YOU LIKE THIS BOOK?

Reader reviews play an important role in a book's success by helping other readers discover stories they might enjoy. Please consider taking a moment to leave a review for *Secrets of the Cronal* on Amazon! You'll be making this author's day :D

ABOUT THE AUTHOR

Jon Wasik has been telling stories since he was a little boy, usually with a cookie and milk at his Great Grandma's kitchen table. It wasn't until 5th grade that he finally put pen to paper, and from that moment on, writing has been his greatest passion.

When he isn't writing, Jon likes to read, play video games, and watch insanely geeky movies with his wife. His Gollum voice impressions are eerie, he quotes Doctor Who like others quote the bible, and he can leap terabytes of data in a single bound!

You can find out more about him by visiting his blog, http://kataar.wordpress.com/

Want to keep up on the latest news about Jon's books? Subscribe to his mailing list! Just go to the Sword of Dragons website and click "Join Mailing List" at the top!
http://www.theswordofdragons.com/
https://jonwasik.com